LITTLE WOMEN

Louisa May Alcott

COLLINS
CLASSICS

Harper Press
An imprint of HarperCollins*Publishers*
1 London Bridge Street
London SE1 9GF

This edition published 2013

Louisa May Alcott asserts the moral right to be
identified as the author of this work

A catalogue record for this book is available from the British Library

ISBN-13: 978-0-00-735099-5

Printed and bound by CPI Group (UK) Ltd, Croydon, CR0 4YY

MIX
Paper from
responsible sources

FSC™ C007454

FSC™ is a non-profit international organisation established to promote
the responsible management of the world's forests. Products carrying the
FSC label are independently certified to assure consumers that they come
from forests that are managed to meet the social, economic and
ecological needs of present and future generations,
and other controlled sources.

Find out more about HarperCollins and the environment at
www.harpercollins.co.uk/green

Life & Times section © HarperCollins*Publishers* Ltd
Gerard Cheshire asserts his moral rights as author of the Life & Times section
Classic Literature: Words and Phrases adapted from
Collins English Dictionary
Typesetting in Kalix by Palimpsest Book Production Limited,
Falkirk, Stirlingshire

History of Collins

In 1819, Millworker William Collins from Glasgow, Scotland, set up a company for printing and publishing pamphlets, sermons, hymn books and prayer books. That company was Collins and was to mark the birth of HarperCollins Publishers as we know it today. The long tradition of Collins dictionary publishing can be traced back to the first dictionary William published in 1824, *Greek and English Lexicon*. Indeed, from 1840 onwards, he began to produce illustrated dictionaries and even obtained a licence to print and publish the Bible.

Soon after, William published the first Collins novel, *Ready Reckoner*, however it was the time of the Long Depression, where harvests were poor, prices were high, potato crops had failed and violence was erupting in Europe. As a result, many factories across the country were forced to close down and William chose to retire in 1846, partly due to the hardships he was facing.

Aged 30, William's son, William II took over the business. A keen humanitarian with a warm heart and a generous spirit, William II was truly 'Victorian' in his outlook. He introduced new, up-to-date steam presses and published affordable editions of Shakespeare's works and *Pilgrim's Progress*, making them available to the masses for the first time. A new demand for educational books meant that success came with the publication of travel books, scientific books, encyclopaedias and dictionaries. This demand to be educated led to the later publication of atlases and Collins also held the monopoly on scripture writing at the time.

In the 1860s Collins began to expand and diversify and the idea of 'books for the millions' was developed. Affordable editions of classical literature were published and in 1903 Collins introduced 10 titles in their Collins Handy Illustrated Pocket Novels. These proved so popular that a few years later this had increased to an output of 50 volumes, selling nearly half a million in their year of publication. In the same year, The Everyman's Library was also instituted, with the idea of publishing an affordable library of the most important classical works, biographies, religious and philosophical treatments, plays, poems, travel and adventure. This series eclipsed all competition at the time and the introduction of paperback books in the 1950s helped to open that market and marked a high point in the industry.

HarperCollins is and has always been a champion of the classics and the current Collins Classics series follows in this tradition – publishing classical literature that is affordable and available to all. Beautifully packaged, highly collectible and intended to be reread and enjoyed at every opportunity.

Life & Times

About the Author

Louisa May Alcott was born into a family of American transcendentalists, the second of four daughters. Transcendentalism was essentially a movement initiated in reaction to a feeling that society was eroding its mores and was consequently in need of reform. Alcott was therefore immersed in an environment of progressive thinking and intellectualization during her formative years. This included a strong moral objection to the notion of slavery, which would become the lynchpin of the American Civil War (1861–5). The Alcott's hid a runaway slave in their house in 1847 such was their level of commitment to the cause.

During the war itself Alcott worked as a nurse and it was her experiences that served to hone her story-telling skill. It wasn't until early middle age, however that she became a success. In 1868 the first part of *Little Women* was published to great acclaim and her reputation grew from there. However, her life was not a long one, for she died of ill health at the age of 55 in 1888.

Apart from the *Little Women* trilogy, she wrote many other novels and children's stories, which are better known in the United States. Her writing style remained more or less similar to *Little Women*, because she was primarily interested in the comings and goings of people in her stories. They are the forerunner of the *cast novels* written by such modern day writers as Maeve Binchy, where the stories are windows into many interrelated lives.

On a socio-political level, Alcott's legacy is that she is held aloft as an early feminist and humanitarian. Her high intellect rendered her unable to resist the testing of conventions in her real life and in her literary alter-egos. She lived through the turbulence of the American Civil War and saw America metamorphose into a modern nation where slaves were freed of their literal chains and women were freed of their metaphorical chains. It was a dual emancipation and Alcott effectively documented the event in her prose.

Little Women

Published in its entirety in 1880, *Little Women* is a novel about an American family from a female perspective. The author, Louisa May Alcott, based the story on the formative years of herself and her three sisters. It is a novel that says a great deal about people and society without requiring a complex or sweeping plot to carry the reader along.

The primary theme is that siblings each have different personalities despite their having been brought up in the same family environment – nature versus nurture. Alcott gives each of the four sisters particular idiosyncrasies that signature their personalities and generate advantages and disadvantages for them. Thus they are each known for being vain, quick tempered, coy and selfish. To some extent the essay is about the extent to which children live up to their ascribed personality traits once they are known for them, or rather are allotted them as if parents need to compartmentalize their children's traits. Alcott generally regards the four specific traits as personality flaws, as opposed to strengths, so the four sisters struggle to overcome them rather than embrace them.

Alcott though, was writing at a time when people held deeply Christian values, where the ideal person was the opposite of all of those traits: modest, level-headed, outgoing and giving. The idea was to pretend to be that ideal, albeit an unattainable synthesis. It was all about being virtuous and wholesome in the eyes of the Christian God, although fundamentally it was about being a good prospect as potential wife or husband material in the eyes of others who held the same views.

The title *Little Women*, has been interpreted in two ways. Firstly, as an expression of the relative unimportance of women in comparison to men, in 19th-century America. Secondly, the title is often read as a statement about the general lack of significance of most people in society. Alcott was certainly a forerunner of the feminist movement, so it seems likely that the title encompasses both meanings: i.e. that women, and especially those of mediocrity, possess a diminutive presence.

The Character of Josephine March

Alcott allegedly based the central character, Josephine March, on herself. She is the one with a furious temper, and acts as a devise by which Alcott can vent her frustrations at the world's unfairness to women. Like Alcott, Josephine is something of a tomboy and therefore cannot appreciate why society draws a distinction between the genders. As far as she is concerned, women can do anything men can do.

The author's intention was to make Josephine the perpetual spinster due to her feminist views, but rather ironically, she ended up marrying her off to keep her readership happy, such was society's desire to see her conform to norms. Josephine struggles throughout the book with the parameters of womanhood. She wishes to take up arms during the civil war and she wishes to attend college, but both ambitions are denied to her. Most of all she is vexed by other people's expectation of her to mellow her extreme views and find a protective husband. Inevitably this makes her ever more bristly. *Little Women* was followed by two sequel volumes that took the life of Josephine into middle age. She becomes the governess of a school where she finds her maternal instinct by teaching and caring for her charges.

In some ways the overall story demonstrates how a strong-willed personality can initially baulk at convention, but eventually capitulate once they realize that they are affecting no one but themselves. It's likely in the modern world that Josephine would be described as 'high maintenance' for her initial efforts at resisting expectations, but instead of becoming the neurotic spinster she finds a way to contain herself by using her teaching as a vehicle to express her views. Her husband, who runs the school with her, is able to tolerate her idiosyncrasies because he is an intellectual and finds her intelligence attractive.

Little Women is a complex web of relationships and in this regard it reads rather like an early soap opera, which would go some way to explaining the mass appeal and popularity of Alcott's books.

LITTLE WOMEN

PREFACE

Go then, my little Book, and show to all
That entertain and bid thee welcome shall,
What thou dost keep close shut up in thy breast;
And wish what thou dost show them may be blest
To them for good, may make them choose to be
Pilgrims better by far, than thee or me.
Tell them of Mercy; she is one
Who early hath her pilgrimage begun.
Yea, let young damsels learn of her to prize
The world which is to come, and so be wise;
For little tripping maids may follow God
Along the ways which saintly feet have trod.

Adapted from John Bunyan

CONTENTS

CHAPTER 1

Playing Pilgrims

'Christmas won't be Christmas without any presents,' grumbled Jo, lying on the rug.

'It's so dreadful to be poor!' sighed Meg, looking down at her old dress.

'I don't think it's fair for some girls to have plenty of pretty things, and other girls nothing at all,' added little Amy, with an injured sniff.

'We've got Father and Mother and each other,' said Beth, contentedly, from her corner.

The four young faces on which the firelight shone brightened at the cheerful words, but darkened again as Jo said sadly:

'We haven't got Father, and shall not have him for a long time.' She didn't say 'perhaps never', but each silently added it, thinking of Father far away, where the fighting was.

Nobody spoke for a minute; then Meg said in an altered tone:

'You know the reason Mother proposed not having any presents this Christmas was because it is going to be a hard winter for everyone; and she thinks we ought not to spend money for pleasure when our men are suffering so in the army. We can't do much, but we can make our little sacrifices, and ought to do it gladly. But I am afraid I don't'; and Meg shook her head, and she thought regretfully of all the pretty things she wanted.

'But I don't think the little we should spend would do any good. We've each got a dollar, and the army wouldn't be much helped by our giving that. I agree not to expect anything from Mother or you, but I do want to buy *Undine and Sintram* for myself; I've wanted it *so* long,' said Jo, who was a bookworm.

'I planned to spend mine on new music,' said Beth, with a little sigh, which no one heard but the hearthbrush and kettle-holder.

'I shall get a nice box of Faber's drawing pencils; I really need them,' said Amy, decidedly.

'Mother didn't say anything about our money, and she won't wish us to give up everything. Let's each buy what we want, and have a little fun; I'm sure we work hard enough to earn it,' cried Jo, examining the heels of her shoes in a gentlemanly manner.

'I know *I* do – teaching those tiresome children nearly all day when I am longing to enjoy myself at home,' began Meg, in the complaining tone again.

'You don't have half such a hard time as I do,' said Jo. 'How would you like to be shut up for hours with a nervous, fussy old lady, who keeps you trotting, is never satisfied, and worries you till you're ready to fly out of the window or cry?'

'It's naughty to fret; but I do think washing dishes and keeping things tidy is the worst work in the world. It makes me cross; and my hands get so stiff, I can't practise well at all'; and Beth looked at her rough hands with a sigh that anyone could hear that time.

'I don't believe any of you suffer as I do,' cried Amy; 'for you don't have to go to school with impertinent girls, who plague you if you don't know your lessons, and laugh at your dresses, and label your father if he isn't rich, and insult you when your nose isn't nice.'

'If you mean *libel*, I'd say so, and not talk about *labels*, as if Papa was a pickle-bottle,' advised Jo, laughing.

'I know what I mean, and you needn't be *statirical* about it. It's proper to use good words, and improve your *vocabulary*,' returned Amy, with dignity.

'Don't peck at one another, children. Don't you wish we had

the money Papa lost when we were little, Jo? Dear me! how happy and good we'd be, if we had no worries!' said Meg, who could remember better times.

'You said, the other day, you thought we were a deal happier than the King children, for they were fighting and fretting all the time, in spite of their money.'

'So I did, Beth. Well, I think we are; for, though we do have to work, we make fun for ourselves, and are a pretty jolly set, as Jo would say.'

'Jo does use such slang words!' observed Amy, with a reproving look at the long figure stretched on the rug. Jo immediately sat up, put her hands in her pockets, and began to whistle.

'Don't, Jo; it's so boyish!'

'That's why I do it.'

'I detest rude, unladylike girls!'

'I hate affected, niminy-piminy chits!'

'"Birds in their little nests agree,"' sang Beth, the peacemaker, with such a funny face that both sharp voices softened to a laugh, and the 'pecking' ended for that time.

'Really, girls, you are both to be blamed,' said Meg, beginning to lecture in her elder-sisterly fashion. 'You are old enough to leave off boyish tricks, and to behave better, Josephine. It didn't matter so much when you were a little girl; but now you are so tall, and turn up your hair, you should remember that you are a young lady.'

'I'm not! and if turning up my hair makes me one, I'll wear it in two tails till I'm twenty,' cried Jo, pulling off her net, and shaking down her chestnut mane. 'I hate to think I've got to grow up, and be Miss March, and wear long gowns, and look as prim as a China-aster! It's bad enough to be a girl, anyway, when I like boys' games and work and manners! I can't get over my disappointment in not being a boy; and it's worse than ever now, for I'm dying to go and fight with Papa, and I can only stay at home and knit, like a poky old woman!' And Jo shook the blue army sock till the needles rattled like castanets, and her ball bounded across the room.

'Poor Jo! It's too bad, but it can't be helped; so you must try to be contented with making your name boyish, and playing brother to us girls,' said Beth, stroking the rough head at her knee with a hand that all the dish-washing and dusting in the world could not make ungentle in its touch.

'As for you, Amy,' continued Meg, 'you are altogether too particular and prim. Your airs are funny now; but you'll grow up an affected little goose, if you don't take care. I like your nice manners and refined ways of speaking when you don't try to be elegant; but your absurd words are as bad as Jo's slang.'

'If Jo is a tomboy and Amy a goose, what am I, please?' asked Beth, ready to share the lecture.

'You're a dear, and nothing else,' answered Meg, warmly; and no one contradicted her, for the 'Mouse' was the pet of the family.

As young readers like to know 'how people look', we will take this moment to give them a little sketch of the four sisters, who sat knitting away in the twilight, while the December snow fell quietly without, and the fire crackled cheerfully within. It was a comfortable old room, though the carpet was faded and the furniture very plain; for a good picture or two hung on the walls, books filled the recesses, chrysanthemums and Christmas roses bloomed in the windows, and a pleasant atmosphere of home-peace pervaded it.

Margaret, the eldest of the four, was sixteen, and very pretty, being plump and fair, with large eyes, plenty of soft, brown hair, a sweet mouth, and white hands, of which she was rather vain. Fifteen-year-old Jo was very tall, thin, and brown, and reminded one of a colt; for she never seemed to know what to do with her long limbs, which were very much in her way. She had a decided mouth, a comical nose, and sharp, grey eyes, which appeared to see everything, and were by turns fierce, funny, or thoughtful. Her long, thick hair was her one beauty; but it was usually bundled in a net, to be out of her way. Round shoulders had Jo, big hands and feet, a fly-away look to her clothes, and the uncomfortable appearance of a girl who was rapidly shooting up into a woman, and didn't like it. Elizabeth – or Beth, as everyone called her – was a rosy, smooth-haired, bright-eyed girl of thirteen, with a shy manner, a timid voice, and a peaceful expression, which was seldom disturbed. Her father called her 'Little Tranquillity', and the name suited her excellently; for she seemed to live in a happy world of her own, only venturing out to meet the few whom she trusted and loved. Amy, though the youngest, was a most important person – in her own opinion at least. A regular snow-maiden, with blue eyes, and yellow hair, curling on her shoulders, pale and slender, and always carrying herself like a young lady mindful of her manners. What the characters of the four sisters were we will leave to be found out.

The clock struck six; and, having swept up the hearth, Beth put a pair of slippers down to warm. Somehow the sight of the old shoes had a good effect upon the girls; for Mother was coming, and everyone brightened to welcome her. Meg stopped lecturing, and lighted the lamp, Amy got out of the easy-chair without being asked, and Jo forgot how tired she was as she sat up to hold the slippers nearer to the blaze.

'They are quite worn out; Marmee must have a new pair.'

'I thought I'd get her some with my dollar,' said Beth.

'No, I shall!' cried Amy.

'I'm the oldest,' began Meg, but Jo cut in with a decided:

'I'm the man of the family now Papa is away, and *I* shall provide the slippers, for he told me to take special care of Mother while he was gone.'

'I'll tell you what we'll do,' said Beth; 'let's each get her something for Christmas, and not get anything for ourselves.'

'That's like you, dear! What will we get?' exclaimed Jo.

Everyone thought soberly for a minute; then Meg announced as if the idea was suggested by the sight of her own pretty hands, 'I shall give her a nice pair of gloves.'

'Army shoes, best to be had,' cried Jo.

'Some handkerchiefs, all hemmed,' said Beth.

'I'll get a little bottle of cologne; she likes it, and it won't cost much, so I'll have some left to buy my pencils,' added Amy.

'How will we give the things?' asked Meg.

'Put them on the table, and bring her in and see her open the bundles. Don't you remember how we used to do on our birthdays?' answered Jo.

'I used to be *so* frightened when it was my turn to sit in the big chair with the crown on, and see you all come marching round to give the presents, with a kiss. I liked the things and the kisses, but it was dreadful to have you sit looking at me while I opened the bundles,' said Beth, who was toasting her face and the bread for tea, at the same time.

'Let Marmee think we are getting things for ourselves, and then surprise her. We must go shopping tomorrow afternoon, Meg; there is so much to do about the play for Christmas night,' said Jo, marching up and down, with her hands behind her back and her nose in the air.

'I don't mean to act any more after this time; I'm getting too old for such things,' observed Meg, who was as much a child as ever about 'dressing-up' frolics.

'You won't stop, I know, as long as you can trail round in a white gown with your hair down, and wear gold-paper jewellery. You are the best actress we've got, and there'll be an end of everything if you quit the boards,' said Jo. 'We ought to rehearse tonight. Come here, Amy, and do the fainting scene, for you are as stiff as a poker in that.'

'I can't help it; I never saw anyone faint, and I don't choose to make myself all black and blue, tumbling flat as you do. If I can go down easily, I'll drop; if I can't, I shall fall into a chair and be graceful; I don't care if Hugo does come at me with a pistol,' returned Amy, who was not gifted with dramatic power, but was chosen because she was small enough to be borne out shrieking by the villain of the piece.

'Do it this way; clasp your hands so, and stagger across the room, crying frantically, "Roderigo! save me! save me!"' and away went Jo, with a melodramatic scream which was truly thrilling.

Amy followed, but she poked her hands out stiffly before her, and jerked herself along as if she went by machinery; and her 'Ow!' was more suggestive of pins being run into her than of fear and anguish. Jo gave a despairing groan, and Meg laughed outright, while Beth let her bread burn as she watched the fun with interest.

'It's no use! Do the best you can when the time comes, and if the audience laugh, don't blame me. Come on, Meg.'

Then things went smoothly, for Don Pedro defied the world in a speech of two pages without a single break; Hagar, the witch, chanted an awful incantation over her kettleful of simmering toads, with weird effect; Roderigo rent his chains asunder manfully, and Hugo died in agonies of remorse and arsenic, with a wild 'Ha! ha!'

'It's the best we've had yet,' said Meg, as the dead villain sat up and rubbed his elbows.

'I don't see how you can write and act such splendid things, Jo. You're a regular Shakespeare!' exclaimed Beth, who firmly believed that her sisters were gifted with wonderful genius in all things.

'Not quite,' replied Jo modestly. 'I do think "*The Witch's Curse*, an Operatic Tragedy*", is rather a nice thing; but I'd like to try *Macbeth*, if we only had a trap-door for Banquo. I always wanted to do the killing part. "Is that a dagger I see before me?"' muttered Jo, rolling her eyes and clutching at the air, as she had seen a famous tragedian do.

'No, it's the toasting fork, with mother's shoe on it instead of the bread. Beth's stage-struck!' cried Meg, and the rehearsal ended in a general burst of laughter.

'Glad to find you so merry, my girls,' said a cheery voice at the door, and actors and audience turned to welcome a tall, motherly lady, with a 'can-I-help-you' look about her which was truly delightful. She was not elegantly dressed, but a noble-looking woman, and the girls thought the grey cloak and unfashionable bonnet covered the most splendid mother in the world.

'Well, dearies, how have you got on today? There was so much to do, getting the boxes ready to go tomorrow, that I didn't come home to dinner. Has anyone called, Beth? How is your cold, Meg? Jo, you look tired to death. Come and kiss me, baby.'

While making these maternal inquiries, Mrs March got her wet things off, her warm slippers on, and sitting down in the easy-chair, drew Amy to her lap, preparing to enjoy the happiest hour of her busy day. The girls flew about, trying to make things comfortable, each in her own way. Meg arranged the tea-table; Jo brought wood and set chairs, dropping, overturning, and clattering everything she touched; Beth trotted to and fro between parlour and kitchen, quiet and busy; while Amy gave directions to everyone, as she sat with her hands folded.

As they gathered about the table, Mrs March said, with a particularly happy face, 'I've got a treat for you after supper.'

A quick, bright smile went round like a streak of sunshine. Beth clapped her hands, regardless of the biscuit she held, and Jo tossed up her napkin, crying, 'A letter! a letter! Three cheers for Father!'

'Yes, a nice long letter. He is well, and thinks he shall get through the cold season better than we feared. He sends all sorts of loving wishes for Christmas, and an especial message to you girls,' said Mrs March, patting her pocket as if she had got a treasure there.

'Hurry and get done! Don't stop to quirk your little finger, and simper over your plate, Amy,' cried Jo, choking in her tea, and dropping her bread, butter side down, on the carpet in her haste to get at the treat.

Beth ate no more, but crept away, to sit in her shadowy corner and brood over the delight to come, till the others were ready.

'I think it was so splendid of Father to go as chaplain when he was too old to be drafted, and not strong enough for a soldier,' said Meg, warmly.

'Don't I wish I could go as a drummer, a *vivan* – what's its name? or a nurse, so I could be near him and help him,' exclaimed Jo, with a groan.

'It must be very disagreeable to sleep in a tent, and eat all sorts of bad-tasting things, and drink out of a tin mug,' sighed Amy.

'When will he come home, Marmee?' asked Beth, with a little quiver in her voice.

'Not for many months, dear, unless he is sick. He will stay

and do his work faithfully as long as he can, and we won't ask for him back a minute sooner than he can be spared. Now come and hear the letter.'

They all drew to the fire, Mother in the big chair, with Beth at her feet, Meg and Amy perched on either arm of the chair, and Jo leaning on the back, where no one would see any sign of emotion if the letter should happen to be touching. Very few letters were written in those hard times that were not touching, especially those which fathers sent home. In this one little was said of the hardships endured, the dangers faced, or the home-sickness conquered; it was a cheerful, hopeful letter, full of lively descriptions of camp life, marches, and military news; and only at the end did the writer's heart overflow with fatherly love and longing for the little girls at home.

'Give them all my dear love and a kiss. Tell them I think of them by day, pray for them by night, and find my best comfort in their affection at all times. A year seems very long to wait before I see them, but remind them that while we wait we may all work, so that these hard days need not be wasted. I know they will remember all I said to them, that they will be loving children to you, will do their duty faithfully, fight their bosom enemies bravely, and conquer themselves so beautifully, that when I come back to them I may be fonder and prouder than ever of my little women.'

Everybody sniffed when they came to that part; Jo wasn't ashamed of the great tear that dropped off the end of her nose, and Amy never minded the rumpling of her curls as she hid her face on her mother's shoulder and sobbed out, 'I *am* a selfish girl! but I'll truly try to be better, so he mayn't be disappointed in me by and by.'

'We all will!' cried Meg. 'I think too much of my looks, and hate to work, but won't any more, if I can help it.'

'I'll try and be what he loves to call me, "a little woman", and not be rough and wild; but do my duty here instead of wanting to be somewhere else,' said Jo, thinking that keeping her temper at home was a much harder task than facing a rebel or two down South.

Beth said nothing, but wiped away her tears with the blue army sock, and began to knit with all her might, losing no time in doing the duty that lay nearest her, while she resolved in her quiet little soul to be all that Father hoped to find her when the year brought round the happy coming home.

Mrs March broke the silence that followed Jo's words, by saying in her cheery voice, 'Do you remember how you used to play *Pilgrim's Progress* when you were little things? Nothing delighted you more than to have me tie my piece-bags on your backs for burdens, give you hats and sticks and rolls of paper, and let you travel through the house from the cellar, which was the City of Destruction, up, up, to the housetop, where you had all the lovely things you could collect to make a Celestial City.'

'What fun it was, especially going by the lions, fighting Apollyon, and passing through the Valley where the hobgoblins were!' said Jo.

'I liked the place where the bundles fell off and tumbled down-stairs,' said Meg.

'My favourite part was when we came out on the flat roof where our flowers and arbours and pretty things were, and all stood and sang for joy up there in the sunshine,' said Beth, smiling, as if that pleasant moment had come back to her.

'I don't remember much about it, except that I was afraid of the cellar and the dark entry, and always liked the cake and milk we had up at the top. If I wasn't too old for such things, I'd rather like to play it over again,' said Amy, who began to talk of renouncing childish things at the mature age of twelve.

'We never are too old for this, my dear, because it is a play we are playing all the time in one way or another. Our burdens are here, our road is before us, and the longing for goodness and happiness is the guide that leads us through many troubles and mistakes to the peace which is a true Celestial City. Now, my little pilgrims, suppose you begin again, not in play, but in earnest, and see how far on you can get before Father comes home.'

'Really, Mother? Where are our bundles?' asked Amy, who was a very literal young lady.

'Each of you told what your burden was just now, except Beth; I rather think she hasn't got any,' said her mother.

'Yes, I have; mine is dishes and dusters, and envying girls with nice pianos, and being afraid of people.'

Beth's bundle was such a funny one that everybody wanted to laugh; but nobody did, for it would have hurt her feelings very much.

'Let us do it,' said Meg, thoughtfully. 'It is only another name for trying to be good, and the story may help us; for though we do want to be good, it's hard work, and we forget, and don't do our best.'

'We were in the Slough of Despond tonight, and Mother came and pulled us out as Help did in the book. We ought to have our roll of directions, like Christian. What shall we do about that?' asked Jo, delighted with the fancy which lent a little romance to the very dull task of doing her duty.

'Look under your pillows, Christmas morning, and you will find your guide-book,' replied Mrs March.

They talked over the new plan while old Hannah cleared the table; then out came the four little work-baskets, and the needles flew as the girls made sheets for Aunt March. It was uninteresting sewing, but tonight no one grumbled. They adopted Jo's plan of dividing the long seams into four parts, and calling the quarters Europe, Asia, Africa, and America, and in that way got on capitally, especially when they talked about the different countries, as they stitched their way through them.

At nine they stopped work, and sang, as usual, before they went to bed. No one but Beth could get much music out of the old piano; but she had a way of softly touching the yellow keys, and making a pleasant accompaniment to the simple songs they sang. Meg had a voice like a flute, and she and her mother led the little choir. Amy chirped like a cricket, and Jo wandered through the airs at her own sweet will, always coming out at the wrong place with a croak or a quaver that spoilt the most pensive tune. They had always done this from the time they could lisp

'Crinkle, crinkle, 'ittle 'tar'

and it had become a household custom, for the mother was a born singer. The first sound in the morning was her voice, as she went about the house singing like a lark; and the last sound at night was the same cheery sound, for the girls never grew too old for that familiar lullaby.

CHAPTER 2

A Merry Christmas

Jo was the first to wake in the grey dawn of Christmas morning. No stockings hung at the fireplace, and for a moment she felt as much disappointed as she did long ago, when her little sock fell down because it was so crammed with goodies. Then she remembered her mother's promise, and, slipping her hand under her pillow, drew out a little crimson-covered book. She knew it very well, for it was that beautiful old story of the best life ever lived, and Jo felt that it was a true guide-book for any pilgrim going the long journey. She woke Meg with a 'Merry Christmas', and bade her see what was under her pillow. A green-covered book appeared, with the same picture inside, and a few words written by their mother, which made their one present very precious in their eyes. Presently Beth and Amy woke, to rummage and find their little books also – one, dove-coloured, the other blue; and all sat looking at and talking about them, while the east grew rosy with the coming day.

In spite of her small vanities, Margaret had a sweet and pious nature, which unconsciously influenced her sisters, especially Jo, who loved her very tenderly, and obeyed her because her advice was so gently given.

'Girls,' said Meg seriously, looking from the tumbled head beside her to the two little night-capped ones in the room beyond, 'Mother wants us to read and love and mind these books, and we must begin at once. We used to be faithful about it; but since Father went away, and all this war trouble unsettled us, we have neglected many things. You can do as you please; but *I* shall keep my book on the table here, and read a little every morning as soon as I wake, for I know it will do me good, and help me through the day.'

Then she opened her new book and began to read. Jo put her arm round her, and, leaning cheek to cheek, read also, with the quiet expression so seldom seen on her restless face.

'How good Meg is! Come, Amy, let's do as they do. I'll help you with the hard words, and they'll explain things if we don't understand,' whispered Beth, very much impressed by the pretty books and her sisters' example.

'I'm glad mine is blue,' said Amy; and then the rooms were very still while the pages were softly turned, and the winter sunshine crept in to touch the bright heads and serious faces with a Christmas greeting.

'Where is Mother?' asked Meg, as she and Jo ran down to thank her for their gifts, half an hour later.

'Goodness only knows. Some poor creeter come a-beggin', and your ma went straight off to see what was needed. There never *was* such a woman for givin' away vittles and drink, clothes, and firin',' replied Hannah, who had lived with the family since Meg was born, and was considered by them all more as a friend than a servant.

'She will be back soon, I think; so fry your cake, and have everything ready,' said Meg, looking over the presents which were collected in a basket and kept under the sofa, ready to be produced at the proper time. 'Why, where is Amy's bottle of cologne?' she added, as the little flask did not appear.

'She took it out a minute ago, and went off with it to put a ribbon on it, or some such notion,' replied Jo, dancing about the room to take the first stiffness off the new army-slippers.

'How nice my handkerchiefs look, don't they! Hannah washed and ironed them for me, and I marked them all myself,' said Beth, looking proudly at the somewhat uneven letters which had cost her such labour.

'Bless the child! she's gone and put "Mother" on them instead of "M. March". How funny!' cried Jo, taking up one.

'Isn't it right? I thought it was better to do it so, because Meg's initials are "M. M.", and I don't want anyone to use these but Marmee,' said Beth, looking troubled.

'It's all right, dear, and a very pretty idea – quite sensible, too, for no one can ever mistake now. It will please her very much, I know,' said Meg, with a frown for Jo and a smile for Beth.

'There's Mother. Hide the basket, quick!' cried Jo, as a door slammed, and steps sounded in the hall.

Amy came in hastily, and looked rather abashed when she saw her sisters all waiting for her.

'Where have you been, and what are you hiding behind you?' asked Meg, surprised to see, by her hood and cloak, that lazy Amy had been out so early.

'Don't laugh at me, Jo! I didn't mean anyone should know till the time came. I only meant to change the little bottle for a big one, and I gave *all* my money to get it, and I'm truly trying not to be selfish any more.'

As she spoke, Amy showed the handsome flask which replaced the cheap one; and looked so earnest and humble in her little effort to forget herself that Meg hugged her on the spot, and Jo pronounced her 'a trump', while Beth ran to the window and picked her finest rose to ornament the stately bottle.

'You see, I felt ashamed of my present, after reading and talking about being good this morning, so I ran round the corner and changed it the minute I was up; and I'm *so* glad, for mine is the handsomest now.'

Another bang of the street door sent the basket under the sofa, and the girls to the table, eager for breakfast.

'Merry Christmas, Marmee! Many of them! Thank you for our books; we read some, and mean to, every day,' they cried, in chorus.

'Merry Christmas, little daughters! I'm glad you began at once, and hope you will keep on. But I want to say one word before we sit down. Not far away from here lies a poor woman with a little new-born baby. Six children are huddled into one bed to keep from freezing, for they have no fire. There is nothing to eat over there; and the oldest boy came to tell me they were suffering hunger and cold. My girls, will you give them your breakfast as a Christmas present?'

They were all unusually hungry, having waited nearly an hour, and for a minute no one spoke; only a minute, for Jo exclaimed impetuously:

'I'm so glad you came before we began!'

'May I go and help carry the things to the poor little children?' said Beth, eagerly.

'*I* shall take the cream and the muffins,' added Amy, heroically, giving up the articles she most liked.

Meg was already covering the buckwheats, and piling the bread into one big plate.

'I thought you'd do it,' said Mrs March, smiling as if satisfied. 'You shall all go and help me, and when we come back we will have bread and milk for breakfast, and make it up at dinner-time.'

They were soon ready, and the procession set out. Fortunately it was early, and they went through back streets, so few people saw them, and no one laughed at the queer party.

A poor, bare, miserable room it was, with broken windows, no fire, ragged bed-clothes, a sick mother, wailing baby, and a group of pale, hungry children cuddled under one old quilt, trying to keep warm.

How the big eyes stared and blue lips smiled as the girls went in!

'*Ach, mein Gott!* it is good angels come to us!' said the poor woman, crying for joy.

'Funny angels in hoods and mittens,' said Jo, and set them laughing.

In a few minutes it really did seem as if kind spirits had been at work there. Hannah, who had carried wood, made a fire, and stopped up the broken panes with old hats and her own cloak. Mrs March gave the mother tea and gruel, and comforted her with promises of help, while she dressed the little baby as tenderly as if it had been her own. The girls, meantime, spread the table, set the children round the fire, and fed them like so many hungry birds – laughing, talking, and trying to understand the funny broken English.

'*Das ist gut!*' '*Die Engelkinder!*' cried the poor things, as they ate, and warmed their purple hands at the comfortable blaze.

The girls had never been called angel children before, and thought it very agreeable, especially Jo, who had been considered a 'Sancho' ever since she was born. That was a very happy breakfast, though they didn't get any of it; and when they went away, leaving comfort behind, I think there were not in all the city four merrier people than the hungry little girls who gave away their breakfasts and contented themselves with bread and milk on Christmas morning.

'That's loving our neighbour better than ourselves, and I like it,' said Meg, as they set out their presents, while their mother was upstairs collecting clothes for the poor Hummels.

Not a very splendid show, but there was a great deal of love done up in the few little bundles; and the tall vase of red roses, white chrysanthemums, and trailing vines, which stood in the middle, gave quite an elegant air to the table.

'She's coming! Strike up, Beth! Open the door, Amy! Three cheers for Marmee!' cried Jo, prancing about, while Meg went to conduct Mother to the seat of honour.

Beth played her gayest march, Amy threw open the door, and Meg enacted escort with great dignity. Mrs March was both surprised and touched; and smiled with her eyes full as she examined her presents, and read the little notes which accompanied them. The slippers went on at once, a new handkerchief was slipped into her pocket, well scented with Amy's cologne, the rose was fastened in her bosom, and the nice gloves were pronounced a 'perfect fit'.

There was a good deal of laughing and kissing and explaining, in the simple, loving fashion which makes these home festivals so pleasant at the time, so sweet to remember long afterwards, and then all fell to work.

The morning charities and ceremonies took so much time that the rest of the day was devoted to preparations for the evening festivities.

Not rich enough to afford any great outlay for private performances, the girls put their wits to work, and – necessity being the mother of invention – made whatever they needed. Very clever were some of their productions – pasteboard guitars, antique lamps made of old-fashioned butter-boats covered with silver paper, gorgeous robes of old cotton glittering with tin spangle from a pickle factory, and armour covered with the same useful diamond-shaped bits, left in the sheets when the lids of tin preserve-pots were cut out. The furniture was used to being turned topsy-turvy, and the big chamber was the scene of many innocent revels.

No gentlemen were admitted; so Jo played male parts to her heart's content, and took immense satisfaction in a pair of russet-leather boots given her by a friend. These boots, an old foil, and a slashed doublet once used by an artist for some picture, were Jo's chief treasures, and appeared on all occasions. The smallness of the company made it necessary for the two principal actors to take several parts apiece; and they certainly deserved some credit for the hard work they did in learning three or four different parts, whisking in and out of various costumes, and managing the stage besides. It was excellent drill for their memories, a harmless amusement, and employed many hours which otherwise would have been idle, lonely, or spent in less profitable society.

On Christmas night, a dozen girls piled on to the bed, which was the dress-circle, and sat before the blue and yellow chintz curtains in a most flattering state of expectancy. There was a good deal of rustling and whispering behind the curtain, a trifle of lamp-smoke, and an occasional giggle from Amy, who was apt to get hysterical in the excitement of the moment. Presently a bell sounded, the curtains flew apart, and the Operatic Tragedy began.

'A gloomy wood', according to the one play-bill, was represented by a few shrubs in pots, green baize on the floor, and a cave in the distance. This cave was made with a clothes-horse for a roof, bureaus for walls; and in it was a small furnace in full blast, with a black spot on it, and an old witch bending over it. The stage was dark, and the glow of the furnace had a fine effect, especially as real steam issued from the kettle when the witch took off the cover. A moment was allowed for the first thrill to subside; then Hugo, the villain, stalked in with a clanking sword at his side, a slouched hat, black beard, mysterious cloak, and the boots. After pacing to and fro in much agitation, he struck his forehead, and burst out in a wild strain, singing of his hatred to Roderigo, his love for Zara, and his pleasing resolution to kill the one and win the other. The gruff tones of Hugo's voice, with an occasional shout when his feelings overcame him, were very impressive, and the audience applauded the moment he paused for breath. Bowing with the air of one accustomed to public praise, he stole to the cavern, and ordered Hagar to come forth with a commanding 'What ho, minion! I need thee!'

Out came Meg, with grey horse-hair hanging about her face, a red and black robe, a staff, and cabbalistic signs upon her cloak. Hugo demanded a potion to make Zara adore him, and one to destroy Roderigo. Hagar, in a fine dramatic melody, promised both, and proceeded to call up the spirit who would bring the love philtre:

> 'Hither, hither, from my home,
> Airy sprite, I bid thee come!
> Born of roses, fed on dew,
> Charms and potions canst thou brew?

> 'Bring me here, with elfin speed,
> The fragrant philtre which I need;
> Make it sweet and swift and strong,
> Spirit, answer now my song!'

A soft strain of music sounded, and then at the back of the cave appeared a little figure in cloudy white, with glittering wings, golden hair, and a garland of roses on its head. Waving a wand, it sang:

'Hither I come,
From my airy home,
Afar in the silver moon.
Take this magic spell,
And use it well,
Or its power will vanish soon!'

And, dropping a small, gilded bottle at the witch's feet, the spirit vanished. Another chant from Hagar produced another apparition – not a lovely one; for, with a bang, an ugly black imp appeared, and, having croaked a reply, tossed a dark bottle at Hugo, and disappeared with a mocking laugh. Having warbled his thanks and put the potions in his boots, Hugo departed; and Hagar informed the audience that, as he had killed a few of her friends in times past, she has cursed him, and intends to thwart his plans, and be revenged on him. Then the curtain fell, and the audience reposed and ate candy while discussing the merits of the play.

A good deal of hammering went on before the curtain rose again; but when it became evident what a masterpiece of stage-carpentering had been got up, no one murmured at the delay. It was truly superb! A tower rose to the ceiling; half-way up appeared a window, with a lamp burning at it, and behind the white curtain appeared Zara in a lovely blue and silver dress, waiting for Roderigo. He came in gorgeous array, with plumed cap, red cloak, chestnut love-locks, a guitar, and the boots, of course. Kneeling at the foot of the tower, he sang a serenade in melting tones. Zara replied, and, after a musical dialogue, consented to fly. Then came the grand effect of the play. Roderigo produced a rope ladder, with five steps to it, threw up one end, and invited Zara to descend. Timidly she crept from her lattice, put her hand on Roderigo's shoulder, and was about to leap gracefully down, when, 'Alas! alas for Zara!' she forgot her train – it caught in the window, the tower tottered, leant forward, fell with a crash, and buried the unhappy lovers in the ruins!

A universal shriek arose as the russet boots waved wildly from the wreck, and a golden head emerged, exclaiming, 'I told you so! I told you so!' With wonderful presence of mind, Don Pedro, the cruel sire, rushed in, dragged out his daughter, with a hasty aside:

'Don't laugh! Act as if it was all right!' – and, ordering Roderigo up, banished him from the kingdom with wrath and scorn. Though decidedly shaken by the fall of the tower upon him, Roderigo defied the old gentleman, and refused to stir. This dauntless example fired Zara: she also defied her sire, and he ordered them both to the deepest dungeons of the castle. A stout little retainer came in with chains, and led them away, looking very much frightened, and evidently forgetting the speech he ought to have made. Act third was the castle hall; and here Hagar appeared, having come to free the lovers and finish Hugo. She hears him coming, and hides; sees him put the potions into two cups of wine, and bid the timid little servant 'Bear them to the captives in their cells, and tell them I shall come anon.' The servant takes Hugo aside to tell him something, and Hagar changes the cups for two others which are harmless. Ferdinando, the 'minion', carries them away, and Hagar puts back the cup which holds the poison meant for Roderigo. Hugo, getting thirsty after a long warble, drinks it, loses his wits, and, after a good deal of clutching and stamping, falls flat and dies; while Hagar informs him what she has done in a song of exquisite power and melody.

This was a truly thrilling scene, though some persons might have thought that the sudden tumbling down of a quantity of long hair rather marred the effect of the villain's death. He was called before the curtain, and with great propriety appeared, leading Hagar, whose singing was considered more wonderful than all the rest of the performance put together.

Act fourth displayed the despairing Roderigo on the point of stabbing himself, because he has been told that Zara has deserted him. Just as the dagger is at his heart, a lovely song is sung under his window, informing him that Zara is true, but in danger, and he can save her, if he will. A key is thrown in, which unlocks the door, and in a spasm of rapture he tears off his chains, and rushes away to find and rescue his lady-love.

Act fifth opened with a stormy scene between Zara and Don Pedro. He wishes her to go into a convent, but she won't hear of it; and, after a touching appeal, is about to faint, when Roderigo dashes in and demands her hand. Don Pedro refuses, because he is not rich. They shout and gesticulate tremendously, but cannot agree, and Roderigo is about to bear away the exhausted Zara, when the timid servant enters with a letter and a bag from Hagar, who has mysteriously disappeared. The latter informs the party that she bequeaths untold wealth to the young pair, and an awful doom to Don Pedro, if he doesn't make them happy. The bag is opened, and several quarts of tin money shower down upon the stage, till it is quite glorified with the glitter. This entirely softens the 'stern sire': he consents without a murmur, all join in a joyful chorus, and the curtain falls upon the lovers kneeling to receive Don Pedro's blessing in attitudes of the most romantic grace.

Tumultuous applause followed, but received an unexpected check; for the cot-bed, on which the 'dress-circle' was built, suddenly shut up, and extinguished the enthusiastic audience. Roderigo and Don Pedro flew to the rescue, and all were taken out unhurt, though many were speechless with laughter. The excitement had hardly subsided, when Hannah appeared, with 'Mrs March's compliments, and would the ladies walk down to supper.'

This was a surprise, even to the actors; and, when they saw the table, they looked at one another in rapturous amazement. It was like Marmee to get up a little treat for them; but anything so fine as this was unheard of since the departed days of plenty. There was ice-cream – actually two dishes of it, pink and white – and cake and fruit and distracting French bonbons, and, in the middle of the table, four great bouquets of hothouse flowers.

It quite took their breath away; and they stared first at the table and then at their mother, who looked as if she enjoyed it immensely.

'Is it fairies?' asked Amy.

'It's Santa Claus,' said Beth.

'Mother did it'; and Meg smiled her sweetest, in spite of her grey beard and white eyebrows.

'Aunt March had a good fit, and sent the supper,' cried Jo, with a sudden inspiration.

'All wrong. Old Mr Laurence sent it,' replied Mrs March.

'The Laurence boy's grandfather! What in the world put such a thing into his head? We don't know him!' exclaimed Meg.

'Hannah told one of his servants about your breakfast party. He is an odd old gentleman, but that pleased him. He knew my father, years ago; and he sent me a polite note this afternoon, saying he hoped I would allow him to express his friendly feeling towards my children by sending them a few trifles in honour of the day. I could not refuse; and so you have a little feast at night to make up for the bread-and-milk breakfast.'

'That boy put it into his head, I know he did! He's a capital fellow, and I wish we could get acquainted. He looks as if he'd like to know us; but he's bashful, and Meg is so prim she won't let me speak to him when we pass,' said Jo, as the plates went round, and the ice began to melt out of sight, with 'Ohs!' and 'Ahs!' of satisfaction.

'You mean the people who live in the big house next door, don't you?' asked one of the girls. 'My mother knows old Mr Laurence; but says he's very proud, and doesn't like to mix with his neighbours. He keeps his grandson shut up, when he isn't riding or walking with his tutor, and makes him study very hard. We invited him to our party, but he didn't come. Mother says he's very nice, though he never speaks to us girls.'

'Our cat ran away once, and he brought her back, and we talked over the fence, and were getting on capitally – all about cricket, and so on – when he saw Meg coming, and walked off. I mean to know him some day; for he needs fun, I'm sure he does,' said Jo decidedly.

'I like his manners, and he looks like a little gentleman; so I've no objection to your knowing him, if a proper opportunity comes.

He brought the flowers himself; and I should have asked him in, if I had been sure what was going on upstairs. He looked so wistful as he went away, hearing the frolic, and evidently having none of his own.'

'It's a mercy you didn't, Mother!' laughed Jo, looking at her boots. 'But we'll have another play, some time, that he *can* see. Perhaps he'll help act; wouldn't that be jolly?'

'I never had such a fine bouquet before! How pretty it is!' And Meg examined her flowers with great interest.

'They *are* lovely. But Beth's roses are sweeter to me,' said Mrs March, smelling the half-dead posy in her belt.

Beth nestled up to her, and whispered softly, 'I wish I could send my bunch to Father. I'm afraid he isn't having such a merry Christmas as we are.'

CHAPTER 3

The Laurence Boy

'Jo! Jo! where are you?' cried Meg, at the foot of the garret stairs.

'Here!' answered a husky voice from above; and, running up, Meg found her sister eating apples and crying over the *Heir of Redclyffe*, wrapped up in a comforter on an old three-legged sofa by the sunny window. This was Jo's favourite refuge; and here she loved to retire with half a dozen russets and a nice book, to enjoy the quiet and the society of a pet rat who lived near by, and didn't mind her a particle. As Meg appeared, Scrabble whisked into his hole. Jo shook the tears off her cheeks, and waited to hear the news.

'Such fun! only see! a regular note of invitation from Mrs Gardiner for tomorrow night!' cried Meg, waving the precious paper, and then proceeding to read it, with girlish delight.

'"Mrs Gardiner would be happy to see Miss March and Miss Josephine at a little dance on New Year's Eve." Marmee is willing we should go; now what *shall* we wear?'

'What's the use of asking that, when you know we shall wear our poplins because we haven't got anything else?' answered Jo, with her mouth full.

'If I only had a silk!' sighed Meg. 'Mother says I may when I'm eighteen, perhaps; but two years is an everlasting time to wait.'

'I'm sure our pops look like silk, and they are nice enough for us. Yours is as good as new, but I forgot the burn and the tear in mine. Whatever shall I do? the burn shows badly and I can't take any out.'

'You must sit still all you can, and keep your back out of sight; the front is all right. I shall have a new ribbon for my hair, and Marmee will lend me her little pearl pin, and my new slippers are lovely, and my gloves will do, though they aren't as nice as I'd like.'

'Mine are spoilt with lemonade, and I can't get any new ones, so I shall have to go without,' said Jo, who never troubled herself much about dress.

'You *must* have gloves, or I won't go,' cried Meg decidedly, 'gloves are more important than anything else. I should be *so* mortified if you didn't have them.'

'Then I'll stay still. I don't care much for company dancing. It's no fun to go sailing round. I like to fly about and cut capers.'

'You can't ask Mother for new ones, they are so expensive, and you are so careless. She said, when you spoilt the others, that she shouldn't get you any more this winter. Can't you make them do?' asked Meg anxiously.

'I can hold them crumpled up in my hand, so no one will know how stained they are; that's all I can do. No, I'll tell you how we can manage – each wear one good one and carry a bad one; don't you see?'

'Your hands are bigger than mine, and you will stretch my glove dreadfully,' began Meg, whose gloves were a tender point with her.

'Then I'll go without. I don't care what people say!' cried Jo, taking up her book.

'You may have it, you may! only don't stain it, and do behave nicely. Don't put your hands behind you, or stare, or say "Christopher Columbus!" will you?'

'Don't worry about me; I'll be as prim as I can, and not get into any scrapes, if I can help it. Now go and answer your note, and let me finish this splendid story.'

So Meg went away to 'accept with thanks', look over her dress, and sing blithely as she did up her one real lace frill; while Jo finished her story, her four apples, and had a game of romps with Scrabble.

On New Year's Eve the parlour was deserted, for the two younger girls played dressing-maids, and the two older were absorbed in the all-important business of 'getting ready for the party'. Simple as the toilets were, there was a great deal of running up and down, laughing and talking, and at one time a strong smell of burnt hair pervaded the house. Meg wanted a few curls about her face, and Jo undertook to pinch the papered locks with a pair of hot tongs.

'Ought they to smoke like that?' asked Beth, from her perch on the bed.

'It's the dampness drying,' replied Jo.

'What a queer smell! it's like burnt feathers,' observed Amy, smoothing her own pretty curls with a superior air.

'There, now I'll take off the papers and you'll see a cloud of little ringlets,' said Jo, putting down the tongs.

She did take off the papers, but no cloud of ringlets appeared, for the hair came with the papers, and the horrified hairdresser laid a row of little scorched bundles on the bureau before her victim.

'Oh, oh, oh! what *have* you done? I'm spoilt! I can't go! My hair, oh, my hair!' wailed Meg, looking with despair at the uneven frizzle on her forehead.

'Just my luck; you shouldn't have asked me to do it; I always spoil everything. I'm so sorry, but the tongs were too hot, and so I've made a mess,' groaned poor Jo, regarding the black pancakes with tears of regret.

'It isn't spoilt: just frizzle it, and tie your ribbon so the ends come on your forehead a bit, and it will look like the last fashion. I've seen many girls do it so,' said Amy, consolingly.

'Serves me right for trying to be fine. I wish I'd let my hair alone,' cried Meg, petulantly.

'So do I, it was so smooth and pretty. But it will soon grow out again,' said Beth, coming to kiss and comfort the shorn sheep.

After various lesser mishaps, Meg was finished at last, and by the united exertions of the family, Jo's hair was got up and her dress on. They looked very well in their simple suits. Meg in silvery drab, with a blue velvet snood, lace frills, and the pearl pin; Jo in maroon, with a stiff, gentlemanly linen collar and a white chrysanthemum or two for her only ornament. Each put on the one nice light glove, and carried one soiled one, and all pronounced the effect 'quite easy and fine'. Meg's high-heeled slippers were very tight, and hurt her, though she would not own it, and Jo's nineteen hairpins all seemed stuck straight into her head, which was not exactly comfortable; but, dear me, let us be elegant or die!

'Have a good time, dearies!' said Mrs March, as the sisters went daintily down the walk. 'Don't eat much supper, and come away at eleven, when I send Hannah for you.' As the gate clashed behind them, a voice cried from a window:

'Girls, girls! *have* you both got nice pocket-handkerchiefs?'

'Yes, yes, spandy nice, and Meg has cologne on hers,' cried Jo, adding with a laugh, as they went on, 'I do believe Marmee would ask that if we were all running away from an earthquake.'

'It is one of her aristocratic tastes, and quite proper, for a real lady is always known by neat boots, gloves, and handkerchief,' replied Meg, who had a good many little 'aristocratic tastes' of her own.

'Now don't forget to keep the bad breadth out of sight, Jo. Is my sash right? and does my hair look *very* bad?' said Meg, as she turned from the glass in Mrs Gardiner's dressing room, after a prolonged prink.

'I know I shall forget. If you see me doing anything wrong just remind me by a wink, will you?' returned Jo, giving her collar a twitch and her hair a hasty brush.

'No, winking isn't lady-like; I'll lift my eyebrows if anything is wrong, and nod if you are all right. Now hold your shoulders straight and take short steps, and don't shake hands if you are introduced to anyone: it isn't the thing.'

'How *do* you learn all the proper ways? I never can. Isn't that music gay?'

Down they went, feeling a trifle timid, for they seldom went to parties, and, informal as this little gathering was, it was an event to them. Mrs Gardiner, a stately old lady, greeted them kindly, and handed them over to the eldest of her six daughters. Meg knew Sallie, and was at her ease very soon; but Jo, who didn't care much for girls or girlish gossip, stood about, with her back carefully against the wall and felt as much out of place as a colt in a flower-garden. Half a dozen jovial lads were talking about skates in another part of the room, and she longed to go and join them, for skating was one of the joys of her life. She telegraphed her wish to Meg, but the eyebrows went up so alarmingly that she dared not stir. No one came to talk to her, and one by one the group near her dwindled away, till she was left alone. She could not roam about and amuse herself, for the burnt breadth would show, so she stared at people rather forlornly till the dancing began. Meg was asked at once, and the tight slippers tripped about so briskly that none would have guessed the pain their wearer suffered smilingly. Jo saw a big red-headed youth approaching her corner, and fearing he meant to engage her, she slipped into a curtained recess, intending to peep and enjoy herself in peace. Unfortunately, another bashful person had chosen the same refuge; for, as the curtain fell behind her, she found herself face to face with the 'Laurence boy'.

'Dear me, I didn't know anyone was here!' stammered Jo, preparing to back out as speedily as she had bounced in.

But the boy laughed, and said pleasantly, though he looked a little startled:

'Don't mind me; stay if you like.'

'Shan't I disturb you?'

'Not a bit; I only came here because I don't know many people, and I felt rather strange at first, you know.'

'So did I. Don't go away, please, unless you'd rather.'

The boy sat down again and looked at his pumps, till Jo said, trying to be polite and easy:

'I think I've had the pleasure of seeing you before; you live near us, don't you?'

'Next door'; and he looked up and laughed outright, for Jo's prim manner was rather funny, when he remembered how they had chatted about cricket when he brought the cat home.

That put Jo at her ease; and she laughed too, as she said, in her heartiest way:

'We did have such a good time over your nice Christmas present.'

'Grandpa sent it.'

'But you put it into his head, didn't you, now?'

'How is your cat, Miss March?' asked the boy, trying to look sober, while his black eyes shone with fun.

'Nicely, thank you, Mr Laurence; but I am not Miss March, I'm only Jo,' returned the young lady.

'I'm not Mr Laurence, I'm only Laurie.'

'Laurie Laurence – what an odd name!'

'My first name is Theodore, but I don't like it, for the fellows called me Dora, so I made them say Laurie instead.'

'I hate my name, too – so sentimental! I wish everyone would say Jo, instead of Josephine. How did you make the boys stop calling you Dora?'

'I thrashed 'em.'

'I can't thrash Aunt March, so I suppose I shall have to bear it'; and Jo resigned herself with a sigh.

'Do you like parties?' she asked in a moment.

'Sometimes; you see I've been abroad a good many years, and haven't been in company enough yet to know how you do things here.'

'Abroad!' cried Jo. 'Oh, tell me about it! I love dearly to hear people describe their travels.'

Laurie didn't seem to know where to begin; but Jo's eager questions soon set him going, and he told her how he had been at school in Vevey, where the boys never wore hats, and had a fleet of boats on the lake, and for holiday fun went on walking trips about Switzerland with their teachers.

'Don't I wish I'd been there!' cried Jo. 'Did you go to Paris?'

'We spent last winter there.'

'Can you talk French?'

'We were not allowed to speak anything else at Vevey.'

'Do say some! I can read it, but can't pronounce.'

'*Quel nom a cette jeune demoiselle en les pantoufles jolies?*' said Laurie, good-naturedly.

'How nicely you do it! Let me see – you said, "Who is the young lady in the pretty slippers," didn't you?'

'*Oui, mademoiselle.*'

'It's my sister Margaret, and you knew it was! Do you think she is pretty?'

'Yes; she makes me think of the German girls, she looks so fresh and quiet.'

Jo quite glowed with pleasure at this boyish praise of her sister, and stored it up to repeat to Meg. Both peeped and criticized and chatted, till they felt like old acquaintances. Laurie's bashfulness soon wore off; for Jo's gentlemanly demeanour amused and set him at his ease, and Jo was her merry self again, because her dress was forgotten, and nobody lifted their eyebrows at her. She liked the 'Laurence boy' better than ever, and took several good looks at him, so that she might describe him to the girls; for they had no brothers, very few male cousins, and boys were almost unknown creatures to them.

'Curly black hair; brown skin; big, black eyes; handsome nose; fine teeth; small hands and feet; taller than I am; very polite for a boy, and altogether jolly. Wonder how old he is?'

It was on the tip of Jo's tongue to ask; but she checked herself in time, and with unusual tact, tried to find out in a roundabout way.

'I suppose you are going to college soon? I see you pegging away at your books – no, I mean studying hard'; and Jo blushed at the dreadful 'pegging' which had escaped her.

Laurie smiled, but didn't seem shocked, and answered, with a shrug:

'Not for a year or two; I won't go before seventeen, anyway.'

'Aren't you but fifteen?' asked Jo, looking at the tall lad, whom she had imagined seventeen already.

'Sixteen, next month.'

'How I wish I was going to college! You don't look as if you liked it.'

'I hate it! Nothing but grinding or skylarking. And I don't like the way fellows do either in this country.'

'What do you like?'

'To live in Italy, and to enjoy myself in my own way.'

Jo wanted very much to ask what his own way was: but his black brows looked rather threatening as he knit them; so she changed the subject by saying, as her foot kept time, 'That's a splendid polka in the next room. Why don't you go and try it?'

'If you will come too,' he answered, with a gallant little bow.

'I can't; for I told Meg I wouldn't, because –' There Jo stopped, and looked undecided whether to tell or to laugh.

'Because what?' asked Laurie, curiously.

'You won't tell?'

'Never!'

'Well, I have a bad trick of standing before the fire, and so I burn my frocks, and I scorched this one; and though it's nicely mended, it shows, and Meg told me to keep still, so no one would see it. You may laugh, if you want to; it is funny, I know.'

But Laurie didn't laugh; he only looked down a minute, and the expression of his face puzzled Jo, when he said very gently: 'Never mind that. I'll tell you how we can manage: there's a long hall out there, and we can dance grandly, and no one will see us. Please come.'

Jo thanked him, and gladly went, wishing she had two neat gloves, when she saw the nice, pearl-coloured ones her partner put on. The hall was empty, and they had a grand polka, for Laurie danced well, and taught her the German step, which delighted Jo, being full of swing and spring.

When the music stopped, they sat down on the stairs to get their breath, and Laurie was in the midst of an account of a students' festival at Heidelberg, when Meg appeared in search of her sister. She beckoned, and Jo reluctantly followed her into a side room, where she found her on a sofa, holding her foot, and looking pale.

'I've sprained my ankle. That stupid high heel turned, and gave me a sad wrench. It aches so I can hardly stand, and I don't know how I'm ever going to get home,' she said, rocking to and fro in pain.

'I knew you'd hurt your feet with those silly shoes. I'm sorry. But I don't see what you can do, except get a carriage, or stay here all night,' answered Jo, softly rubbing the poor ankle as she spoke.

'I can't have a carriage, without its costing ever so much. I daresay I can't get one at all; for most people come in their own, and it's a long way to the stable, and no one to send.'

'I'll go.'

'No, indeed! It's past nine, and dark as Egypt. I can't stop here, for the house is full. Sallie has some girls staying with her. I'll rest till Hannah comes, and then do the best I can.'

'I'll ask Laurie; he will go,' said Jo, looking relieved as the idea occurred to her.

'Mercy, no! Don't ask or tell anyone. Get me my rubbers, and put these slippers with our things. As soon as supper is over, watch for Hannah, and tell me the minute she comes.'

'They are going out to supper now. I'll stay with you; I'd rather.'

'No, dear, run along, and bring me some coffee. I'm so tired, I can't stir!'

So Meg reclined, with rubbers well hidden, and Jo went blundering away to the dining room, which she found after going into a china-closet, and opening the door of a room where old Mr Gardiner was taking a little private refreshment. Making a dart at the table, she secured the coffee, which she immediately spilt, making the front of her dress as bad as the back.

'Oh, dear, what a blunderbuss I am!' exclaimed Jo, finishing Meg's glove by scrubbing her gown with it.

'Can I help you?' said a friendly voice; and there was Laurie, with a full cup in one hand, and a plate of ice in the other.

'I was trying to get something for Meg, who is very tired, and someone shook me; and here I am, in a nice state,' answered Jo, glancing dismally from the stained skirt to the coffee-coloured glove.

'Too bad! I was looking for someone to give this to. May I take it to your sister?'

'Oh, thank you! I'll show you where she is. I don't offer to take it myself, for I should only get into another scrape if I did.'

Jo led the way; and, as if used to waiting on ladies, Laurie drew up a little table, brought a second instalment of coffee and ice for Jo, and was so obliging that even particular Meg pronounced him a 'nice boy'. They had a merry time over the bonbons and mottoes, and were in the midst of a quiet game of 'Buzz', with two or three other young people who had strayed in, when Hannah appeared. Meg forgot her foot, and rose so quickly that she was forced to catch hold of Jo, with an exclamation of pain.

'Hush! Don't say anything,' she whispered, adding aloud, 'It's nothing. I turned my foot a little, that's all'; and limped upstairs to put her things on.

Hannah scolded, Meg cried, and Jo was at her wit's end, till she decided to take things into her own hands. Slipping out, she ran down, and, finding a servant, asked if he could get her a carriage. It happened to be a hired waiter, who knew nothing about the neighbourhood; and Jo was looking round for help, when Laurie, who had heard what she said, came up, and offered his grandfather's carriage, which had just come for him, he said.

'It's so early! You can't mean to go yet?' began Jo, looking relieved, but hesitating to accept the offer.

'I always go early – I do, truly! Please let me take you home. It's all on my way, you know, and it rains, they say.'

That settled it; and, telling him of Meg's mishap, Jo gratefully accepted, and rushed up to bring down the rest of the party. Hannah hated rain as much as a cat does; so she made no trouble, and they rolled away in the luxurious close carriage, feeling very festive and elegant. Laurie went on the box; so Meg could keep her foot up, and the girls talked over their party in freedom.

'I had a capital time. Did you?' asked Jo, rumpling up her hair, and making herself comfortable.

'Yes, till I hurt myself. Sallie's friend, Annie Moffat, took a fancy to me, and asked me to come and spend a week with her when Sallie does. She is going in the spring, when the opera comes; and it will be perfectly splendid, if Mother only lets me go,' answered Meg, cheering up at the thought.

'I saw you with the red-headed man I ran away from. Was he nice?'

'Oh, very! His hair is auburn, not red; and he was very polite, and I had a delicious redowa with him.'

'He looked like a grasshopper in a fit when he did the new step. Laurie and I couldn't help laughing. Did you hear us?'

'No; but it was very rude. What *were* you about all that time, hidden away there?'

Jo told her adventures, and, by the time she had finished, they were at home. With many thanks, they said 'Good night', and crept in, hoping to disturb no one; but the instant their door creaked, two little night-caps bobbed up, and two sleepy but eager voices cried out:

'Tell about the party! tell about the party!'

With what Meg called 'a great want of manners', Jo had saved some bonbons for the little girls; and they soon subsided, after hearing the most thrilling events of the evening.

'I declare, it really seems like being a fine young lady to come home from the party in a carriage, and sit in my dressing-gown with a maid to wait on me,' said Meg, as Jo bound up her foot with arnica, and brushed her hair.

'I don't believe fine young ladies enjoy themselves a bit more than we do, in spite of our burnt hair, old gowns, one glove apiece, and tight slippers that sprain our ankles when we are silly enough to wear them.' And I think Jo was quite right.

CHAPTER 4

Burdens

'Oh, dear, how hard it does seem to take up our packs and jog on,' sighed Meg, the morning after the party; for, now the holidays were over, the week of merry-making did not fit her for going on easily with the task she never liked.

'I wish it was Christmas or New Year all the time; wouldn't it be fun?' answered Jo, yawning dismally.

'We shouldn't enjoy ourselves half so much as we do now. But it does seem so nice to have little suppers and bouquets, and go to parties, and drive home, and read and rest, and not work. It's like other people, you know, and I always envy girls who do such things; I'm so fond of luxury,' said Meg, trying to decide which of two shabby gowns was the least shabby.

'Well, we can't have it, so don't let us grumble, but shoulder our bundles and trudge along as cheerfully as Marmee does. I'm sure Aunt March is a regular Old Man of the Sea to me, but I suppose when I've learnt to carry her without complaining, she will tumble off, or get so light that I shan't mind her.'

This idea tickled Jo's fancy, and put her in good spirits; but Meg didn't brighten, for her burden, consisting of four spoilt children, seemed heavier than ever. She hadn't heart enough even to make herself pretty, as usual, by putting on a blue neck-ribbon, and dressing her hair in the most becoming way.

'Where's the use of looking nice, when no one sees me but those cross midgets, and no one cares whether I'm pretty or not?' she muttered, shutting her drawer with a jerk. 'I shall have to toil and moil all my days, with only little bits of fun now and then, and get old and ugly and sour, because I'm poor, and can't enjoy my life as other girls do. It's a shame!'

So Meg went down, wearing an injured look, and wasn't at all agreeable at breakfast-time. Everyone seemed rather out of sorts, and inclined to croak. Beth had a headache, and lay on the sofa, trying to comfort herself with the cat and three kittens; Amy was fretting because her lessons were not learned, and she couldn't find her rubbers; Jo *would* whistle and make a great racket getting ready; Mrs March was very busy trying to finish a letter which must go at once; and Hannah had the grumps, for being up late didn't suit her.

'There never *was* such a cross family!' cried Jo, losing her temper when she had upset an inkstand, broken both bootlacings, and sat down upon her hat.

'You're the crossest person in it!' returned Amy, washing out the sum, that was all wrong, with the tears that had fallen on her slate.

'Beth, if you don't keep these horrid cats down in the cellar I'll have them drowned,' exclaimed Meg, angrily, as she tried to get rid of the kitten, which had scrambled up her back, and stuck like a burr just out of reach.

Jo laughed, Meg scolded, Beth implored, and Amy wailed, because she couldn't remember how much nine times twelve was.

'Girls, girls, do be quiet one minute! I *must* get this off by the early mail, and you drive me distracted with your worry,' cried Mrs March, crossing out the third spoilt sentence in her letter.

There was a momentary lull, broken by Hannah, who stalked in, laid two hot turnovers on the table, and stalked out again. These turnovers were an institution; and the girls called them 'muffs', for they had no others, and found the hot pies very comforting to their hands on cold mornings. Hannah never forgot to make them, no matter how busy or grumpy she might be, for the walk was long and bleak; the poor things got no other lunch, and were seldom home before two.

'Cuddle your cats, and get over your headache, Bethy. Good-bye, Marmee; we are a set of rascals this morning, but we'll come home regular angels. Now then, Meg!' and Jo tramped away, feeling that the pilgrims were not setting out as they ought to do.

They always looked back before turning the corner, for their mother was always at the window, to nod and smile, and wave her hand to them. Somehow it seemed as if they couldn't have got through the day without that; for, whatever their mood might be, the last glimpse of that motherly face was sure to affect them like sunshine.

'If Marmee shook her fist instead of kissing her hand to us, it would serve us right, for more ungrateful wretches than we are were never seen,' cried Jo, taking a remorseful satisfaction in the snowy walk and bitter wind.

'Don't use such dreadful expressions,' said Meg, from the depths of the veil in which she had shrouded herself like a nun sick of the world.

'I like good strong words that mean something,' replied Jo, catching her hat as it took a leap off her head, preparatory to flying away altogether.

'Call yourself any names you like; but *I* am neither a rascal nor a wretch, and I don't choose to be called so.'

'You're a blighted being, and decidedly cross today, because you can't sit in the lap of luxury all the time. Poor dear, just wait till I make my fortune, and you shall revel in carriages and ice-cream and high heeled slippers and posies and red-headed boys to dance with.'

'How ridiculous you are, Jo!' but Meg laughed at the nonsense, and felt better in spite of herself.

'Lucky for you I am; for if I put on crushed airs, and tried to be dismal, as you do, we should be in a nice state. Thank goodness, I can always find something funny to keep me up. Don't croak any more but come home jolly, there's a dear.'

Jo gave her sister an encouraging pat on the shoulder as they parted for the day, each going a different way, each hugging her little warm turnover, and each trying to be cheerful in spite of wintry weather, hard work, and the unsatisfied desires of pleasure-loving youth.

When Mr March lost his property in trying to help an unfortunate friend, the two oldest girls begged to be allowed to do something towards their own support, at least. Believing that they could not begin too early to cultivate energy, industry, and independence, their parents consented, and both fell to work with the hearty goodwill which, in spite of all obstacles, is sure to succeed at last. Margaret found a place as nursery governess, and felt rich with her small salary. As she said, she *was* 'fond of luxury', and her chief trouble was poverty. She found it harder to bear than the others, because she could remember a time when home was beautiful, life full of ease and pleasure, and want of any kind unknown. She tried not to be envious or discontented but it was very natural that the young girl should long for pretty things, gay friends, accomplishments, and a happy life. At the Kings' she daily saw all she wanted, for the children's older sisters were just out, and Meg caught frequent glimpses of dainty party-dresses and bouquets, heard lively gossip about theatres, concerts, sleighing parties, and merry-makings of all kinds, and saw money lavished on trifles which would have been so precious to her. Poor Meg seldom complained, but a sense of injustice made her feel bitter towards everyone sometimes, for she had not yet learned to know how rich she was in the blessings which alone can make life happy.

Jo happened to suit Aunt March, who was lame, and needed an active person to wait upon her. The childless old lady had offered to adopt one of the girls when the troubles came, and was much offended because her offer was declined. Other friends told the Marches that they had lost all chance of being remembered in the rich old lady's will; but the unworldly Marches only said:

'We can't give up our girls for a dozen fortunes. Rich or poor, we will keep together and be happy in one another.'

The old lady wouldn't speak to them for a time, but, happening to meet Jo at a friend's, something in her comical face and blunt manners struck the old lady's fancy, and she proposed to take her for a companion. This did not suit Jo at all; but she accepted the place since nothing better appeared, and, to everyone's surprise, got on remarkably well with her irascible relative. There was an occasional tempest, and once Jo had marched home, declaring she couldn't bear it any longer; but Aunt March always cleared up quickly, and sent for her back again with such urgency that she could not refuse, for in her heart she rather liked the peppery old lady.

I suspect that the real attraction was a large library of fine books, which was left to dust and spiders since Uncle March died. Jo remembered the kind old gentleman, who used to let her build railroads and bridges with his big dictionaries, tell her stories about the queer pictures in his Latin books, and buy her cards of gingerbread whenever he met her in the street. The dim, dusty room, with the busts staring down from the tall bookcases, the cosy chairs, the globes, and, best of all, the wilderness of books, in which she could wander where she liked, made the library a region of bliss to her. The moment Aunt March took her nap or was busy with company Jo hurried to this quiet place, and curling herself up in the easy-chair, devoured poetry, romance, history, travels, and pictures, like a regular book-worm. But, like all happiness, it did not last long; for as sure as she had just reached the heart of the story, the sweetest verse of the song, or the most perilous adventure of her traveller, a shrill voice called, 'Josy-phine! Josy-phine!' and she had to leave her paradise to wind yarn, wash the poodle, or read Belsham's Essays by the hour together.

Jo's ambition was to do something very splendid; what it was she had no idea, as yet, but left it for time to tell her; and, meanwhile, found her greatest affliction in the fact that she couldn't read, run, and ride as much as she liked. A quick temper, sharp tongue, and restless spirit were always getting her into scrapes, and her life was a series of ups and downs, which were both comic and pathetic. But the training she received at Aunt March's was just what she needed; and the thought that she was doing something to support herself made her happy, in spite of the perpetual 'Josy-phine!'

Beth was too bashful to go to school; it had been tried, but she suffered so much that it was given up, and she did her lessons at home with her father. Even when he went away, and her mother was called to devote her skill and energy to Soldiers' Aid Societies, Beth went faithfully on by herself, and did the best she could. She was a housewifely little creature, and helped Hannah keep home neat and comfortable for the workers, never thinking of any reward but to be loved. Long, quiet days she spent, not lonely nor idle, for her little world was peopled with imaginary friends, and she was by nature a busy bee. There were six dolls to be taken up and dressed every morning, for Beth was a child still, and loved her pets as well as ever. Not one whole or handsome one among them; all were outcasts till Beth took them in; for, when her sisters outgrew these idols, they passed to her, because Amy would have nothing old or ugly. Beth cherished them all the more tenderly for that very reason, and set up a hospital for infirm dolls. No pins were ever stuck into their cotton vitals; no harsh words or blows were ever given them; no neglect ever saddened the heart of the most repulsive: but all were fed and clothed, nursed and caressed, with an affection which never failed.

One forlorn fragment of *dollanity* had belonged to Jo; and, having led a tempestuous life, was left a wreck in the ragbag, from which dreary poor-house it was rescued by Beth, and taken to her refuge. Having no top to its head, she tied on a neat little cap, and, as both arms and legs were gone, she hid these deficiencies by folding it in a blanket, and devoting her best bed to this chronic invalid. If anyone had known the care lavished on that dolly, I think it would have touched their hearts, even while they laughed. She brought it bits of bouquets; she read to it, took it out to breathe the air, hidden under her coat; she sang it lullabies, and never went to bed without kissing its dirty face, and whispering tenderly, 'I hope you'll have a good night, my poor dear.'

Beth had her troubles as well as the others; and not being an angel, but a very human little girl, she often 'wept a little weep', as Jo said, because she couldn't take music lessons and have a fine piano. She loved music so dearly, tried so hard to learn, and practised away so patiently at the jingling old instrument, that it did seem as if someone (not to hint Aunt March) ought to help her. Nobody did, however, and nobody saw Beth wipe the tears off the yellow keys, that wouldn't keep in tune, when she was all alone. She sang like a little lark about her work, never was too tired to play for Marmee and the girls, and day after day said hopefully to herself, 'I know I'll get my music some time, if I'm good.'

There are many Beths in the world, shy and quiet, sitting in corners till needed, and living for others so cheerfully that no one sees the sacrifices till the little cricket on the hearth stops chirping, and the sweet, sunshiny presence vanishes, leaving silence and shadow behind.

If anybody had asked Amy what the greatest trial of her life was, she would have answered at once, 'My nose'. When she was a baby, Jo had accidentally dropped her into the coal-hod, and Amy insisted that the fall had ruined her nose for ever. It was not big, nor red, like poor 'Petrea's'; it was only rather flat, and all the pinching in the world could not give it an aristocratic point. No one minded it but herself, and it was doing its best to grow, but Amy felt deeply the want of a Grecian nose, and drew whole sheets of handsome ones to console herself.

'Little Raphael', as her sisters called her, had a decided talent for drawing, and was never so happy as when copying flowers, designing fairies, or illustrating stories with queer specimens of art. Her teachers complained that, instead of doing her sums, she covered her slate with animals; the blank pages of her atlas were used to copy maps on; and caricatures of the most ludicrous description came fluttering out of all her books at unlucky moments. She got through her lessons as well as she could, and managed to escape reprimands by being a model of deportment. She was a great favourite with her mates, being good-tempered and possessing the happy art of pleasing without effort. Her little airs and graces were much admired, so were her accomplishments; for beside her drawing, she could play twelve tunes, crochet, and read French without mispronouncing more than two-thirds of the words. She had a plaintive way of saying 'When Papa was rich we did so-and-so,' which was very touching; and her long words were considered 'perfectly elegant' by the girls.

Amy was in a fair way to be spoilt; for everyone petted her, and her small vanities and selfishness were growing nicely. One thing, however, rather quenched the vanities; she had to wear her cousin's clothes. Now Florence's mamma hadn't a particle of taste, and Amy suffered deeply at having to wear a red instead of a blue bonnet, unbecoming gowns, and fussy aprons that did not fit. Everything was good, well made, and little worn; but Amy's artistic eyes were much afflicted, especially this winter, when her school dress was a dull purple, with yellow dots, and no trimming.

'My only comfort,' she said to Meg, with tears in her eyes, 'is that Mother don't take tucks in my dresses whenever I'm naughty, as Maria Park's mother does. My dear, it's really dreadful; for sometimes she is so bad, her frock is up to her knees, and she can't come to school. When I think of this *deggerredation*, I feel that I can bear even my flat nose and purple gown, with yellow sky-rockets on it.'

Meg was Amy's confidante and monitor, and, by some strange attraction of opposites, Jo was gentle Beth's. To Jo alone did the shy child tell her thoughts; and over her big harum-scarum sister Beth unconsciously exercised more influence than anyone in the family. The two elder girls were a great deal to one another, but each took one of the younger into her keeping, and watched over her in her own way; 'playing mother' they called it, and put their sisters in the places of discarded dolls, with the maternal instincts of little women.

'Has anybody got anything to tell? It's been such a dismal day I'm really dying for some amusement,' said Meg, as they sat sewing together that evening.

'I had a queer time with aunt today, and, as I got the best of it, I'll tell you about it,' began Jo, who dearly loved to tell stories.

'I was reading that everlasting Belsham, and droning away as I always do, for aunt soon drops off, and then I take out some nice book, and read like fury till she wakes up. I actually made myself sleepy; and, before she began to nod, I gave such a gape that she asked me what I meant by opening my mouth wide enough to take the whole book in at once.

'"I wish I could and be done with it," said I, trying not to be saucy.

'Then she gave me a long lecture on my sins, and told me to sit and think them over while she just "lost" herself for a moment. She never finds herself very soon; so the minute her cap began to bob, like a top-heavy dahlia, I whipped the *Vicar of Wakefield* out of my pocket, and read away, with one eye on him, and one on aunt. I'd just got to where they all tumbled into the water, when I forgot, and laughed out loud. Aunt woke up; and, being more good-natured after her nap, told me to read a bit, and show what frivolous work I preferred to the worthy and instructive Belsham. I did my very best, and she liked it, though she only said:

'"I don't understand what it's all about. Go back and begin it, child."

'Back I went, and made the Primroses as interesting as ever I could. Once I was wicked enough to stop in a thrilling place, and say meekly, "I'm afraid it tires you, ma'am; shan't I stop now?"

'She caught up her knitting, which had dropped out of her hands, gave me a sharp look through her specs, and said, in her short way:

'"Finish the chapter, and don't be impertinent, miss."'

'Did she own she liked it?' asked Meg.

'Oh, bless you, no! but she let old Belsham rest; and, when I ran back after my gloves this afternoon, there she was, so hard at the Vicar that she didn't hear me laugh as I danced a jig in the hall, because of the good time coming. What a pleasant life she might have, if she only chose. I don't envy her much, in spite of her money, for after all, rich people have about as many worries as poor ones, I think,' added Jo.

'That reminds me,' said Meg, 'that I've got something to tell. It isn't funny, like Jo's story, but I thought about it a good deal as I came home. At the Kings' today I found everybody in a flurry, and one of the children said that her oldest brother had done something dreadful, and papa had sent him away. I heard Mrs King crying and Mr King talking very loud, and Grace and Ellen turned away their faces when they passed me, so I shouldn't see how red their eyes were. I didn't ask any questions, of course; but I felt so sorry for them, and was rather glad I hadn't any wild brothers to do wicked things and disgrace the family.'

'I think being disgraced in school is a great deal *tryinger* than anything bad boys can do,' said Amy, shaking her head, as if her experience of life had been a deep one. 'Susie Perkins came to school today with a lovely red carnelian ring; I wanted it dreadfully, and wished I was her with all my might. Well, she drew a picture of Mr Davis, with a monstrous nose and a hump, and the words, "Young ladies, my eye is upon you!" coming out of his mouth in a balloon thing. We were laughing over it, when all of a sudden his eye *was* on us, and he ordered Susie to bring up her slate. She was *parrylized* with fright, but she went, and oh, what *do* you think he did? He took her by the ear – the ear! just fancy how horrid! – and led her to the recitation platform, and made her stand there half an hour, holding that slate so everyone could see it.'

'Didn't the girls laugh at the picture?' asked Jo, who relished the scrape.

'Laugh! Not one! They sat as still as mice; and Susie cried quarts, I know she did. I didn't envy her then; for I felt that millions of carnelian rings wouldn't have made me happy after that. I never, never should have got over such an agonizing mortification.' And Amy went on with her work, in the proud consciousness of virtue, and the successful utterance of two long words in a breath.

'I saw something that I liked this morning, and I meant to tell it at dinner, but I forgot,' said Beth, putting Jo's topsy-turvy basket in order as she talked. 'When I went to get some oysters for Hannah, Mr Laurence was in the fish-shop; but he didn't see me, for I kept behind a barrel, and he was busy with Mr Cutter, the fish-man. A poor woman came in, with a pail and a mop, and asked Mr Cutter if he would let her do some scrubbing for a bit of fish, because she hadn't any dinner for her children, and had been disappointed of a day's work. Mr Cutter was in a hurry, and said "No," rather crossly; so she was going away, looking hungry and sorry, when Mr Laurence hooked up a big fish with the crooked end of his cane, and held it out to her. She was so glad and surprised, she took it right in her arms, and thanked him over and over. He told her to "go along and cook it", and she hurried off, so happy! Wasn't it good of him? Oh, she did look so funny, hugging the big, slippery fish, and hoping Mr Laurence's bed in heaven would be "aisy".'

When they had laughed at Beth's story, they asked their mother for one; and, after a moment's thought, she said soberly:

'As I sat cutting out blue flannel jackets today, at the rooms, I felt very anxious about Father, and thought how lonely and help-less we should be if anything happened to him. It was not a wise thing to do; but I kept on worrying till an old man came in, with an order for some clothes. He sat down near me, and I began to talk to him; for he looked poor and tired and anxious.

'"Have you sons in the army?" I asked; for the note he brought was not to me.

'"Yes, ma'am. I had four, but two were killed, one is a pris-oner, and I'm going to the other, who is very sick in a Washington hospital," he answered, quietly.

'"You have done a great deal for your country, sir," I said, feeling respect now instead of pity.

'"Not a mite more than I ought, ma'am. I'd go myself, if I was any use; as I ain't, I give my boys, and give 'em free."

'He spoke so cheerfully, looked so sincere, and seemed so glad to give his all, that I was ashamed of myself. I'd given one man, and thought it too much, while he gave four without grudging them. I had all my girls to comfort me at home; and his last son was waiting, miles away, to say "good-bye" to him, perhaps! I felt so rich, so happy, thinking of my blessings, that I made him a nice bundle, gave him some money, and thanked him heartily for the lesson he had taught me.'

'Tell another story, Mother – one with a moral to it, like this. I like to think about them afterwards, if they are real, and not too preachy,' said Jo, after a minute's silence.

Mrs March smiled, and began at once; for she had told stories to this little audience for many years, and knew how to please them.

'Once upon a time, there were four girls, who had enough to eat and drink and wear, a good many comforts and pleasures, kind friends and parents, who loved them dearly, and yet they were not contented.' (Here the listeners stole sly looks at one another, and began to sew diligently.) 'These girls were anxious to be good, and made many excellent resolutions; but they did not keep them very well, and were constantly saying, "If we only had this," or "If we could only do that," quite forgetting how much they already had, and how many pleasant things they actually could do. So they asked an old woman what spell they could use to make them happy, and she said, "When you feel discontented, think over your blessings and be grateful."' (Here Jo looked up quickly, as if about to speak, but changed her mind, seeing that the story was not done yet.)

'Being sensible girls, they decided to try her advice, and soon were surprised to see how well off they were. One discovered that money couldn't keep shame and sorrow out of rich people's houses; another that, though she was poor, she was a great deal happier, with her youth, health, and good spirits, than a certain fretful, feeble old lady, who couldn't enjoy her comforts; a third, that, disagreeable as it was to help get dinner, it was harder still to have to go begging for it; and the fourth, that even carnelian rings were not so valuable as good behaviour. So they agreed to stop complaining, to enjoy the blessings already possessed, and try to deserve them, lest they should be taken away entirely, instead of increased; and I believe they were never disappointed, or sorry that they took the old woman's advice.'

'Now, Marmee, that is very cunning of you to turn our own stories against us, and give us a sermon instead of a romance!' cried Meg.

'I like that kind of sermon. It's the sort Father used to tell us,' said Beth, thoughtfully, putting the needles straight on Jo's cushion.

'I don't complain near as much as the others do, and I shall be more careful than ever now; for I've had warning from Susie's downfall,' said Amy, morally.

'We needed that lesson, and we won't forget it. If we do, you just say to us, as old Chloe did in *Uncle Tom*, "Tink ob yer marcies, chillen! tink ob yer marcies!"' added Jo, who could not for the life of her help getting a morsel of fun out of the little sermon, though she took it to heart as much as any of them.

CHAPTER 5

Being Neighbourly

'What in the world are you going to do now, Jo?' asked Meg, one snowy afternoon, as her sister came tramping through the hall, in rubber boots, old sack and hood, with a broom in one hand and a shovel in the other.

'Going out for exercise,' answered Jo, with a mischievous twinkle in her eyes.

'I should think two long walks this morning would have been enough! It's cold and dull out; and I advise you to stay warm and dry, by the fire, as I do,' said Meg, with a shiver.

'Never take advice! Can't keep still all day, and, not being a pussy-cat, I don't like to doze by the fire. I like adventures, and I'm going to find some.'

Meg went back to toast her feet and read *Ivanhoe*; and Jo began to dig paths with great energy. The snow was light, and with her broom she soon swept a path all round the garden, for Beth to walk in when the sun came out; and the invalid dolls needed air. Now the garden separated the Marches' house from that of Mr Laurence. Both stood in a suburb of the city, which was still country-like, with groves and lawns, large gardens, and quiet streets. A low hedge parted the two estates. On one side was an old, brown house, looking rather bare and shabby, robbed of the vines that in summer covered its walls, and the flowers which then surrounded it. On the other side was a stately stone mansion, plainly betokening every sort of comfort and luxury, from the big coach-house and well-kept grounds to the conservatory and the glimpses of lovely things one caught between the rich curtains. Yet it seemed a lonely, lifeless sort of house; for no children frolicked on the lawn, no motherly face ever smiled at the windows, and few people went in and out, except the old gentleman and his grandson.

To Jo's lively fancy, this fine house seemed a kind of enchanted palace, full of splendours and delights, which no one enjoyed. She had long wanted to behold these hidden glories, and to know the 'Laurence boy', who looked as if he would like to be known, if he only knew how to begin. Since the party, she had been more eager than ever, and had planned many ways of making friends with him; but he had not been seen lately, and Jo began to think he had gone away, when she one day spied a brown face at an upper window, looking wistfully down into their garden, where Beth and Amy were snowballing one another.

'That boy is suffering for society and fun,' she said to herself. 'His grandpa does not know what's good for him, and keeps him shut up all alone. He needs a party of jolly boys to play with, or somebody young and lively. I've a great mind to go over and tell the old gentleman so!'

The idea amused Jo, who liked to do daring things, and was always scandalizing Meg by her queer performances. The plan of 'going over' was not forgotten; and when the snowy afternoon came, Jo resolved to try what could be done. She saw Mr Laurence drive off, and then sallied out to dig her way down to the hedge, where she paused and took a survey. All quiet – curtains down at the lower windows; servants out of sight, and nothing human visible but a curly black head leaning on a thin hand at the upper window.

'There he is,' thought Jo, 'poor boy! all alone and sick this dismal day. It's a shame! I'll toss up a snowball, and make him look out, and then say a kind word to him.'

Up went a handful of soft snow, and the head turned at once, showing a face which lost its listless look in a minute, as the big eyes brightened and the mouth began to smile. Jo nodded and laughed, and flourished her broom as she called out:

'How do you do? Are you sick?'

Laurie opened the window, and croaked out as hoarsely as a raven,

'Better, thank you. I've had a bad cold, and been shut up a week.'

'I'm sorry. What do you amuse yourself with?'

'Nothing; it's as dull as tombs up here.'

'Don't you read?'

'Not much; they won't let me.'

'Can't somebody read to you?'

'Grandpa does, sometimes; but my books don't interest him and I hate to ask Brooke all the time.'

'Have someone come and see you, then.'

'There isn't anyone I'd like to see. Boys make such a row, and my head is weak.'

'Isn't there some nice girl who'd read and amuse you? Girls are quiet, and like to play nurse.'

'Don't know any.'

'You know us,' began Jo, then laughed, and stopped.

'So I do! Will you come, please?' cried Laurie.

'I'm not quiet and nice; but I'll come, if Mother will let me. I'll go ask her. Shut that window, like a good boy, and wait till I come.'

With that, Jo shouldered her broom and marched into the house, wondering what they would all say to her. Laurie was in a flutter of excitement at the idea of having company, and flew about to get ready; for, as Mrs March said, he was 'a little gentleman', and did honour to the coming guest by brushing his curly pate, putting on a fresh collar, and trying to tidy up the room, which, in spite of half a dozen servants, was anything but neat. Presently there came a loud ring, then a decided voice, asking for 'Mr Laurie', and a surprised-looking servant came running up to announce a young lady.

'All right, show her up, it's Miss Jo,' said Laurie, going to the door of his little parlour to meet Jo, who appeared, looking rosy and kind and quite at her ease, with a covered dish in one hand and Beth's three kittens in the other.

'Here I am, bag and baggage,' she said briskly. 'Mother sent her love, and was glad if I could do anything for you. Meg wanted me to bring some of her blancmange; she makes it very nicely, and Beth thought her cats would be comforting. I knew you'd laugh at them, but I couldn't refuse, she was so anxious to do something.'

It so happened that Beth's funny loan was just the thing; for, in laughing over the kits, Laurie forgot his bashfulness, and grew sociable at once.

'That looks too pretty to eat,' he said, smiling with pleasure, as Jo uncovered the dish, and showed the blancmange, surrounded by a garland of green leaves, and the scarlet flowers of Amy's pet geranium.

'It isn't anything, only they all felt kindly, and wanted to show it. Tell the girl to put it away for your tea; it's so simple, you can eat it; and, being soft, it will slip down without hurting your sore throat. What a cosy room this is!'

'It might be if it was kept nice; but the maids are lazy, and I don't know how to make them mind. It worries me, though.'

'I'll right it up in two minutes; for it only needs to have the hearth brushed, so – and the things made straight on the mantel-piece, so – and the books put here and the bottles there, and your sofa turned from the light, and the pillows plumped up a bit. Now, then, you're fixed.'

And so he was; for, as she laughed and talked, Jo had whisked things into place, and given quite a different air to the room. Laurie watched her in respectful silence; and when she beckoned him to his sofa, he sat down with a sigh of satisfaction, saying gratefully:

'How kind you are! Yes, that's what it wanted. Now please take the big chair, and let me do something to amuse my company.'

'No. I came to amuse you. Shall I read aloud?' and Jo looked affectionately towards some inviting books near by.

'Thank you; I've read all those, and if you don't mind I'd rather talk,' answered Laurie.

'Not a bit; I'll talk all day if you'll only set me going. Beth says I never know when to stop.'

'Is Beth the rosy one, who stays at home a good deal, and sometimes goes out with a little basket?' asked Laurie, with interest.

'Yes, that's Beth; she's my girl, and a regular good one she is, too.'

'The pretty one is Meg, and the curly-haired one is Amy, I believe?'

'How did you find that out?'

Laurie coloured up, but answered frankly, 'Why, you see, I often hear you calling to one another, and when I'm alone up here, I can't help looking over at your house, you always seem to be having such good times. I beg your pardon for being so rude, but sometimes you forget to put down the curtain at the window where the flowers are; and when the lamps are lighted, it's like looking at a picture to see the fire, and you all round the table with your mother; her face is right opposite, and it looks so sweet behind the flowers, I can't help watching it. I haven't got any mother, you know,' and Laurie poked the fire to hide a little twitching of the lips that he could not control.

The solitary, hungry look in his eyes went straight to Jo's warm heart. She had been so simply taught that there was no nonsense in her head, and at fifteen she was as innocent and frank as any child. Laurie was sick and lonely; and, feeling how rich she was in home-love and happiness, she gladly tried to share it with him. Her face was very friendly and her sharp voice unusually gentle as she said:

'We'll never draw that curtain any more, and I give you leave to look as much as you like. I just wish, though, instead of peeping, you'd come over and see us. Mother is so splendid, she'd do you heaps of good, and Beth would sing to you if *I* begged her to, and Amy would dance; Meg and I would make you laugh over our funny stage properties, and we'd have jolly times. Wouldn't your grandpa let you?'

'I think he would, if your mother asked him. He's very kind, though he does not look so; and he lets me do what I like, pretty much, only he's afraid *I* might be a bother to strangers,' began Laurie, brightening more and more.

'We are not strangers, we are neighbours, and you needn't think you'd be a bother. We want to know you, and I've been trying to do this ever so long. We haven't been here a great while, you know, but we have got acquainted with all our neighbours but you.'

'You see grandpa lives among his books, and doesn't mind much what happens outside. Mr Brooke, my tutor, doesn't stay here, you know, and I have no one to go about with me, so I just stop at home and get on as I can.'

'That's bad. You ought to make an effort, and go visiting everywhere you are asked; then you'll have plenty of friends, and pleasant places to go to. Never mind being bashful; it won't last long if you keep going.'

Laurie turned red again, but wasn't offended at being accused of bashfulness; for there was so much goodwill in Jo, it was impossible not to take her blunt speeches as kindly as they were meant.

'Do you like your school?' asked the boy, changing the subject, after a little pause, during which he stared at the fire, and Jo looked about her, well pleased.

'Don't go to school; I'm a business man – girl, I mean. I go to wait on my great-aunt, and a dear, cross old soul she is, too,' answered Jo.

Laurie opened his mouth to ask another question; but remembering just in time that it wasn't manners to make too many inquiries into people's affairs, he shut it again, and looked uncomfortable. Jo liked his good breeding, and didn't mind having a laugh at Aunt March, so she gave him a lively description of the fidgety old lady, her fat poodle, the parrot that talked Spanish, and the library where she revelled. Laurie enjoyed that immensely; and when she told about the prim old gentleman who came once to woo Aunt March, and in the middle of a fine speech, how Polly had tweaked his wig off, to his great dismay, the boy lay back and laughed till the tears ran down his cheeks, and a maid popped her head in to see what was the matter.

'Oh! that does me no end of good. Tell on, please,' he said, taking his face out of the sofa cushions, red and shining with merriment.

Much elated with her success, Jo did 'tell on', all about their plays and plans, their hopes and fears for Father, and the most interesting events of the little world in which the sisters lived. Then they got to talking about books; and to Jo's delight, she found that Laurie loved them as well as she did, and had read even more than herself.

'If you like them so much, come down and see ours. Grandpa is out, so you needn't be afraid,' said Laurie, getting up.

'I'm not afraid of anything,' returned Jo, with a toss of the head.

'I don't believe you are!' exclaimed the boy, looking at her with much admiration, though he privately thought she would have good reason to be a trifle afraid of the old gentleman, if she met him in some of his moods.

The atmosphere of the whole house being summer-like, Laurie led the way from room to room, letting Jo stop to examine whatever struck her fancy; and so at last they came to the library, where she clapped her hands, and pranced, as she always did when especially delighted. It was lined with books, and there were pictures and statues and distracting little cabinets full of coins and curiosities, and sleepy-hollow chairs and queer tables, and bronzes; and, best of all, a great open fireplace, with quaint tiles all round it.

'What richness!' sighed Jo, sinking into the depth of a velvet chair, and gazing about her with an air of intense satisfaction. 'Theodore Laurence, you ought to be the happiest boy in the world,' she added impressively.

'A fellow can't live on books,' said Laurie, shaking his head, as he perched on a table opposite.

Before he could say more, a bell rang, and Jo flew up, exclaiming with alarm, 'Mercy me! it's your grandpa!'

'Well, what if it is? You are not afraid of anything, you know,' returned the boy, looking wicked.

'I think I am a little bit afraid of him, but I don't know why I should be. Marmee said I might come, and I don't think you're any the worse for it,' said Jo, composing herself, though she kept her eyes on the door.

'I'm a great deal better for it, and ever so much obliged. I'm only afraid you are very tired talking to me; it was so pleasant, I couldn't bear to stop,' said Laurie, gratefully.

'The doctor to see you, sir,' and the maid beckoned as she spoke.

'Would you mind if I left you for a minute? I suppose I must see him,' said Laurie.

'Don't mind me. I'm as happy as a cricket here,' answered Jo.

Laurie went away, and his guest amused herself in her own way. She was standing before a fine portrait of the old gentleman, when the door opened again, and without turning, she said decidedly, 'I'm sure now that I shouldn't be afraid of him, for he's got kind eyes, though his mouth is grim, and he looks as if he had a tremendous will of his own. He isn't as handsome as *my* grandfather, but I like him.'

'Thank you, ma'am,' said a gruff voice behind her; and there, to her great dismay, stood old Mr Laurence.

Poor Jo blushed till she couldn't blush any redder, and her heart began to beat uncomfortably fast as she thought what she had said. For a minute a wild desire to run away possessed her; but that was cowardly, and the girls would laugh at her; so she resolved to stay, and get out of the scrape if she could. A second look showed her that the living eyes, under the bushy grey eyebrows, were kinder even than the painted ones; and there was a sly twinkle in them which lessened her fear a good deal. The gruff voice was gruffer than ever, as the old gentleman said abruptly, after that dreadful pause, 'So you're not afraid of me, hey?'

'Not much, sir.'

'And you don't think me as handsome as your grandfather?'

'Not quite, sir.'

'And I've got a tremendous will, have I?'

'I only said I thought so.'

'But you like me, in spite of it?'

'Yes, I do, sir.'

That answer pleased the old gentleman; he gave a short laugh, shook hands with her, and, putting his fingers under her chin, turned up her face, examined it gravely, and let it go, saying, with a nod, 'You've got your grandfather's spirit, if you haven't his face. He *was* a fine man, my dear; but, what is better, he was a brave and honest one, and I was proud to be his friend.'

'Thank you, sir'; and Jo was quite comfortable after that, for it suited her exactly.

'What have you been doing to this boy of mine, hey?' was the next question, sharply put.

'Only trying to be neighbourly, sir'; and Jo told how her visit came about.

'You think he needs cheering up a bit, do you?'

'Yes, sir; he seems a little lonely, and young folks would do him good, perhaps. We are only girls, but we should be glad to help if we could, for we don't forget the splendid Christmas present you sent us,' said Jo, eagerly.

'Tut, tut, tut! that was the boy's affair. How is the poor woman?'

'Doing nicely, sir'; and off went Jo, talking very fast, as she told all about the Hummels, in whom her mother had interested richer friends than they were.

'Just her father's way of doing good. I shall come and see your mother some fine day. Tell her so. There's the tea-bell; we have it early, on the boy's account. Come down, and go on being neighbourly.'

'If you'd like to have me, sir.'

'Shouldn't ask you if I didn't'; and Mr Laurence offered her his arm with old-fashioned courtesy.

'What *would* Meg say to this?' thought Jo, as she was marched away, while her eyes danced with fun as she imagined herself telling the story at home.

'Hey! Why, what the dickens has come to the fellow?' said the old gentleman, as Laurie came running downstairs, and brought up with a start of surprise at the astonishing sight of Jo arm-in-arm with his redoubtable grandfather.

'I didn't know you'd come, sir,' he began, as Jo gave him a triumphant little glance.

'That's evident, by the way you racket downstairs. Come to your tea, sir, and behave like a gentleman'; and having pulled the boy's hair by way of a caress, Mr Laurence walked on, while Laurie went through a series of comic evolutions behind their backs, which nearly produced an explosion of laughter from Jo.

The old gentleman did not say much as he drank his four cups of tea, but he watched the young people, who soon chatted away like old friends, and the change in his grandson did not escape him. There was colour, light, and life in the boy's face now, vivacity in his manner, and genuine merriment in his laugh.

'She's right; the lad *is* lonely. I'll see what these little girls can do for him,' thought Mr Laurence, as he looked and listened. He liked Jo, for her odd, blunt ways suited him; and she seemed to understand the boy almost as well as if she had been one herself.

If the Laurences had been what Jo called 'prim and poky' she would not have got on at all, for such people always made her shy and awkward; but finding them free and easy, she was so herself, and made a good impression. When they rose, she proposed to go, but Laurie said he had something more to show her, and took her away to the conservatory, which had been lighted for her benefit. It seemed quite fairylike to Jo, as she went up and down the walks, enjoying the blooming walls on either side, the soft light, the damp, sweet air, and the wonderful vines and trees that hung above her – while her new friend cut the finest flowers till his hands were full; then he tied them up, saying, with the happy look Jo liked to see, 'Please give these to your mother, and tell her I like the medicine she sent me very much.'

They found Mr Laurence standing before the fire in the great drawing room, but Jo's attention was entirely absorbed by a grand piano, which stood open.

'Do you play?' she asked, turning to Laurie with a respectful expression.

'Sometimes,' he answered, modestly.

'Please do now. I want to hear it so I can tell Beth.'

'Won't you first?'

'Don't know how; too stupid to learn, but I love music dearly.'

So Laurie played, and Jo listened, with her nose luxuriously buried in heliotrope and tea-roses. Her respect and regard for the 'Laurence boy' increased very much, for he played remarkably well, and didn't put on any airs. She wished Beth could hear him, but she did not say so; only praised him till he was quite abashed and his grandfather came to the rescue. 'That will do, that will do, young lady. Too many sugar-plums are not good for him. His music isn't bad, but I hope he will do as well in more important things. Going? Well, I'm much obliged to you, and I hope you'll come again. My respects to your mother. Good night, Doctor Jo.'

He shook hands kindly, but looked as if something did not please him. When they got into the hall, Jo asked Laurie if she had said anything amiss. He shook his head.

'No, it was me; he doesn't like to hear me play.'

'Why not?'

'I'll tell you some day. John is going home with you, as I can't.'

'No need of that; I am not a young lady, and it's only a step. Take care of yourself, won't you?'

'Yes; but you will come again, I hope?'

'If you promise to come and see us after you are well.'

'I will.'

'Good night, Laurie!'

'Good night, Jo, good night!'

When all the afternoon's adventures had been told, the family felt inclined to go visiting in a body, for each found something very attractive in the big house on the other side of the hedge: Mrs March wanted to talk of her father with the old man who had not forgotten him; Meg longed to walk in the conservatory; Beth sighed for the grand piano; and Amy was eager to see the fine pictures and statues.

'Mother, why didn't Mr Laurence like to have Laurie play?' asked Jo, who was of an inquiring disposition.

'I am not sure, but I think it was because his son, Laurie's father, married an Italian lady, a musician, which displeased the old man, who is very proud. The lady was good and lovely and accomplished, but he did not like her, and never saw his son after he married. They both died when Laurie was a little child, and then his grandfather took him home. I fancy the boy, who was born in Italy, is not very strong, and the old man is afraid of losing him, which makes him so careful. Laurie comes naturally by his love of music, for he is like his mother, and I dare say his grandfather fears that he may want to be a musician; at any rate, his skill reminds him of the woman he did not like, and so he "glowered", as Jo said.'

'Dear me, how romantic!' exclaimed Meg.

'How silly!' said Jo. 'Let him be a musician, if he wants to, and not plague his life out sending him to college, when he hates to go.'

'That's why he has such handsome black eyes and pretty manners, I suppose. Italians are always nice,' said Meg, who was a little sentimental.

'What do you know about his eyes and his manners? You never spoke to him, hardly,' cried Jo, who was *not* sentimental.

'I saw him at the party, and what you tell shows that he knows how to behave. That was a nice little speech about the medicine Mother sent him.'

'He meant the blancmange, I suppose.'

'How stupid you are, child! He meant you, of course.'

'Did he?' and Jo opened her eyes as if it had never occurred to her before.

'I never saw such a girl! You don't know a compliment when you get it,' said Meg, with the air of a young lady who knew all about the matter.

'I think they are great nonsense, and I'll thank you not to be silly, and spoil my fun. Laurie's a nice boy, and I like him, and I won't have any sentimental stuff about compliments and such rubbish.

We'll all be good to him, because he hasn't got any mother, and he *may* come over and see us, mayn't he, Marmee?'

'Yes, Jo, your little friend is very welcome, and I hope Meg will remember that children should be children as long as they can.'

'I don't call myself a child, and I'm not in my teens yet,' observed Amy. 'What do you say, Beth?'

'I was thinking about our *Pilgrim's Progress*,' answered Beth, who had not heard a word. 'How we got out of the Slough and through the Wicket Gate by resolving to be good, and up the steep hill by trying; and that maybe the house over there full of splendid things, is going to be our Palace Beautiful.'

'We have got to get by the lions, first,' said Jo, as if she rather liked the prospect.

CHAPTER 6

Beth Finds the Palace Beautiful

The big house did prove a Palace Beautiful, though it took some time for all to get in, and Beth found it very hard to pass the lions. Old Mr Laurence was the biggest one; but after he had called, said something funny or kind to each one of the girls, and talked over old times with their mother, nobody felt much afraid of him, except timid Beth. The other lion was the fact that they were poor and Laurie rich; for this made them shy of accepting favours which they could not return. But, after a while they found that he considered them the benefactors, and could not do enough to show how grateful he was for Mrs March's motherly welcome, their cheerful society, and the comfort he took in that humble home of theirs. So they soon forgot their pride, and interchanged kindnesses without stopping to think which was the greater.

All sorts of pleasant things happened about that time; for the new friendship flourished like grass in spring. Everyone liked Laurie, and he privately informed his tutor that 'the Marches were regular splendid girls'. With the delightful enthusiasm of youth they took the solitary boy into their midst, and made much of him, and he found something very charming in the innocent companionship of these simple-hearted girls. Never having known mother or sisters, he was quick to feel the influences they brought about him; and their busy, lively ways made him ashamed of the indolent life he led. He was tired of books, and found people so interesting now that Mr Brooke was obliged to make very unsatisfactory reports; for Laurie was always playing truant and running over to the Marches'.

'Never mind; let him take a holiday, and make it up afterwards,' said the old gentleman. 'The good lady next door says he is studying too hard, and needs young society, amusement, and exercise. I suspect she is right, and that I've been coddling the fellow as if I'd been his grandmother. Let him do what he likes, as long as he is happy. He can't get into mischief in that little nunnery over there; and Mrs March is doing more for him than we can.'

What good times they had, to be sure! Such plays and tableaux, such sleigh-rides and skating frolics, such pleasant evenings in the old parlour, and now and then such gay little parties at the great house. Meg could walk in the conservatory whenever she liked, and revel in bouquets; Jo browsed over the new library voraciously, and convulsed the old gentleman with her criticisms. Amy copied pictures and enjoyed beauty to her heart's content; and Laurie played 'lord of the manor' in the most delightful style.

But Beth, though yearning for the grand piano, could not pluck up courage to go to the 'Mansion of Bliss', as Meg called it. She went once with Jo; but the old gentleman, not being aware of her infirmity, stared at her so hard from under his heavy eyebrows, and said 'Hey!' so loud, that he frightened her so much her 'feet chattered on the floor', she told her mother; and she ran away, declaring she would never go there any more, not even for the dear piano. No persuasions or enticements could overcome her fears, till the fact coming to Mr Laurence's ear in some mysterious way, he set about mending matters. During one of the brief calls he made, he artfully led the conversation to music, and talked away about great singers whom he had seen, fine organs he had heard, and told such charming anecdotes that Beth found it impossible to stay in her distant corner, but crept nearer and nearer, as if fascinated. At the back of his chair she stopped, and stood listening, with her great eyes wide open, and her cheeks red with the excitement of this unusual performance. Taking no more notice of her than if she had been a fly, Mr Laurence talked on about Laurie's lessons and teachers; and presently, as if the idea had just occurred to him, he said to Mrs March:

'The boy neglects his music now, and I'm glad of it, for he was getting too fond of it. But the piano suffers for want of use. Wouldn't some of your girls like to run over, and practise on it now and then, just to keep it in tune, you know, ma'am?'

Beth took a step forward, and pressed her hands tightly together to keep from clapping them, for this was an irresistible temptation; and the thought of practising on that splendid instrument quite took her breath away. Before Mrs March could reply, Mr Laurence went on with an odd little nod and smile:

'They needn't see or speak to anyone, but run in at any time; for I'm shut up in my study at the other end of the house, Laurie is out a great deal, and the servants are never near the drawing room after nine o'clock.'

Here he rose, as if going, and Beth made up her mind to speak, for that last arrangement left nothing to be desired. 'Please tell the young ladies what I say; and if they don't care to come, why, never mind.' Here a little hand slipped into his, and Beth looked up at him with a face full of gratitude, as she said, in her earnest, yet timid way:

'Oh, sir, they do care, very, very much!'

'Are you the musical girl?' he asked, without any startling 'Hey!' as he looked down at her very kindly.

'I'm Beth. I love it dearly, and I'll come, if you are quite sure nobody will hear me – and be disturbed,' she added, fearing to be rude, and trembling at her own boldness as she spoke.

'Not a soul, my dear. The house is empty half the day; so come and drum away as much as you like, and I shall be obliged to you.'

'How kind you are, sir!'

Beth blushed like a rose under the friendly look he wore; but she was not frightened now, and gave the big hand a grateful squeeze, because she had no words to thank him for the precious gift he had given her. The old gentleman softly stroked the hair of her forehead, and stooping down, he kissed her, saying, in a tone few people ever heard:

'I had a little girl once, with eyes like these. God bless you, my dear! Good day, madam'; and away he went, in a great hurry.

Beth had a rapture with her mother, and then rushed up to impart the glorious news to her family of invalids, as the girls were not at home. How blithely she sang that evening, and how they all laughed at her, because she woke Amy in the night by playing the piano on her face in her sleep. Next day, having seen both the old and the young gentlemen out of the house, Beth, after two or three retreats, fairly got in at the side-door and made her way, as noiselessly as any mouse, to the drawing room where her idol stood. Quite by accident of course, some pretty, easy music lay on the piano; and, with trembling fingers, and frequent stops to listen and look about, Beth at last touched the great instrument, and straightway forgot her fear, herself, and everything else but the unspeakable delight which the music gave her, for it was like the voice of a beloved friend.

She stayed till Hannah came to take her home to dinner; but she had no appetite, and could only sit and smile upon everyone in a general state of beatitude.

After that, the little brown hood slipped through the hedge nearly every day, and the great drawing room was haunted by a tuneful spirit that came and went unseen. She never knew that Mr Laurence often opened his study door to hear the old-fashioned airs he liked; she never saw Laurie mount guard in the hall to warn the servants away; she never suspected that the exercise-books and new songs which she found in the rack were put there for her especial benefit; and when he talked to her about music at home, she only thought how kind he was to tell things that helped her so much. So she enjoyed herself heartily, and found, what isn't always the case, that her granted wish was all she had hoped. Perhaps it was because she was so grateful for this blessing that a greater was given her; at any rate she deserved both.

'Mother, I'm going to work Mr Laurence a pair of slippers.

He is so kind to me, I must thank him, and I don't know any other way. Can I do it?' asked Beth, a few weeks after that eventful call of his.

'Yes, dear. It will please him very much, and be a nice way of thanking him. The girls will help you about them, and I will pay for the making up,' replied Mrs March, who took peculiar pleasure in granting Beth's requests, because she so seldom asked anything for herself.

After many serious discussions with Meg and Jo, the pattern was chosen, the materials bought, and the slippers begun. A cluster of grave yet cheerful pansies on a deeper purple ground, was pronounced very appropriate and pretty; and Beth worked away early and late, with occasional lifts over hard parts. She was a nimble little needle-woman, and they were finished before anyone got tired of them. Then she wrote a very short, simple note, and, with Laurie's help, got them smuggled on to the study-table one morning before the old gentleman was up.

When this excitement was over, Beth waited to see what would happen. All that day passed, and a part of the next, before any acknowledgement arrived, and she was beginning to fear she had offended her crotchety friend. On the afternoon of the second day, she went out to do an errand, and give poor Joanna, the invalid doll, her daily exercise. As she came up the street, on her return, she saw three, yes, four, heads popping in and out of the parlour windows, and the moment they saw her, several hands were waved, and several joyful voices screamed:

'Here's a letter from the old gentleman! Come quick, and read it!'

'Oh, Beth, he's sent you –' began Amy, gesticulating with unseemly energy; but she got no further, for Jo quenched her by slamming down the window.

Beth hurried on in a flutter of suspense. At the door, her sisters seized and bore her to the parlour in a triumphal procession, all pointing, and all saying at once, 'Look there! look there!' Beth did look, and turned pale with delight and surprise; for there stood a little cabinet piano, with a letter lying on the glossy lid, directed, like a signboard, to 'Miss Elizabeth March.'

'For me?' gasped Beth, holding on to Jo, and feeling as if she should tumble down, it was such an overwhelming thing altogether.

'Yes; all for you, my precious! Isn't it splendid of him? Don't you think he's the dearest old man in the world? Here's the key in the letter. We didn't open it, but we are dying to know what he says,' cried Jo, hugging her sister, and offering the note.

'You read it! I can't! I feel so queer! Oh, it is too lovely!' and Beth hid her face in Jo's apron, quite upset by her present.

Jo opened the paper, and began to laugh, for the first words she saw were:

'Miss March:
'Dear Madam' –
'How nice it sounds! I wish someone would write to me so!' said Amy, who thought the old-fashioned address very elegant.

'"I have had many pairs of slippers in my life, but I never had any that suited me so well as yours,"' continued Jo. '"Heart's ease is my favourite flower, and these will always remind of the gentle giver. I like to pay my debts; so I know you will allow 'the old gentleman' to send you something which once belonged to the little granddaughter he lost. With hearty thanks and best wishes, I remain, your grateful friend and humble servant,
'"James Laurence."'

'There, Beth, that's an honour to be proud of, I'm sure. Laurie told me how fond Mr Laurence used to be of the child who died, and how he kept all her little things carefully. Just think, he's given you her piano. That comes of having big blue eyes, and loving music,' said Jo, trying to soothe Beth, who trembled, and looked more excited than she had ever been before.

'See the cunning brackets to hold candles, and the nice green silk, puckered up, with a gold rose in the middle, and the pretty rack and stool, all complete,' added Meg, opening the instrument and displaying its beauties.

'"Your humble servant, James Laurence"; only think of his writing that to you. I'll tell the girls. They'll think it's splendid,' said Amy, much impressed by the note.

'Try it, honey. Let's hear the sound of the baby pianny,' said Hannah, who always took a share in the family joys and sorrows.

So Beth tried it; and everyone pronounced it the most remarkable piano ever heard. It had evidently been newly tuned and put in apple-pie order; but perfect as it was, I think the real charm of it lay in the happiest of all happy faces which leaned over it, as Beth lovingly touched the beautiful black and white keys and pressed the bright pedals.

'You'll have to go and thank him,' said Jo, by way of a joke; for the idea of the child's really going never entered her head.

'Yes, I mean to. I guess I'll go now, before I get frightened thinking about it.' And, to the utter amazement of the assembled family, Beth walked deliberately down the garden, through the hedge, and in at the Laurences' door.

'Well, I wish I may die if it ain't the queerest thing I ever see. The pianny has turned her head! She'd never have gone in her right mind,' cried Hannah, staring after her, while the girls were rendered quite speechless by the miracle.

They would have been still more amazed if they had seen what Beth did afterwards. If you will believe me, she went and knocked at the study door before she gave herself time to think; and when a gruff voice called out, 'Come in!' she did go in, right up to Mr Laurence, who looked quite taken aback, and held out her hand, saying, with only a small quaver in her voice, 'I came to thank you, sir, for –' But she didn't finish; for he looked so friendly, that she forgot her speech, and, only remembering that he had lost the little girl he loved, she put both arms round his neck, and kissed him.

If the roof of the house had suddenly flown off, the old gentleman wouldn't have been more astonished; but he liked it – oh, dear, yes, he liked it amazingly! – and was so touched and pleased by that confiding little kiss, that all his crustiness vanished; and he just set her on his knee, and laid his wrinkled cheek against her rosy one, feeling as if he had got his own little granddaughter back again. Beth ceased to fear him from that moment and sat there talking to him as cosily as if she had known him all her life; for love casts out fear, and gratitude can conquer pride. When she went home, he walked with her to her own gate, shook hands cordially, and touched his hat as he marched back again, looking very stately and erect, like a handsome, soldierly old gentleman, as he was.

When the girls saw that performance, Jo began to dance a jig, by way of expressing her satisfaction; Amy nearly fell out of the window in her surprise; and Meg exclaimed, with uplifted hands, 'Well, I do believe the world is coming to an end!'

CHAPTER 7

Amy's Valley of Humiliation

'That boy is a perfect Cyclops, isn't he?' said Amy, one day, as Laurie clattered by on horseback, with a flourish of his whip as he passed.

'How dare you say so, when he's got both his eyes? and very handsome ones they are, too,' cried Jo, who resented any slighting remarks about her friend.

'I didn't say anything about his eyes, and I don't see why you need fire up when I admire his riding.'

'Oh, my goodness! that little goose means a centaur, and she called him a Cyclops,' exclaimed Jo, with a burst of laughter.

'You needn't be so rude; it's only a "lapse of lingy," as Mr Davis says,' retorted Amy, finishing Jo with her Latin. 'I just wish I had a little of the money Laurie spends on that horse,' she added, as if to herself, yet hoping her sisters would hear.

'Why?' asked Meg, kindly, for Jo had gone off in another laugh at Amy's second blunder.

'I need it so much; I'm dreadfully in debt, and it won't be my turn to have the rag-money for a month.'

'In debt, Amy? What do you mean?' and Meg looked sober.

'Why, I owe at least a dozen pickled limes, and I can't pay them, you know, till I have money, for Marmee forbade my having anything charged at the shop.'

'Tell me all about it. Are limes the fashion now? It used to be pickling bits of rubber to make balls'; and Meg tried to keep her countenance, Amy looked so grave and important.

'Why, you see, the girls are always buying them, and unless you want to be thought mean, you must do it too. It's nothing but limes now, for everyone is sucking them in their desks in school-time, and trading them off for pencils, bead-rings, paper dolls, or something else at recess. If one girl likes another she gives her a lime; if she's mad with her she eats one before her face, and don't offer even a suck. They treat by turns; and I've had ever so many, but haven't returned them; and I ought, for they are debts of honour, you know.'

'How much will pay them off, and restore your credit?' asked Meg, taking out her purse.

'A quarter would more than do it, and leave a few cents over for a treat for you. Don't you like limes?'

'Not much; you may have my share. Here's the money. Make it last as long as you can, for it isn't very plenty, you know.'

'Oh, thank you! It must be so nice to have pocket-money! I'll have a grand feast, for I haven't tasted a lime this week. I felt deli-cate about taking any, as I couldn't return them, and I'm actually suffering for one.'

Next day Amy was rather late at school; but could not resist the temptation of displaying, with pardonable pride, a moist, brown-paper parcel, before she consigned it to the inmost recesses of her desk. During the next few minutes the rumour that Amy March had got twenty-four delicious limes (she ate one on the way), and was going to treat, circulated through her 'set', and the attentions of her friends became quite overwhelming. Katy Brown invited her to her next party on the spot; Mary Kingsley insisted on lending her her watch till recess; and Jenny Snow, a satirical young lady, who had basely twitted Amy upon her limeless state, promptly buried the hatchet, and offered to furnish answers to certain appalling sums. But Amy had not forgotten Miss Snow's cutting remarks about 'some persons whose noses were not too flat to smell other people's limes, and stuck-up people who were not too proud to ask for them'; and she instantly crushed that 'Snow girl's' hopes by the withering telegram, 'You needn't be so polite all of a sudden, for you won't get any.'

A distinguished personage happened to visit the school that morning, and Amy's beautifully drawn maps received praise, which honour to her foe rankled in the soul of Miss Snow, and caused Miss March to assume the airs of a studious young peacock. But, alas, alas! pride goes before a fall, and the revengeful Snow turned the tables with disastrous success. No sooner had the guest paid the usual stale compliments, and bowed himself out than Jenny, under pretence of asking an important question, informed Mr Davis, the teacher, that Amy March had pickled limes in her desk.

Now Mr Davis had declared limes a contraband article, and solemnly vowed to ferrule publicly the first person who was found breaking the law. This much-enduring man had succeeded in banishing chewing-gum after a long and stormy war, and had made a bonfire of the confiscated novels and newspapers, had suppressed a private post-office, had forbidden distortions of the face, nick-names, and caricatures, and done all that one man could do to keep half-a-hundred rebellious girls in order. Boys are trying enough to human patience, goodness knows! but girls are infinitely more so, especially to nervous gentlemen, with tyrannical tempers, and no more talent for teaching than Dr Blimber. Mr Davis knew any quantity of Greek, Latin, Algebra, and ologies of all sorts, so he was called a fine teacher, and manners, morals, feelings, and examples were not considered of any particular importance. It was a most unfortunate moment for denouncing Amy, and Jenny knew it. Mr Davis had evidently taken his coffee too strong that morning; there was an east wind, which always affected his neuralgia; and his pupils had not done him the credit which he felt he deserved: therefore, to use the expressive, if not elegant, language of a schoolgirl, 'he was as nervous as a witch, and as cross as a bear'. The word 'limes' was like fire to powder; his yellow face flushed, and he rapped on his desk with an energy which made Jenny skip to her seat with unusual rapidity.

'Young ladies, attention, if you please!'

At the stern order the buzz ceased, and fifty pairs of blue, black, grey, and brown eyes were obediently fixed upon his awful countenance.

'Miss March, come to the desk.'

Amy rose to comply with outward composure, but a secret fear oppressed her, for the limes weighed upon her conscience.

'Bring with you the limes you have in your desk,' was the unexpected command which arrested her before she got out of her seat.

'Don't take all,' whispered her neighbour, a young lady of great presence of mind.

Amy hastily shook out half a dozen, and laid the rest down before Mr Davis, feeling that any man possessing a human heart would relent when that delicious perfume met his nose. Unfortunately Mr Davis particularly detested the odour of the fashionable pickle, and disgust added to his wrath.

'Is that all?'

'Not quite,' stammered Amy.

'Bring the rest immediately.'

With a despairing glance at her set, she obeyed.

'You are sure there are no more?'

'I never lie, sir.'

'So I see. Now take these disgusting things two by two, and throw them out of the window.'

There was a simultaneous sigh, which created quite a little gust, as the last hope fled, and the treat was ravished from their longing lips. Scarlet with shame and anger, Amy went to and fro six dreadful times; and as each doomed couple – looking oh! so plump and juicy – fell from her reluctant hands, a shout from the street completed the anguish of the girls, for it told them that their feast was being exulted over by the little Irish children, who were their sworn foes. This – this was too much; all flashed indignant or appealing glances at the inexorable Davis, and one passionate lime-lover burst into tears.

As Amy returned from her last trip, Mr Davis gave a porten-tous 'Hem!' and said, in his most impressive manner – 'Young ladies, you remember what I said to you a week ago. I am sorry this has happened; but I never allow my rules to be infringed, and I *never* break my word. Miss March, hold out your hand.'

Amy started and put both hands behind her, turning on him an imploring look which pleaded for her better than the words she could not utter. She was rather a favourite with 'old Davis', as, of course, he was called, and it's my private belief that he *would* have broken his word if the indignation of one irrepressible young lady had not found vent in a hiss. That hiss, faint as it was, irritated the irascible gentleman, and sealed the culprit's fate.

'Your hand, Miss March!' was the only answer her mute appeal received; and, too proud to cry or beseech, Amy set her teeth, threw back her head defiantly, and bore without flinching several tingling blows on her little palm. They were neither many nor heavy, but that made no difference to her. For the first time in her life she had been struck; and the disgrace, in her eyes, was as deep as if he had knocked her down.

'You will now stand on the platform till recess,' said Mr Davis, resolved to do the thing thoroughly, since he had begun.

That was dreadful. It would have been bad enough to go to her seat, and see the pitying faces of her friends, or the satisfied ones of her few enemies; but to face the whole school with that shame fresh upon her, seemed impossible, and for a second she felt as if she could only drop down where she stood, and break her heart with crying. A bitter sense of wrong, and the thought of Jenny Snow, helped her to bear it; and, taking the ignominious place, she fixed her eyes on the stove-funnel above what now seemed a sea of faces, and stood there, so motionless and white that the girls found it very hard to study, with that pathetic figure before them.

During the fifteen minutes that followed, the proud and sensi-tive little girl suffered a shame and pain which she never forgot. To others it might seem a ludicrous or trivial affair, but to her it was a hard experience; for during the twelve years of her life she had been governed by love alone, and a blow of that sort had never touched her before. The smart of her hand and the ache of her heart were forgotten in the sting of the thought – 'I shall have to tell at home, and they will be so disappointed in me!'

The fifteen minutes seemed an hour; but they came to an end at last, and the word 'Recess!' had never seemed so welcome to her before.

'You can go, Miss March,' said Mr Davis, looking, as he felt, uncomfortable.

He did not soon forget the reproachful glance Amy gave him, as she went, without a word to anyone, straight into the ante-room, snatched her things, and left the place 'for ever', as she passionately declared to herself. She was in a sad state when she got home; and when the older girls arrived, some time later, an indignation meeting was held at once. Mrs March did not say much, but looked disturbed, and comforted her afflicted little daughter in her tenderest manner. Meg bathed the insulted hand with glycerine and tears; Beth felt that even her beloved kittens would fail as a balm for griefs like this; Jo wrathfully proposed that Mr Davis be arrested without delay; and Hannah shook her fist at the 'villain', and pounded potatoes for dinner as if she had him under her pestle. No notice was taken of Amy's flight, except by her mates; but the sharp-eyed demoiselles discovered that Mr Davis was quite benignant in the afternoon, also unusually nervous. Just before school closed Jo appeared, wearing a grim expression, as she stalked up to the desk, and delivered a letter from her mother; then collected Amy's property and departed, carefully scraping the mud from her boots on the door-mat, as if she shook the dust of the place off her feet.

'Yes, you can have a vacation from school, but I want you to study a little every day with Beth,' said Mrs March that evening. 'I don't approve of corporal punishment, especially for girls. I dislike Mr Davis's manner of teaching, and don't think the girls you associate with are doing you any good, so I shall ask your father's advice before I send you anywhere else.'

'That's good! I wish all the girls would leave, and spoil his old school. It's perfectly maddening to think of those lovely limes,' sighed Amy, with the air of a martyr.

'I am not sorry you lost them, for you broke the rules, and deserved some punishment for disobedience,' was the severe reply, which rather disappointed the young lady, who expected nothing but sympathy.

'Do you mean you are glad I was disgraced before the whole school?' cried Amy.

'I should not have chosen that way of mending a fault,' replied her mother; 'but I'm not sure that it won't do you more good than a milder method. You are getting to be rather conceited, my dear, and it is quite time you set about correcting it. You have a good many little gifts and virtues, but there is no need of parading them, for conceit spoils the finest genius. There is not much danger that real talent or goodness will be overlooked long; even if it is, the consciousness of possessing and using it well should satisfy one, and the great charm of all power is modesty.'

'So it is!' cried Laurie, who was playing chess in a corner with Jo. 'I knew a girl, once, who had a really remarkable talent for music, and she didn't know it, never guessed what sweet little things she composed when she was alone, and wouldn't have believed it if anyone had told her.'

'I wish I'd known that nice girl; maybe she would have helped me, I'm so stupid,' said Beth, who stood beside him, listening eagerly.

'You do know her, and she helps you better than anyone else could,' answered Laurie, looking at her with such mischievous meaning in his merry black eyes, that Beth suddenly turned very red, and hid her face in the sofa-cushion, quite overcome by such an unexpected discovery.

Jo let Laurie win the game, to pay for that praise of her Beth, who could not be prevailed upon to play for them after her compliment. So Laurie did his best, and sang delightfully, being in a particularly lively humour, for to the Marches he seldom showed the moody side of his character. When he was gone, Amy, who had been pensive all the evening, said suddenly, as if busy over some new idea: 'Is Laurie an accomplished boy?'

'Yes; he has had an excellent education, and has much talent; he will make a fine man, if not spoilt by petting,' replied her mother.

'And he isn't conceited, is he?' asked Amy.

'Not in the least; that is why he is so charming, and we all like him so much.'

'I see; it's nice to have accomplishments, and be elegant; but not to show off, or get perked up,' said Amy, thoughtfully.

'These things are always seen and felt in a person's manner and conversation, if modestly used; but it is not necessary to display them,' said Mrs March.

'Any more than it's proper to wear all your bonnets and gowns and ribbons at once, that folks may know you've got them,' added Jo; and the lecture ended in a laugh.

CHAPTER 8

Jo Meets Apollyon

'Girls, where are you going?' asked Amy, coming into their room one Saturday afternoon, and finding them getting ready to go out, with an air of secrecy, which excited her curiosity.

'Never mind; little girls shouldn't ask questions,' returned Jo, sharply.

Now if there *is* anything mortifying to our feelings, when we are young, it is to be told that; and to be bidden to 'run away, dear', is still more trying to us. Amy bridled up at this insult, and determined to find out the secret, if she teased for an hour. Turning to Meg, who never refused her anything very long, she said coaxingly, 'Do tell me! I should think you might let me go too; for Beth is fussing over her piano, and I haven't got anything to do, and am *so* lonely.'

'I can't, dear, because you aren't invited,' began Meg; but Jo broke in impatiently, 'Now, Meg, be quiet, or you will spoil it all. You can't go, Amy; so don't be a baby and whine about it.'

'You are going somewhere with Laurie, I know you are; you were whispering and laughing together, on the sofa, last night, and you stopped when I came in. Aren't you going with him?'

'Yes, we are; now do be still and stop bothering.'

Amy held her tongue, but used her eyes, and saw Meg slip a fan into her pocket.

'I know! I know! you're going to the hall to see "The Seven Castles!"' she cried, adding resolutely, 'and I *shall* go, for Mother said I might see it; and I've got my rag-money, and it was mean not to tell me in time.'

'Just listen to me a minute, and be a good child,' said Meg, soothingly. 'Mother doesn't wish you to go this week, because your eyes are not well enough yet to bear the light of this fairy piece. Next week you can go with Beth and Hannah, and have a nice time.'

'I don't like that half as well as going with you and Laurie. Please let me; I've been sick with this cold so long, and shut up, I'm dying for some fun. Do, Meg! I'll be ever so good,' pleaded Amy, looking as pathetic as she could.

'Suppose we take her. I don't believe Mother would mind, if we bundle her up well,' began Meg.

'If *she* goes *I* shan't; and if I don't, Laurie won't like it; and it will be very rude, after he invited only us, to go and drag in Amy. I should think she'd hate to poke herself where she isn't wanted,' said Jo, crossly, for she disliked the trouble of overseeing a fidgety child, when she wanted to enjoy herself.

Her tone and manner angered Amy, who began to put her boots on, saying, in her most aggravating way, 'I *shall* go; Meg says I may; and if I pay for myself, Laurie hasn't anything to do with it.'

'You can't sit with us, for our seats are reserved, and you mustn't sit alone; so Laurie will give you his place, and that will spoil our pleasure; or he'll get another seat for you, and that isn't proper, when you weren't asked. You shan't stir a step; so you may just stay where you are,' scolded Jo, crosser than ever, having just pricked her finger in her hurry.

Sitting on the floor, with one boot on, Amy began to cry, and Meg to reason with her, when Laurie called from below, and the two girls hurried down, leaving their sister wailing; for now and then she forgot her grown-up ways, and acted like a spoilt child. Just as the party were setting out, Amy called over the bannisters, in a threatening voice, 'You'll be sorry for this, Jo March; see if you ain't.'

'Fiddlesticks!' returned Jo, slamming the door.

They had a charming time, for 'The Seven Castles of the Diamond Lake' was as brilliant and wonderful as heart could wish. But, in spite of the comical red imps, sparkling elves, and gorgeous princes and princesses, Jo's pleasure had a drop of bitterness in it; the fairy queen's yellow curls reminded her of Amy; and between the acts she amused herself with wondering what her sister would do to make her 'sorry for it'. She and Amy had had many lively skirmishes in the course of their lives, for both had quick tempers, and were apt to be violent when fairly roused. Amy teased Jo, Jo irritated Amy, and semi-occasional explosions occurred, of which both were much ashamed afterwards. Although the oldest, Jo had the least self-control, and had hard times trying to curb the fiery spirit which was continually getting her into trouble; her anger never lasted long, and having humbly confessed her fault she sincerely repented and tried to do better. Her sisters used to say that they rather liked to get Jo into a fury because she was such an angel afterwards. Poor Jo tried desperately to be good, but her bosom enemy was always ready to flame up and defeat her; and it took years of patient effort to subdue it.

When they got home they found Amy reading in the parlour. She assumed an injured air as they came in; never lifted her eyes from her book, or asked a single question. Perhaps curiosity might have conquered resentment, if Beth had not been there to inquire, and receive a glowing description of the play. On going up to put away her best hat, Jo's first look was towards the bureau; for, in their last quarrel, Amy had soothed her feelings by turning Jo's top drawer upside down on the floor. Everything was in its place, however, and after a hasty glance into her various closets, bags, and boxes, Jo decided that Amy had forgiven and forgotten her wrongs.

There Jo was mistaken; for next day she made a discovery which produced a tempest. Meg, Beth, and Amy were sitting together, late in the afternoon, when Jo burst into the room, looking excited, and demanding breathlessly, 'Has anyone taken my book?'

Meg and Beth said 'No,' at once, and looked surprised;

Amy poked the fire, and said nothing. Jo saw her colour rise, and was down upon her in a minute.

'Amy, you've got it.'

'No, I haven't.'

'You know where it is, then!'

'No, I don't.'

'That's a fib!' cried Jo, taking her by the shoulders and looking fierce enough to frighten a much braver child than Amy.

'It isn't. I haven't got it, don't know where it is now, and don't care.'

'You know something about it, and you'd better tell at once, or I'll make you,' and Jo gave her a slight shake.

'Scold as much as you like, you'll never see your silly old book again,' cried Amy, getting excited in her turn.

'Why not?'

'I burnt it up.'

'What! my little book I was so fond of, and worked over, and meant to finish before Father got home! Have you really burnt it?' said Jo, turning very pale, while her eyes kindled and her hands clutched Amy nervously.

'Yes, I did! I told you I'd make you pay for being so cross yesterday, and I have, so –'

Amy got no further, for Jo's hot temper mastered her, and she shook Amy till her teeth chattered in her head; crying in a passion of grief and anger:

'You wicked, wicked girl! I never can write it again and I'll never forgive you as long as I live.'

Meg flew to rescue Amy, and Beth to pacify Jo, but Jo was quite beside herself; and with a parting box on her sister's ear, she rushed out of the room up to the old sofa in the garret, and finished her fight alone.

The storm cleared up below, for Mrs March came home, and, having heard the story, soon brought Amy to a sense of the wrong she had done her sister. Jo's book was the pride of her heart, and was regarded by her family as a literary sprout of great promise.

It was only half a dozen little fairy tales, but Jo had worked over them patiently, putting her whole heart into her work, hoping to make something good enough to print. She had just copied them with great care, and had destroyed the old manuscript, so that Amy's bonfire had consumed the loving work of several years. It seemed a small loss to others, but to Jo it was a dreadful calamity, and she felt that it never could be made up to her. Beth mourned as for a departed kitten, and Meg refused to defend her pet; Mrs March looked grave and grieved, and Amy felt that no one would love her till she had asked pardon for the act which she now regretted more than any of them.

When the tea-bell rang Jo appeared, looking so grim and un-approachable, that it took all Amy's courage to say meekly:

'Please forgive me, Jo; I'm very, very sorry.'

'I never shall forgive you,' was Jo's stern answer; and from that moment she ignored Amy entirely.

No one spoke of the great trouble – not even Mrs March – for all had learned by experience that when Jo was in that mood words were wasted; and the wisest course was to wait till some little accident, or her own generous nature, softened Jo's resentment, and healed the breach. It was not a happy evening; for though they sewed as usual, while their mother read aloud from Bremer, Scott, or Edgeworth, something was wanting and the sweet home peace was disturbed. They felt this most when singing time came; for Beth could only play, Jo stood dumb as a stone, and Amy broke down, so Meg and Mother sang alone. But in spite of their efforts to be as cheery as larks, the flute-like voices did not seem to chord as well as usual, and all felt out of tune.

As Jo received her good-night kiss, Mrs March whispered gently: 'My dear, don't let the sun go down upon your anger; forgive each other, help each other, and begin again tomorrow.'

Jo wanted to lay her head down on that motherly bosom, and cry her grief and anger all away, but tears were an unmanly weakness, and she felt so deeply injured that she really *couldn't* quite forgive yet. So she winked hard, shook her head, and said gruffly, because Amy was listening: 'It was an abominable thing, and she don't deserve to be forgiven.'

With that she marched off to bed, and there was no merry or confidential gossip that night.

Amy was much offended that her overtures of peace had been repulsed, and began to wish she had not humbled herself, to feel more injured than ever, and to plume herself on her superior virtue in a way which was particularly exasperating. Jo still looked like a thundercloud, and nothing went well all day. It was bitter cold in the morning, she dropped her precious turnover in the gutter, Aunt March had an attack of fidgets, Meg was pensive, Beth *would* look grieved and wistful when she got home, and Amy kept making remarks about people who were always talking about being good, and yet wouldn't try, when other people set them a virtuous example.

'Everybody is so hateful, I'll ask Laurie to go skating. He is always kind and jolly, and will put me to rights, I know,' said Jo to herself, and off she went.

Amy heard the clash of skates, and looked out with an impatient exclamation: 'There! she promised I should go next time, for this is the last ice we shall have. But it's no use to ask such a cross-patch to take me.'

'Don't say that; you *were* very naughty, and it *is* hard to forgive the loss of her precious little book; but I think she might do it now, and I guess she will, if you try her at the right minute,' said Meg. 'Go after them; don't say anything till Jo has got good-natured with Laurie, then take a quiet minute, and just kiss her, or do some kind thing, and I'm sure she'll be friends again with all her heart.'

'I'll try,' said Amy, for the advice suited her; and, after a flurry to get ready, she ran after the friends, who were just disappearing over the hill.

It was not far to the river, but both were ready before Amy reached them. Jo saw her coming, and turned her back; Laurie did not see, for he was carefully skating along the shore, sounding the ice, for a warm spell had preceded the cold snap.

'I'll go on the first bend, and see if it's all right, before we begin to race,' Amy heard him say, as he shot away, looking like a young Russian, in his fur-trimmed coat and cap.

Jo heard Amy panting after her run, stamping her feet and blowing her fingers, as she tried to put her skates on; but Jo never turned, and went slowly zigzagging down the river, taking a bitter, unhappy sort of satisfaction in her sister's troubles. She had cherished her anger till it grew strong, and took possession of her, as evil thoughts and feelings always do, unless cast out at once. As Laurie turned the bend, he shouted back: 'Keep near the shore, it isn't safe in the middle.'

Jo heard, but Amy was just struggling to her feet, and did not catch a word. Jo glanced over her shoulder, and the little demon she was harbouring said in her ear: 'No matter whether she heard or not, let her take care of herself.'

Laurie had vanished round the bend; Jo was just at the turn, and Amy, far behind, striking out towards the smoother ice in the middle of the river. For a minute Jo stood still, with a strange feeling at her heart; then she resolved to go on, but something held and turned her round, just in time to see Amy throw up her hands and go down, with a sudden crash of rotten ice, the splash of water, and a cry that made Jo's heart stand still with fear. She tried to call Laurie, but her voice was gone; she tried to rush forward, but her feet seemed to have no strength in them; and, for a second, she could only stand motionless, staring, with a terror-stricken face, at the little blue hood above the black water. Something rushed swiftly by her, and Laurie's voice cried out: 'Bring a rail; quick, quick!'

How she did it, she never knew; but for the next few minutes she worked as if possessed, blindly obeying Laurie, who was quite self-possessed, and, lying flat, held Amy up by his arm and hockey till Jo dragged a rail from the fence, and together they got the child out, more frightened than hurt.

'Now then, we must walk her home as fast as we can; pile our things on her, while I get off these confounded skates,' cried Laurie, wrapping his coat round Amy, and tugging away at the straps, which never seemed so intricate before.

Shivering, dripping, and crying, they got Amy home; and, after an exciting time of it, she fell asleep, rolled in blankets, before a hot fire. During the bustle Jo had scarcely spoken, but flown about looking pale and wild, with her things half off, her dress torn, and her hands cut and bruised by ice and rails and refractory buckles. When Amy was comfortably asleep, the house quiet, and Mrs March sitting by the bed, she called Jo to her, and began to bind up the hurt hands.

'Are you sure she is safe?' whispered Jo, looking remorsefully at the golden head, which might have been swept away from her sight for ever under the treacherous ice.

'Quite safe, dear; she is not hurt, and won't even take cold, I think, you were so sensible in covering and getting her home quickly,' replied her mother, cheerfully.

'Laurie did it all; I only let her go. Mother, if she *should* die, it would be my fault'; and Jo dropped down beside the bed, in a passion of penitent tears, telling all that had happened, bitterly condemning her hardness of heart, and sobbing out her gratitude for being spared the heavy punishment which might have come upon her.

'It's my dreadful temper! I try to cure it; I think I have, and then it breaks out worse than ever. Oh, Mother, what shall I do? what shall I do?' cried poor Jo, in despair.

'Watch and pray, dear; never get tired of trying; and never think it is impossible to conquer your fault,' said Mrs March, drawing the blowzy head to her shoulder, and kissing the wet cheek so tenderly that Jo cried harder than ever.

'You don't know, and you can't guess how bad it is! It seems as if I could do anything when I'm in a passion; I get so savage, I could hurt anyone, and enjoy it. I'm afraid I *shall* do something dreadful some day, and spoil my life, and make everybody hate me. Oh, Mother, help me, do help me!'

'I will, my child, I will. Don't cry so bitterly, but remember this day, and resolve, with all your soul, that you will never know another like it. Jo, dear, we all have our temptations, some far greater than yours, and it often takes us all our lives to conquer them. You think your temper is the worst in the world; but mine used to be just like it.'

'Yours, Mother? Why, you are never angry!' and, for the moment, Jo forgot remorse in surprise.

'I've been trying to cure it for forty years, and have only succeeded in controlling it. I am angry nearly every day of my life, Jo; but I have learned not to show it; and I still hope to learn not to feel it, though it may take me another forty years to do so.'

The patience and the humility of the face she loved so well was a better lesson to Jo than the wisest lecture, the sharpest reproof. She felt comforted at once by the sympathy and confidence given her; the knowledge that her mother had a fault like hers, and tried to mend it, made her own easier to bear and strengthened her resolution to cure it; though forty years seemed rather a long time to watch and pray, to a girl of fifteen.

'Mother, are you angry when you fold your lips tight together, and go out of the room sometimes, when Aunt March scolds, or people worry you?' asked Jo, feeling nearer and dearer to her mother than ever before.

'Yes, I've learned to check the hasty words that rise to my lips; and when I feel that they mean to break out against my will, I just go away a minute, and give myself a little shake for being so weak and wicked,' answered Mrs March, with a sigh and a smile, as she smoothed and fastened up Jo's dishevelled hair.

'How did you learn to keep still? That is what troubles me – for the sharp words fly out before I know what I'm about; and the more I say the worse I get, till it's a pleasure to hurt people's feelings, and say dreadful things. Tell me how you do it, Marmee dear.'

'My good mother used to help me –'

'As you do us –' interrupted Jo, with a grateful kiss.

'But I lost her when I was a little older than you are, and for years had to struggle on alone, for I was too proud to confess my weakness to anyone else. I had a hard time, Jo, and shed a good many bitter tears over my failures; for, in spite of my efforts, I never seemed to get on. Then your father came, and I was so happy that I found it easy to be good. But by and by, when I had four little daughters round me, and we were poor, then the old trouble began again; for I am not patient by nature, and it tried me very much to see my children wanting anything.'

'Poor Mother! What helped you then?'

'Your father, Jo. He never loses patience – never doubts or complains – but always hopes and works and waits so cheerfully that one is ashamed to do otherwise before him. He helped and comforted me, and showed me that I must try to practise all the virtues I would have my little girls possess, for I was their example. It was easier to try for your sakes than for my own; a startled or surprised look from one of you, when I spoke sharply, rebuked me more than any words could have done; and the love, respect, and confidence of my children was the sweetest reward I could receive for my efforts to be the woman I would have them copy.'

'Oh Mother, if I'm ever half as good as you, I shall be satisfied,' cried Jo, much touched.

'I hope you will be a great deal better, dear; but you must keep watch over your "bosom enemy" as Father calls it, or it may sadden, if not spoil your life. You have had a warning; remember it, and try with heart and soul to master this quick temper, before it brings you greater sorrow and regret than you have known today.'

'I will try, Mother: I truly will. But you must help me, remind me, and keep me from flying out. I used to see Father sometimes put his finger on his lips, and look at you with a very kind but sober face, and you always folded your lips tight or went away: was he reminding you then?' asked Jo, softly.

'Yes, I asked him to help me so, and he never forgot it, but saved me from many a sharp word by that little gesture and kind look.'

Jo saw that her mother's eyes filled and her lips trembled as she spoke; and, fearing that she had said too much, she whispered, anxiously, 'Was it wrong to watch you, and to speak of it? I didn't mean to be rude, but it's so comfortable to say all I think of you, and feel so safe and happy here.'

'My Jo, you may say anything to your mother, for it is my greatest happiness and pride to feel that my girls confide in me, and know how much I love them.'

'I thought I'd grieved you.'

'No, dear; but speaking of Father reminded me how much I miss him, how much I owe him, and how faithfully I should watch and work to keep his little daughters safe and good for him.'

'Yet you told him to go, Mother, and didn't cry when he went, and never complain now, or seem as if you needed any help,' said Jo, wondering.

'I gave my best to the country I love, and kept my tears till he was gone. Why should I complain, when we both have merely done our duty, and will surely be the happier for it in the end? If I don't seem to need help, it is because I have a better friend even than Father to comfort and sustain me. My child, the troubles and temptations of your life are beginning, and may be many; but you can overcome and outlive them all if you learn to feel the strength and tenderness of your Heavenly Father as you do that of your earthly one. The more you love and trust him, the nearer you will feel to him, and the less you will depend on human power and wisdom. His love and care never tire or change, can never be taken from you, but may become the source of lifelong peace, happiness, and strength. Believe this heartily, and go to God with all your little cares, and hopes, and sins, and sorrows, as freely and confidingly as you come to your mother.'

Jo's only answer was to hold her mother close, and, in the silence which followed, the sincerest prayer she had ever prayed left her heart without words; for in that sad yet happy hour she had learned not only the bitterness of remorse and despair, but the sweetness of self-denial and self-control; and, led by her mother's hand, she had drawn nearer to the friend who welcomes every child with a love stronger than that of any father, tenderer than that of any mother.

Amy stirred, and sighed in her sleep; and, as if eager to begin at once to mend her fault, Jo looked up with an expression on her face which it had never worn before.

'I let the sun go down on my anger; I wouldn't forgive her, and today, if it hadn't been for Laurie, it might have been too late! How could I be so wicked?' said Jo, half aloud, as she leaned over her sister, softly stroking the wet hair scattered on the pillow.

As if she heard, Amy opened her eyes, and held out her arms, with a smile that went straight to Jo's heart. Neither said a word, but they hugged one another close, in spite of the blankets, and everything was forgiven and forgotten in one hearty kiss.

CHAPTER 9

Meg Goes to Vanity Fair

'I do think it was the most fortunate thing in the world that those children should have the measles just now,' said Meg, one April day, as she stood packing the 'go abroady' trunk in her room, surrounded by her sisters.

'And so nice of Annie Moffat not to forget her promise. A whole fortnight of fun will be regularly splendid,' replied Jo, looking like a windmill, as she folded skirts, with her long arms.

'And such lovely weather; I'm so glad of that,' added Beth, tidily sorting neck and hair ribbons in her best box, lent for the great occasion.

'I wish I was going to have a fine time, and wear all these nice things,' said Amy, with her mouth full of pins, as she artistically replenished her sister's cushion.

'I wish you were all going; but as you can't, I shall keep my adventures to tell you when I come back. I'm sure it's the least I can do, when you have been so kind, lending me things, and helping me get ready,' said Meg, glancing round the room at the very simple outfit, which seemed nearly perfect in their eyes.

'What did Mother give you out of the treasure-box?' asked Amy, who had not been present at the opening of a certain cedar chest, in which Mrs March kept a few relics of past splendour as gifts for her girls when the proper time came.

'A pair of silk stockings, that pretty carved fan, and a lovely blue sash. I wanted the violet silk; but there isn't time to make it over, so I must be contented with my old tarlatan.'

'It will look nicely over my new muslin skirt, and the sash will set it off beautifully. I wish I hadn't smashed my coral bracelet, for you might have had it,' said Jo, who loved to give and lend, but whose possessions were usually too dilapidated to be of much use.

'There is a lovely old-fashioned pearl set in the treasure-box; but Mother said real flowers were the prettiest ornament for a young girl, and Laurie promised to send me all I want,' replied Meg. 'Now, let me see; there's my new grey walking-suit – just curl up the feather in my hat, Beth – then my poplin, for Sunday, and the small party – it looks heavy for spring, doesn't it? The violet silk would be so nice; oh dear.'

'Never mind; you've got the tarlatan for the big party, and you always look like an angel in white,' said Amy, brooding over the little store of finery in which her soul delighted.

'It isn't low-necked, and it doesn't sweep enough, but it will have to do. My blue house-dress looks so well, turned and freshly trimmed, that I feel as if I'd got a new one. My silk sacque isn't a bit the fashion, and my bonnet doesn't look like Sallie's; I didn't like to say anything, but I was sadly disappointed in my umbrella. I told Mother black, with a white handle, but she forgot and bought a green one, with a yellowish handle. It's strong and neat, so I ought not to complain, but I know I shall feel ashamed of it beside Annie's silk one with a gold top,' sighed Meg, surveying the little umbrella with great disfavour.

'Change it,' advised Jo.

'I won't be so silly, or hurt Marmee's feelings, when she took so much pains to get my things. It's a nonsensical notion of mine, and I'm not going to give up to it. My silk stockings and two pairs of new gloves are my comfort. You are a dear, to lend me yours, Jo. I feel so rich, and sort of elegant, with two new pairs, and the old ones cleaned up for common'; and Meg took a refreshing peep at her glove box.

'Annie Moffat has blue and pink bows on her night-caps; would you put some on mine?' she asked, as Beth brought up a pile of snowy muslins, fresh from Hannah's hands.

'No, I wouldn't; for the smart caps won't match the plain gowns, without any trimming on them. Poor folks shouldn't rig,' said Jo, decidedly.

'I wonder if I shall *ever* be happy enough to have real lace on my clothes, and bows on my caps?' said Meg, impatiently.

'You said the other day that you'd be perfectly happy if you could only go to Annie Moffat's,' observed Beth, in her quiet way.

'So I did! Well, I *am* happy and I *won't* fret; but it does seem as if the more one gets the more one wants, doesn't it? There now, the trays are ready, and everything in but my ball-dress, which I shall leave for Mother to pack,' said Meg, cheering up, as she glanced from the half filled trunk to the many-times pressed and mended white tarlatan, which she called her 'ball-dress', with an important air.

The next day was fine, and Meg departed in style, for a fortnight of novelty and pleasure. Mrs March had consented to the visit rather reluctantly, fearing that Margaret would come back more discontented than she went. But she had begged so hard, and Sallie had promised to take good care of her, and a little pleasure seemed so delightful after a winter of irksome work, that the mother yielded, and the daughter went to take her first taste of fashionable life.

The Moffats *were* very fashionable, and simple Meg was rather daunted, at first, by the splendour of the house and the elegance of its occupants. But they were kindly people in spite of the frivolous life they led, and soon put their guest at her ease. Perhaps Meg felt, without understanding why, that they were not particularly cultivated or intelligent people and that all their gilding could not quite conceal the ordinary material of which they were made. It certainly was agreeable to fare sumptuously, drive in a fine carriage, wear her best frock every day, and do nothing but enjoy herself. It suited her exactly; and soon she began to imitate the manners and conversation of those about her; to put on little airs and graces, use French phrases, crimp her hair, take in her dresses, and talk about the fashions as well as she could. The more she saw of Annie Moffat's pretty things, the more she envied her, and sighed to be rich. Home now looked bare and dismal as she thought of it, work grew harder than ever, and she felt that she was a very destitute and much-injured girl, in spite of the new gloves and silk stockings.

She had not much time for repining, however, for the three young girls were busily employed in 'having a good time'. They shopped, walked, rode, and called all day; went to theatres and operas, or frolicked at home in the evening; for Annie had many friends, and knew how to entertain them. Her older sisters were very fine young ladies, and one was engaged, which was extremely interesting and romantic, Meg thought. Mr Moffat was a fat, jolly old gentleman, who knew her father; and Mrs Moffat a fat, jolly old lady, who took as great a fancy to Meg as her daughter had done. Everyone petted her; and 'Daisy', as they called her, was in a fair way to have her head turned.

When the evening for the 'small party' came, she found that the poplin wouldn't do at all, for the other girls were putting on thin dresses, and making themselves very fine indeed; so out came the tarlatan, looking older, limper, and shabbier than ever, beside Sallie's crisp new one. Meg saw the girls glance at it and then at one another, and her cheeks began to burn, for, with all her gentleness, she was very proud. No one said a word about it, but Sallie offered to dress her hair, and Annie to tie her sash, and Belle, the engaged sister, praised her white arms; but in their kindness Meg saw only pity for her poverty, and her heart felt very heavy as she stood by herself, while the others laughed, chattered, and flew about like gauzy butterflies. The hard, bitter feeling was getting pretty bad, when the maid brought in a box of flowers. Before she could speak, Annie had the cover off, and all were exclaiming at the lovely roses, heath, and ferns within.

'It's for Belle, of course; George always sends her some, but these are altogether ravishing,' cried Annie, with a great sniff.

'They are for Miss March, the man said. And here's a note,' put in the maid, holding it to Meg.

'What fun! Who are they from? Didn't know you had a lover,' cried the girls, fluttering about Meg in a high state of curiosity and surprise.

'The note is from Mother, and the flowers from Laurie,' said Meg, simply, yet much gratified that he had not forgotten her.

'Oh, indeed!' said Annie, with a funny look, as Meg slipped the note in her pocket, as a sort of talisman against envy, vanity, and false pride; for the few loving words had done her good, and the flowers cheered her up by their beauty.

Feeling almost happy again, she laid by a few ferns and roses for herself, and quickly made up the rest in dainty bouquets for the breasts, hair, or skirts of her friends, offering them so prettily that Clara, the elder sister, told her she was 'the sweetest little thing she ever saw'; and they looked quite charmed with her small attention. Somehow the kind act finished her despondency, and when all the rest went to show themselves to Mrs Moffat, she saw a happy, bright-eyed face in the mirror, as she laid her ferns against her rippling hair, and fastened the roses in the dress that didn't strike her as so *very* shabby now.

She enjoyed herself very much that evening, for she danced to her heart's content; everyone was very kind, and she had three compliments. Annie made her sing, and someone said she had a remarkably fine voice; Major Lincoln asked who the 'fresh little girl, with the beautiful eyes' was; and Mr Moffat insisted on dancing with her because she 'didn't dawdle, but had some spring in her' as he gracefully expressed it. So, altogether, she had a very nice time, till she overheard a bit of a conversation, which disturbed her extremely. She was sitting just inside the conservatory, waiting for her partner to bring her an ice, when she heard a voice ask, on the other side of the flowery wall: 'How old is he?'

'Sixteen or seventeen, I should say,' replied another voice.

'It would be a grand thing for one of those girls, wouldn't it? Sallie says they are very intimate now, and the old man quite dotes on them.'

'Mrs M. has made her plans, I dare say, and will play her cards well, early as it is. The girl evidently doesn't think of it yet,' said Mrs Moffat.

'She told that fib about her mamma as if she did know, and coloured up when the flowers came quite prettily. Poor thing! she'd be so nice if she was only got up in style. Do you think she'd be offended if we offered to lend her a dress for Thursday?' asked another voice.

'She's proud, but I don't believe she'd mind, for that dowdy tarlatan is all she has got. She may tear it tonight, and that will be a good excuse for offering a decent one.'

'We'll see. I shall ask young Laurence, as a compliment to her, and we'll have fun about it afterwards.'

Here Meg's partner appeared, to find her looking much flushed and rather agitated. She *was* proud, and her pride was useful just then, for it helped her hide her mortification, anger, and disgust at what she had just heard; for innocent and unsuspicious as she was, she could not help understanding the gossip of her friends. She tried to forget it, but could not, and kept repeating to herself, 'Mrs M. has made her plans,' 'that fib about her mamma', and 'dowdy tarlatan', till she was ready to cry, and rush home to tell her troubles and ask for advice. As that was impossible, she did her best to seem gay, and, being rather excited, she succeeded so well that no one dreamed what an effort she was making. She was very glad when it was all over, and she was quiet in her bed, where she could think and wonder and fume till her head ached, and her hot cheeks were cooled by a few natural tears. Those foolish, yet well-meant words had opened a new world to Meg, and much disturbed the peace of the old one, in which, till now, she had lived as happily as a child. Her innocent friendship with Laurie was spoilt by the silly speeches she had overheard; her faith in her mother was a little shaken by the worldly plans attributed to her by Mrs Moffat, who judged others by herself; and the sensible resolution to be contented with the simple wardrobe which suited a poor man's daughter was weakened by the unnecessary pity of girls who thought a shabby dress one of the greatest calamities under heaven.

Poor Meg had a restless night, and got up heavy-eyed, unhappy, half resentful towards her friends, and half ashamed of herself for not speaking out frankly and setting everything right. Everybody dawdled that morning, and it was noon before the girls found energy enough even to take up their worsted work. Something in the manner of her friends struck Meg at once; they treated her with more respect, she thought, took quite a tender interest in what she said, and looked at her with eyes that plainly betrayed curiosity. All this surprised and flattered her, though she did not understand it till Miss Belle looked up from her writing and said, with a sentimental air:

'Daisy, dear, I've sent an invitation to your friend, Mr Laurence, for Thursday. We should like to know him, and it's only a proper compliment to you.'

Meg coloured, but a mischievous fancy to tease the girls made her reply, demurely:

'You are very kind, but I'm afraid he won't come.'

'Why not, *chérie?*' asked Miss Belle.

'He's too old.'

'My child, what do you mean? What is his age, I beg to know!' cried Miss Clara.

'Nearly seventy, I believe,' answered Meg, counting stitches to hide the merriment in her eyes.

'You sly creature! Of course we meant the young man,' exclaimed Miss Belle, laughing.

'There isn't any, Laurie is only a little boy,' and Meg laughed also at the queer look which the sisters exchanged as she thus described her supposed lover.

'About your age,' Nan said.

'Nearer my sister Jo's; *I* am seventeen in August,' returned Meg, tossing her head.

'It's very nice of him to send you flowers, isn't it?' said Annie, looking wise about nothing.

'Yes, he often does to all of us, for their house is full and we are so fond of them. My mother and old Mr Laurence are friends, you know, so it is quite natural that we children should play together'; and Meg hoped they would say no more.

'It's evident Daisy isn't out yet,' said Miss Clara to Belle, with a nod.

'Quite a pastoral state of innocence all round,' returned Miss Belle, with a shrug.

'I'm going out to get some little matters for my girls; can I do anything for you, young ladies?' asked Mrs Moffat, lumbering in, like an elephant, in silk and lace.

'No, thank you, ma'am,' replied Sallie. 'I've got my new pink silk for Thursday, and don't want a thing.'

'Nor I –' began Meg, but stopped, because it occurred to her that she *did* want several things, and could not have them.

'What shall you wear?' asked Sallie.

'My old white one again, if I can mend it fit to be seen; it got sadly torn last night,' said Meg, trying to speak quite easily, but feeling very uncomfortable.

'Why don't you send home for another?' said Sallie, who was not an observing young lady.

'I haven't got any other.' It cost Meg an effort to say that, but Sallie did not see it, and exclaimed, in amiable surprise:

'Only that? How funny –' She did not finish her speech, for Belle shook her head at her, and broke in, saying kindly:

'Not at all; where is the use of having a lot of dresses when she isn't out? There's no need of sending home, Daisy, even if you had a dozen, for I've got a sweet blue silk laid away, which I've outgrown, and you shall wear it to please me, won't you, dear?'

'You are very kind, but I don't mind my old dress, if you don't; it does well enough for a little girl like me,' said Meg.

'Now do let me please myself by dressing you up in style. I admire to do it, and you'd be a regular little beauty with a touch here and there. I shan't let anyone see you till you are done, and then we'll burst upon them like Cinderella and her godmother going to the ball,' said Belle, in her persuasive tone.

Meg couldn't refuse the offer so kindly made, for a desire to see if she would be 'a little beauty' after touching up, caused her to accept, and forget all her former uncomfortable feelings towards the Moffats.

On the Thursday evening Belle shut herself up with her maid; and between them they turned Meg into a fine lady. They crimped and curled her hair, they polished her neck and arms with some fragrant powder, touched her lips with coralline salve, to make them redder, and Hortense would have added 'a *soupçon* of rouge', if Meg had not rebelled. They laced her into a sky-blue dress which was so tight she could hardly breathe, and so low in the neck that modest Meg blushed at herself in the mirror. A set of silver filagree was added, bracelets, necklace, brooch, and even earrings, for Hortense tied them on with a bit of pink silk which did not show. A cluster of tea-rosebuds at the bosom and a *ruche* reconciled Meg to the display of her pretty white shoulders, and a pair of high-heeled blue silk boots satisfied the last wish of her heart. A laced handkerchief, a plumy fan, and a bouquet in a silver holder finished her off; and Miss Belle surveyed her with the satisfaction of a little girl with a newly dressed doll.

'Mademoiselle is *charmante, très jolie*, is she not?' cried Hortense, clasping her hands in an affected rapture.

'Come and show yourself,' said Miss Belle, leading the way to the room where the others were waiting.

As Meg went rustling after her, with her long skirts trailing, her earrings tinkling, her curls waving, and her heart beating, she felt as if her 'fun' had really begun at last, for the mirror had plainly told her that she *was* 'a little beauty'. Her friends repeated the pleasing phrase enthusiastically; and for several minutes she stood, like the jackdaw in the fable, enjoying her borrowed plumes, while the rest chattered like a party of magpies. 'While I dress, do you drill her, Nan, in the management of her skirt, and those French heels, or she will trip herself up. Take your silver butterfly, and catch up that long curl on the left side of her head, Clara, and don't any of you disturb the charming work of my hands,' said Belle, as she hurried away, looking well pleased with her success.

'I'm afraid to go down, I feel so queer and stiff and half-dressed,' said Meg to Sallie, as the bell rang, and Mrs Moffat sent to ask the young ladies to appear at once.

'You don't look a bit like yourself, but you are very nice. I'm nowhere beside you, for Belle has heaps of taste, and you're quite French, I assure you. Let your flowers hang; don't be so careful of them, and be sure you don't trip,' returned Sallie; trying not to care that Meg was prettier than herself.

Keeping that warning carefully in mind, Margaret got safely downstairs, and sailed into the drawing rooms, where the Moffats and a few early guests were assembled. She very soon discovered that there is a charm about fine clothes which attracts a certain class of people, and secures their respect. Several young ladies who had taken no notice of her before, were very affectionate all of a sudden; several young gentlemen, who had only stared at her at the other party, now not only stared, but asked to be introduced, and said all manner of foolish but agreeable things to her; and several old ladies, who sat on sofas and criticized the rest of the party, inquired who she was, with an air of interest. She heard Mrs Moffat reply to one of them: 'Daisy March – father a colonel in the army – one of our first families, but reverses of fortune, you know; intimate friends of the Laurences; sweet creature, I assure you; my Ned is quite wild about her.'

'Dear me!' said the old lady, putting up her glass for another observation of Meg, who tried to look as if she had not heard, and been rather shocked at Mrs Moffat's fibs.

The 'queer feeling' did not pass away, but she imagined herself acting the new part of a fine lady, and so got on pretty well, though the tight dress gave her a side-ache, the train kept getting under her feet, and she was in constant fear lest her earrings should fly off, and get lost or broken. She was flirting her fan, and laughing at the feeble jokes of a young gentleman who tried to be witty, when she suddenly stopped laughing, and looked confused; for, just opposite, she saw Laurie. He was staring at her with undisguised surprise, and disapproval also, she thought, for, though he bowed and smiled, yet something in his honest eyes made her blush, and wish she had her old dress on. To complete her confusion, she saw Belle nudge Annie, and both glance from her to Laurie, who, she was happy to see, looked unusually boyish and shy.

'Silly creatures, to put such thoughts into my head! I won't care for it, or let it change me a bit,' thought Meg, and rustled across the room to shake hands with her friend.

'I'm glad you've come, I was afraid you wouldn't,' she said, with her most grown-up air.

'Jo wanted me to come, and tell her how you looked, so I did,' answered Laurie, without turning his eyes upon her, though he half smiled at her maternal tone.

'What shall you tell her?' asked Meg, full of curiosity to know his opinion of her, yet feeling ill at ease with him, for the first time.

'I shall say I didn't know you; for you look so grown-up, and unlike yourself, I'm quite afraid of you,' he said, fumbling at his glove-button.

'How absurd of you! The girls dressed me up for fun, and I rather like it. Wouldn't Jo stare if she saw me?' said Meg, bent on making him say whether he thought her improved or not.

'Yes, I think she would,' returned Laurie, gravely.

'Don't you like me so?' asked Meg.

'No, I don't,' was the blunt reply.

'Why not?' in an anxious tone.

He glanced at her frizzled head, bare shoulders, and fantastically trimmed dress, with an expression that abashed her more than his answer, which had not a particle of his usual politeness about it.

'I don't like fuss and feathers.'

That was altogether too much from a lad younger than herself, and Meg walked away, saying petulantly: 'You are the rudest boy I ever saw.'

Feeling very much ruffled, she went and stood at a quiet window to cool her cheeks, for the tight dress gave her an uncomfortably brilliant colour. As she stood there, Major Lincoln passed by, and, a minute after, she heard him saying to his mother: 'They are making a fool of that little girl; I wanted you to see her, but they have spoilt her entirely; she's nothing but a doll tonight.'

'Oh dear!' sighed Meg; 'I wish I'd been sensible, and worn my own things; then I should not have disgusted other people or felt so uncomfortable and ashamed of myself.'

She leaned her forehead on the cool pane, and stood half hidden by the curtains, never minding that her favourite song had begun, till someone touched her; and, turning, she saw Laurie, looking penitent, as he said, with his very best bow, and his hand out: 'Please forgive my rudeness, and come and dance with me.'

'I'm afraid it will be too disagreeable to you,' said Meg, trying to look offended, and failing entirely.

'Not a bit of it, I'm dying to do it. Come, I'll be good; I don't like your gown, but I do think you are – just splendid'; and he waved his hands, as if words failed to express his admiration.

Meg smiled and relented, and whispered, as they stood waiting: 'Take care my skirt don't trip you up; it's the plague of my life, and I was a goose to wear it.'

'Pin it round your neck, and then it will be useful,' said Laurie, looking down at the little blue boots, which he evidently approved of.

Away they went fleetly and gracefully, for, having practised at home, they were well matched, and the blithe young couple were a pleasant sight to see, as they twirled merrily round and round, feeling more friendly than ever after their small tiff.

'Laurie, I want you to do me a favour; will you?' said Meg, as he stood fanning her when her breath gave out, which it did very soon though she would not own why.

'Won't I!' said Laurie, with alacrity.

'Please don't tell them at home about my dress tonight. They won't understand the joke, and it will worry Mother.'

'Then why did you do it?' said Laurie's eyes, so plainly that Meg hastily added: 'I shall tell them myself all about it and "'fess" to Mother how silly I've been. But I'd rather do it myself; so you'll not tell, will you?'

'I give you my word I won't; only what shall I say when they ask me?'

'Just say I looked nice, and was having a good time.'

'I'll say the first with all my heart; but how about the other? You don't look as if you were having a good time; are you?' and Laurie looked at her with an expression which made her answer, in a whisper: 'No, not just now. Don't think I'm horrid; I only wanted a little fun, but this sort doesn't pay, I find, and I'm getting tired of it.'

'Here comes Ned Moffat; what does he want?' said Laurie, knitting his black brows as if he did not regard his young host in the light of a pleasant addition to the party.

'What a bore!' said Meg, assuming a languid air, which amused Laurie immensely.

He did not speak to her again till supper-time, when he saw her drinking champagne with Ned and his friend Fisher, who were behaving 'like a pair of fools', as Laurie said to himself, for he felt a brotherly sort of right to watch over the Marches, and fight their battles whenever a defender was needed.

'You'll have a splitting headache tomorrow, if you drink that stuff. I wouldn't, Meg; your mother doesn't like it, you know,' he whispered, leaning over her chair, as Ned turned to refill her glass, and Fisher stooped to pick up her fan.

'I'm not Meg tonight; I'm a "doll", who does all sorts of crazy things. Tomorrow I shall put away my "fuss and feathers", and be desperately good again,' she answered, with an affected little laugh.

'Wish tomorrow was here, then,' muttered Laurie, walking off, ill-pleased at the change he saw in her.

Meg danced and flirted, chattered and giggled, as the other girls did; after supper she undertook the German, and blundered through it, nearly upsetting her partner with her long skirt, and romping in a way that scandalized Laurie, who looked on, and meditated a lecture. But he got no chance to deliver it, for Meg kept away from him till he came to say good night.

'Remember!' she said, trying to smile, for the splitting headache had already begun.

'Silence *à la mort*,' replied Laurie, with a melodramatic flourish, as he went away.

This little bit of byplay excited Annie's curiosity; but Meg was too tired for gossip, and went to bed feeling as if she had been to a masquerade, and hadn't enjoyed herself as much as she expected. She was sick all the next day, and on Saturday went home, quite used up with her fortnight's fun, and feeling that she had 'sat in the lap of luxury' long enough.

'It does seem pleasant to be quiet, and not have company manners on all the time. Home *is* a nice place, though it isn't splendid,' said Meg, looking about her with a restful expression as she sat with her mother and Jo on the Sunday evening.

'I'm glad to hear you say so, dear, for I was afraid home would seem dull and poor to you after your fine quarters,' replied her mother, who had given her many anxious looks that day; for motherly eyes are quick to see any change in children's faces.

Meg had told her adventures gaily, and said over and over what a charming time she had had; but something still seemed to weigh upon her spirits, and, when the younger girls were gone to bed, she sat thoughtfully staring at the fire, saying little, and looking worried. As the clock struck nine, and Jo proposed bed, Meg suddenly left her chair, and taking Beth's stool, leaned her elbows on her mother's knee, saying bravely:

'Marmee, I want to "'fess".'

'I thought so; what is it, dear?'

'Shall I go away?' asked Jo, discreetly.

'Of course not; don't I always tell you everything? I was ashamed to speak of it before the children, but I want you to know all the dreadful things I did at the Moffats'.'

'We are prepared,' said Mrs March, smiling, but looking a little anxious.

'I told you they dressed me up, but I didn't tell you that they powdered and squeezed and frizzled, and made me look like a fashion-plate. Laurie thought I wasn't proper; I know he did, though he didn't say so, and one man called me "a doll". I knew it was silly, but they flattered me, and said I was a beauty, and quantities of nonsense, so I let them make a fool of me.'

'Is that all?' asked Jo, as Mrs March looked silently at the downcast face of her pretty daughter, and could not find it in her heart to blame her little follies.

'No; I drank champagne, and romped, and tried to flirt and was altogether abominable,' said Meg, self-reproachfully.

'There is something more, I think,' and Mrs March smoothed the soft cheek, which suddenly grew rosy, as Meg answered slowly:

'Yes; it's very silly, but I want to tell it, because I hate to have people say and think such things about us and Laurie.'

Then she told the various bits of gossip she had heard at the Moffats'; and, as she spoke, Jo saw her mother fold her lips tightly, as if ill pleased that such ideas should be put into Meg's innocent mind.

'Well, if that isn't the greatest rubbish I ever heard,' cried Jo, indignantly. 'Why didn't you pop out and tell them so, on the spot?'

'I couldn't, it was so embarrassing for me. I couldn't help hearing at first, and then I was so angry and ashamed, I didn't remember that I ought to go away.'

'Just wait till *I* see Annie Moffat, and I'll show you how to settle such ridiculous stuff. The idea of having "plans", and being kind to Laurie because he's rich, and may marry us by and by! Won't he shout when I tell him what those silly things say about us poor children?' and Jo laughed, as if, on second thoughts, the thing struck her as a good joke.

'If you tell Laurie, I'll never forgive you! She mustn't, must she, Mother?' said Meg, looking distressed.

'No; never repeat that foolish gossip, and forget it as soon as you can,' said Mrs March, gravely. 'I was very unwise to let you go among people of whom I know so little – kind, I dare say, but worldly, ill-bred, and full of these vulgar ideas about young people. I am more sorry than I can express for the mischief this visit may have done you, Meg.'

'Don't be sorry, I won't let it hurt me; I'll forget all the bad, and remember only the good; for I did enjoy a great deal, and thank you very much for letting me go. I'll not be sentimental or dissatisfied, Mother; I know I'm a silly little girl, and I'll stay with you till I'm fit to take care of myself. But it *is* nice to be praised and admired, and I can't help saying I like it,' said Meg, looking half ashamed of the confession.

'That is perfectly natural, and quite harmless, if the liking does not become a passion, and lead one to do foolish or unmaidenly things. Learn to know and value the praise which is worth having, and to excite the admiration of excellent people by being modest as well as pretty, Meg.'

Margaret sat thinking a moment, while Jo stood with her hands behind her, looking both interested and a little perplexed; for it was a new thing to see Meg blushing and talking about admiration, lovers, and things of that sort; and Jo felt as if, during that fortnight, her sister had grown up amazingly, and was drifting away from her into a world where she could not follow.

'Mother, do you have "plans", as Mrs Moffat said?' asked Meg, bashfully.

'Yes, my dear, I have a great many; all mothers do, but mine differ somewhat from Mrs Moffat's, I suspect. I will tell you some of them, for the time has come when a word may set this romantic little head and heart of yours right on a very serious subject. You are young, Meg, but not too young to understand me; and mother's lips are the fittest to speak of such things to girls like you. Jo, your turn will come in time, perhaps, so listen to my "plans", and help me carry them out if they are good.'

Jo went and sat on one arm of the chair, looking as if she thought they were about to join in some very solemn affair. Holding a hand of each, and watching the two young faces wistfully, Mrs March said, in her serious yet cheery way:

'I want my daughters to be beautiful, accomplished, and good; to be admired, loved, and respected; to have a happy youth, to be well and wisely married, and to lead useful, pleasant lives, with as little care and sorrow to try them as God sees fit to send. To be loved and chosen by a good man is the best and sweetest thing which can happen to a woman; and I sincerely hope my girls may know this beautiful experience. It is natural to think of it, Meg; right to hope and wait for it, and wise to prepare for it; so that, when the happy time comes, you may feel ready for the duties and worthy of the joy. My dear girls, I *am* ambitious for you, but not to have you make a dash in the world – marry rich men merely because they are rich, or have splendid houses, which are not homes because love is wanting. Money is a needful and precious thing – and, when well used, a noble thing – but I never want you to think of it as the first or only prize to strive for. I'd rather see you poor men's wives, if you were happy, beloved, contented, than queens on thrones, without self-respect and peace.'

'Poor girls don't stand any chance, Belle says, unless they put themselves forward,' sighed Meg.

'Then we'll be old maids,' said Jo, stoutly.

'Right, Jo; better be happy old maids than unhappy wives or unmaidenly girls, running about to find husbands,' said Mrs March, decidedly. 'Don't be troubled, Meg; poverty seldom daunts a sincere lover. Some of the best and most honoured women I know were poor girls, but so love-worthy that they were not allowed to be old maids. Leave these things to time. Make this home happy, so that you may be fit for homes of your own if they are offered you, and contented here if they are not. One thing remember, my girls; Mother is always ready to be your confidante, Father to be your friend; and both of us trust and hope that our daughters, whether married or single, will be the pride and comfort of our lives.'

'We will, Marmee, we will!' cried both, with all their hearts, as she bade them good night.

CHAPTER 10

The P.C. and P.O.

As spring came on, a new set of amusements became the fashion, and the lengthening days gave long afternoons for work and play of all sorts. The garden had to be put in order, and each sister had a quarter of the little plot to do what she liked with. Hannah used to say, 'I'd know which each of them gardings belonged to, ef I see 'em in Chiny'; and so she might, for the girls' tastes differed as much as their characters. Meg's had roses and heliotrope, myrtle, and a little orange tree in it. Jo's bed was never alike two seasons, for she was always trying experiments; this year it was to be a plantation of sunflowers, the seeds of which cheerful and aspiring plant were to feed 'Aunt Cockle-top' and her family of chicks. Beth had old-fashioned, fragrant flowers in her garden – sweet peas and mignonette, larkspur, pinks, pansies, and southernwood, with chickweed for the bird, and catnip for the pussies. Amy had a bower in hers – rather small and earwiggy, but very pretty to look at – with honeysuckles and morning-glories hanging their coloured horns and bells in graceful wreaths all over it; tall white lilies, delicate ferns, and as many brilliant, picturesque plants as would consent to blossom there.

Gardening, walks, rows on the river, and flower-hunts employed the fine days; and for rainy ones they had house diversions, some old, some new – all more or less original. One of these was the 'P.C.'; for, as secret societies were the fashion, it was thought proper to have one;

and, as all of the girls admired Dickens, they called themselves the Pickwick Club. With a few interruptions, they had kept this up for a year, and met every Saturday evening in the big garret, on which occasions the ceremonies were as follows: Three chairs were arranged in a row before a table, on which was a lamp, also four white badges, with a big 'P.C.' in different colours on each, and the weekly newspaper, called *The Pickwick Portfolio*, to which all contributed something; while Jo, who revelled in pens and ink, was the editor. At seven o'clock the four members ascended to the club room, tied their badges round their heads, and took their seats with great solemnity. Meg, as the eldest, was Samuel Pickwick; Jo, being of a literary turn, Augustus Snodgrass; Beth, because she was round and rosy, Tracy Tupman; and Amy, who was always trying to do what she couldn't, was Nathaniel Winkle. Pickwick, the president, read the paper, which was filled with original tales, poetry, local news, funny advertisements, and hints, in which they good-naturedly reminded each other of their faults and shortcomings. On one occasion Mr Pickwick put on a pair of spectacles without any glasses, rapped upon the table, hemmed, and, having stared hard at Mr Snodgrass, who was tilting back in his chair till he arranged himself properly, began to read:

The Pickwick Portfolio.

May 20, 18—

Poet's Corner.

ANNIVERSARY ODE.
—

Again we meet to celebrate,
  With badge and solemn rite,
Our fifty-second anniversary,
  In Pickwick Hall, to-night.

We all are here in perfect
  health,

None gone from our small
  band;
Again we see each well-known
  face,
And press each friendly hand.

Our Pickwick, always at his
  post,
  With reverence we greet,
As, spectacles on nose, he
  reads

Our well-filled weekly sheet.

Although he suffers from a
  cold,
  We joy to hear him speak,
For words of wisdom from
  him fall,
  In spite of croak or squeak.

Old six-foot Snodgrass looms
  on high
  With elephantine grace,
And beams upon the
  company
  With brown and jovial face.

Poetic fire lights up his eye,
  He struggles 'gainst his lot
Behold ambition on his brow,
  And on his nose a blot!

Next out peaceful Tupman
  comes,
  So rosy, plump, and sweet,
Who chokes with laughter at
  the puns,
  And tumbles off his seat.

Prim little Winkle too is
  here,
  With every hair in place,
A model of propriety,
  Though he hates to wash
  his face.

The year is gone, we still unite
  To joke and laugh and read,
And tread the path of literature
  That doth to glory lead.

Long may our paper prosper
  well,
  Our club unbroken be,
And coming years their
  blessings pour
  On the useful gay 'P.C.'
              A. SNODGRASS.

♣

THE MASKED MARRIAGE.
A TALE OF VENICE.
—

Gondola after gondola swept up to the marble steps, and left its lovely load to swell the brilliant throng that filled the stately halls of Count de Adelon. Knights and ladies, elves and pages, monks and flower-girls, mingled gaily in the dance. Sweet voices and rich melody filled the air; and so with mirth and music the masquerade went on.

'Has your Highness seen the Lady Viola tonight?' asked a gallant troubadour of the fairy queen who floated down the hall upon his arm.

'Yes; is she not lovely, though so sad? Her dress is well chosen, too, for in a week she weds Count Antonio, whom she passionately hates.'

'By my faith, I envy him. Yonder he comes arrayed like a bridegroom, except the black mask. When that is off we shall see how he regards the fair maid whose heart he cannot win, though her stern father bestows her hand,' returned the troubadour.

''Tis whispered that she loves the young English artist who haunts her steps, and is spurned by the old count,' said the lady, as they joined the dance.

The revel was at its height when a priest appeared, and, withdrawing the young pair to an alcove hung with purple velvet, he motioned them to kneel. Instant silence fell upon the gay throng; and not a sound, but the dash of fountains or the rustle of orange-groves sleeping in the moonlight, broke the hush, as Count de Adelon spoke thus –

'My lords and ladies, pardon the ruse by which I have gathered you here to witness the marriage of my daughter. Father we wait your services.'

All eyes turned toward the bridal party, and a low murmur of amazement went through the throng, for neither bride nor groom removed their masks. Curiosity and wonder possessed all hearts, but respect restrained all tongues till the holy rite was over. Then the eager spectators gathered round the count, demanding an explanation.

'Gladly would I give it if I could; but I only know that it was the whim of my timid Viola, and I yielded to it. Now, my children, let the play end. Unmask, and receive my blessing.'

But neither bent the knee; for the young bridegroom replied, in a tone that startled all listeners, as the mask fell, disclosing the noble face of Ferdinand Devereux, the artist lover; and, leaning on the breast where now flashed the star of an English earl, was the lovely Viola, radiant with joy and beauty.

'My lord, you scornfully bade me claim your daughter when I could boast as high a name and vast a fortune as the Count Antonio. I can do more; for even your ambitious soul cannot refuse the Earl of Devereux and De Vere, when he gives his ancient name and boundless wealth in return for the beloved hand of this fair lady now my wife.'

The count stood like one changed to stone; and, turning to the bewildered crowd, Ferdinand added, with a gay smile of triumph, 'To you, my gallant friends, I can only wish that your wooing may prosper as mine has done; and that you may all win as fair a bride as I have by this masked marriage.'

S. PICKWICK.

♣

grocerman bought and put it in his shop. That same morning, a little girl, in a brown hat and blue dress, with a round face and a snub nose, went and bought it for her mother. She lugged it home, cut it up, and boiled it in the big pot; mashed some of it, with salt and butter, for dinner; and to the rest she added a pint of milk, two eggs, four spoons of sugar, nutmeg, and some crackers; put it in a deep dish, and baked it till it was brown and nice; and next day it was eaten by a family named March.

T. TUPMAN.

♣

Why is the P.C. like the Tower of Babel? It is full of unruly members.

♣

THE HISTORY OF A SQUASH.

——

Once upon a time a farmer planted a little seed in his garden, and after a while it sprouted and became a vine, and bore many squashes. One day in October, when they were ripe, he picked one and took it to market. A

MR PICKWICK, *Sir*:–

I address you upon the subject of sin the sinner I mean is a man named Winkle who makes trouble in his club by laughing and sometimes won't write his piece in this fine paper I hope you will pardon his badness and let him send a French fable because he can't write out of his head as he has so many lessons to do and no brains in future I will try to take time by the fetlock and prepare some work which will be all *commy la fo* that means all right I am in haste as it is nearly school time.

Yours respectably,

N. WINKLE.

[The above is a manly and handsome acknowledgement of past misdemeanours. If our young friend studied punctuation, it would be well.]

♣

A SAD ACCIDENT

—

On Friday last we were startled by a violent shock in our basement, followed by cries of distress. On rushing, in a body, to the cellar, we discovered our beloved President prostrate on the floor, having tripped and fallen while getting wood for domestic purposes. A perfect scene of ruin met our eyes; for in his fall Mr Pickwick had plunged his head and shoulders into a tub of water, upset a keg of soft soap upon his manly form, and torn his garments badly. On being removed from his perilous situation, it was discovered that he had suffered no injury but several bruises; and, we are happy to add, is now doing well.

ED.

♣

The Public Bereavement.

It is our painful duty to record the sudden and mysterious disappearance of our cherished friend, Mrs Snowball Pat Paw. This lovely and beloved cat was the pet of a large circle of warm and admiring friends; for her beauty attracted all eyes, her grace and virtues endeared her to all hearts, and her loss is deeply felt by the whole community.

When last seen, she was sitting at the gate, watching the butcher's cart; and it is feared that some villain, tempted by her charms, basely stole her. Weeks have passed but no trace of her has been discovered; and we relinquish all hope, tie a black ribbon to her basket, set aside her dish, and weep for her as one lost to us for ever.

A sympathizing friend sends the following gem:–

A LAMENT.

FOR S. B. PAT PAW.

———

We mourn the loss of our little
pet,
   And sigh o'er her hapless fate,
For never more by the fire she'll
sit,
   Nor play by the old green
gate.

The little grave where her
infant sleeps
   Is 'neath the chestnut tree;
But o'er her grave we may
not weep,
   We know not where it may
be.

Her empty bed, her idle ball,
   Will never see her more;
No gentle tap, no loving purr
   Is heard at the parlour door.

Another cat comes after her
mice,
   A cat with a dirty face;
But she does not hunt as our
darling did,
   Nor play with her airy
grace.

Her stealthy paws tread the
very hall

Where Snowball used to
play,
But she only spits at the dogs
our pet
   So gallantly drove away.

She is useful and mild, and
does her best,
   But she is not fair to see;
And we cannot give her your
place, dear,
   Nor worship her as we
worship thee.

A. S.

ADVERTISEMENTS.

MISS ORANTHY BLUGGAGE, the accomplished Strong-Minded Lecturer, will deliver her famous Lecture on 'WOMAN AND HER POSITION', at Pickwick Hall, next Saturday Evening, after the usual performances.

———

A WEEKLY MEETING will be held at Kitchen Place, to teach young ladies how to cook. Hannah Brown will preside; and all are invited to attend.

THE DUSTPAN SOCIETY will meet on Wednesday next, and

parade in the upper story of the Club House. All members to appear in uniform and shoulder their brooms at nine precisely.

MRS BETH BOUNCER will open her new assortment of Doll's Millinery next week. The latest Paris Fashions have arrived, and orders are respectfully solicited.

A NEW PLAY will appear at the Barnville Theatre, in the course of a few weeks, which will surpass anything ever seen on the American stage. 'THE GREEK SLAVE, or Constantine the Avenger', is the name of this thrilling drama!!!

HINTS.

If S. P. didn't use so much soap on his hands, he wouldn't always be late at breakfast. A. S. is requested not to whistle in the street. T. T. please don't forget Amy's napkin. A. W. must not fret because his dress has not nine tucks.

—

WEEKLY REPORT.
Meg—Good.
Jo—Bad.
Beth—Very good.
Amy—Middling.

As the President finished reading the paper (which I beg leave to assure my readers is a bona fide copy of one written by bona fide girls once upon a time), a round of applause followed and then Mr Snodgrass rose to make a proposition.

'Mr President and gentlemen,' he began, assuming a parliamentary attitude and tone, 'I wish to propose the admission of a new member – one who highly deserves the honour, would be deeply grateful for it, and would add immensely to the spirit of the club, the literary value of the paper, and be no end jolly and nice. I propose Mr Theodore Laurence as an honorary member of the P.C. Come now, do have him.'

Jo's sudden change of tone made the girls laugh; but all looked rather anxious, and no one said a word, as Snodgrass took his seat.

'We'll put it to the vote,' said the President. 'All in favour of this motion please to manifest it by saying "Ay".'

A loud response from Snodgrass, followed, to everybody's surprise, by a timid one from Beth.

'Contrary minded say "No".'

Meg and Amy were contrary minded; and Mr Winkle rose to say, with great eloquence, 'We don't wish any boys; they only joke and bounce about. This is a ladies' club, and we wish to be private and proper.'

'I'm afraid he'll laugh at our paper, and make fun of us afterwards,' observed Pickwick, pulling the little curl on her forehead, as she always did when doubtful.

Up rose Snodgrass, very much in earnest. 'Sir, I give you my word as a gentleman, Laurie won't do anything of the sort. He likes to write, and he'll give a tone to our contributions, and keep us from being sentimental, don't you see? We can do so little for him, and he does so much for us, I think the least we can do is to offer him a place here, and make him welcome if he comes.'

This artful allusion to benefits conferred brought Tupman to his feet, looking as if he had quite made up his mind.

'Yes, we ought to do it, even if we *are* afraid. I say he *may* come, and his grandpa too, if he likes.'

This spirited outburst from Beth electrified the club, and Jo left her seat to shake hands approvingly. 'Now then, vote again. Everybody remember it's our Laurie, and say "Ay!"' cried Snodgrass, excitedly.

'Ay! ay! ay!' replied three voices at once.

'Good! Bless you! Now, as there's nothing like "taking time by the *fetlock*", as Winkle characteristically observes, allow me to present the new member'; and, to the dismay of the rest of the club, Jo threw open the door of the closet, and displayed Laurie sitting on a rag-bag, flushed and twinkling with suppressed laughter.

'You rogue! you traitor! Jo, how could you?' cried the three girls, as Snodgrass led her friend triumphantly forth; and, producing both a chair and a badge, installed him in a jiffy.

'The coolness of you two rascals is amazing,' began Mr Pickwick, trying to get up an awful frown, and only succeeding in producing an amiable smile. But the new member was equal to the occasion; and, rising, with a graceful salutation to the Chair, said, in the most engaging manner, 'Mr President and ladies – I beg pardon, gentlemen – allow me to introduce myself as Sam Weller, the very humble servant of the club.'

'Good! good!' cried Jo, pounding with the handle of the old warming-pan, on which she leaned.

'My faithful friend and noble patron,' continued Laurie, with a wave of the hand, 'who has so flatteringly presented me, is not to be blamed for the base stratagem of tonight. I planned it, and she only gave in after lots of teasing.'

'Come now, don't lay it all on yourself; you know I proposed the cupboard,' broke in Snodgrass, who was enjoying the joke amazingly.

'Never you mind what she says. I'm the wretch that did it, sir,' said the new member, with a Welleresque nod to Mr Pickwick. 'But on my honour I never will do so again, and henceforth *dewote* myself to the interest of this immortal club.'

'Hear! hear!' cried Jo, clashing the lid of the warming-pan like a cymbal.

'Go on, go on!' added Winkle and Tupman, while the President bowed benignly.

'I merely wish to say, that as a slight token of my gratitude for the honour done me, and as a means of promoting friendly relations between adjoining nations, I have set up a post-office in the hedge in the lower corner of the garden; a fine, spacious building, with padlocks on the doors, and every convenience for the mails – also the females, if I may be allowed the expression. It's the old martin-house; but I've stopped up the door, and made the roof open, so it will hold all sorts of things, and save our valuable time. Letters, manuscripts, books, and bundles can be passed in there; and, as each nation has a key, it will be uncommonly nice, I fancy. Allow me to present the club key; and, with many thanks for your favour, take my seat.'

Great applause as Mr Weller deposited a little key on the table, and subsided; the warming-pan clashed and waved wildly, and it was some time before order could be restored. A long discussion followed, and everyone came out surprising, for everyone did her best; so it was an unusually lively meeting, and did not adjourn till a late hour, when it broke up with three shrill cheers for the new member. No one ever regretted the admittance of Sam Weller, for a more devoted, well-behaved, and jovial member no club could have. He certainly did add 'spirit' to the meeting and 'a tone' to the paper; for his orations convulsed his hearers, and his contributions were excellent, being patriotic, classical, comical, or dramatic, but never sentimental. Jo regarded them as worthy of Bacon, Milton, or Shakespeare; and remodelled her own works with good effect, she thought.

The P.O. was a capital little institution, and flourished wonderfully, for nearly as many queer things passed through it as through the real office. Tragedies and cravats, poetry and pickles, garden-seeds and long letters, music and gingerbread, rubbers, invitations, scoldings and puppies. The old gentleman liked the fun, and amused himself by sending odd bundles, mysterious messages, and funny telegrams; and his gardener, who was smitten with Hannah's charms, actually sent a love-letter to Jo's care. How they laughed when the secret came out, never dreaming how many love-letters that little post-office would hold in the years to come!

CHAPTER 11

Experiments

'The first of June! The Kings are off to the seashore tomorrow, and I'm free. Three months' vacation – how I shall enjoy it!' exclaimed Meg, coming home one warm day to find Jo laid upon the sofa in an unusual state of exhaustion, while Beth took off her dusty boots, and Amy made lemonade for the refreshment of the whole party.

'Aunt March went today, for which, oh, be joyful!' said Jo. 'I was mortally afraid she'd ask me to go with her; if she had, I should have felt as if I ought to do it; but Plumfield is about as gay as a churchyard, you know, and I'd rather be excused. We had a flurry getting the old lady off, and I had a fright every time she spoke to me, for I was in such a hurry to be through that I was uncommonly helpful and sweet, and feared she'd find it impossible to part from me. I quaked till she was fairly in the carriage, and had a final fright, for, as it drove off, she popped out her head, saying, "Josyphine, won't you –?" I didn't hear any more, for I basely turned and fled; I did actually run, and whisked round the corner, where I felt safe.'

'Poor old Jo! she came in looking as if bears were after her,' said Beth, as she cuddled her sister's feet with a motherly air.

'Aunt March is a regular *samphire*, is she not?' observed Amy, tasting her mixture critically.

'She means *vampire*, not seaweed; but it doesn't matter; it's too warm to be particular about one's parts of speech,' murmured Jo.

'What shall you do all your vacation?' asked Amy, changing the subject, with tact.

'I shall lie abed late and do nothing,' replied Meg, from the depths of the rocking-chair. 'I've been routed up early all winter, and had to spend my days working for other people; so now I'm going to rest and revel to my heart's content.'

'No,' said Jo; 'that dozy way wouldn't suit me. I've laid in a heap of books, and I'm going to improve my shining hours reading on my perch in the old apple-tree, when I'm not having l –'

'Don't say "larks"!' implored Amy, as a return snub for the 'samphire' correction.

'I'll say "nightingales", then, with Laurie; that's proper and appropriate, since he's a warbler.'

'Don't let us do any lessons, Beth, for a while, but play all the time, and rest, as the girls mean to,' proposed Amy.

'Well, I will, if Mother doesn't mind. I want to learn some new songs, and my children need fitting up for the summer; they are dreadfully out of order, and really suffering for clothes.'

'May we, Mother?' asked Meg, turning to Mrs March, who sat sewing in what they called 'Marmee's corner'.

'You may try your experiment for a week, and see how you like it. I think by Saturday night you will find that all play and no work is as bad as all work and no play.'

'Oh, dear, no! it will be delicious, I'm sure,' said Meg, complacently.

'I now propose a toast, as my "friend and pardner, Sairy Gamp", says. Fun for ever, and no grubbing!' cried Jo, rising, glass in hand, as the lemonade went round.

They all drank it merrily, and began the experiment by lounging for the rest of the day. Next morning Meg did not appear till ten o'clock; her solitary breakfast did not taste nice and the room seemed lonely and untidy; for Jo had not filled the vases, Beth had not dusted, and Amy's books lay scattered about. Nothing was neat and pleasant but 'Marmee's corner', which looked as usual; and there Meg sat, to 'rest and read', which meant yawn, and imagine what pretty summer dresses she would get with her salary. Jo spent the morning on the river with Laurie, and the afternoon reading and crying over *The Wide, Wide World*, up in the apple-tree. Beth began by rummaging everything out of the big closet where her family resided; but, getting tired before half done, she left her establishment topsy-turvy, and went to her music, rejoicing that she had no dishes to wash. Amy arranged her bower, put on her best white frock, smoothed her curls, and sat down to draw, under the honeysuckles, hoping someone would see and inquire who the young artist was. As no one appeared but an inquisitive daddy long-legs, who examined her work with interest, she went for a walk, got caught in a shower, and came home dripping.

At tea-time they compared notes, and all agreed that it had been a delightful, though unusually long day. Meg, who went shopping in the afternoon, and got a 'sweet blue muslin', had discovered, after she had cut the breadths off, that it wouldn't wash, which mishap made her slightly cross. Jo had burnt the skin off her nose boating, and got a raging headache by reading too long. Beth was worried by the confusion of her closet, and the difficulty of learning three or four songs at once; and Amy deeply regretted the damage done her frock, for Katy Brown's party was to be the next day, and now, like Flora M'Flimsey, she had 'nothing to wear'. But these were mere trifles; and they assured their mother that the experiment was working finely. She smiled, said nothing, and, with Hannah's help, did their neglected work, keeping home pleasant, and the domestic machinery running smoothly. It was astonishing what a peculiar and uncomfortable state of things was produced by the 'resting and revelling' process. The days kept getting longer and longer; the weather was unusually variable, and so were tempers; an unsettled feeling possessed everyone, and Satan found plenty of mischief for the idle hands to do. As the height of luxury, Meg put out some of her sewing, and then found time hang so heavily that she fell to snipping and spoiling her clothes, in her attempts to furbish them up *à la* Moffat. Jo read till her eyes gave out, and she was sick of books; got so fidgety that even good-natured Laurie had a quarrel with her, and so reduced in spirits that she desperately wished she had gone out with Aunt March. Beth got on pretty well, for she was constantly forgetting that it was to be *all play, and no work*, and fell back into her old ways now and then; but something in the air affected her, and more than once her tranquillity was much disturbed; so much so, that, on one occasion, she actually shook poor dear Joanna, and told her she was a 'fright'. Amy fared worst of all, for her resources were small; and when her sisters left her to amuse and care for herself, she soon found that accomplished and important little self a great burden. She didn't like dolls, fairy tales were childish, and one couldn't draw all the time; tea parties didn't amount to much, neither did picnics, unless very well conducted. 'If one could have a fine house, full of nice girls, or go travelling, the summer would be delightful; but to stay at home with three selfish sisters and a grown-up boy was enough to try the patience of a "Boaz"', complained Miss Malaprop, after several days devoted to pleasure, fretting, and *ennui*.

No one would own that they were tired of the experiment; but, by Friday night, each acknowledged to herself that she was glad the week was nearly done. Hoping to impress the lesson more deeply, Mrs March, who had a good deal of humour, resolved to finish off the trial in an appropriate manner; so she gave Hannah a holiday, and let the girls enjoy the full effect of the play system.

When they got up on Saturday morning, there was no fire in the kitchen, no breakfast in the dining room, and no mother anywhere to be seen.

'Mercy on us! what *has* happened?' cried Jo, staring about her in dismay.

Meg ran upstairs, and soon came back again, looking relieved, but rather bewildered, and a little ashamed.

'Mother isn't sick, only very tired, and she says she is going to stay quietly in her room all day, and let us do the best we can. It's a very queer thing for her to do, she doesn't act a bit like herself; but she says it has been a hard week for her, so we mustn't grumble, but take care of ourselves.'

'That's easy enough, and I like the idea; I'm aching for something to do – that is, some new amusement, you know,' added Jo, quickly.

In fact it *was* an immense relief to them all to have a little work, and they took hold with a will, but soon realized the truth of Hannah's saying, 'Housekeeping ain't no joke.' There was plenty of food in the larder, and, while Beth and Amy set the table, Meg and Jo got breakfast, wondering, as they did so, why servants ever talked about hard work.

'I shall take some up to Mother, though she said we were not to think of her, for she'd take care of herself,' said Meg, who presided, and felt quite matronly behind the teapot.

So a tray was fitted out before anyone began, and taken up with the cook's compliments. The boiled tea was very bitter, the omelette scorched, and the biscuits speckled with saleratus; but Mrs March received her repast with thanks, and laughed heartily over it after Jo was gone.

'Poor little souls, they will have a hard time, I'm afraid; but they won't suffer, and it will do them good,' she said, producing the more palatable viands with which she had provided herself, and disposing of the bad breakfast, so that their feelings might not be hurt – a motherly little deception for which they were grateful.

Many were the complaints below, and great the chagrin of the head cook at her failures, 'Never mind, I'll get the dinner and be servant; you be mistress, keep your hands nice, see company, and give orders,' said Jo, who knew still less than Meg about culinary affairs.

This obliging offer was gladly accepted; and Margaret retired to the parlour, which she hastily put in order by whisking the litter under the sofa, and shutting the blinds, to save the trouble of dusting. Jo, with perfect faith in her own powers, and a friendly desire to make up the quarrel, immediately put a note in the office, inviting Laurie to dinner.

'You'd better see what you have got before you think about having company,' said Meg, when informed of the hospitable but rash act.

'Oh, there's corned beef and plenty of potatoes; and I shall get some asparagus, and a lobster, "for a relish", as Hannah says. We'll have lettuce, and make a salad. I don't know how, but the book tells. I'll have blancmange and strawberries for dessert; and coffee, too, if you want to be elegant.'

'Don't try too many messes, Jo, for you can't make anything but gingerbread and molasses candy fit to eat. I wash my hands of the dinner-party; and since you have asked Laurie on your own responsibility, you may just take care of him.'

'I don't want you to do anything but be civil to him, and help with the pudding. You'll give me your advice if I get in a muddle, won't you?' asked Jo, rather hurt.

'Yes; but I don't know much, except about bread, and a few trifles. You had better ask Mother's leave before you order anything,' returned Meg, prudently.

'Of course I shall; I'm not a fool,' and Jo went off in a huff at the doubts expressed of her powers.

'Get what you like, and don't disturb me; I'm going out to dinner, and can't worry about things at home,' said Mrs March, when Jo spoke to her. 'I never enjoyed housekeeping, and I'm going to take a vacation today, and read, and write, go visiting, and amuse myself.'

The unusual spectacle of her busy mother rocking comfortably and reading, early in the morning, made Jo feel as if some natural phenomenon had occurred; for an eclipse, an earthquake, or a volcanic eruption would hardly have seemed stranger.

'Everything is out of sorts somehow,' she said to herself, going downstairs. 'There's Beth crying; that's a sure sign that something is wrong with this family. If Amy is bothering, I'll shake her.'

Feeling very much out of sorts herself, Jo hurried into the parlour to find Beth sobbing over Pip, the canary, who lay dead in the cage, with his little claws pathetically extended, as if imploring the food for want of which he had died.

'It's all my fault – I forgot him – there isn't a seed or a drop left. O Pip! O Pip! how could I be so cruel to you?' cried Beth, taking the poor thing in her hands, and trying to restore him.

Jo peeped into his half-open eye, felt his little heart, and finding him stiff and cold shook her head, and offered her domino box for a coffin.

'Put him in the oven, and maybe he will get warm and revive,' said Amy, hopefully.

'He's been starved, and he shan't be baked, now he's dead. I'll make him a shroud, and he shall be buried in the garden; and I'll never have another bird, never, my Pip! for I'm too bad to own one,' murmured Beth, sitting on the floor with her pet folded in her hands.

'The funeral shall be this afternoon, and we will all go. Now, don't cry, Betty; it's a pity, but nothing goes right this week, and Pip has had the worst of the experiment. Make the shroud, and lay him in my box; and, after the dinner party, we'll have a nice little funeral,' said Jo, beginning to feel as if she had undertaken a good deal.

Leaving the others to console Beth, she departed to the kitchen, which was in a most discouraging state of confusion. Putting on a big apron she fell to work, and got the dishes piled up ready for washing, when she discovered that the fire was out. 'Here's a sweet prospect!' muttered Jo, slamming the stove-door open, and poking vigorously among the cinders.

Having rekindled the fire, she thought she would go to market while the water heated. The walk revived her spirits; and flattering herself that she had made good bargains, she trudged home again, after buying a very young lobster, some very old asparagus, and two boxes of acid strawberries. By the time she got cleared up the dinner arrived, and the stove was red-hot. Hannah had left a pan of bread to rise, Meg had worked it up early, set it on the hearth for a second rising, and forgotten it. Meg was entertaining Sallie Gardiner in the parlour, when the door flew open, and a floury, crocky, flushed, and dishevelled figure appeared, demanding tartly:

'I say, isn't bread "riz" enough when it runs over the pans?'

Sallie began to laugh; but Meg nodded, and lifted her eyebrows as high as they would go, which caused the apparition to vanish, and put the sour bread into the oven without further delay. Mrs March went out, after peeping here and there to see how matters went, also saying a word of comfort to Beth, who sat making a winding sheet, while the dear departed lay in state in the domino box. A strange sense of helplessness fell upon the girls as the grey bonnet vanished round the corner; and despair seized them when, a few minutes later, Miss Crocker appeared, and said she'd come to dinner. Now, this lady was a thin, yellow spinster, with a sharp nose and inquisitive eyes, who saw everything, and gossiped about all she saw. They disliked her, but had been taught to be kind to her, simply because she was old and poor, and had few friends. So Meg gave her the easy-chair, and tried to entertain her, while she asked questions, criticized everything, and told stories of the people who she knew.

Language cannot describe the anxieties, experiences, and exertions which Jo underwent that morning; and the dinner she served up became a standing joke. Fearing to ask any more advice, she did her best alone, and discovered that something more than energy and goodwill is necessary to make a cook. She boiled the asparagus for an hour, and was grieved to find the heads cooked off and the stalks harder than ever. The bread burnt black, for the salad-dressing so aggravated her that she let everything else go till she had convinced herself that she could not make it fit to eat. The lobster was a scarlet mystery to her, but she hammered and poked till it was unshelled, and its meagre proportions concealed in a grove of lettuce leaves. The potatoes had to be hurried, not to keep the asparagus waiting, and were not done at last. The blancmange was lumpy, and the strawberries not as ripe as they looked, having been skilfully 'deaconed'.

'Well, they can eat beef, and bread and butter, if they are hungry; only it's mortifying to have to spend your whole morning for nothing,' thought Jo, as she rang the bell half an hour later than usual, and stood, hot, tired, and dispirited, surveying the feast spread for Laurie, accustomed to all sorts of elegance, and Miss Crocker, whose curious eyes would mark all failures, and whose tattling tongue would report them far and wide.

Poor Jo would gladly have gone under the table, as one thing

after another was tasted and left; while Amy giggled, Meg looked
distressed, Miss Crocker pursed up her lips, and Laurie talked and
laughed with all his might, to give a cheerful tone to the festive
scene. Jo's one strong point was the fruit, for she had sugared it
well, and had a pitcher of rich cream to eat with it. Her hot cheeks
cooled a trifle, and she drew a long breath, as the pretty glass plates
went round, and everyone looked graciously at the little rosy islands
floating in a sea of cream. Miss Crocker tasted first, made a wry
face, and drank some water hastily. Jo, who had refused, thinking
there might not be enough, for they dwindled sadly after the picking
over, glanced at Laurie, but he was eating away manfully, though
there was a slight pucker about his mouth, and he kept his eye fixed
on his plate. Amy, who was fond of delicate fare, took a heaping
spoonful, choked, hid her face in her napkin, and left the table
precipitately.

'Oh, what is it?' exclaimed Jo, trembling.

'Salt instead of sugar, and the cream is sour,' replied Meg,
with a tragic gesture.

Jo uttered a groan, and fell back in her chair; remembering
that she had given a last hasty powdering to the berries out of one
of the two boxes on the kitchen table, and had neglected to put the
milk in the refrigerator. She turned scarlet, and was on the verge
of crying, when she met Laurie's eyes, which *would* look merry in
spite of his heroic efforts; the comical side of the affair suddenly
struck her, and she laughed till the tears ran down her cheeks. So
did everyone else, even 'Croaker', as the girls called the old lady;
and the unfortunate dinner ended gaily, with bread and butter,
olives, and fun.

'I haven't strength of mind enough to clear up now, so we will
sober ourselves with a funeral,' said Jo, as they rose; and Miss
Crocker made ready to go, being eager to tell the new story at
another friend's dinner-table.

They did sober themselves for Beth's sake; Laurie dug a grave
under the ferns in the grove, little Pip was laid in, with many
tears, by his tender-hearted mistress, and covered with moss, while

a wreath of violets and chickweed was hung on the stone which bore his epitaph, composed by Jo while she struggled with the dinner:

> Here lies Pip March,
> Who died the 7th of June;
> Loved and lamented sore,
> And not forgotten soon.

At the conclusion of the ceremonies, Beth retired to her room, overcome with emotion and lobster; but there was no place of repose, for the beds were not made, and she found her grief much assuaged by beating up pillows and putting things in order. Meg helped Jo clear away the remains of the feast, which took half the afternoon, and left them so tired that they agreed to be contented with tea and toast for supper. Laurie took Amy for a drive, which was a deed of charity, for the sour cream seemed to have had a bad effect upon her temper. Mrs March came home to find the three older girls hard at work in the middle of the afternoon, and a glance at the closet gave her an idea of the success of one part of the experiment.

Before the housewives could rest several people called, and there was a scramble to get ready to see them; then tea must be got, errands done; and one or two necessary bits of sewing neglected till the last minute. As twilight fell, dewy and still, one by one they gathered in the porch where the June roses were budding beautifully, and each groaned or sighed as she sat down as if tired or troubled.

'What a dreadful day this has been!' began Jo, usually the first to speak.

'It has seemed shorter than usual, but *so* uncomfortable,' said Meg.

'Not a bit like home,' added Amy.

'It can't seem so without Marmee and little Pip,' sighed Beth, glancing with full eyes at the empty cage above her head.

'Here's Mother, dear; and you shall have another bird tomorrow, if you want it.'

As she spoke, Mrs March came and took her place among them, looking as if her holiday had not been much pleasanter than theirs.

'Are you satisfied with your experiment, girls, or do you want another week of it?' she asked, as Beth nestled up to her, and the rest turned towards her with brightening faces, as flowers turn towards the sun.

'I don't,' cried Jo, decidedly.

'Nor I,' echoed the others.

'You think, then, that it is better to have a few duties, and live a little for others, do you?'

'Lounging and larking doesn't pay,' observed Jo, shaking her head. 'I'm tired of it, and mean to go to work at something right off.'

'Suppose you learn plain cooking; that's a useful accomplishment which no woman should be without,' said Mrs March, laughing inaudibly at the recollection of Jo's dinner-party; for she had met Miss Crocker, and heard her account of it.

'Mother, did you go away and let everything be, just to see how we'd get on?' cried Meg, who had had suspicions all day.

'Yes; I wanted you to see how the comfort of all depends on each doing her share faithfully. While Hannah and I did your work you got on pretty well, though I don't think you were very happy or amiable; so I thought, as a little lesson, I would show you what happens when everyone thinks only of herself. Don't you feel that it is pleasanter to help one another, to have daily duties which make leisure sweet when it comes, and to bear and forbear, that home may be comfortable and lovely to us all?'

'We do, Mother, we do!' cried the girls.

'Then let me advise you to take up your little burdens again; for though they seem heavy sometimes, they are good for us, and lighten as we learn to carry them. Work is wholesome, and there is plenty for everyone; it keeps us from *ennui* and mischief, is good for health and spirits, and gives us a sense of power and independence better than money or fashion.'

'We'll work like bees, and love it too; see if we don't!' said Jo.

'I'll learn plain cooking for my holiday task; and the next dinner-party I have shall be a success.'

'I'll make the set of shirts for Father, instead of letting you do it, Marmee. I can and I will, though I'm not fond of sewing; that will be better than fussing over my own things, which are plenty nice enough as they are,' said Meg.

'I'll do my lessons every day, and not spend so much time with my music and dolls. I am a stupid thing, and ought to be studying, not playing,' was Beth's resolution; while Amy followed their example by heroically declaring, 'I shall learn to make button-holes, and attend to my parts of speech.'

'Very good! then I am quite satisfied with the experiment, and fancy that we shall not have to repeat it; only don't go to the other extreme, and delve like slaves. Have regular hours for work and play; make each day both useful and pleasant, and prove that you understand the worth of time by employing it well. Then youth will be delightful, old age will bring few regrets, and life become a beautiful success, in spite of poverty.'

'We'll remember, Mother!' and they did.

CHAPTER 12

Camp Laurence

Beth was postmistress, for, being most at home, she could attend to it regularly, and dearly liked the daily task of unlocking the little door and distributing the mail. One July day she came in with her hands full, and went about the house leaving letters and parcels like the penny post.

'Here's your posy, Mother! Laurie never forgets that,' she said, putting the fresh nosegay in the vase that stood in 'Marmee's corner', and was kept supplied by the affectionate boy.

'Miss Meg March, one letter and a glove,' continued Beth, delivering the article to her sister, who sat near her mother, stitching wristbands.

'Why, I left a pair over there, and here is only one,' said Meg, looking at the grey cotton glove. 'Didn't you drop the other in the garden?'

'No, I'm sure I didn't; for there was only one in the office.'

'I hate to have odd gloves! Never mind, the other may be found. My letter is only a translation of the German song I wanted; I think Mr Brooke did it, for this isn't Laurie's writing.'

Mrs March glanced at Meg, who was looking very pretty in her gingham morning gown, with the little curls blowing about her forehead, and very womanly, as she sat sewing at her little work-table, full of tiny white rolls; so unconscious of the thought in her mother's mind as she sewed and sung, while her fingers flew, and her thoughts were busied with girlish fancies as innocent and fresh as the pansies in her belt, that Mrs March smiled, and was satisfied.

'Two letters for Doctor Jo, a book, and a funny old hat, which covered the whole post-office, stuck outside,' said Beth, laughing, as she went into the study, where Jo sat writing.

'What a sly fellow Laurie is! I said I wished bigger hats were the fashion, because I burn my face every hot day. He said, "Why mind the fashion? Wear a big hat and be comfortable!" I said I would if I had one, and he has sent me this to try me. I'll wear it, for fun, and show him I don't care for the fashion'; and hanging the antique broad-brim on a bust of Plato, Jo read her letters.

One from her mother made her cheeks glow and her eyes fill, for it said to her:

> MY DEAR – I write a little word to tell you with how
> much satisfaction I watch your efforts to control your
> temper. You say nothing about your trials, failures, or
> successes, and think, perhaps, that no one sees them but
> the friend whose help you daily ask, if I may trust the
> well-worn cover of your guide book. *I*, too, have seen
> them all, and heartily believe in the sincerity of your
> resolution, since it begins to bear fruit. Go on, dear,
> patiently and bravely, and always believe that no one
> sympathizes more tenderly with you than your loving
> MOTHER

'That does me good! that's worth millions of money and pecks of praise. Oh, Marmee, I do try! I will keep on trying, and not get tired, since I have you to help me.'

Laying her head on her arm, Jo wet her little romance with a few happy tears, for she *had* thought no one saw and appreciated her efforts to do good; and this assurance was doubly precious, doubly encouraging, because unexpected, and from the person whose commendation she most valued. Feeling stronger than ever to meet and subdue her Apollyon, she pinned the note inside her frock, as a shield and a reminder, lest she be taken unawares, and proceeded to open her other letter, quite ready for either good or bad news. In a big, dashing hand, Laurie wrote:

> Dear Jo,
> What ho!
> Some English girls and boys are coming to see me
> tomorrow, and I want to have a jolly time. If it's fine,
> I'm going to pitch my tent in Longmeadow, and row up
> the whole crew to lunch and croquet – have a fire, make
> messes, gipsy fashion, and all sorts of larks. They are
> nice people, and like such things. Brooke will go, to keep
> us boys steady, and Kate Vaughn will play propriety for
> the girls. I want you all to come; can't let Beth off at any
> price, and nobody shall worry her. Don't bother about
> rations – I'll see to that, and everything else – only do
> come, there's a good fellow!
> In a tearing hurry,
> Yours ever, LAURIE

'Here's richness!' cried Jo, flying in to tell the news to Meg. 'Of course we can go, Mother? it will be such a help to Laurie, for I can row, and Meg see to the lunch, and the children be useful in some way.'

'I hope the Vaughns are not fine, grown-up people. Do you know anything about them, Jo?' asked Meg.

'Only that there are four of them. Kate is older than you, Fred and Frank (twins) about my age, and a little girl (Grace), who is nine or ten. Laurie knew them abroad, and liked the boys; I fancied, from the way he primmed up his mouth in speaking of her, that he didn't admire Kate much.'

'I'm so glad my French print is clean; it's just the thing, and so becoming!' observed Meg complacently. 'Have you anything decent, Jo?'

'Scarlet and grey boating suit, good enough for me. I shall row and tramp about, so I don't want any starch to think of. You'll come, Betty?'

'If you won't let any of the boys talk to me.'

'Not a boy!'

'I like to please Laurie; and I'm not afraid of Mr Brooke, he is so kind; but I don't want to play, or sing, or say anything. I'll work hard and not trouble anyone; and you'll take care of me, Jo, so I'll go.'

'That's my good girl; you do try to fight off your shyness, and I love you for it. Fighting faults isn't easy, as I know; and a cheery word kind of gives a lift. Thank you, Mother,' and Jo gave the thin cheek a grateful kiss, more precious to Mrs March than if it had given back the rosy roundness of her youth.

'I had a box of chocolate drops, and the picture I wanted to copy,' said Amy, showing her mail.

'And I got a note from Mr Laurence asking me to come over and play to him tonight before the lamps are lighted, and I shall go,' added Beth, whose friendship with the old gentleman prospered finely.

'Now let's fly round and do double duty today, so that we can play tomorrow with free minds,' said Jo, preparing to replace her pen with a broom.

When the sun peeped into the girls' room early the next morning, to promise them a fine day, he saw a comical sight. Each had made such preparation for the *fête* as seemed necessary and proper. Meg had an extra row of little curl papers across her forehead, Jo had copiously anointed her afflicted face with cold cream, Beth had taken Joanna to bed with her to atone for the approaching separation, and Amy had capped the climax by putting a clothes-pin on her nose, to uplift the offending feature. It was one of the kind artists used to hold the paper on their drawing-boards, therefore quite appropriate and effective for the purpose to which it was now put. This funny spectacle appeared to amuse the sun, for he burst out with such radiance that Jo woke up, and roused all her sisters by a hearty laugh at Amy's ornament.

Sunshine and laughter were good omens for a pleasure party, and soon a lively bustle began in both houses. Beth, who was ready first, kept reporting what went on next door, and enlivened her sisters' toilets by frequent telegrams from the window.

'There goes the man with the tent! I see Mrs Barker doing up the lunch in a hamper and a great basket. Now Mr Laurence is looking up at the sky and the weathercock; I wish he would go too. There's Laurie, looking like a sailor – nice boy! Oh, mercy me! here's a carriage full of people – a tall lady, a little girl, and two dreadful boys. One is lame; poor thing, he's got a crutch. Laurie didn't tell us that. Be quick, girls! it's getting late. Why, there is Ned Moffat, I do declare. Look, Meg, isn't that the man who bowed to you one day when we were shopping?'

'So it is. How queer that he should come. I thought he was at the Mountains. There is Sallie; I'm glad she's got back in time. Am I all right, Jo?' cried Meg, in a flutter.

'A regular daisy. Hold up your dress and put your hat straight; it looks sentimental tipped that way, and will fly off at the first puff. Now then, come on!'

'Oh, Jo, you are not going to wear that awful hat? It's too absurd! You shall *not* make a guy of yourself,' remonstrated Meg, as Jo tied down, with a red ribbon, the broad-brimmed old-fashioned Leghorn Laurie had sent for a joke.

'I just will, though, for it's capital – so shady, light, and big. It will make fun; and I don't mind being a guy if I'm comfortable.' With that Jo marched straight away, and the rest followed – a bright little band of sisters, all looking their best, in summer suits, with happy faces under the jaunty hat-brims.

Laurie ran to meet and present them to his friends in the most cordial manner. The lawn was the reception room, and for several minutes a lively scene was enacted there. Meg was grateful to see that Miss Kate, though twenty, was dressed with a simplicity that American girls would do well to imitate; and she was much flattered by Mr Ned's assurances that he came especially to see her. Jo understood why Laurie 'primmed up his mouth' when speaking of Kate, for that young lady had a stand-off-don't-touch-me air, which contrasted strongly with the free and easy demeanour of the other girls. Beth took an observation of the new boys, and decided that the lame one was not 'dreadful', but gentle and feeble, and she would be kind to him on that account. Amy found Grace a well-mannered, merry little person; and after staring dumbly at one another for a few minutes, they suddenly became very good friends.

Tents, lunch, and croquet utensils had been sent on beforehand, the party was soon embarked, and the two boats pushed off together, leaving Mr Laurence waving his hat on the shore. Laurie and Jo rowed one boat; Mr Brooke and Ned the other; while Fred Vaughn, the riotous twin, did his best to upset both by paddling about in a wherry like a disturbed water-bug. Jo's funny hat deserved a word of thanks, for it was of general utility; it broke the ice in the beginning, by producing a laugh; it created quite a refreshing breeze, flapping to and fro as she rowed, and would make an excellent umbrella for the whole party if a shower came up, she said. Kate looked rather amazed at Jo's proceedings, especially as she exclaimed 'Christopher Columbus!' when she lost her oar; and Laurie said, 'My dear fellow, did I hurt you?' when he tripped over her feet in taking his place. But after putting up her glass to examine the queer girl several times, Miss Kate decided that she was 'odd, but rather clever,' and smiled upon her from afar.

Meg, in the other boat, was delightfully situated, face to face with the rowers, who both admired the prospect, and feathered their oars with uncommon 'skill and dexterity'. Mr Brooke was a grave, silent young man, with handsome brown eyes and a pleasant voice. Meg liked his quiet manners, and considered him a walking encyclopedia of useful knowledge. He never talked to her much, but he looked at her a good deal, and she felt sure that he did not regard her with aversion. Ned, being in college, of course put on all the airs which freshmen think it their bounden duty to assume; he was not very wise, but very good-natured, and altogether an excellent person to carry on a picnic. Sallie Gardiner was absorbed in keeping her white piqué dress clean, and chattering with the ubiquitous Fred, who kept Beth in constant terror by his pranks.

It was not far to Longmeadow; but the tent was pitched and the wickets down by the time they arrived. A pleasant green field, with three wide-spreading oaks in the middle, and a smooth strip of turf for the croquet.

'Welcome to Camp Laurence!' said the young host, as they landed, with exclamations of delight.

'Brooke is commander-in-chief; I am commissary-general; the other fellows are staff-officers; and you, ladies, are company. The tent is for your especial benefit, and that oak is your drawing room; this is the messroom, and the third is the camp-kitchen. Now, let's have a game before it gets hot, and then we'll see about dinner.'

Frank, Beth, Amy, and Grace sat down to watch the game played by the other eight. Mr Brooke chose Meg, Kate, and Fred; Laurie took Sallie, Jo, and Ned. The Englishers played well; but the Americans played better, and contested every inch of the ground as strongly as if the spirit of '76 inspired them. Jo and Fred had several skirmishes, and once narrowly escaped high words. Jo was through the last wicket, and had missed the stroke, which failure ruffled her a good deal. Fred was close behind her, and his turn came before hers; he gave a stroke, his ball hit the wicket, and stopped an inch on the wrong side. No one was very near; and running up to examine, he gave it a sly nudge with his toe, which put it just an inch on the right side.

'I'm through! Now, Miss Jo, I'll settle you, and get in first,' cried the young gentleman, swinging his mallet for another blow.

'You pushed it; I saw you; it's my turn now,' said Jo, sharply.

'Upon my word, I didn't move it; it rolled a bit, perhaps, but that is allowed; so stand off, please, and let me have a go at the stake.'

'We don't cheat in America, but you can, if you choose,' said Jo, angrily.

'Yankees are a deal the most tricky, everybody knows. There you go!' returned Fred, croqueting her ball far away.

Jo opened her lips to say something rude, but checked herself in time, coloured up to her forehead, and stood a minute hammering down a wicket with all her might, while Fred hit the stake, and declared himself out with much exultation. She went off to get her ball, and was a long time finding it among the bushes; but she came back, looking cool and quiet, and waited her turn patiently. It took several strokes to regain the place she had lost; and, when she got there, the other side had nearly won, for Kate's ball was the last but one, and lay near the stake.

'By George, it's all up with us! Good-bye, Kate. Miss Jo owes me one, so you are finished,' cried Fred, excitedly, as they all drew near to see the finish.

'Yankees have a trick of being generous to their enemies,' said Jo, with a look that made the lad redden, 'especially when they beat them,' she added, as, leaving Kate's ball untouched, she won the game by a clever stroke.

Laurie threw up his hat; then remembering that it wouldn't do to exult over the defeat of his guests, he stopped in the middle of a cheer to whisper to his friend: 'Good for you, Jo! He did cheat, I saw him; we can't tell him so, but he won't do it again, take my word for it.'

Meg drew her aside, under pretence of pinning up a loose braid, and said approvingly: 'It was dreadfully provoking; but you kept your temper, and I'm so glad, Jo.'

'Don't praise me, Meg, for I could box his ears this minute. I should certainly have boiled over if I hadn't stayed among the nettles till I got my rage under enough to hold my tongue. It's simmering now, so I hope he'll keep out of my way,' returned Jo, biting her lips, as she glowered at Fred from under her big hat.

'Time for lunch,' said Mr Brooke, looking at his watch. 'Commissary-general, will you make the fire and get water, while Miss March, Miss Sallie and I spread the table? Who can make good coffee?'

'Jo can!' said Meg, glad to recommend her sister. So Jo, feeling that her late lessons in cookery were to do her honour, went to preside over the coffee-pot, while the children collected dry sticks, and the boys made a fire, and got water from a spring near by. Miss Kate sketched, and Frank talked to Beth, who was making little mats of braided rushes to serve as plates.

The commander-in-chief and his aides soon spread the tablecloth with an inviting array of eatables and drinkables, prettily decorated with green leaves. Jo announced that the coffee was ready, and everyone settled themselves to a hearty meal; for youth is seldom dyspeptic, and exercise develops wholesome appetites. A very merry lunch it was; for everything seemed fresh and funny, and frequent peals of laughter startled a venerable horse who fed near by. There was a pleasing inequality in the table, which produced many mishaps to cups and plates; acorns dropped into the milk, little black ants partook of the refreshments without being invited, and fuzzy caterpillars swung down from the tree to see what was going on. Three white-headed children peeped over the fence, and an objectionable dog barked at them from the other side of the river with all his might and main.

'There's salt here, if you prefer it,' said Laurie, as he handed Jo a saucer of berries.

'Thank you, I prefer spiders,' she replied, fishing up two unwary little ones who had gone to a creamy death. 'How dare you remind me of that horrid dinner-party, when yours is so nice in every way?' added Jo, as they both laughed, and ate out of one plate, the china having run short.

'I had an uncommonly good time that day, and haven't got over it yet. This is no credit to me, you know; I don't do anything; it's you and Meg and Brooke who make it go, and I'm no end obliged to you. What shall we do when we can't eat any more?' asked Laurie, feeling that his trump card had been played when lunch was over.

'Have games till it's cooler. I brought "Authors", and I dare say Miss Kate knows something new and nice. Go and ask her; she's company, and you ought to stay with her more.'

'Aren't you company, too? I thought she'd suit Brooke; but he keeps talking to Meg, and Kate just stares at them through that ridiculous glass of hers. I'm going, so you needn't try to preach propriety, for you can't do it, Jo.'

Miss Kate did know several new games; and as the girls would not, and the boys could not, eat any more, they all adjourned to the drawing room to play 'Rigmarole'.

'One person begins a story, any nonsense you like, and tells as long as he pleases, only taking care to stop short at some exciting point, when the next takes it up and does the same. It's very funny when well done, and makes a perfect jumble of tragical comical stuff to laugh over. Please start it, Mr Brooke,' said Kate with a commanding air, which surprised Meg, who treated the tutor with as much respect as any other gentleman.

Lying on the grass at the feet of the two young ladies, Mr Brooke obediently began the story, with the handsome brown eyes steadily fixed upon the sunshiny river.

'Once upon a time a knight went out into the world to seek his fortune, for he had nothing but his sword and his shield. He travelled a long while, nearly eight-and-twenty years, and had a hard time of it, till he came to the palace of a good old king, who had offered a reward to any who would tame and train a fine but unbroken colt of which he was very fond. The knight agreed to try, and got on slowly but surely; for the colt was a gallant fellow, and soon learned to love his new master, though he was freakish and wild. Every day, when he gave his lessons to this pet of the king's, the knight rode him through the city; and, as he rode, he looked everywhere for a certain beautiful face, which he had seen many times in his dreams, but never found. One day, as he went prancing down a quiet street, he saw at the window of a ruinous castle the lovely face. He was delighted, inquired who lived in this old castle, and was told that several captive princesses were kept there by a spell, and spun all day to lay up money to buy their liberty. The knight wished intensely that he could free them; but he was poor, and could only go by each day, watching for the sweet face, and longing to see it out in the sunshine. At last he resolved to get into the castle and ask how he could help them. He went and knocked; the great door flew open, and he beheld –'

'A ravishingly lovely lady, who exclaimed, with a cry of rapture, "At last! at last"' continued Kate, who had read French novels, and admired the style. ""Tis she!" cried Count Gustave, and fell at her feet in an ecstasy of joy. "Oh, rise!" she said, extending a hand of marble fairness. "Never! till you tell me how I may rescue you," swore the knight, still kneeling. "Alas, my cruel fate condemns me to remain here till my tyrant is destroyed." "Where is the villain!" "In the mauve salon. Go, brave heart, and save me from despair." "I obey, and return victorious or dead!" With these thrilling words he rushed away, and flinging open the door of the mauve salon, was about to enter, when he received –'

'A stunning blow from the big Greek lexicon, which an old fellow in a black gown fired at him,' said Ned. 'Instantly Sir What's-his-name recovered himself, pitched the tyrant out of the window, and turned to join the lady victorious, but with a bump on his brow; found the door locked, tore up the curtains, made a rope ladder, got half way down when the ladder broke, and he went head first into the moat, sixty feet below. Could swim like a duck, paddled round the castle till he came to a little door guarded by two stout fellows; knocked their heads together till they cracked like a couple of nuts, then, by a trifling exertion of his prodigious strength, he smashed in the door, went up a pair of stone steps covered with dust a foot thick, toads as big as your fist, and spiders that would frighten you into hysterics, Miss March. At the top of these steps he came plump upon a sight that took his breath away and chilled his blood –'

'A tall figure, all in white, with a veil over its face, and a lamp in its wasted hand,' went on Meg. 'It beckoned, gliding noiselessly before him down a corridor as dark and cold as any tomb. Shadowy effigies in armour stood on either side, a dead silence reigned, the lamp burned blue, and the ghostly figure ever and anon turned its face towards him showing the glitter of awful eyes through its white veil. They reached a curtained door, behind which sounded lovely music; he sprang forward to enter, but the spectre plucked him back, and waved threateningly before him a –'

'Snuff-box,' said Jo, in a sepulchral tone, which convulsed the audience. '"Thankee," said the knight, politely, as he took a pinch, and sneezed seven times so violently that his head fell off. "Ha! ha!" laughed the ghost; and having peeped through the keyhole at the princesses spinning away for dear life, the evil spirit picked up her victim and put him in a large tin box, where there were eleven other knights packed together without their heads, like sardines, who all rose and began to –'

'Dance a hornpipe,' cut in Fred, as Jo paused for breath; 'and, as they danced, the rubbishy old castle turned to a man-of-war in full sail. "Up with the jib, reef the tops'l halliards, helm hard a-lee, and man the guns!" roared the captain, as a Portuguese pirate hove in sight, with a flag black as ink flying from her foremast. "Go in and win my hearties!" says the captain; and a tremendous fight began. Of course the British beat; they always do.'

'No, they don't,' cried Jo, aside.

'Having taken the pirate captain prisoner, sailed slap over the schooner, whose decks were piled with dead, and whose leescuppers ran blood, for the order had been "Cutlasses, and die hard!" "Bosun's mate, take a bight of the flying-jib sheet, and start this villain if he don't confess his sins double quick," said the British captain. The Portuguese held his tongue like a brick, and walked the plank, while the jolly tars cheered like mad. But the sly dog dived, came up under the man-of-war, scuttled her, and down she went, with all sail set, "To the bottom of the sea, sea, sea," where –'

'Oh, gracious! what *shall* I say?' cried Sallie, as Fred ended his rigmarole, in which he had jumbled together, pell-mell, nautical phrases and facts out of one of his favourite books. 'Well, they went to the bottom, and a nice mermaid welcomed them, but was much grieved on finding the box of headless knights, and kindly pickled them in brine, hoping to discover the mystery about them, for, being a woman, she was curious. By and by, a diver came down, and the mermaid said, "I'll give you this box of pearls if you can take it up"; for she wanted to restore the poor things to life, and couldn't raise the heavy load herself. So the diver hoisted it up, and was much disappointed, on opening it, to find no pearls. He left it in a great lonely field, where it was found by a –'

'Little goosegirl, who kept a hundred fat geese in the field,' said Amy, when Sallie's invention gave out. 'The little girl was sorry for them, and asked an old woman what she should do to help them. "Your geese will tell you, they know everything," said the old woman. So she asked what she should use for new heads, since the old ones were lost, and all the geese opened their hundred mouths and screamed –'

'"Cabbages!"' continued Laurie, promptly. '"Just the thing," said the girl, and ran to get twelve fine ones from her garden. She put them on, the knights revived at once, thanked her, and went on their way rejoicing, never knowing the difference, for there were so many other heads like them in the world that no one thought anything of it. The knight in whom I'm interested went back to find the pretty face, and learned that the princesses had spun themselves free, and all gone to be married but one. He was in a great state of mind at that; and mounting the colt, who stood by him through thick and thin, rushed to the castle to see which was left. Peeping over the hedge, he saw the queen of his affections picking flowers in her garden. "Will you give me a rose?" said he. "You must come and get it. I can't come to you; it isn't proper," said she, as sweet as honey. He tried to climb over the hedge, but it seemed to grow higher and higher; then he tried to push through, but it grew thicker and thicker and he was in despair. So he patiently broke twig after twig till he had made a little hole, through which he peeped, saying imploringly, "Let me in! let me in." But the pretty princess did not seem to understand, for she picked her roses quietly, and left him to fight his way in. Whether he did or not, Frank will tell you.'

'I can't; I'm not playing, I never do,' said Frank, dismayed at the sentimental predicament out of which he was to rescue the absurd couple. Beth had disappeared behind Jo, and Grace was asleep.

'So the poor knight is to be left sticking in the hedge, is he?' asked Mr Brooke, still watching the river and playing with the wild rose in his buttonhole.

'I guess the princess gave him a posy, and opened the gate after a while,' said Laurie, smiling to himself, as he threw acorns at his tutor.

'What a piece of nonsense we have made! With practice we might do something quite clever. Do you know "Truth"?' asked Sallie, after they had laughed over their story.

'I hope so,' said Meg, soberly.

'The game, I mean?'

'What is it?' said Fred.

'Why, you pile up your hands, choose a number, and draw out in turn, and the person who draws out the number has to answer truly any questions put by the rest. It's great fun.'

'Let's try it,' said Jo, who liked new experiments.

Miss Kate and Mr Brooke, Meg, and Ned declined, but Fred, Sallie, Jo, and Laurie piled and drew; and the lot fell to Laurie.

'Who are your heroes?' asked Jo.

'Grandfather and Napoleon.'

'Which lady here do you think prettiest?' said Sallie.

'Margaret.'

'Which do you like best?' from Fred.

'Jo, of course.'

'What silly questions you ask!' and Jo gave a disdainful shrug, as the rest laughed at Laurie's matter-of-fact tone.

'Try again; Truth isn't a bad game,' said Fred.

'It's a very good one for you,' retorted Jo, in a low voice.

Her turn came next.

'What is your greatest fault?' asked Fred, by way of testing in her the virtue he lacked himself.

'A quick temper.'

'What do you most wish for?' said Laurie.

'A pair of boot-lacings,' returned Jo, guessing and defeating his purpose.

'Not a true answer; you must say what you really do want most.'

'Genius; don't you wish you could give it to me, Laurie?' and she slyly smiled in his disappointed face.

'What virtues do you most admire in a man?' asked Sallie.

'Courage and honesty.'

'Now my turn,' said Fred, as his hand came last.

'Let's give it to him,' whispered Laurie to Jo, who nodded, and asked at once: 'Didn't you cheat at croquet?'

'Well, yes, a little bit.'

'Good! Didn't you take your story out of *The Sea-Lion*?' said Laurie.

'Rather.'

'Don't you think the English nation perfect in every respect?' asked Sallie.

'I should be ashamed of myself if I didn't.'

'He's a true John Bull. Now, Miss Sallie, you shall have a chance without waiting to draw. I'll harrow up your feelings first by asking if you don't think you are something of a flirt,' said Laurie, as Jo nodded to Fred, as a sign that peace was declared.

'You impertinent boy! of course I'm not,' exclaimed Sallie, with an air that proved the contrary.

'What do you hate most?' asked Fred.

'Spiders and rice-pudding.'

'What do you like best?' asked Jo.

'Dancing and French gloves.'

'Well, *I* think Truth is a very silly play; let's have a sensible game of Authors, to refresh our minds,' proposed Jo.

Ned, Frank, and the little girls joined in this, and while it went on the three elder sat apart talking. Miss Kate took out her sketch again, and Margaret watched her, while Mr Brooke lay on the grass, with a book which he did not read.

'How beautifully you do it! I wish I could draw,' said Meg, with mingled admiration and regret in her voice.

'Why don't you learn? I should think you had taste and talent for it,' replied Miss Kate, graciously.

'I haven't time.'

'Your mamma prefers other accomplishments, I fancy. So did mine; but I proved to her that I had talent by taking a few lessons privately, and then she was quite willing I should go on. Can't you do the same with your governess?'

'I have none.'

'I forgot; young ladies in America go to school more than with us. Very fine schools they are, too, papa says. You go to a private one, I suppose?'

'I don't go at all; I am a governess myself.'

'Oh, indeed!' said Miss Kate; but she might as well have said, 'Dear me, how dreadful!' for her tone implied it, and something in her face made Meg colour, and wish she had not been so frank.

Mr Brooke looked up, and said quickly, 'Young ladies in America love independence as much as their ancestors did, and are admired and respected for supporting themselves.'

'Oh, yes; of course it's very nice and proper in them to do so. We have many most respectable and worthy young women who do the same, and are employed by the nobility, because, being the daughters of gentlemen, they are both well-bred and accomplished, you know,' said Miss Kate in a patronizing tone, that hurt Meg's pride, and made her work seem not only more distasteful, but degrading.

'Did the German song suit, Miss March?' inquired Mr Brooke, breaking an awkward pause.

'Oh yes; it was very sweet, and I'm much obliged to whoever translated it for me'; and Meg's downcast face brightened as she spoke.

'Don't you read German?' asked Miss Kate, with a look of surprise.

'Not very well. My father, who taught me, is away, and I don't get on very fast alone, for I've no one to correct my pronunciation.'

'Try a little now; here is Schiller's *Mary Stuart*, and a tutor who loves to teach,' and Mr Brooke laid his book on her lap, with an inviting smile.

'It's so hard, I'm afraid to try,' said Meg, grateful, but bashful in the presence of the accomplished young lady beside her.

'I'll read a bit to encourage you'; and Miss Kate read one of the most beautiful passages in a perfectly correct but perfectly expressionless manner.

Mr Brooke made no comment as she returned the book to Meg, who said innocently:

'I thought it was poetry.'

'Some of it is. Try this passage.'

There was a queer smile about Mr Brooke's mouth as he opened at poor Mary's lament.

Meg, obediently following the long grass blade which her new tutor used to point with, read slowly and timidly, unconsciously making poetry of the hard words by the soft intonation of her musical voice. Down the page went the green guide, and presently forgetting her listener in the beauty of the sad scene Meg read as if alone, giving a little touch of tragedy to the words of the unhappy queen. If she had seen the brown eyes then, she would have stopped short; but she never looked up, and the lesson was not spoiled for her.

'Very well indeed!' said Mr Brooke, as she paused, quite ignoring her many mistakes, and looking as if he did, indeed, 'love to teach'.

Miss Kate put up her glass, and having taken a survey of the little tableau before her, shut her sketchbook, saying, with condescension:

'You've a nice accent, and in time will be a clever reader. I advise you to learn, for German is a valuable accomplishment to teachers. I must look after Grace, she is romping'; and Miss Kate strolled away adding to herself, with a shrug, 'I didn't come to chaperone a governess, though she *is* young and pretty. What odd people these Yankees are; I'm afraid Laurie will be quite spoilt among them.'

'I forgot that English people rather turn up their noses at

governesses, and don't treat them as we do,' said Meg, looking after the retreating figure with an annoyed expression.

'Tutors, also, have rather a hard time of it there, as I know to my sorrow. There's no place like America for us workers, Miss Margaret'; and Mr Brooke looked so contented and cheerful, that Meg was ashamed to lament her hard lot.

'I'm glad I live in it, then. I don't like my work, but I get a good deal of satisfaction out of it after all, so I won't complain; I only wish I liked teaching as you do.'

'I think you would if you had Laurie for a pupil. I shall be very sorry to lose him next year,' said Mr Brooke, busily punching holes in the turf.

'Going to college, I suppose?' Meg's lips asked that question, but her eyes added, 'And what becomes of you?'

'Yes; it's high time he went, for he is ready; and as soon as he is off I shall turn soldier. I am needed.'

'I am glad of that!' exclaimed Meg. 'I should think every young man would want to go; though it is hard for the mothers and sisters who stay at home,' she added, sorrowfully.

'I have neither, and very few friends, to care whether I live or die,' said Mr Brooke, rather bitterly, as he absently put the dead rose in the hole he had made and covered it up, like a little grave.

'Laurie and his grandfather would care a great deal, and we should all be very sorry to have any harm happen to you,' said Meg, heartily.

'Thank you; that sounds pleasant,' began Mr Brooke, looking cheerful again; but before he could finish his speech, Ned, mounted on the old horse, came lumbering up to display his equestrian skill before the young ladies, and there was no more quiet that day.

'Don't you love to ride?' asked Grace of Amy, as they stood resting, after a race round the field with the others, led by Ned.

'I dote upon it; my sister Meg used to ride when papa was rich but we don't keep any horses now, except Ellen Tree,' added Amy, laughing.

'Tell me about Ellen Tree; is it a donkey?' asked Grace, curiously.

'Why, you see, Jo is crazy about horses, and so am *I*, but we've only got an old side-saddle, and no horse. But in our garden is an apple-tree, that has a nice low branch; so Jo put the saddle on it, fixed some reins on the part that turns up, and we bounce away on Ellen Tree whenever we like.'

'How funny!' laughed Grace. 'I have a pony at home, and ride nearly every day in the park, with Fred and Kate; it's very nice, for my friends go too, and the Row is full of ladies and gentlemen.'

'Dear, how charming! I hope I shall go abroad some day; but I'd rather go to Rome than the Row,' said Amy, who had not the remotest idea what the Row was, and wouldn't have asked for the world.

Frank, sitting just behind the little girls, heard what they were saying, and pushed his crutch away from him with an impatient gesture, as he watched the active lads going through all sorts of comical gymnastics. Beth, who was collecting the scattered Authorcards, looked up, and said, in her shy yet friendly way:

'I'm afraid you are tired; can I do anything for you?'

'Talk to me, please; it's dull, sitting by myself,' answered Frank, who had evidently been used to being made much of at home.

If he had asked her to deliver a Latin oration, it would not have seemed a more impossible task to bashful Beth; but there was no place to run to, no Jo to hide behind now, and the poor boy looked so wistfully at her, that she bravely resolved to try.

'What do you like to talk about?' she asked, fumbling over the cards, and dropping half as she tried to tie them up.

'Well, I like to hear about cricket and boating and hunting,' said Frank, who had not yet learnt to suit his amusements to his strength.

'My heart! what shall I do? I don't know anything about them,' thought Beth; and, forgetting the boy's misfortune in her flurry, she said, hoping to make him talk, 'I never saw any hunting, but I suppose you know all about it.'

'I did once; but I can never hunt again, for I got hurt leaping a confounded five-barred gate; so there are no more horses and hounds for me,' said Frank, with a sigh that made Beth hate herself for her innocent blunder.

'Your deer are much prettier than our ugly buffaloes,' she said, turning to the prairies for help, and feeling glad that she had read one of the boy's books in which Jo delighted.

Buffaloes proved soothing and satisfactory; and, in her eagerness to amuse another, Beth forgot herself, and was quite unconscious of her sisters' surprise and delight at the unusual spectacle of Beth talking away to one of the dreadful boys, against whom she had begged protection.

'Bless her heart! She pities him, so she is good to him,' said Jo, beaming at her from the croquet ground.

'I always said she was a little saint,' added Meg, as if there could be no further doubt about it.

'I haven't heard Frank laugh so much for ever so long,' said Grace to Amy, as they sat discussing dolls, and making tea-sets out of the acorn-cups.

'My sister Beth is a very *fastidious* girl when she likes to be,' said Amy, well pleased at Beth's success. She meant 'fascinating', but as Grace didn't know the exact meaning of either word 'fastidious' sounded well, and made a good impression.

An impromptu circus, fox and geese, and an amicable game of croquet finished the afternoon. At sunset the tent was struck, hampers packed, wickets pulled up, boats loaded, and the whole party floated down the river, singing at the tops of their voices. Ned, getting sentimental, warbled a serenade with the pensive refrain:

'Alone, alone, ah! woe, alone,'

and at the lines:

'We each are young, we each have a heart,
Oh, why should we thus stand coldly apart,'

he looked at Meg with such a lackadaisical expression that she laughed outright and spoilt his song.

'How can you be so cruel to me?' he whispered, under cover of a lively chorus. 'You've kept close to that starched-up English woman all day, and now you snub me.'

'I didn't mean to; but you looked so funny I really couldn't help it,' replied Meg passing over the first part of his reproach; for it was quite true that she *had* shunned him, remembering the Moffat party and the talk after it.

Ned was offended, and turned to Sallie for consolation, saying to her, rather pettishly, 'There isn't a bit of flirt in that girl, is there?'

'Not a particle; but she's a dear,' returned Sallie, defending her friend, even while confessing her shortcomings.

'She's not a stricken deer, anyway,' said Ned, trying to be witty, and succeeding as well as very young gentlemen usually do.

On the lawn, where it had gathered, the little party separated, with cordial good nights and good-byes, for the Vaughns were going to Canada. As the four sisters went home through the garden, Miss Kate looked after them, saying, without the patronizing tone in her voice, 'In spite of their demonstrative manners, American girls are very nice when one knows them.'

'I quite agree with you,' said Mr Brooke.

CHAPTER 13

Castles in the Air

Laurie lay luxuriously swinging to and fro in his hammock one warm September afternoon, wondering what his neighbours were about, but too lazy to go and find out. He was in one of his moods; for the day had been both unprofitable and unsatisfactory, and he was wishing he could live it over again. The hot weather made him indolent, and he had shirked his studies, tried Mr Brooke's patience to the utmost, displeased his grandfather by practising half the afternoon, frightened the maid-servants half out of their wits by mischievously hinting that one of his dogs was going mad, and, after high words with the stableman about some fancied neglect of his horse, he had flung himself into his hammock, to fume over the stupidity of the world in general, till the peace of the lovely day quieted him in spite of himself. Staring up into the green gloom of the horse-chestnut trees above him, he dreamed dreams of all sorts, and was just imagining himself tossing on the ocean, in a voyage round the world, when the sound of voices brought him ashore in a flash. Peeping through the meshes of his hammock, he saw the Marches coming out, as if bound on some expedition.

'What in the world are those girls about now?' thought Laurie, opening his sleepy eyes to take a good look, for there was something rather peculiar in the appearance of his neighbours. Each wore a large, flapping hat, a brown linen pouch slung over one shoulder, and carried a long staff. Meg had a cushion, Jo a book, Beth a basket, and Amy a portfolio. All walked quietly through the garden, out at the little back gate, and began to climb the hill that lay between the house and the river.

'Well, that's cool!' said Laurie to himself, 'to have a picnic and never ask me. They can't be going in the boat, for they haven't got the key. Perhaps they forgot it; I'll take it to them, and see what's going on.'

Though possessed of half a dozen hats, it took him some time to find one; then there was a hunt for the key, which was at last discovered in his pocket; so that the girls were quite out of sight when he leaped the fence and ran after them. Taking the shortest way to the boathouse, he waited for them to appear: but no one came, and he went up the hill to take an observation. A group of pines covered one part of it, and from the heart of his green spot came a clearer sound than the soft sigh of the pines or the drowsy chirp of the crickets.

'Here's a landscape!' thought Laurie, peeping through the bushes, and looking wide awake and good-natured already.

It *was* rather a pretty little picture; for the sisters sat together in the shady nook, with sun and shadow flickering over them, the aromatic wind lifting their hair and cooling their hot cheeks, and all the little wood-people going on with their affairs, as if these were no strangers, but old friends. Meg sat upon her cushion, sewing daintily with her white hands, and looking as fresh and as sweet as a rose, in her pink dress among the green. Beth was sorting the cones that lay thick under the hemlock near by, for she made pretty things of them. Amy was sketching a group of ferns, and Jo was knitting as she read aloud. A shadow passed over the boy's face as he watched them, feeling that he ought to go away, because uninvited; yet lingering, because home seemed very lonely, and this quiet party in the woods most attractive to his restless spirit. He stood so still that a squirrel, busy with its harvesting, ran down a pine close beside him, saw him suddenly and skipped back, scolding so shrilly that Beth looked up, espied the wistful face behind the birches, and beckoned with a reassuring smile.

'May I come in, please? or shall I be a bother?' he asked advancing slowly.

Meg lifted her eyebrows, but Jo scowled at her defiantly, and said at once, 'Of course you may. We should have asked you before, only we thought you wouldn't care for such a girl's game as this.'

'I always liked your games; but if Meg doesn't want me, I'll go away.'

'I've no objection, if you do something; it's against the rules to be idle here,' replied Meg, gravely but graciously.

'Much obliged; I'll do anything if you'll let me stop a bit, for it's as dull as the Desert of Sahara down there. Shall I sew, read, cone, draw, or do all at once? Bring on your bears; I'm ready,' and Laurie sat down, with a submissive expression delightful to behold.

'Finish this story while I set my heel,' said Jo, handing him the book.

'Yes'm,' was the meek answer, as he began, doing his best to prove his gratitude for the favour of an admission into the 'Busy Bee Society'.

The story was not a long one, and, when it was finished, he ventured to ask a few questions, as a reward of merit.

'Please, ma'am, could I inquire if this highly instructive and charming institution is a new one?'

'Would you tell him?' asked Meg of her sisters.

'He'll laugh,' said Amy, warningly.

'Who cares?' said Jo.

'I guess he'll like it,' added Beth.

'Of course I shall! I give you my word I won't laugh. Tell away, Jo, and don't be afraid.'

'The idea of being afraid of you! Well, you see, we used to play *Pilgrim's Progress*, and we have been going on with it in earnest all winter and summer.'

'Yes, I know,' said Laurie, nodding wisely.

'Who told you?' demanded Jo.

'Spirits.'

'No, I did; I wanted to amuse him one night when you were

all away, and he was rather dismal. He did like it, so don't scold, Jo,' said Beth, meekly.

'You can't keep a secret. Never mind; it saves trouble now.'

'Go on, please,' said Laurie, as Jo became absorbed in her work, looking a trifle displeased.

'Oh, didn't she tell you about this new plan of ours? Well, we have tried not to waste our holiday, but each has had a task, and worked at it with a will. The vacation is nearly over, the stints are all done, and we are ever so glad that we didn't dawdle.'

'Yes, I should think so'; and Laurie thought regretfully of his own idle ways.

'Mother likes to have us out of doors as much as possible; so we bring our work here, and have nice times. For the fun of it we bring our things in these bags, wear the old hats, use poles to climb the hill, and play pilgrims, as we used to do years ago. We call this hill the "Delectable Mountain", for we can look far away and see the country where we hope to live some time.'

Jo pointed, and Laurie sat up to examine; for through an opening in the wood one could look across the wide blue river, the meadows on the other side, far over the outskirts of the great city, to the green hills that rose to meet the sky. The sun was low, and the heavens glowed with the splendour of an autumn sunset. Gold and purple clouds lay on the hilltops; and rising high into the ruddy light were silvery white peaks, that shone like the airy spires of some Celestial City.

'How beautiful that is!' said Laurie, softly, for he was quick to see and feel beauty of any kind.

'It's often so; and we like to watch it, for it is never the same, but always splendid,' replied Amy, wishing she could paint it.

'Jo talks about the country where we hope to live some time – the real country, she means, with pigs and chickens and haymaking. It would be nice, but I wish the beautiful country up there was real, and we could ever go to it,' said Beth, musingly.

'There is a lovelier country even than that, where we *shall* go by and by, when we are good enough,' answered Meg, with her sweet voice.

'It seems so long to wait, so hard to do; I want to fly away at once, as those swallows fly, and go in at that splendid gate.'

'You'll get there, Beth, sooner or later; no fear of that,' said Jo; 'I'm the one that will have to fight and work, and climb and wait, and maybe never get in after all.'

'You'll have me for company, if that's any comfort. I shall have to do a deal of travelling before I come in sight of your Celestial City. If I arrive late, you'll say a good word for me, won't you, Beth?'

Something in the boy's face troubled his little friend; but she said cheerfully, with her quiet eyes on the changing clouds, 'If people really want to go, and really try all their lives, I think they will get in; for I don't believe there are any locks on that door, or any guards at the gate. I always imagine it is as it is in the picture, where the shining ones stretch out their hands to welcome poor Christian, as he comes up from the river.'

'Wouldn't it be fun if all the castles in the air which we make could come true, and we could live in them?' said Jo, after a little pause.

'I've made such quantities it would be hard to choose which I'd have,' said Laurie, lying flat, and throwing cones at the squirrel who had betrayed him.

'You'd have to take your favourite one. What is it?' asked Meg.

'If I tell mine, will you tell yours?'

'Yes, if the girls will too.'

'We will. Now, Laurie.'

'After I'd seen as much of the world as I want to, I'd like to settle in Germany, and have just as much music as I choose. I'm to be a famous musician myself, and all creation is to rush to hear me; and I'm never to be bothered about money or business, but just enjoy myself, and live for what I like. That's my favourite castle. What's yours, Meg?'

Margaret seemed to find it a little hard to tell hers, and waved a brake before her face, as if to disperse imaginary gnats, while she said slowly, 'I should like a lovely house, full of all sorts of luxurious things – nice food, pretty clothes, handsome furniture, pleasant people, and heaps of money. I am to be mistress of it, and manage it as I like, with plenty of servants, so I never need work a bit. How I should enjoy it! for I wouldn't be idle, but do good and make everyone love me dearly.'

'Wouldn't you have a master for your castle in the air?' asked Laurie, slyly.

'I said "pleasant people", you know'; and Meg carefully tied up her shoe as she spoke, so that no one saw her face.

'Why don't you say you'd have a splendid, wise, good husband, and some angelic little children? You know your castle wouldn't be perfect without,' said blunt Jo, who had no tender fancies yet, and rather scorned romance, except in books.

'You'd have nothing but horses, inkstands, and novels in yours,' answered Meg, petulantly.

'Wouldn't I, though? I'd have a stable full of Arabian steeds, rooms piled with books, and I'd write out of a magic inkstand, so that my works should be as famous as Laurie's music. I want to do something splendid before I go into my castle – something heroic or wonderful, that won't be forgotten after I'm dead. I don't know what, but I'm on the watch for it, and mean to astonish you all some day. I think I shall write books, and get rich and famous: that would suit me, so that is *my* favourite dream.'

'Mine is to stay at home safe with Father and Mother, and help take care of the family,' said Beth, contentedly.

'Don't you wish for anything else?' asked Laurie.

'Since I had my little piano, I am perfectly satisfied. I only wish we may all keep well and be together; nothing else.'

'I have ever so many wishes; but the pet one is to be an artist, and go to Rome, and do fine pictures, and be the best artist in the whole world,' was Amy's modest desire.

'We're an ambitious set, aren't we? Every one of us, but Beth, wants to be rich and famous, and gorgeous in every respect. I do wonder if any of us will ever get our wishes,' said Laurie, chewing grass, like a meditative calf.

'I've got the key to my castle in the air; but whether I can unlock the door remains to be seen,' observed Jo, mysteriously.

'I've got the key to mine, but I'm not allowed to try it. Hang college!' muttered Laurie, with an impatient sigh.

'Here's mine!' and Amy waved her pencil.

'I haven't got any,' said Meg, forlornly.

'Yes, you have,' said Laurie at once.

'Where?'

'In your face.'

'Nonsense; that's of no use.'

'Wait and see if it doesn't bring you something worth having,' replied the boy, laughing at the thought of a charming little secret which he fancied he knew.

Meg coloured behind the brake, but asked no questions, and looked across the river with the same expectant expression which Mr Brooke had worn when he told the story of the knight.

'If we are all alive ten years hence, let's meet, and see how many of us have got our wishes, or how much nearer we are then than now,' said Jo, always ready with a plan.

'Bless me! how old I shall be – twenty-seven!' exclaimed Meg, who felt grown up already, having just reached seventeen.

'You and I will be twenty-six, Teddy, Beth twenty-four, and Amy twenty-two. What a venerable party!' said Jo.

'I hope I shall have done something to be proud of by that time; but I'm such a lazy dog, I'm afraid I shall "dawdle", Jo.'

'You need a motive, Mother says; and when you get it she is sure you'll work splendidly.'

'Is she? By Jupiter! I will, if I only get the chance!' cried Laurie, sitting up with sudden energy. 'I ought to be satisfied to please Grandfather, and I do try, but it's working against the grain, you see, and comes hard. He wants me to be an India merchant, as he was, and I'd rather be shot. I hate tea and silk and spices, and every sort of rubbish his old ships bring, and I don't care how soon they go to the bottom when I own them. Going to college ought to satisfy him, for if I give him four years he ought to let me off from business;

but he's set, and I've got to do just as he did, unless I break away and please myself, as my father did. If there was anyone left to stay with the old gentleman, I'd do it tomorrow.'

Laurie spoke excitedly, and looked ready to carry his threat into execution on the slightest provocation; for he was growing up very fast, and, in spite of his indolent ways, had a young man's hatred of subjection, a young man's restless longing to try the world for himself.

'I advise you to sail away in one of your ships, and never come home again till you have tried your own way,' said Jo, whose imagination was fired by the thought of such a daring exploit, and whose sympathy was excited by what she called 'Teddy's wrongs'.

'That's not right, Jo; you mustn't talk in that way, and Laurie mustn't take your bad advice. You should do just what your grandfather wishes, my dear boy,' said Meg, in her most maternal tone. 'Do your best at college, and when he sees that you try to please him, I'm sure he won't be hard or unjust to you. As you say, there is no one else to stay with and love him, and you'd never forgive yourself if you left him without his permission. Don't be dismal, or fret, but do your duty; and you'll get your reward, as good Mr Brooke has, by being respected and loved.'

'What do you know about him?' asked Laurie, grateful for the good advice, but objecting to the lecture, and glad to turn the conversation from himself, after his unusual outbreak.

'Only what your grandpa told us about him – how he took good care of his own mother till she died, and wouldn't go abroad as tutor to some nice person, because he wouldn't leave her; and how he provides now for an old woman who nursed his mother; and never tells anyone, but is just as generous and patient and good as he can be.'

'So he is, dear old fellow!' said Laurie, heartily, as Meg paused, looking flushed and earnest with her story. 'It's like Grandpa to find out all about him without letting him know, and to tell all his goodness to others, so that they might like him. Brooke couldn't understand why your mother was so kind to him, asking him over with me, and treating him in her beautiful, friendly way. He thought she was just perfect, and talked about it for days and days, and went on about you all in flaming style. If ever I get my wish, you see what I'll do for Brooke.'

'Begin to do something now, by not plaguing his life out,' said Meg, sharply.

'How do you know I do, Miss?'

'I can always tell by his face when he goes away. If you have been good, he looks satisfied and walks briskly; if you have plagued him, he's sober and walks slowly, as if he wanted to go back and do his work better.'

'Well, I like that! So you keep an account of my good and bad marks in Brooke's face, do you! I see him bow and smile as he passes your window, but I didn't know you'd got up a telegraph.'

'We haven't; don't be angry, and oh, don't tell him I said anything! It was only to show that I cared how you get on, and what is said here is said in confidence, you know,' cried Meg, much alarmed at the thought of what might follow from her careless speech.

'*I* don't tell tales,' replied Laurie, with his 'high and mighty' air, as Jo called a certain expression which he occasionally wore, 'only, if Brooke is going to be a barometer, I must mind and have fair weather for him to report.'

'Please don't be offended. I didn't mean to preach or tell tales or be silly; I only thought Jo was encouraging you in a feeling which you'd be sorry for by and by. You are so kind to us, we feel as if you were our brother, and say just what we think. Forgive me. I meant it kindly.' And Meg offered her hand with a gesture both affectionate and timid.

Ashamed of his momentary pique, Laurie squeezed the kind little hand, and said frankly, 'I'm the one to be forgiven; I'm cross, and have been out of sorts all day. I like to have you tell me my faults and be sisterly, so don't mind if I am grumpy sometimes; I thank you all the same.'

Bent on showing that he was not offended, he made himself

agreeable as possible – wound cotton for Meg, recited poetry to please Jo, shook down cones for Beth, and helped Amy with her ferns, proving himself a fit person to belong to the 'Busy Bee Society'. In the midst of an animated discussion on the domestic habits of turtles (one of those amiable creatures having strolled up from the river), the faint sound of a bell warned them that Hannah had put the tea 'to draw', and they would just have time to get home to supper.

'May I come again?' asked Laurie.

'Yes, if you are good, and love your book, as the boys in the primer are told to do,' said Meg, smiling.

'I'll try.'

'Then you may come, and I'll teach you to knit as the Scotchmen do; there's a demand for socks just now,' added Jo, waving hers, like a big, blue worsted banner, as they parted at the gate.

That night, when Beth played to Mr Laurence in the twilight, Laurie, standing in the shadow of the curtain, listened to the little David, whose simple music always quieted his moody spirit, and watched the old man, who sat with his grey head on his hand, thinking tender thoughts of the dead child he had loved so much. Remembering the conversation of the afternoon, the boy said to himself, with the resolve to make the sacrifice cheerfully, 'I'll let my castle go, and stay with the dear old gentleman while he needs me, for I am all he has.'

CHAPTER 14

Secrets

Jo was very busy in the garret, for the October days began to grow chilly, and the afternoons were short. For two or three hours the sun lay warmly in the high window, showing Jo seated on the old sofa, writing busily, with her papers spread out upon a trunk before her, while Scrabble, the pet rat, promenaded the beams overhead, accompanied by his young fellow, who was evidently very proud of his whiskers. Quite absorbed in her work, Jo scribbled away till the last page was filled, when she signed her name with a flourish, and threw down her pen, exclaiming:

'There, I've done my best! If this won't suit, I shall have to wait till I can do better.'

Lying back on the sofa, she read the manuscript carefully through, making dashes here and there, and putting in many exclamation points, which looked like little balloons; then she tied it up with a smart, red ribbon, and sat a minute looking at it with a sober, wistful expression, which plainly showed how earnest her work had been. Jo's desk up here was an old tin kitchen, which hung against the wall. In it she kept her papers and a few books, safely shut away from Scrabble, who, being likewise of a literary turn, was fond of making a circulating library of such books as were left in his way, by eating the leaves. From this tin receptable, Jo produced another manuscript; and, putting both in her pocket, crept quietly downstairs, leaving her friends to nibble her pens and taste her ink.

She put on her hat and jacket as noiselessly as possible, and, going to the back entry window, got out upon the roof of a low porch, swung herself down to the grassy bank, and took a round-about way to the road. Once there, she composed herself, hailed a passing omnibus, and rolled away to town, looking very merry and mysterious.

If anyone had been watching her he would have thought her movements decidedly peculiar; for, on alighting, she went off at a great pace till she reached a certain number in a certain busy street; having found the place with some difficulty, she went into the doorway, looked up the dirty stairs, and, after standing stock still a minute, suddenly dived into the street, and walked away as rapidly as she came. This manoeuvre she repeated several times, to the great amusement of a black-eyed young gentleman lounging in the window of the building opposite. On returning for the third time, Jo gave herself a shake, pulled her hat over her eyes, and walked up the stairs, looking as if she were going to have all her teeth out.

There was a dentist's sign, among others which adorned the entrance, and, after staring a minute at the pair of artificial jaws which slowly opened and shut to draw attention to a fine set of teeth, the young gentleman put on his coat, took his hat, and went down to post himself in the opposite doorway, saying, with a smile and a shiver:

'It's like her to come alone, but if she has a bad time she'll need someone to help her home.'

In ten minutes Jo came running downstairs with a very red face, and the general appearance of a person who had just passed through a trying ordeal of some sort. When she saw the young gentleman she looked anything but pleased, and passed him with a nod; but he followed, asking with an air of sympathy:

'Did you have a bad time?'

'Not very.'

'You got through quickly.'

'Yes, thank goodness!'

'Why did you go alone?'

'Didn't want anyone to know.'

'You're the oddest fellow I ever saw. How many did you have out?'

Jo looked at her friend as if she did not understand him; then began to laugh, as if mightily amused at something.

'There are two which I want to have come out, but I must wait a week.'

'What are you laughing at? You are up to some mischief, Jo,' said Laurie, looking mystified.

'So are you. What were you doing, sir, up in that billiard saloon?'

'Begging your pardon, ma'am, it wasn't a billiard saloon, but a gymnasium, and I was taking a lesson in fencing.'

'I'm glad of that.'

'Why?'

'You can teach me, and then when we play *Hamlet*, you can be Laertes, and we'll make a fine thing of the fencing scene.'

Laurie burst out with a hearty boy's laugh, which made several passers-by smile in spite of themselves.

'I'll teach you, whether we play *Hamlet* or not; it's grand fun, and will straighten you up capitally. But I don't believe that was your reason for saying "I'm glad", in that decided way; was it, now?'

'No, I was glad that you were not in the saloon, because I hope you never go to such places. Do you?'

'Not often.'

'I wish you wouldn't.'

'It's no harm, Jo. I have billiards at home, but it's no fun unless you have good players, so, as I'm fond of it, I come sometimes and have a game with Ned Moffat or some of the other fellows.'

'Oh dear, I'm so sorry, for you'll get to liking it better and better, and will waste time and money, and grow like those dreadful boys. I did hope you'd stay respectable, and be a satisfaction to your friends,' said Jo, shaking her head.

'Can't a fellow take a little innocent amusement now and then without losing his respectability?' asked Laurie, looking nettled.

'That depends upon how and where he takes it. I don't like Ned and his set, and wish you'd keep out of it. Mother won't let us have him at our house, though he wants to come; and if you grow like him she won't be willing to have us frolic together as we do now.'

'Won't she?' asked Laurie, anxiously.

'No, she can't bear fashionable young men, and she'd shut us all up in bandboxes rather than have us associate with them.'

'Well, she needn't get out her bandboxes yet; I'm not a fashionable party, and don't mean to be; but I do like harmless larks now and then, don't you?'

'Yes, nobody minds them, so lark away, but don't get wild, will you? or there will be an end of all our good times.'

'I'll be a double-distilled saint.'

'I can't bear saints; just be a simple, honest, respectable boy, and we'll never desert you. I don't know what I *should* do if you acted like Mr King's son; he had plenty of money, but didn't know how to spend it, and got tipsy, and gambled, and ran away, and forged his father's name, I believe, and was altogether horrid.'

'You think I'm likely to do the same? Much obliged.'

'No, I don't – oh, *dear*, no! – but I hear people talking about money being such a temptation, and I sometimes wish you were poor; I shouldn't worry then.'

'Do you worry about me, Jo?'

'A little, when you look moody or discontented, as you sometimes do; for you've got such a strong will, if you once get started wrong, I'm afraid it would be hard to stop you.'

Laurie walked in silence for a few minutes, and Jo watched him, wishing she had held her tongue, for his eyes looked angry though his lips still smiled as if at her warnings.

'Are you going to deliver lectures all the way home?' he asked presently.

'Of course not; why?'

'Because, if you are, I'll take a bus; if you are not, I'd like to walk with you, and tell you something very interesting.'

'I won't preach any more, and I'd like to hear the news immensely.'

'Very well, then; come on. It's a secret, and if I tell you, you must tell me yours.'

'I haven't got any,' began Jo, but stopped suddenly, remembering that she had.

'You know you have – you can't hide anything; so up and 'fess, or I won't tell,' cried Laurie.

'Is your secret a nice one?'

'Oh, isn't it! all about people you know, and such fun! You ought to hear it, and I've been aching to tell it this long time. Come, you begin.'

'You'll not say anything about it at home, will you?'

'Not a word.'

'And you won't tease me in private?'

'I never tease.'

'Yes, you do; you get everything you want out of people. I don't know how you do it, but you are a born wheedler.'

'Thank you; fire away.'

'Well, I've left two stories with a newspaper man, and he's to give his answer next week,' whispered Jo, in her confidant's ear.

'Hurrah for Miss March, the celebrated American authoress!' cried Laurie, throwing up his hat and catching it again, to the great delight of two ducks, four cats, five hens, and half a dozen Irish children; for they were out of the city now.

'Hush! It won't come to anything, I dare say; but I couldn't rest till I had tried, and I said nothing about it, because I didn't want anyone else to be disappointed.'

'It won't fail. Why, Jo, your stories are works of Shakespeare, compared to half the rubbish that is published every day. Won't it be fun to see them in print; and shan't we feel proud of our authoress?'

Jo's eyes sparkled, for it is always pleasant to be believed in; and a friend's praise is always sweeter than a dozen newspaper puffs.

'Where's *your* secret? Play fair, Teddy, or I'll never believe you again,' she said, trying to extinguish the brilliant hopes that blazed up at a word of encouragement.

'I may get into a scrape for telling; but I didn't promise not to, so I will, for I never feel easy in my mind till I've told you any plummy bit of news I get. I know where Meg's glove is.'

'Is that all?' said Jo, looking disappointed, as Laurie nodded and twinkled, with a face full of mysterious intelligence.

'It's quite enough for the present, as you'll agree when I tell you where it is.'

'Tell then.'

Laurie bent, and whispered three words in Jo's ear, which produced a comical change. She stood and stared at him for a minute, looking both surprised and displeased, then walked on, saying sharply, 'How do you know?'

'Saw it.'

'Where?'

'Pocket.'

'All this time?'

'Yes; isn't that romantic?'

'No, it's horrid.'

'Don't you like it?'

'Of course I don't. It's ridiculous; it won't be allowed. My patience! what would Meg say?'

'You are not to tell anyone; mind that.'

'I didn't promise.'

'That was understood, and I trusted you.'

'Well, I won't for the present, anyway; but I'm disgusted, and wish you hadn't told me.'

'I thought you'd be pleased.'

'At the idea of anybody coming to take Meg away? No, thank you.'

'You'll feel better about it when somebody comes to take you away.'

'I'd like to see anyone try it,' cried Jo, fiercely.

'So should I!' and Laurie chuckled at the idea.

'I don't think secrets agree with me; I feel rumpled up in my mind since you told me that,' said Jo, rather ungratefully.

'Race down this hill with me, and you'll be all right,' suggested Laurie.

No one was in sight; the smooth road sloped invitingly before her; and finding the temptation irresistible, Jo darted away, soon leaving hat and comb behind her, and scattering hairpins as she ran. Laurie reached the goal first, and was quite satisfied with the success of his treatment; for his Atalanta came panting up, with flying hair, bright eyes, ruddy cheeks, and no signs of dissatisfaction in her face.

'I wish I was a horse; then I could run for miles in this splendid air, and not lose my breath. It was capital; but see what a guy it's made me. Go, pick up my things, like a cherub as you are,' said Jo, dropping down under a maple-tree which was carpeting the bank with crimson leaves.

Laurie leisurely departed to recover the lost property, and Jo bundled up her braids, hoping no one would pass by till she was tidy again. But someone did pass by, and who should it be but Meg, looking particularly ladylike in her state and festival suit, for she had been making calls.

'What in the world are you doing here?' she asked, regarding her dishevelled sister with well-bred surprise.

'Getting leaves,' meekly answered Jo, sorting the rosy handful she had just swept up.

'And hairpins,' added Laurie, throwing half a dozen into Jo's lap. 'They grow on this road, Meg; so do combs and brown straw hats.'

'You have been running, Jo; how could you? When *will* you be stopping such romping ways?' said Meg, reprovingly, as she settled her cuffs, and smoothed her hair, with which the wind had taken liberties.

'Never till I'm stiff and old, and have to use a crutch. Don't try to make me grow up before my time, Meg; it's hard enough to have you change all of a sudden; let me be a little girl as long as I can.'

As she spoke, Jo bent over the leaves to hide the trembling of her lips; for lately she had felt that Margaret was fast getting to be a woman, and Laurie's secret made her dread the separation which must surely come sometime, and now seemed very near. He saw the trouble in her face, and drew Meg's attention from it by asking quickly, 'Where have you been calling all so fine?'

'At the Gardiners', and Sallie has been telling me all about Belle Moffat's wedding. It was very splendid, and they have gone to spend the winter in Paris. Just think how delightful that must be!'

'Do you envy her, Meg?' said Laurie.

'I'm afraid I do.'

'I'm glad of it,' muttered Jo, tying on her hat with a jerk.

'Why?' asked Meg, looking surprised.

'Because if you care much about riches, you will never go and marry a poor man,' said Jo, frowning at Laurie, who was mutely warning her to mind what she said.

'I shall never "*go* and marry" anyone,' observed Meg, walking on with great dignity, while the others followed, laughing, whispering, skipping stones, and 'behaving like children', as Meg said to herself, though she might have been tempted to join them if she had not had her best dress on.

For a week or two, Jo behaved so queerly that her sisters were quite bewildered. She rushed to the door when the postman rang; was rude to Mr Brooke whenever they met; would sit looking at Meg with a woebegone face, occasionally jumping up to shake, and then to kiss her, in a very mysterious manner; Laurie and she were always making signs to one another and talking about 'Spread Eagles' till the girls declared they had both lost their wits. On the second Saturday after Jo got out of the window, Meg, as she sat sewing at her window, was scandalized by the sight of Laurie chasing Jo all over the garden, and finally capturing her in Amy's bower. What went on there, Meg could not see; but shrieks of laughter were heard, followed by the murmur of voices and a great flapping of newspapers.

'What shall we do with that girl? She never *will* behave like a young lady,' sighed Meg, as she watched the race with a disapproving face.

'I hope she won't; she is so funny and dear as she is,' said Beth, who had never betrayed that she was a little hurt at Jo's having secrets with anyone but her.

'It's very trying, but we can never make her *commy la fo*,' added Amy, who sat making some new frills for herself, with her curls tied up in a very becoming way – two agreeable things, which made her feel unusually elegant and ladylike.

In a few minutes Jo bounced in, laid herself on the sofa, and affected to read.

'Have you anything interesting there?' asked Meg, with condescension.

'Nothing but a story; won't amount to much, I guess,' returned Jo, carefully keeping the name of the paper out of sight.

'You'd better read it aloud; that will amuse us and keep you out of mischief,' said Amy, in her most grown-up tone.

'What's the name?' asked Beth, wondering why Jo kept her face behind the sheet.

'*The Rival Painters.*'

'That sounds well; read it,' said Meg.

With a loud 'Hem!' and a long breath, Jo began to read very fast. The girls listened with interest, for the tale was romantic, and somewhat pathetic, as most of the characters died in the end.

'I like that about the splendid picture,' was Amy's approving remark, as Jo paused.

'I prefer the lovering part. Viola and Angelo are two of our favourite names; isn't that queer?' said Meg, wiping her eyes, for the 'lovering part' was tragical.

'Who wrote it?' asked Beth, who had caught a glimpse of Jo's face.

The reader suddenly sat up, cast away the paper, displaying a flushed countenance, and, with a funny mixture of solemnity and excitement, replied in a loud voice, 'Your sister.'

'You?' cried Meg, dropping her work.

'It's very good,' said Amy, critically.

'I knew it! I knew it! Oh, my Jo, I *am* so proud!' and Beth began to hug her sister, and exult over this splendid success.

Dear me, how delighted they all were, to be sure! how Meg wouldn't believe it till she saw the words 'Miss Josephine March' actually printed in the paper; how graciously Amy criticized the artistic parts of the story, and offered hints for a sequel, which unfortunately couldn't be carried out, as the hero and heroine were dead; how Beth got excited, and skipped and sung with joy; how Hannah came in to exclaim 'Sakes alive, well I never!' in great astonishment at 'that Jo's doin's'; how proud Mrs March was when she knew it; how Jo laughed, with tears in her eyes, as she declared she might as well be a peacock and done with it; and how the 'Spread Eagle' might be said to flap his wings triumphantly over the House of March, as the paper passed from hand to hand.

'Tell us all about it.' 'When did it come?' 'How much did you get for it?' 'What *will* Father say?' 'Won't Laurie laugh?' cried the family, all in one breath, as they clustered about Jo; for these foolish, affectionate people made a jubilee of every little household joy.

'Stop jabbering, girls, and I'll tell you everything,' said Jo, wondering if Miss Burney felt any grander over her *Evelina*, than she did over her *Rival Painters*. Having told how she disposed of her tales, Jo added, 'And when I went to get my answer, the man said he liked them both, but didn't pay beginners, only let them print in his paper, and noticed the stories. It was good practice, he said; and when the beginners improved, anyone would pay. So I let him have the two stories, and today this was sent to me, and Laurie caught me with it, and insisted on seeing it, so I let him; and he said it was good, and I shall write more, and he's going to get the next paid for, and I *am* so happy, for in time I may be able to support myself and help the girls.'

Jo's breath gave out here; and, wrapping her head in the paper, she bedewed her little story with a few natural tears; for to be independent, and earn the praise of those she loved, were the dearest wishes of her heart, and this seemed to be the first step towards that happy end.

CHAPTER 15

A Telegram

'November is the most disagreeable month in the whole year,' said Margaret, standing at the window one dull afternoon, looking out at the frost-bitten garden.

'That's the reason I was born in it,' observed Jo, pensively, quite unconscious of the blot on her nose.

'If something very pleasant should happen now, we should think it a delightful month,' said Beth, who took a hopeful view of everything, even November.

'I dare say; but nothing pleasant ever *does* happen in this family,' said Meg, who was out of sorts. 'We go grubbing along day after day, without a bit of change, and very little fun. We might as well be in a treadmill.'

'My patience, how blue we are!' cried Jo. 'I don't much wonder, poor dear, for you see other girls having splendid times, while you grind, grind, year in and year out. Oh, don't I wish I could manage things for you as I do for my heroines! You're pretty enough and good enough already, so I'd have some rich relation leave you a fortune unexpectedly; then you'd dash out as an heiress, scorn everyone who has slighted you, go abroad and come home my Lady Something, in a blaze of splendour and elegance.'

'People don't have fortunes left them in that style nowadays;

men have to work, and women to marry for money. It's a dreadful unjust world,' said Meg, bitterly.

'Jo and I are going to make fortunes for you all; just wait ten years, and see if we don't,' said Amy, who sat in a corner, making mud pies, as Hannah called her little clay models of birds, fruit, and faces.

'Can't wait, and I'm afraid I haven't much faith in ink and dirt, though I'm grateful for your good intentions.'

Meg sighed, and turned to the frost-bitten garden again; Jo groaned, and leaned both elbows on the table, in a despondent attitude, but Amy patted away energetically; and Beth, who sat at the other window, said, smiling, 'Two pleasant things are going to happen right away; Marmee is coming down the street, and Laurie is tramping through the garden as if he had something nice to tell.'

In they both came, Mrs March with her usual question, 'Any letter from Father, girls?' and Laurie to say in his persuasive way, 'Won't some of you come for a drive? I've been working away at mathematics till my head is in a muddle, and I'm going to freshen my wits by a brisk turn. It's a dull day, but the air isn't bad, and I'm going to take Brooke home, so it will be gay inside, if it isn't out. Come, Jo, you and Beth will go, won't you?'

'Of course we will.'

'Much obliged, but I'm busy'; and Meg whisked out her work-basket, for she had agreed with her mother that it was best, for her at least, not to drive often with the young gentleman.

'We three will be ready in a minute,' cried Amy, running away to wash her hands.

'Can I do anything for you, Madam Mother?' asked Laurie, leaning over Mrs March's chair, with the affectionate look and tone he always gave her.

'No, thank you, except call at the office, if you'll be so kind, dear. It's our day for a letter, and the postman hasn't been. Father is as regular as the sun, but there's some delay on the way, perhaps.'

A sharp ring interrupted her, and a minute after Hannah came in with a letter.

'It's one of them horrid telegraph things, mum,' she said, handling it as if she was afraid it would explode and do some damage.

At the word 'telegraph', Mrs March snatched it, read the two lines it contained, and dropped back into her chair as white as if the little paper had sent a bullet to her heart. Laurie dashed downstairs for water, while Meg and Hannah supported her, and Jo read aloud, in a frightened voice:

'MRS MARCH:
Your husband is very ill. Come at once.
S. HALE,
Blank Hospital, Washington.'

How still the room was as they listened breathlessly, how strangely the day darkened outside, and how suddenly the whole world seemed to change, as the girls gathered about their mother, feeling as if all the happiness and support of their lives was about to be taken from them. Mrs March was herself again directly; read the message over, and stretched out her arms to her daughters, saying, in a tone they never forgot, 'I shall go at once, but it may be too late. Oh, children, children, help me to bear it!'

For several minutes there was nothing but the sound of sobbing in the room, mingled with broken words of comfort, tender assurances of help, and hopeful whispers that died away in tears. Poor Hannah was the first to recover, and with unconscious wisdom she set all the rest a good example; for, with her, work was the panacea for most afflictions.

'The Lord keep the dear man! I won't waste no time a cryin', but git your things ready right away, mum,' she said, heartily, as she wiped her face on her apron, gave her mistress a warm shake of the hand with her own hard one, and went away, to work like three women in one.

'She's right; there's no time for tears now. Be calm, girls, and let me think.'

They tried to be calm, poor things, as their mother sat up,

looking pale, but steady, and put away her grief to think and plan for them.

'Where's Laurie?' she asked presently, when she had collected her thoughts, and decided on the first duties to be done.

'Here, ma'am. Oh, let me do something!' cried the boy, hurrying from the next room, whither he had withdrawn, feeling that their first sorrow was too sacred for even his friendly eyes to see.

'Send a telegram saying I will come at once. The next train goes early in the morning. I'll take that.'

'What else? The horses are ready; I can go anywhere, do anything,' he said, looking ready to fly to the ends of the earth.

'Leave a note at Aunt March's. Jo, give me that pen and paper.'

Tearing off the blank side of one of her newly-copied pages, Jo drew the table before her mother, well knowing that money for the long, sad journey must be borrowed, and feeling as if she could do anything to add a little to the sum for her father.

'Now go, dear; but don't kill yourself driving at a desperate pace; there is no need of that.'

Mrs March's warning was evidently thrown away; for five minutes later Laurie tore by the window on his own fleet horse, riding as if for his life.

'Jo, run to the rooms, and tell Mrs King that I can't come. On the way get these things. I'll put them down; they'll be needed, and I must go prepared for nursing. Hospital stores are not always good. Beth, go and ask Mr Laurence for a couple of bottles of old wine: I'm not too proud to beg for Father; he shall have the best of everything. Amy, tell Hannah to get down the black trunk; and Meg, come and help me find my things, for I'm half bewildered.'

Writing, thinking, and directing, all at once, might well bewilder the poor lady, and Meg begged her to sit down quietly in her room for a little while, and let them work. Everyone scattered like leaves before a gust of wind; and the quiet, happy household was broken up as suddenly as if the paper had been an evil spell.

Mr Laurence came hurrying back with Beth, bringing every comfort the kind old gentleman could think of for the invalid, and friendliest promises of protection for the girls during the mother's absence, which comforted her very much. There was nothing he didn't offer, from his own dressing-gown to himself as escort. But that last was impossible. Mrs March would not hear of the old gentleman's undertaking the long journey; yet an expression of relief was visible when he spoke of it, for anxiety ill fits one for travelling. He saw the look, knit his heavy eyebrows, rubbed his hands, and marched abruptly away, saying he'd be back directly. No one had time to think of him again till, as Meg ran through the entry, with a pair of rubbers in one hand and a cup of tea in the other, she came suddenly upon Mr Brooke.

'I'm very sorry to hear of this, Miss March,' he said, in the kind, quiet tone which sounded pleasantly to her perturbed spirit. 'I came to offer myself as escort to your mother. Mr Laurence has commissions for me in Washington, and it will give me real satisfaction to be of service to her there.'

Down dropped the rubbers, and the tea was very near following, as Meg put out her hand, with a face so full of gratitude, that Mr Brooke would have felt repaid for a much greater sacrifice than the trifling one of time and comfort which he was about to make.

'How kind you all are! Mother will accept, I'm sure; and it will be such a relief to know that she has someone to take care of her. Thank you very, very much!'

Meg spoke earnestly, and forgot herself entirely, till something in the brown eyes looking down at her made her remember the cooling tea, and lead the way into the parlour, saying she would call her mother.

Everything was arranged by the time Laurie returned with a note from Aunt March enclosing the desired sum, and a few lines repeating what she had often said before – that she had always told them it was absurd for March to go into the army, always predicted that no good would come of it, and she hoped they would take her advice next time. Mrs March put the note in the fire, the money in her purse, and went on with her preparations, with her lips folded tightly, in a way which Jo would have understood if she had been there.

The short afternoon wore away; all the other errands were done, and Meg and her mother busy at some necessary needlework, while Beth and Amy got tea, and Hannah finished her ironing with what she called a 'slap and a bang', but still Jo did not come. They began to get anxious; and Laurie went off to find her, for no one ever knew what freak Jo might take into her head. He missed her, however, and she came walking in with a very queer expression of countenance, for there was a mixture of fun and fear, satisfaction and regret in it, which puzzled the family as much as did the roll of bills she laid before her mother, saying, with a little choke in her voice, 'That's my contribution towards making Father comfortable, and bringing him home!'

'My dear, where did you get it? Twenty-five dollars? Jo, I hope you haven't done anything rash?'

'No, it's mine honestly; I didn't beg, borrow, or steal it. I earned it; and I don't think you'll blame me, for I only sold what was my own.'

As she spoke, Jo took off her bonnet, and a general outcry arose, for all her abundant hair was cut short.

'Your hair! Your beautiful hair!' 'Oh, Jo, how could you? Your one beauty.' 'My dear girl, there was no need of this.' 'She doesn't look like my Jo any more, but I love her dearly for it!'

As everyone exclaimed, and Beth hugged the cropped head tenderly, Jo assumed an indifferent air, which did not deceive anyone a particle, and said, rumpling up the brown bush, and trying to look as if she liked it, 'It doesn't affect the fate of the nation, so don't wail, Beth. It will be good for my vanity; I was getting too proud of my wig. It will do my brains good to have that mop taken off; my head feels deliciously light and cool, and the barber said I could soon have a curly crop, which will be boyish, becoming, and easy to keep in order. I'm satisfied; so please take the money, and let's have supper.'

'Tell me all about it, Jo. *I* am not quite satisfied, but I can't blame you, for I know how willingly you sacrificed your vanity, as you call it, to your love. But, my dear, it was not necessary, and I'm afraid you will regret it, one of these days,' said Mrs March.

'No, I won't!' returned Jo, stoutly, feeling much relieved that her prank was not entirely condemned.

'What made you do it?' asked Amy, who would as soon have thought of cutting off her head as her pretty hair.

'Well, I was wild to do something for Father,' replied Jo, as they gathered about the table, for healthy young people can eat even in the midst of trouble. 'I hate to borrow as much as Mother does, and I knew Aunt March would croak; she always does, if you ask for a ninepence. Meg gave all her quarterly salary toward the rent, and I only got some clothes with mine, so I felt wicked, and was bound to have some money, if I sold the nose off my face to get it.'

'You needn't feel wicked, my child; you had no winter things, and got the simplest with your own hard earnings,' said Mrs March, with a look that warmed Jo's heart.

'I hadn't the least idea of selling my hair at first, but as I went along I kept thinking what I could do, and feeling as if I'd like to dive into some of the rich stores and help myself. In a barber's window I saw tails of hair with the prices marked; and one black tail, not so thick as mine, was forty dollars. It came over me all of a sudden that I had one thing to make money out of, and without stopping to think, I walked in, asked if they bought hair, and what they would give for mine.'

'I don't see how you dared to do it,' said Beth, in a tone of awe.

'Oh, he was a little man who looked as if he merely lived to oil his hair. He rather stared, at first, as if he wasn't used to having girls bounce into his shop and ask him to buy their hair. He said he didn't care about mine, it wasn't the fashionable colour, and he never paid much for it in the first place; the work put into it made it dear, and so on. It was getting late, and I was afraid, if it wasn't done right away, that I shouldn't have it done at all, and you know when I start to do a thing, I hate to give it up; so I begged him to take it, and told him why I was in such a hurry. It was silly, I dare say, but it changed his mind, for I got rather excited, and told the story in my topsy-turvy way, and his wife heard, and said so kindly: "Take it, Thomas, and oblige the young lady; I'd do as much for our Jimmy any day if I had a spire of hair worth selling."'

'Who was Jimmy?' asked Amy, who liked to have things explained as they went along.

'Her son, she said, who was in the army. How friendly such things make strangers feel, don't they? She talked away all the time the man clipped, and diverted my mind nicely.'

'Didn't you feel dreadfully when the first cut came?' asked Meg, with a shiver.

'I took a last look at my hair while the man got his things, and that was the end of it. I never snivel over trifles like that; I will confess, though, I felt queer when I saw the dear old hair laid out on the table, and felt only the short, rough ends on my head. It almost seemed as if I'd an arm or a leg off. The woman saw me look at it, and picked out a long lock for me to keep. I'll give it to you, Marmee, just to remember past glories by; for a crop is so comfortable I don't think I shall ever have a mane again.'

Mrs March folded the wavy chestnut lock, and laid it away with a short grey one in her desk. She only said, 'Thank you, deary', but something in her face made the girls change the subject, and talk as cheerfully as they could about Mr Brooke's kindness, the prospect of a fine day tomorrow, and the happy times they would have when Father came home to be nursed.

No one wanted to go to bed, when, at ten o'clock, Mrs March put by the last finished job, and said, 'Come, girls.' Beth went to the piano and played the father's favourite hymn; all began bravely, but broke down one by one, till Beth was left alone, singing with all her heart, for to her music was always a sweet consoler.

'Go to bed and don't talk, for we must be up early, and shall need all the sleep we can get. Good night, my darlings,' said Mrs March, as the hymn ended, for no one cared to try another.

They kissed her quietly, and went to bed as silently as if the dear invalid lay in the next room. Beth and Amy soon fell asleep in spite of the great trouble, but Meg lay awake, thinking the most serious thoughts she had ever known in her short life. Jo lay motionless, and her sister fancied that she was asleep, till a stifled sob made her exclaim, as she touched a wet cheek: 'Jo, dear, what is it? Are you crying about Father?'

'No, not now.'

'What then?'

'My – my hair!' burst out poor Jo, trying vainly to smother her emotion in the pillow.

It did not sound at all comical to Meg, who kissed and caressed the afflicted heroine in the tenderest manner.

'I'm not sorry,' protested Jo, with a choke. 'I'd do it again tomorrow, if I could. It's only the vain, selfish part of me that goes and cries in this silly way. Don't tell anyone, it's all over now. I thought you were asleep, so I just made a little private moan for my one beauty. How came you to be awake?'

'I can't sleep, I'm so anxious,' said Meg.

'Think about something pleasant, and you'll soon drop off.'

'I tried it, but felt wider awake than ever.'

'What did you think of?'

'Handsome faces – eyes particularly,' answered Meg, smiling to herself, in the dark.

'What colour do you like best?'

'Brown – that is, sometimes; blue are lovely.'

Jo laughed, and Meg sharply ordered her not to talk, then amiably promised to make her hair curl, and fell asleep to dream of living in her castle in the air.

The clocks were striking midnight, and the rooms were very still, as a figure glided quietly from bed to bed, smoothing a coverlid here, settling a pillow there, and pausing to look long and tenderly at each unconscious face, to kiss each with lips that mutely blessed, and to pray the fervent prayers which only mothers utter. As she lifted the curtain to look out into the dreary night, the moon broke suddenly from behind the clouds, and shone upon her like a bright, benignant face, which seemed to whisper in the silence, 'Be comforted, dear soul! There is always light behind the clouds.'

CHAPTER 16

Letters

In the cold grey dawn the sisters lit their lamp, and read their chapter with an earnestness never felt before; for now the shadow of a real trouble had come, the little books were full of help and comfort; and, as they dressed, they agreed to say good-bye cheerfully and hopefully, and send their mother on her anxious journey unsaddened by tears or complaints from them. Everything seemed very strange when they went down – so dim and still outside, so full of light and bustle within. Breakfast at that early hour seemed odd, and even Hannah's familiar face looked unnatural as she flew about her kitchen with her night-cap on. The big trunk stood ready in the hall, Mother's cloak and bonnet lay on the sofa, and Mother herself sat trying to eat, but looking so pale and worn, with sleeplessness and anxiety, that the girls found it very hard to keep their resolution. Meg's eyes kept filling in spite of herself; Jo was obliged to hide her face in the kitchen roller more than once; and the little girls wore a grave, troubled expression, as if sorrow was a new experience to them.

Nobody talked much, but as the time drew very near, and they sat waiting for the carriage, Mrs March said to the girls, who were all busied about her, one folding her shawl, another smoothing out the strings of her bonnet, a third putting on her overshoes, and a fourth fastening up her travelling bag:

'Children, I leave you to Hannah's care and Mr Laurence's protection. Hannah is faithfulness itself, and our good neighbour will guard you as if you were his own. I have no fears for you, yet I am anxious that you should take this trouble rightly. Don't grieve and fret when I am gone, or think that you can comfort yourselves by being idle and trying to forget. Go on with your work as usual, for work is a blessed solace. Hope and keep busy; and whatever happens, remember that you never can be fatherless.'

'Yes, Mother.'

'Meg, dear, be prudent, watch over your sisters, consult Hannah, and, in any perplexity, go to Mr Laurence. Be patient, Jo, don't get despondent or do rash things; write to me often, and be my brave girl, ready to help and cheer us all. Beth, comfort yourself with your music, and be faithful to the little home duties; and you, Amy, help all you can, be obedient, and keep happy safe at home.'

'We will, Mother! we will!'

The rattle of an approaching carriage made them all start and listen. That was the hard minute, but the girls stood it well; no one cried, no one ran away or uttered a lamentation, though their hearts were very heavy as they sent loving messages to Father, remembering, as they spoke, that it might be too late to deliver them. They kissed their mother quietly, clung about her tenderly, and tried to wave their hands cheerfully when she drove away.

Laurie and his grandfather came over to see her off, and Mr Brooke looked so strong and sensible and kind that the girls christened him 'Mr Greatheart' on the spot.

'Good-bye, my darlings! God bless and keep us all!' whispered Mrs March, as she kissed one dear little face after the other, and hurried into the carriage.

As she rolled away, the sun came out, and, looking back, she saw it shining on the group at the gate, like a good omen. They saw it also, and smiled and waved their hands; and the last thing she beheld, as she turned the corner, was the four bright faces, and behind them, like a bodyguard, old Mr Laurence, faithful Hannah, and devoted Laurie.

'How kind everyone is to us!' she said, turning to find fresh proof of it in the respectful sympathy of the young man's face.

'I don't see how they can help it,' returned Mr Brooke, laughing so infectiously that Mrs March could not help smiling; and so the long journey began with the good omens of sunshine, smiles, and cheerful words.

'I feel as if there had been an earthquake,' said Jo, as their neighbours went home to breakfast, leaving them to rest and refresh themselves.

'It seems as if half the house was gone,' added Meg, forlornly.

Beth opened her lips to say something, but could only point to the pile of nicely mended hose which lay on Mother's table, showing that even in her last hurried moments she had thought and worked for them. It was a little thing, but it went straight to their hearts; and, in spite of their brave resolutions, they all broke down and cried bitterly.

Hannah wisely allowed them to relieve their feelings, and, when the shower showed signs of clearing up, she came to the rescue, armed with a coffee-pot.

'Now, my dear young ladies, remember what your ma said, and don't fret. Come and have a cup of coffee all round, and then let's fall to work and be a credit to the family.'

Coffee was a treat, and Hannah showed great tact in making it that morning. No one could resist her persuasive nods, or the fragrant invitation issuing from the nose of the coffee-pot. They drew up to the table, exchanged their handkerchiefs for napkins, and in ten minutes were all right again.

'"Hope and keep busy", that's the motto for us, so let's see who will remember it best. I shall go to Aunt March, as usual. Oh, won't she lecture though!' said Jo, as she sipped with returning spirit.

'I shall go to my Kings, though I'd much rather stay at home and attend to things here,' said Meg, wishing she hadn't made her eyes so red.

'No need of that, Beth and I can keep house perfectly well,' put in Amy, with an important air.

'Hannah will tell us what to do, and we'll have everything nice when you come home,' added Beth, getting out her mop and dish-tub without delay.

'I think anxiety is very interesting,' observed Amy, eating sugar, pensively.

The girls couldn't help laughing, and felt better for it, though Meg shook her head at the young lady who could find consolation in a sugar-bowl.

The sight of the turnovers made Jo sober again; and when the two went out to their daily tasks, they looked sorrowfully back at the window where they were accustomed to see their mother's face. It was gone; but Beth had remembered the little household ceremony, and there she was, nodding away at them like a rosy-faced mandarin.

'That's so like my Beth!' said Jo, waving her hat, with a grateful face. 'Good-bye, Meggy; I hope the Kings won't train today. Don't fret about Father, dear,' she added, as they parted.

'And I hope Aunt March won't croak. Your hair *is* becoming, and it looks very boyish and nice,' returned Meg, trying not to smile at the curly head, which looked comically small on her tall sister's shoulders.

'That's my only comfort'; and, touching her hat, *à la* Laurie, away went Jo, feeling like a shorn sheep on a wintry day.

News from their father comforted the girls very much; for, though dangerously ill, the presence of the best and tenderest of nurses had already done him good. Mr Brooke sent a bulletin every day, and, as the head of the family, Meg insisted on reading the dispatches, which grew more and more cheering as the week passed. At first, everyone was eager to write, and plump envelopes were carefully poked into the letterbox by one or other of the sisters, who felt rather important with their Washington correspondence. As one of these packets contained characteristic notes from the party, we will rob an imaginary mail, and read them:

MY DEAREST MOTHER – It is impossible to tell you how happy your last letter made us, for the news was so good

we couldn't help laughing and crying over it. How very kind Mr Brooke is, and how fortunate that Mr Laurence's business detains him near you so long, since he is so useful to you and Father. The girls are all as good as gold. Jo helps me with the sewing, and insists on doing all sorts of hard jobs. I should be afraid she might overdo, if I didn't know that her 'moral fit' wouldn't last long. Beth is as regular about her tasks as a clock, and never forgets what you told her. She grieves about Father, and looks sober except when she is at her little piano. Amy minds me nicely, and I take great care of her. She does her own hair, and I am teaching her how to make buttonholes, and mend her stockings. She tries very hard, and I know you will be pleased with her improvement when you come. Mr Laurence watches over us like a motherly old hen, as Jo says; and Laurie is very kind and neighbourly. He and Jo keep us merry, for we get pretty blue sometimes, and feel like orphans, with you so far away. Hannah is a perfect saint; she does not scold at all, and always calls me Miss 'Margaret', which is quite proper, you know, and treats me with respect. We are all well and busy; but we long day and night to have you back. Give my dearest love to Father, and believe me, ever your own
MEG.

This note, prettily written on scented paper, was a great contrast to the next, which was scribbled on a big sheet of thin foreign paper, ornamented with blots and all manner of flourishes and curly-tailed letters:

MY PRECIOUS MARMEE – Three cheers for dear Father. Brooke was a trump to telegraph right off, and let us know the minute he was better. I rushed up garret when the letter came and tried to thank God for being so good

to us; but I could only cry, and say, 'I'm glad! I'm glad!'
Didn't that do as well as a regular prayer? for I felt a great
many in my heart. We have such funny times; and now I
can enjoy them, for everyone is so desperately good, it's
like living in a nest of turtle doves. You'd laugh to see
Meg head the table and try to be motherish. She gets
prettier every day, and I'm in love with her sometimes.
The children are regular archangels, and I – well, I'm Jo,
and never shall be anything else. Oh, I must tell you that
I came near having a quarrel with Laurie. I freed my
mind about a silly little thing, and he was offended. I was
right, but didn't speak as I ought, and he marched home,
saying he wouldn't come again till I begged pardon. I
declared I wouldn't and got mad. It lasted all day; I felt
bad, and wanted you very much. Laurie and I are both so
proud, it's hard to beg pardon; but I thought he'd come to
it, for I *was* in the right. He didn't come; and just at night
I remembered what you said when Amy fell into the
river. I read my little book, felt better, resolved not to let
the sun set on *my* anger, and ran over to tell Laurie I was
sorry. I met him at the gate, coming for the same thing.
We both laughed, begged each other's pardon, and felt all
good and comfortable again.

I made a 'pome' yesterday, when I was helping Hannah
wash; and, as Father likes my silly little things, I put it
in to amuse him. Give him the lovingest hug that ever
was, and kiss yourself a dozen times for your

Topsy-Turvy Jo.

A SONG FROM THE SUDS

    Queen of my tub, I merrily sing,
    While the white foam rises high;
    And sturdily wash and rinse and wring,

And fasten the clothes to dry;
Then out in the free, fresh air they swing,
Under the sunny sky.

I wish we could wash from our hearts and souls
The stains of the week away,
And let water and air by their magic make
Ourselves as pure as they;
Then on the earth there would be indeed
A glorious washing day!

Along the path of a useful life,
Will heart's-ease ever bloom;
The busy mind has no time to think
Of sorrow or care or gloom;
And anxious thoughts may be swept away,
As we bravely wield a broom.

I am glad a task to me is given,
To labour at day by day;
For it brings me health and strength and hope,
And I cheerfully learn to say, –
'Head, you may think, Heart, you may feel,
But, Hand, you shall work alway!'

DEAR MOTHER – There is only room for me to send my
love and some pressed pansies from the root I have been
keeping safe in the house for Father to see. I read every
morning, try to be good all day, and sing myself to sleep
with Father's tune. I can't sing 'Land of the Leal' now; it
makes me cry. Everyone is very kind, and we are as happy
as we can be without you. Amy wants the rest of the page,
so I must stop. I didn't forget to cover the holders, and I
wind the clock and air the rooms every day.
Kiss dear Father on the cheek he calls mine. Oh, do

come soon to your loving
LITTLE BETH.

MA CHÈRE MAMMA – We are all well I do my lessons
always and never corroberate the girls – Meg says I mean
contradick so I put in both words and you can take the
properest. Meg is a great comfort to me and lets me have
jelly every night at tea its so good for me Jo says because
it keeps me sweet tempered. Laurie is not as respeckful
as he ought to be now I am almost in my teens, he calls
me Chick and hurts my feelings by talking French to me
very fast when I say Merci or Bon jour as Hattie King
does. The sleeves of my blue dress were all worn out, and
Meg put in new ones, but the full front came wrong and
they are more blue than the dress. I felt bad but did not
fret I bear my troubles well but I do wish Hannah would
put more starch in my aprons and have buckwheats
every day. Can't she? Didn't I make that interrigation
point nice? Meg says my punchtuation and spelling are
disgraceful and I am mortyfied but dear me I have so
many things to do, I can't stop. Adieu, I send heaps of
love to Papa – Your affectionate daughter
AMY CURTIS MARCH.

DEAR MIS MARCH – I jes drop a line to say we git on fust
rate. The girls is clever and fly round right smart. Miss
Meg is going to make a proper good housekeeper; she hes
the liking for it, and gits the hang of things surprisin
quick. Jo doos beat all for going ahead, but she don't stop
to cal'k'late fust, and you never know where she's like to
bring up. She done out a tub of clothes on Monday, but
she starched em afore they was wrenched, and blued a
pink calico dress till I thought I should a died a laughin.
Beth is the best of little creeters, and a sight of help to me,
bein so forehanded and dependable. She tries to learn

everything, and really goes to market beyond her years;
likewise keeps accounts, with my help, quite wonderful.
We have got on very economical so fur; I don't let the
girls hev coffee only once a week, accordin to your wish,
and keep em on plain wholesome vittles. Amy does well
about frettin, wearin her best clothes and eatin sweet
stuff. Mr Laurie is as full of didoes as usual, and turns the
house upside down frequent; but he heartens up the girls,
and so I let em hev full swing. The old gentleman sends
heaps of things, and is rather wearin, but means wal, and
it aint my place to say nothin. My bread is riz, so no more
at this time. I send my duty to Mr March, and hope he's
seen the last of his Pewmonia – Yours Respectful,
HANNAH MULLET.

HEAD NURSE OF WARD No. 2 – All serene on the
Rappahannock, troops in fine condition, commissary
department well conducted, the Home Guard under
Colonel Teddy always on duty, Commander-in-Chief
General Laurence reviews the army daily, Quartermaster
Mullet keeps order in camp, and Major Lion does picket
duty at night. A salute of twenty-four guns was fired on
receipt of good news from Washington, and a dress
parade took place at head-quarters. Commander-in-chief
sends best wishes, in which he is heartily joined by
COLONEL TEDDY.

DEAR MADAM – The little girls are well; Beth and my boy
report daily; Hannah is a model servant, and guards
pretty Meg like a dragon. Glad the fine weather holds;
pray make Brooke useful, and draw on me for funds if
expenses exceed your estimate. Don't let your husband
want anything. Thank God he is mending – Your sincere
friend and servant,
JAMES LAURENCE.

CHAPTER 17

Little Faithful

For a week the amount of virtue in the old house would have supplied the neighbourhood. It was really amazing, for everyone seemed in a heavenly frame of mind, and self-denial was all the fashion. Relieved of their first anxiety about their father the girls insensibly relaxed their praise-worthy efforts a little, and began to fall back into the old ways. They did not forget their motto, but hoping and keeping busy seemed to grow easier; and after such tremendous exertions, they felt that Endeavour deserved a holiday, and gave it a good many.

Jo caught a bad cold through neglect to cover the shorn head enough, and was ordered to stay at home till she was better, for Aunt March didn't like to hear people read with cold in their heads. Jo liked this, and after an energetic rummage from garret to cellar, subsided on the sofa to nurse her cold with arsenicum and books. Amy found that house-work and art did not go well together, and returned to her mud pies. Meg went daily to her pupils, and sewed, or thought she did, at home, but much time was spent in writing long letters to her mother, or reading the Washington dispatches over and over. Beth kept on, with only slight relapses into idleness or grieving.

All the little duties were faithfully done each day, and many of her sisters' also, for they were forgetful, and the house seemed like a clock whose pendulum was gone a-visiting. When her heart got heavy with longings for Mother or fears for Father, she went away into a certain closet, hid her face in the folds of a certain dear old gown, and made her little moan and prayed her little prayer quietly by herself. Nobody knew what cheered her up after a sober fit, but everyone felt how sweet and helpful Beth was, and fell into a way of going to her for comfort or advice in their small affairs.

All were unconscious that this experience was a test of character; and when the first excitement was over, felt that they had done well, and deserved praise. So they did; but their mistake was in ceasing to do well, and they learned this lesson through much anxiety and regret.

'Meg, I wish you'd go and see the Hummels; you know Mother told us not to forget them,' said Beth, ten days after Mrs March's departure.

'I'm too tired to go this afternoon,' replied Meg, rocking comfortably as she sewed.

'Can't you, Jo?' asked Beth.

'Too stormy for me with my cold.'

'I thought it was almost well.'

'It's well enough for me to go out with Laurie, but not well enough to go to the Hummels',' said Jo, laughing, but looking a little ashamed of her inconsistency.

'Why don't you go yourself?' asked Meg.

'I *have* been every day, but the baby is sick, and I don't know what to do for it. Mrs Hummel goes away to work, and Lottchen takes care of it; but it gets sicker and sicker, and I think you or Hannah ought to go.'

Beth spoke earnestly, and Meg promised she would go tomorrow.

'Ask Hannah for some nice little mess, and take it round, Beth; the air will do you good,' said Jo, adding apologetically, 'I'd go, but I want to finish my writing.'

'My head aches and I'm tired, so I thought maybe some of you would go,' said Beth.

LITTLE WOMEN

'Amy will be in presently, and she will run down for us,' suggested Meg.

'Well, I'll rest a little and wait for her.'

So Beth lay down on the sofa, and others returned to their work, and the Hummels were forgotten. An hour passed: Amy did not come; Meg went to her room to try on a new dress; Jo was absorbed in her story, and Hannah was sound asleep before the kitchen fire, when Beth quietly put on her hood, filled her basket with odds and ends for the poor children, and went out into the chilly air, with a heavy head, and a grieved look in her patient eyes. It was late when she came back, and no one saw her creep upstairs and shut herself into her mother's room. Half an hour after, Jo went to 'Mother's closet' for something, and there found Beth sitting on the medicine chest looking very grave, with red eyes, and a camphor-bottle in her hand.

'Christopher Columbus! What's the matter?' cried Jo, as Beth put out her hand as if to warn her off, and asked quickly:

'You've had the scarlet fever, haven't you?'

'Years ago, when Meg did. Why?'

'Then I'll tell you. Oh, Jo, the baby's dead!'

'What baby?'

'Mrs Hummel's; it died in my lap before she got home,' cried Beth, with a sob.

'My poor dear, how dreadful for you! I ought to have gone,' said Jo, taking her sister in her arms as she sat down in her mother's big chair, with a remorseful face.

'It wasn't dreadful, Jo, only so sad! I saw in a minute that it was sicker, but Lottchen said her mother had gone for a doctor, so I took baby and let Lotty rest. It seemed asleep, but all of a sudden it gave a little cry, and trembled, and then lay very still. I tried to warm its feet, and Lotty gave it some milk, but it didn't stir, and I knew it was dead.'

'Don't cry, dear! What did you do?'

'I just sat and held it softly till Mrs Hummel came with the doctor. He said it was dead, and looked at Heinrich and Minna, who have got sore throats. "Scarlet fever, ma'am. Ought to have called me before," he said, crossly. Mrs Hummel told him she was poor, and had tried to cure baby herself, but now it was too late, and she could only ask him to help the others, and trust to charity for his pay. He smiled then, and was kinder; but it was very sad, and I cried with them till he turned round, all of a sudden, and told me to go home and take belladonna right away, or I'd have the fever.'

'No, you won't!' cried Jo, hugging her close, with a frightened look. 'Oh, Beth, if you should be sick I never could forgive myself! What *shall* we do?'

'Don't be frightened, I guess I shan't have it badly. I looked in Mother's book, and saw that it begins with headache, sore throat, and queer feelings like mine, so I did take some belladonna, and I feel better,' said Beth, laying her cold hands on her hot forehead, and trying to look well.

'If Mother was only at home!' exclaimed Jo, seizing the book, and feeling that Washington was an immense way off. She read a page, looked at Beth, felt her head, peeped into her throat, and then said gravely, 'You've been over the baby for more than a week, and among the others who are going to have it; so I'm afraid *you* are going to have it, Beth. I'll call Hannah, she knows all about sickness.'

'Don't let Amy come: she never had it, and I should hate to give it to her. Can't you and Meg have it over again?' asked Beth anxiously.

'I guess not; don't care if I do; serve me right, selfish pig, to let you go, and stay writing rubbish myself!' muttered Jo, as she went to consult Hannah.

The good soul was wide awake in a minute, and took the lead at once, assuring Jo that there was no need to worry, everyone had scarlet fever, and, if rightly treated, nobody died – all of which Jo believed, and felt much relieved as they went up to call Meg.

'Now I'll tell you what we'll do,' said Hannah, when she had examined and questioned Beth; 'we will have Dr Bangs, just to take a look at you, dear, and see that we start right; then we'll send

Amy off to Aunt March's for a spell, to keep her out of harm's way, and one of you girls can stay at home and amuse Beth for a day or two.'

'I shall stay, of course; I'm oldest,' began Meg, looking anxious and self-reproachful.

'*I* shall, because it's my fault she is sick; I told Mother I'd do the errands, and I haven't,' said Jo, decidedly.

'Which will you have, Beth? there ain't no need of but one,' said Hannah.

'Jo, please,' and Beth leaned her head against her sister, with a contented look, which effectually settled that point.

'I'll go and tell Amy,' said Meg, feeling a little hurt, yet rather relieved on the whole, for she did not like nursing, and Jo did.

Amy rebelled outright, and passionately declared that she had rather have the fever than go to Aunt March. Meg reasoned, pleaded, and commanded: all in vain. Amy protested that she would *not* go; and Meg left her in despair, to ask Hannah what should be done. Before she came back, Laurie walked into the parlour to find Amy sobbing, with her head in the sofa cushions. She told her story, expecting to be consoled; but Laurie only put his hands in his pockets, and walked about the room, whistling softly, as he knit his brows in deep thought. Presently he sat down beside her, and said, in his most wheedlesome tone, 'Now, be a sensible little woman, and do as they say. No, don't cry, but hear what a jolly plan I've got. You go to Aunt March's, and I'll come and take you out every day driving or walking, and we'll have capital times. Won't that be better than moping here?'

'I don't wish to be sent off as if I was in the way,' began Amy, in an injured voice.

'Bless your heart, child, it's to keep you well. You don't want to be sick, do you?'

'No, I'm sure I don't; but I dare say I shall be, for I've been with Beth all the time.'

'That's the very reason you ought to go away at once, so that you may escape it. Change of air and care will keep you well, I dare say; or, if it does not entirely, you will have the fever more lightly. I advise you to be off as soon as you can, for scarlet fever is no joke, miss.'

'But it's dull at Aunt March's, and she is so cross,' said Amy, looking rather frightened.

'It won't be dull with me popping in every day to tell you how Beth is, and take you out gallivanting. The old lady likes me, and I'll be as sweet as possible to her, so she won't peck at us, whatever we do.'

'Will you take me out in the trotting waggon with Puck?'

'On my honour as a gentleman.'

'And come every single day?'

'See if I don't.'

'And bring me back the minute Beth is well?'

'The identical minute.'

'And go to the hall, truly?'

'A dozen halls, if we may.'

'Well – I guess – I will,' said Amy, slowly.

'Good girl! Call Meg, and tell her you'll give in,' said Laurie, with an approving pat, which annoyed Amy more than the 'giving in'.

Meg and Jo came running down to behold the miracle which had been wrought and Amy, feeling very precious and self-sacrificing, promised to go, if the doctor said Beth was going to be ill.

'How is the little dear?' asked Laurie; for Beth was his especial pet, and he felt more anxious about her than he liked to show.

'She is lying down on Mother's bed, and feels better. The baby's death troubled her, but I dare say she has only got cold. Hannah *says* she thinks so; but she *looks* worried, and that makes me fidgety,' answered Meg.

'What a trying world it is!' said Jo, rumpling up her hair in a fretful sort of way. 'No sooner do we get out of one trouble than down comes another. There doesn't seem to be anything to hold on to when Mother's gone; so I'm all at sea.'

'Well, don't make a porcupine of yourself, it isn't becoming. Settle your wig, Jo, and tell me if I shall telegraph to your mother or do anything?' asked Laurie, who never had been reconciled to the loss of his friend's one beauty.

'That is what troubles me,' said Meg. 'I think we ought to tell her if Beth is really ill, but Hannah says we mustn't, for Mother can't leave Father, and it will only make them anxious. Beth won't be sick long, and Hannah knows just what to do, and Mother said we were to mind her, so I suppose we must, but it doesn't seem quite right to me.'

'Hum, well, I can't say; suppose you ask grandfather after the doctor has been.'

'We will. Jo, go and get Dr Bangs at once,' commanded Meg; 'we can't decide anything till he has been.'

'Stay where you are, Jo; I'm errand-boy to this establishment,' said Laurie, taking up his cap.

'I'm afraid you are busy,' began Meg.

'No, I've done my lessons for today.'

'Do you study in vacation time?' asked Jo.

'I follow the good example my neighbours set me,' was Laurie's answer, as he swung himself out of the room.

'I have great hopes of my boy,' observed Jo, watching him fly over the fence with an approving smile.

'He does very well – for a boy,' was Meg's somewhat ungracious answer, for the subject did not interest her.

Dr Bangs came, said Beth had symptoms of the fever, but thought she would have it lightly, though he looked sober over the Hummel story. Amy was ordered off at once, and, provided with something to ward off danger, she departed in great state, with Jo and Laurie as escort.

Aunt March received them with her usual hospitality.

'What do you want now?' she asked, looking sharply over her spectacles, while the parrot, sitting on the back of her chair, called out:

'Go away. No boys allowed here.'

Laurie retired to the window, and Jo told her story.

'No more than I expected, if you are allowed to go poking

about among poor folks. Amy can stay and make herself useful, if she isn't sick, which I've no doubt she will be – looks like it now. Don't cry, child, it worries me to hear people sniff.'

Amy *was* on the point of crying, but Laurie slyly pulled the parrot's tail, which caused Polly to utter an astonished croak, and call out, 'Bless my boots!' in such a funny way, that she laughed instead.

'What do you hear from your mother?' asked the old lady, gruffly.

'Father is much better,' replied Jo, trying to keep sober.

'Oh, is he? Well, that won't last long, I fancy; March never had any stamina,' was the cheerful reply.

'Hah, ha! never say die, take a pinch of snuff, good-bye, good-bye!' squalled Polly, dancing on her perch, and clawing at the old lady's cap as Laurie tweaked him in the rear.

'Hold your tongue, you disrespectful old bird! and, Jo, you'd better go at once; it isn't proper to be gadding about so late with a rattle-pated boy like –'

'Hold your tongue, you disrespectful old bird!' cried Polly, tumbling off the chair with a bounce, and running to peck the 'rattle-pated boy', who was shaking with laughter at the last speech.

'I don't think I *can* bear it, but I'll try,' thought Amy, as she was left alone with Aunt March.

'Get along, you fright!' screamed Polly; and at that rude speech Amy could not restrain a sniff.

CHAPTER 18

Dark Days

Beth did have the fever, and was much sicker than anyone but Hannah and the doctor suspected. The girls knew nothing about illness, and Mr Laurence was not allowed to see her, so Hannah had everything all her own way, and busy Dr Bangs did his best, but left a good deal to the excellent nurse. Meg stayed at home, lest she should infect the Kings, and kept house, feeling very anxious and a little guilty when she wrote letters in which no mention was made of Beth's illness. She could not think it right to deceive her mother, but she had been bidden to mind Hannah, and Hannah wouldn't hear of 'Mrs March bein' told, and worried just for sech a trifle'. Jo devoted herself to Beth day and night; not a hard task, for Beth was very patient, and bore her pain uncomplainingly, as long as she could control herself. But there came a time when during the fever fits she began to talk in a hoarse, broken voice, to play on the coverlet, as if on her beloved little piano, and try to sing with a throat so swollen that there was no music left; a time when she did not know the familiar faces round her, but addressed them by wrong names, and called imploringly for her mother. Then Jo grew frightened, Meg begged to be allowed to write the truth, and even Hannah said she 'would think of it, though there was no danger *yet*'. A letter from Washington added to their trouble, for Mr March had had a relapse, and could not think of coming home for a long while.

How dark the days seemed now, how sad and lonely the house, and how heavy were the hearts of the sisters as they worked and waited, while the shadow of death hovered over the once happy home! Then it was that Margaret, sitting alone with tears dropping often on her work, felt how rich she had been in things more precious than any luxuries money could buy – in love, protection, peace, and health, the real blessings of life. Then it was that Jo, living in the darkened room with that suffering little sister always before her eyes, and that pathetic voice sounding in her ears, learned to see the beauty and the sweetness of Beth's nature, to feel how deep and tender a place she filled in all hearts, and to acknowledge the worth of Beth's unselfish ambition to live for others, and make home happy by the exercise of those simple virtues which all may possess, and which all should love and value more than talent, wealth, or beauty. And Amy, in her exile, longed eagerly to be at home, that she might work for Beth, feeling now that no service would be hard or irksome, and remembering, with regretful grief, how many neglected tasks those willing hands had done for her. Laurie haunted the house like a restless ghost, and Mr Laurence locked the grand piano, because he could not bear to be reminded of the young neighbour who used to make the twilight pleasant for him. Everyone missed Beth. The milkman, baker, grocer, and butcher inquired how she did; poor Mrs Hummel came to beg pardon for her thoughtlessness, and to get a shroud for Minna; the neighbours sent all sorts of comforts and good wishes, and even those who knew her best, were surprised to find how many friends shy little Beth had made.

Meanwhile she lay on her bed with old Joanna at her side, for even in her wanderings she did not forget her forlorn protégée. She longed for her cats, but would not have them brought, lest they should get sick; and, in her quiet hours, she was full of anxiety about Jo. She sent loving messages to Amy, bade them tell her mother that she would write soon; and often begged for pencil and paper to try and say a word, that Father might not think she had neglected him. But soon even these intervals of consciousness ended, and she lay hour after hour, tossing to and fro, with incoherent words on her lips, or sank into a heavy sleep which brought her no refreshment. Dr Bangs came twice a day, Hannah sat up at night, Meg kept a telegram in her desk all ready to send off at any minute, and Jo never stirred from Beth's side.

The first of December was a wintry day indeed to them, for a bitter wind blew, snow fell fast, and the year seemed getting ready for its death. When Dr Bangs came that morning, he looked long at Beth, held the hot hand in both his own a minute, and laid it gently down, saying, in a low tone, to Hannah: 'If Mrs March *can* leave her husband she'd better be sent for.'

Hannah nodded without speaking, for her lips twitched nervously; Meg dropped down into a chair as the strength seemed to go out of her limbs at the sound of those words: and Jo, after standing with a pale face for a minute, ran to the parlour, snatched up the telegram, and, throwing on her things, rushed out into the storm. She was soon back, and, while noiselessly taking off her cloak, Laurie came in with a letter, saying that Mr March was mending again. Jo read it thankfully, but the heavy weight did not seem lifted off her heart, and her face was so full of misery that Laurie asked quickly: 'What is it? is Beth worse?'

'I've sent for Mother,' said Jo, tugging at her rubber boots with a tragical expression.

'Good for you, Jo! Did you do it on your own responsibility?' asked Laurie, as he seated her in the hall chair, and took off the rebellious boots, seeing how her hands shook.

'No, the doctor told us to.'

'Oh, Jo, it's not so bad as that?' cried Laurie, with a startled face.

'Yes, it is; she doesn't know us, she doesn't even talk about the flocks of green doves, as she calls the vine leaves on the wall; she doesn't look like my Beth, and there's nobody to help us bear it; Mother and Father both gone, and God seems so far away I can't find him.'

As the tears streamed fast down poor Jo's cheeks, she stretched out her hand in a helpless sort of way, as if groping in the dark, and Laurie took it in his, whispering as well as he could, with a lump in his throat: 'I'm here. Hold on to me, Jo, dear!'

She could not speak, but she did 'Hold on', and the warm grasp of the friendly human hand comforted her sore heart, and seemed to lead her nearer to the Divine arm which alone could uphold her in her trouble. Laurie longed to say something tender and comfortable, but no fitting words came to him, so he stood silent, gently stroking her bent head as her mother used to do. It was the best thing he could have done; far more soothing than the most eloquent words, for Jo felt the unspoken sympathy, and in the silence, learned the sweet solace which affection administers to sorrow. Soon she dried the tears which had relieved her, and looked up with a grateful face.

'Thank you, Teddy, I'm better now; I don't feel so forlorn, and will try to bear it if it comes.'

'Keep hoping for the best; that will help you, Jo. Soon your mother will be here, and then everything will be right.'

'I'm so glad Father is better; now she won't feel so bad about leaving him. Oh, me! it does seem as if all the troubles came in a heap, and I got the heaviest part on my shoulders,' sighed Jo, spreading her wet handkerchief over her knees to dry.

'Doesn't Meg pull fair?' asked Laurie, looking indignant.

'Oh, yes; she tries to, but she can't love Bethy as I do; and she won't miss her as I shall. Beth is my conscience, and I *can't* give her up. I can't! I can't!'

Down went Jo's face into the wet handkerchief, and she cried despairingly; for she had kept up bravely till now, and never shed a tear. Laurie drew his hand across his eyes, but could not speak till he had subdued the choking feeling in his throat and steadied his lips. It might be unmanly, but he couldn't help it, and I'm glad of it. Presently as Jo's sobs quieted, he said hopefully, 'I don't think she will die; she's so good, and we all love her so much, I don't believe God will take her away yet.'

'The good and dear people always do die,' groaned Jo, but she stopped crying, for her friend's words cheered her up, in spite of her own doubts and fears.

'Poor girl, you're worn out. It isn't like you to be forlorn. Stop a bit; I'll hearten you up in a jiffy.'

Laurie went off two stairs at a time, and Jo laid her wearied head down on Beth's little brown hood, which no one had thought of moving from the table where she left it. It must have possessed some magic, for the submissive spirit of its gentle owner seemed to enter into Jo; and, when Laurie came running down with a glass of wine, she took it with a smile and said bravely, 'I drink health to my Beth! You are a good doctor, Teddy, and *such* a comfortable friend; how can I ever pay you?' she added; the kind words had refreshed her troubled mind.

'I'll send in my bill, by and by; and tonight I'll give you something that will warm the cockles of your heart better than quarts of wine,' said Laurie, beaming at her with a face of suppressed satisfaction at something.

'What is it?' cried Jo, forgetting her woes for a minute, in her wonder.

'I telegraphed to your mother yesterday, and Brooke answered she'd come at once, and she'll be here tonight, and everything will be all right. Aren't you glad I did it?'

Laurie spoke very fast, and turned red and excited all in a minute, for he had kept his plot a secret, for fear of disappointing the girls or harming Beth. Jo grew quite white, flew out of her chair, and the moment he stopped speaking she electrified him by throwing her arms round his neck, and crying out, with a joyful cry, 'Oh, Laurie! Oh, Mother! I *am* so glad!' She did not weep again, but laughed hysterically, and trembled and clung to her friend as if she was a little bewildered by the sudden news.

Laurie, though decidedly amazed, behaved with great presence of mind; he patted her back soothingly and, finding that she was recovering, followed it up by a bashful kiss or two, which brought Jo round at once. Holding on to the bannisters, she put him gently away, saying breathlessly, 'Oh, don't! I didn't mean to; it was dreadful of me; but you were such a dear to go and do it in spite of Hannah that I couldn't help flying at you. Tell me all about it, and don't give me wine again; it makes me act so stupidly.'

'I don't mind,' laughed Laurie, as he settled his tie. 'Why, you see I got fidgety, and so did grandpa. We thought Hannah was over-doing the authority business, and your mother ought to know. She'd never forgive us if Beth – well, if anything happened, you know. So I got grandpa to say it was high time we did something, and off I pelted to the office yesterday, for the doctor looked sober, and Hannah 'most took my head off when I proposed a telegram. I *never* can bear to be "lorded" over, so that settled my mind, and I did it. Your mother will come, I know, and the late train is in at 2 a.m. I shall go for her, and you've only got to bottle up your rapture, and keep Beth quiet, till that blessed lady gets here.'

'Laurie, you're an angel! How shall I ever thank you?'

'Fly at me again; I rather like it,' said Laurie, looking mischievous – a thing he had not done for a fortnight.

'No, thank you. I'll do it by proxy, when your grandpa comes. Don't tease, but go home and rest, for you'll be up half the night. Bless you, Teddy, bless you!'

Jo had backed into a corner; and, as she finished her speech, she vanished precipitately into the kitchen, where she sat down upon a dresser, and told the assembled cats, that she was 'happy, oh, *so* happy!' while Laurie departed, feeling that he had made rather a neat thing of it.

'That's the interferingest chap I ever see; but I forgive him, and do hope Mrs March is coming on right away,' said Hannah, with an air of relief, when Jo told the good news.

Meg had a quiet rapture, and then brooded over the letter, while Jo set the sickroom in order, and Hannah 'knocked up a couple of pies in case of company unexpected'. A breath of fresh air seemed to blow through the house, and something better than sunshine brightened the quiet rooms. Everything appeared to feel the hopeful change; Beth's bird began to chirp again, and a half-blown rose was discovered on Amy's bush in the window, and fires seemed to burn with unusual cheeriness; and every time the girls met, their pale faces broke into smiles as they hugged one another, whispering encouragingly, 'Mother's coming, dear! Mother's coming!' Everyone rejoiced but Beth; she lay in that heavy stupor, alike unconscious of hope and joy, doubt and anger. It was a piteous sight – the once rosy face so changed and vacant, the once busy hands so weak and wasted, the once smiling lips quite dumb, and the once pretty, well-kept hair scattered rough and tangled on the pillow. All day she lay so, only rousing now and then to mutter, 'Water!' with lips so parched they could hardly shape the word; all day Jo and Meg hovered over her, watching, waiting, hoping, and trusting in God and Mother; and all day the snow fell, the bitter wind raged, and the hours dragged slowly by. But night came at last; and every time the clock struck, the sisters, still sitting on either side of the bed, looked at each other with brightening eyes, for each hour brought help nearer. The doctor had been in to say that some change, for better or worse, would probably take place about midnight, at which time he would return.

Hannah, quite worn out, lay down on the sofa at the bed's foot, and fell fast asleep; Mr Laurence marched to and fro in the parlour, feeling that he would rather face a rebel battery than Mrs March's anxious countenance as she entered; Laurie lay on the rug, pretending to rest, but staring into the fire with the thoughtful look which made his black eyes beautifully soft and clear.

The girls never forgot that night, for no sleep came to them, as they kept their watch with that dreadful sense of powerlessness which comes to us in hours like those.

'If God spares Beth I never will complain again,' whispered Meg, earnestly.

'If God spares Beth I'll try to love and serve him all my life,' answered Jo, with equal fervour.

'I wish I had no heart, it aches so,' sighed Meg, after a pause.

'If life is often as hard as this, I don't see how we ever shall get through it,' added her sister, despondently.

Here the clock struck twelve, and both forgot themselves in watching Beth, for they fancied a change passed over her wan face.

The house was still as death, and nothing but the wailing of the wind broke the deep hush. Weary Hannah slept on, and no one but the sisters saw the pale shadow which seemed to fall upon the little bed. An hour went by, and nothing happened except Laurie's quiet departure for the station. Another hour – still no one came; and anxious fears of delay in the storm or accidents by the way, or, worst of all, a great grief at Washington, haunted the poor girls.

It was past two, when Jo, who stood at the window thinking how dreary the world looked in its winding-sheet of snow, heard a movement by the bed, and, turning quickly, saw Meg kneeling before her mother's easy-chair, with her face hidden. A dreadful fear passed coldly over Jo, as she thought, 'Beth is dead, and Meg is afraid to tell me.'

She was back in her post in an instant, and to her excited eyes a great change seemed to have taken place. The fever flush and the look of pain were gone, and the beloved little face looked so pale and peaceful in its utter repose, that Jo felt no desire to weep or to lament. Leaning low over this dearest of her sisters, she kissed the damp forehead with her heart on her lips, and softly whispered, 'Good-bye, my Beth; goodbye!'

As if waked by the stir, Hannah started out of her sleep, hurried to the bed, looked at Beth, felt her hands, listened at her lips, and then, throwing her apron over her head, sat down to rock to and fro, exclaiming, under her breath, 'The fever's turned; she's sleeping nat'ral; her skin's damp, and she breathes easy. Praise be given! Oh, my goodness me!'

Before the girls could believe the happy truth, the doctor came to confirm it. He was a homely man, but they thought his face quite heavenly when he smiled, and said, with a fatherly look at them, 'Yes, my dears, I think the little girl will pull through this time. Keep the house quiet; let her sleep, and when she wakes, give her –'

What they were to give, neither heard; for both crept into the dark hall, and sitting on the stairs, held each other close, rejoicing with hearts too full for words. When they went back to be kissed and cuddled by faithful Hannah, they found Beth lying, as she used to do, with her cheek pillowed on her hand, the dreadful pallor gone, and breathing quietly, as if just fallen asleep.

'If Mother would only come now!' said Jo, as the winter night began to wane.

'See,' said Meg, coming up with a white, half-opened rose, 'I thought this would hardly be ready to lay in Beth's hand tomorrow if she – went away from us. But it has blossomed in the night, and now I mean to put it in my vase here, so that when the darling wakes, the first things she sees will be the little rose, and Mother's face.'

Never had the sun risen so beautifully, and never had the world seemed so lovely, as it did to the heavy eyes of Meg and Jo, as they looked out in the early morning, when their long, sad vigil was done.

'It looks like a fairy world,' said Meg, smiling to herself, as she stood behind the curtain, watching the dazzling sight.

'Hark!' cried Jo, starting to her feet.

Yes, there was a sound of bells at the door below, a cry from Hannah, and then Laurie's voice saying, in a joyful whisper, 'Girls, she's come! she's come!'

CHAPTER 19

Amy's Will

While these things were happening at home, Amy was having hard times at Aunt March's. She felt her exile deeply, and, for the first time in her life, realized how much she was beloved and petted at home. Aunt March never petted anyone; she did not approve of it; but she meant to be kind, for the well-behaved little girl pleased her very much, and Aunt March had a soft place in her old heart for her nephew's children, though she didn't think proper to confess it. She really did her best to make Amy happy, but, dear me, what mistakes she made! Some old people keep young at heart in spite of wrinkles and grey hair, can sympathize with children's little cares and joys, make them feel at home, and can hide wise lessons under pleasant plays, giving and receiving friendship in the sweetest way. But Aunt March had not this gift, and she worried Amy very much with her rules and orders, her prim ways, and long, prosy talks. Finding the child more docile and amiable than her sister, the old lady felt it her duty to try and counteract, as far as possible, the bad effects of home freedom and indulgence. So she took Amy in hand, and taught her as she herself had been taught sixty years ago – a process which carried dismay to Amy's soul, and made her feel like a fly in the web of a very strict spider.

She had to wash the cups every morning, and polish up the old-fashioned spoons, the fat silver tea-pot, and the glasses, till they shone. Then she must dust the room, and what a trying job that was! Not a speck escaped Aunt March's eye, and all the furniture had claw legs, and much carving, which was never dusted to suit. Then Polly must be fed, the lap-dog combed, and a dozen trips upstairs and down, to get things, to deliver orders, for the old lady was very lame, and seldom left her big chair. After these tiresome labours, she must do her lessons, which was a daily trial of every virtue she possessed. Then she was allowed one hour for exercise or play, and didn't she enjoy it? Laurie came every day, and wheedled Aunt March, till Amy was allowed to go out with him, when they walked and rode, and had capital times. After dinner, she had to read aloud, and sit still while the old lady slept, which she usually did for an hour, as she dropped off over the first page. Then patchwork or towels appeared, and Amy sewed with outward meekness and inward rebellion till dusk, when she was allowed to amuse herself as she liked till tea-time. The evenings were the worst of all, for Aunt March fell to telling long stories about her youth, which were so unutterably dull that Amy was always ready to go to bed, intending to cry over her hard fate, but usually going to sleep before she had squeezed out more than a tear or two.

If it had not been for Laurie, and old Esther, the maid, she felt that she never could have got through that dreadful time. The parrot alone was enough to drive her distracted, for he soon felt that she did not admire him, and revenged himself by being as mischievous as possible. He pulled her hair whenever she came near him, upset his bread and milk to plague her when she had newly cleaned his cage, made Mop bark by pecking at him while Madam dozed; called her names before company, and behaved in all respects like a reprehensible old bird. Then she could not endure the dog – a fat, cross beast, who snarled and yelped at her when she made his toilet, and who lay on his back, with all his legs in the air and a most idiotic expression of countenance when he wanted something to eat, which was about a dozen times a day. The cook was bad-tempered, the old coachman deaf, and Esther the only one who ever took any notice of the young lady.

Esther was a Frenchwoman, who had lived with 'Madame,' as she called her mistress, for many years, and who rather tyrannized over the old lady, who could not get along without her. Her real name was Estelle, but Aunt March ordered her to change it, and she obeyed, on condition that she was never asked to change her religion. She took a fancy to Mademoiselle, and amused her very much, with odd stories of her life in France, when Amy sat with her while she got up Madame's laces. She also allowed her to roam about the great house, and examine the curious and pretty things stored away in the big wardrobes and the ancient chests; for Aunt March hoarded like a magpie. Amy's chief delight was an Indian cabinet, full of queer drawers, little pigeon-holes, and secret places, in which were kept all sorts of ornaments, some precious, some merely curious, all more or less antique. To examine and arrange these things gave Amy great satisfaction, especially the jewel-cases, in which, on velvet cushions, reposed the ornaments which had adorned a belle forty years ago. There was the garnet set which Aunt March wore when she came out, the pearls her father gave her on her wedding day, her lover's diamonds, the jet mourning rings and pins, and queer lockets, with portraits of dead friends, and weeping willows made of hair inside; the baby bracelets her one little daughter had worn; Uncle March's big watch, with the red seal so many childish hands had played with, and in a box, all by itself, lay Aunt March's wedding-ring, too small now for her fat finger, but put carefully away, like the most precious jewel of them all.

'Which would Mademoiselle choose if she had her will?' asked Esther, who always sat near to watch over and lock up the valuables.

'I liked the diamonds best, but there is no necklace among them, and I'm fond of necklaces, they are so becoming. I should choose this if I might,' replied Amy, looking with great admiration at a string of gold and ebony beads, from which hung a heavy cross of the same.

'I, too, covet that, but not as a necklace; ah, no! to me it is a rosary, and as such I should use it like a good Catholic,' said Esther, eyeing the handsome thing wistfully.

'Is it meant to use as you use the string of good-smelling wooden beads hanging over your glass?' asked Amy.

'Truly, yes, to pray with. It would be pleasing to the saints if one used so fine a rosary as this, instead of wearing it as a vain bijou. If Mademoiselle went apart each day to meditate and pray, as did the good mistress whom I served before Madame, it would be well. She had a little chapel, and in it found solacement for much trouble.'

'Would it be right for me to do so too?' asked Amy, who, in her loneliness, felt the need of help of some sort, and found that she was apt to forget her little book, now that Beth was not there to remind her of it.

'It would be excellent and charming; and I shall gladly arrange the little dressing-room for you if you like it. Say nothing to Madame, but when she sleeps go you and sit alone a while to think good thoughts, and pray the dear God to preserve your sister.'

Esther was truly pious, and quite sincere in her advice; for she had an affectionate heart, and felt much for the sisters in their anxiety. Amy liked the idea and gave her leave to arrange the light closet next her room, hoping it would do her good.

'I wish I knew where all these pretty things would go when Aunt March dies,' she said, as she slowly replaced the shining rosary, and shut the jewel-cases one by one.

'To you and your sisters. I know it; Madame confides in me; I witnessed her will, and it is to be so,' whispered Esther, smiling.

'How nice! but I wish she'd let us have them now. Pro-cras-ti-nation is not agreeable,' observed Amy, taking a last look at the diamonds.

'It is too soon yet for the young ladies to wear these things. The first one who is affianced will have the pearls – Madame has said it; and I have a fancy that the little turquoise ring will be given to you when you go, for Madame approves your good behaviour and charming manners.'

'Do you think so? Oh, I'll be a lamb, if I can only have that lovely ring! It's ever so much prettier than Kitty Bryant's. I do like Aunt March after all'; and Amy tried on the blue ring with a delightful face, and a firm resolve to earn it.

From that day she was a model of obedience, and the old lady complacently admired the success of her training. Esther fitted up the closet with a little table, placed a footstool before it, and over it a picture taken from one of the shut-up rooms. She thought it was of no great value, but, being appropriate, she borrowed it, well knowing that Madame would never know it, nor care if she did. It was, however, a very valuable copy of one of the famous pictures of the world, and Amy's beauty-loving eyes were never tired of looking up at the sweet face of the divine mother, while tender thoughts of her own were busy at her heart. On the table she laid her little testament and hymn-book, kept a vase always full of the best flowers Laurie brought her, and came every day to sit alone, 'thinking good thoughts, and praying the dear God to preserve her sister'. Esther had given her a rosary of black beads, with a silver cross, but Amy hung it up and did not use it, feeling more than doubtful as to its fitness for Protestant prayers.

The little girl was very sincere in all this, for, being left alone outside the safe home-nest, she felt the need of some kind hand to hold by so sorely, that she instinctively turned to the strong and tender friend, whose fatherly love most closely surrounds his little children. She missed her mother's help to understand and rule herself, but having been taught where to look, she did her best to find the way, and walk in it confidingly. But Amy was a young pilgrim, and just now her burden seemed very heavy. She tried to forget herself, to keep cheerful, and be satisfied with doing right, though no one saw or praised her for it. In her first effort at being very, very good, she decided to make her will, as Aunt March had done; so that if she *did* fall ill and die, her possessions might be justly and generously divided. It cost her a pang even to think of giving up the little treasures which in her eyes were as precious as the old lady's jewels.

During one of her play-hours she wrote out the important document as well as she could, with some help from Esther as to certain legal terms, and, when the good-natured Frenchwoman had signed her name, Amy felt relieved, and laid it by to show Laurie, whom she wanted as a second witness. As it was a rainy day, she went upstairs to amuse herself in one of the large chambers, and took Polly with her for company. In this room there was a wardrobe full of old-fashioned costumes, with which Esther allowed her to play, and it was her favourite amusement to array herself in the faded brocades, and parade up and down before the long mirror, making stately courtesies, and sweeping her train about, with a rustle which delighted her ears. So busy was she on this day that she did not hear Laurie's ring, nor see his face peeping in at her, as she gravely promenaded to and fro, flirting her fan and tossing her head, on which she wore a great pink turban, contrasting oddly with her blue brocade dress and yellow quilted petticoat. She was obliged to walk carefully, for she had on high-heeled shoes, and, as Laurie told Jo afterwards, it was a comical sight to see her mince along in her gay suit, with Polly sidling and bridling just behind her, imitating her as well as he could, and occasionally stopping to laugh or exclaim, 'Ain't we fine? Get along, you fright! Hold your tongue! Kiss me, dear! Ha! ha!'

Having with difficulty restrained an explosion of merriment lest it should offend her majesty, Laurie tapped, and was graciously received.

'Sit down and rest while I put these things away; then I want to consult you about a very serious matter,' said Amy, when she had shown her splendour, and driven Polly into a corner. 'That bird is the trial of my life,' she continued, removing the pink mountain from her head, while Laurie seated himself astride of a chair. 'Yesterday, when Aunt was asleep, and I was trying to be as still as a mouse, Polly began to squall and flap about in his cage; so I went to let him out, and found a big spider there. I poked it out, and it ran under the book-case; Polly marched straight after it, stooped down and peeped under the book-case, saying, in his funny way, with a cock of his eye, "Come out and take a walk, my dear." I *couldn't* help laughing, which made Poll swear, and Aunt woke up and scolded us both.'

'Did the spider accept the old fellow's invitation?' asked Laurie, yawning.

'Yes; out it came, and away ran Polly, frightened to death, and scrambled up on Aunt's chair, calling out, "Catch her! catch her! catch her!" as I chased the spider.'

'That's a lie! Oh, lor!' cried the parrot, pecking at Laurie's toes.

'I'd wring your neck if you were mine, you old torment,' cried Laurie, shaking his fist at the bird, who put his head on one side, and gravely croaked, 'Allyluyer! bless your buttons, dear!'

'Now I'm ready,' said Amy, shutting the wardrobe, and taking a paper out of her pocket. 'I want you to read that, please, and tell me if it is legal and right. I felt that I ought to do it, for life is uncertain and I don't want any ill-feeling over my tomb.'

Laurie bit his lips, and turning a little from the pensive speaker read the following document with praiseworthy gravity, considering the spelling:

'MY LAST WILL AND TESTAMENT'

'I, Amy Curtis March, being in my sane mind, do give and bequeath all my earthly property – viz., to wit: – namely

'To my Father, my best pictures, sketches, maps, and works of art, including frames. Also my $100, to do what he likes with.

'To my Mother, all my clothes, except the blue apron with pockets – also my likeness, and my medal, with much love.

'To my dear sister Margaret, I give my turkquoise ring (if I get it), also my green box with the doves on it, also my piece of real lace for her neck, and my sketch of her as a memorial of her "little girl".

'To Jo I leave my breast-pin, the one mended with sealing wax, also my bronze inkstand – she lost the cover – and my most precious plaster rabbit, because I am sorry I burnt up her story.

'To Beth (if she lives after me) I give my dolls and the little bureau, my fan, my linen collars, and my new slippers if she can wear them being thin when she gets well. And I herewith also leave her my regret that I ever made fun of old Joanna.

'To my friend and neighbour Theodore Laurence I bequeath my paper marshay portfolio, my clay model of a horse though he did say it hadn't any neck. Also in return for his great kindness in the hour of affliction any one of my artistic works he likes, Noter Dame is the best.

'To our venerable benefactor Mr Laurence I leave my purple box with a looking glass in the cover which will be nice for his pens and remind him of the departed girl who thanks him for his favours to her family, specially Beth.

'I wish my favourite play mate Kitty Bryant to have the blue silk apron and my gold bead ring with a kiss.

'To Hannah I give the bandbox she wanted and all the patch work I leave hoping she will "remember me, when it you see".

'And now having disposed of my most valuable property I hope all will be satisfied and not blame the dead. I forgive everyone, and trust we may all meet when the trump shall sound. Amen.

'To this will and testament I set my hand and seal on this 20th day of Nov. Anni Domino 1861.

'AMY CURTIS MARCH.'

'*Witnesses* } ESTELLE VALNOR,
                THEODORE LAURENCE.'

The last name was written in pencil, and Amy explained that he was to rewrite it in ink, and seal it up for her properly.

'What put it into your head? Did anyone tell you about Beth's giving away her things?' asked Laurie, soberly, as Amy laid a bit of red tape, with sealing-wax, a taper, and a standish before him.

She explained; and then asked anxiously, 'What about Beth?'

'I'm sorry I spoke: but as I did I'll tell you. She felt so ill one day that she wanted to give her piano to Meg, her cats to you, and the poor old doll to Jo, who would love it for her sake. She was sorry she had so little to give, and left locks of hair to the rest of us, and her best love to grandpa. *She* never thought of a will.'

Laurie was signing and sealing as he spoke, and did not look up till a great tear dropped on the paper. Amy's face was full of trouble; but she only said, 'Don't people put sort of postscripts to their wills, sometimes?'

'Yes; "codicils", they call them.'

'Put one in mine, then – that I wish *all* my curls cut off, and given round to my friends. I forgot it; but I want it done, though it will spoil my looks.'

Laurie added it, smiling at Amy's last and greatest sacrifice. Then he amused her for an hour, and was much interested in all her trials. But when he came to go, Amy held him back to whisper, with trembling lips, 'Is there really any danger about Beth?'

'I'm afraid there is; but we must hope for the best, so don't cry, dear'; and Laurie put his arm about her with a brotherly gesture which was very comforting.

When he had gone, she went to her little room, and sitting in the twilight, prayed for Beth, with streaming tears and an aching heart, feeling that a million turquoise rings would not console her for the loss of her gentle little sister.

CHAPTER 20

Confidential

I don't think I have any words in which to tell the meeting of the mother and daughters; such hours are beautiful to live, but very hard to describe, so I will leave it to the imagination of my readers, merely saying that the house was full of genuine happiness, and that Meg's tender hope was realized; for when Beth woke from that long, healing sleep, the first object on which her eyes fell *were* the little rose and Mother's face. Too weak to wonder at anything, she only smiled, and nestled close into the loving arms about her, feeling that the hungry longing was satisfied at last. Then she slept again, and the girls waited upon their mother; for she would not unclasp the thin hand which clung to hers even in sleep.

Hannah had 'dished up' an astonishing breakfast for the traveller, finding it impossible to vent her excitement in any other way; and Meg and Jo fed their mother like dutiful young storks, while they listened to her whispered account of Father's state, Mr Brooke's promise to stay and nurse him, the delays which the storm occasioned on the homeward journey, and the unspeakable comfort Laurie's hopeful face had given her when she arrived, worn out with fatigue, anxiety, and cold.

What a strange, yet pleasant day that was! so brilliant and gay without, for all the world seemed abroad to welcome the first snow; so quiet and reposeful within, for everyone slept, spent with

watching, and a sabbath stillness reigned through the house, while
nodding Hannah mounted guard at the door. With a blissful sense
of burdens lifted off, Meg and Jo closed their weary eyes, and lay
at rest, like storm-beaten boats, safe at anchor in a quiet harbour.
Mrs March would not leave Beth's side, but rested in the big chair,
waking often to look at, touch, and brood over her child, like a miser
over some recovered treasure.

Laurie, meanwhile, posted off to comfort Amy, and told his
story so well that Aunt March actually 'sniffed' herself, and never
once said, 'I told you so'. Amy came out so strong on this occasion
that I think the good thoughts in the little chapel really began to
bear fruit. She dried her tears quickly, restrained her impatience to
see her mother, and never even thought of the turquoise ring, when
the old lady heartily agreed in Laurie's opinion, that she behaved
'like a capital little woman'. Even Polly seemed impressed, for he
called her 'good girl', blessed her buttons, and begged her to 'come
and take a walk, dear!' in his most affable tone. She would very
gladly have gone out to enjoy the bright wintry weather; but, discov-
ering that Laurie was dropping with sleep in spite of manful efforts
to conceal the fact, she persuaded him to rest on the sofa, while she
wrote a note to her mother. She was a long time about it, and, when
she returned, he was stretched out, with both arms under his head,
sound asleep, while Aunt March had pulled down the curtains, and
sat doing nothing in an unusual fit of benignity.

After a while, they began to think he was not going to wake till
night, and I'm not sure that he would, had he not been effectually
roused by Amy's cry of joy at sight of her mother. There probably
were a good many happy little girls in and about the city that day, but
it is my private opinion that Amy was the happiest of all, when she
sat in her mother's lap and told her trials, receiving consolation and
compensation in the shape of approving smiles and fond caresses. They
were alone together in the little room, to which her mother did not
object when its purpose was explained to her.

'On the contrary, I like it very much, dear,' looking from the
footstool to the well-worn little book, and the lovely picture with

its garland of evergreen. 'It is an excellent plan to have some place where we can go to be quiet, when things vex or grieve us. There are a good many hard times in this life of ours, but we can always bear them if we ask help in the right way. I think my little girl is learning this?'

'Yes, Mother; and when I go home I mean to have a corner in the big closet to put my books, and the copy of that picture which I've tried to make. The woman's face is not good – it's too beautiful for me to draw – but the baby is done better, and I love it very much. I like to think he was a little child once, for then I don't seem so far away, and that helps me.'

As Amy pointed to the smiling Christ-child on his mother's knee, Mrs March saw something on the lifted hand that made her smile. She said nothing, but Amy understood the look, and, after a minute's pause, she added, gravely:

'I wanted to speak to you about this, but I forgot it. Aunt gave me the ring today; she called me to her and kissed me, and put it on my finger, and said I was a credit to her, and she'd like to keep me always. She gave me that funny guard to keep the turquoise on, as it's too big. I'd like to wear them, Mother; can I?'

'They are very pretty, but I think you're rather too young for such ornaments, Amy,' said Mrs March, looking at the plump little hand, with the band of skyblue stones on the forefinger, and the quaint guard, formed of two tiny golden hands clasped together.

'I'll try not to be vain,' said Amy. 'I don't think I like it only because it's so pretty; but I want to wear it as the girl in the story wore her bracelets, to remind me of something.'

'Do you mean Aunt March?' asked her mother, laughing.

'No, to remind me not to be selfish.' Amy looked so earnest and sincere about it, that her mother stopped laughing, and listened respectfully to the little plan.

'I've thought a great deal lately about my "bundle of naughties", and being selfish is the largest one on it; so I'm going to try hard to cure it, if I can. Beth isn't selfish, and that's the reason everyone loves her and feels so bad at the thought of losing her.

People wouldn't feel half so bad about me if I was sick, and I don't deserve to have them; but I'd like to be loved and missed by a great many friends, so I'm going to try and be like Beth all I can. I'm apt to forget my resolutions; but if I had something always about me to remind me, I guess I should do better. May I try this way?'

'Yes; but I have more faith in the corner of the big closet. Wear your ring, dear, and do your best; I think you will prosper, for the sincere wish to be good is half the battle. Now I must go back to Beth. Keep up your heart, little daughter, and we will soon have you home again.'

That evening, while Meg was writing to her father, to report the traveller's safe arrival, Jo slipped upstairs into Beth's room, and, finding her mother in her usual place, stood a minute twisting her fingers in her hair, with a worried gesture and an undecided look.

'What is it, deary?' asked Mrs March, holding out her hand, with a face which invited confidence.

'I want to tell you something, Mother.'

'About Meg?'

'How quickly you guessed! Yes, it's about her, and though it's a little thing, it fidgets me.'

'Beth is asleep; speak low, and tell me all about it. That Moffat hasn't been here, I hope?' asked Mrs March, rather sharply.

'No, I should have shut the door in his face if he had,' said Jo, settling herself on the floor at her mother's feet. 'Last summer Meg left a pair of gloves over at the Laurences', and only one was returned. We forgot all about it, till Teddy told me that Mr Brooke had it. He kept it in his waistcoat pocket, and once it fell out, and Teddy joked him about it, and Mr Brooke owned that he liked Meg, but didn't dare say so, she was so young and he so poor. Now, isn't it a *dreadful* state of things?'

'Do you think Meg cares for him?' asked Mrs March, with an anxious look.

'Mercy me! I don't know anything about love and such nonsense!' cried Jo, with a funny mixture of interest and contempt. 'In novels, the girls show it by starting and blushing, fainting away, growing thin, and acting like fools. Now Meg does not do anything of the sort; she eats and drinks and sleeps, like a sensible creature; she looks straight in my face when I talk about that man, and only blushes a little bit when Teddy jokes about lovers. I forbid him to do it, but he doesn't mind me as he ought.'

'Then you fancy that Meg is *not* interested in John?'

'Who?' cried Jo, staring.

'Mr Brooke. I call him "John" now; we fell into the way of doing so at the hospital, and he likes it.'

'Oh, dear! I know you'll take his part: he's been good to Father, and you won't send him away, but let Meg marry him, if she wants to. Mean thing! to go petting Papa and helping you, just to wheedle you into liking him'; and Jo pulled her hair again with a wrathful tweak.

'My dear, don't get angry about it, and I will tell you how it happened. John went with me at Mr Laurence's request, and was so devoted to poor Father that we couldn't help getting fond of him. He was perfectly open and honourable about Meg, for he told us he loved her, but would earn a comfortable home before he asked her to marry him. He only wanted our leave to love her and work for her, and the right to make her love him if he could. He is a truly excellent young man, and we could not refuse to listen to him; but I will not consent to Meg engaging herself so young.'

'Of course not; it would be idiotic! I knew there was mischief brewing; I felt it; and now it's worse than I imagined. I just wish I could marry Meg myself, and keep her safe in the family.'

This odd arrangement made Mrs March smile; but she said gravely, 'Jo, I confide in you, and don't wish you to say anything to Meg yet. When John comes back, and I see them together, I can judge better of her feelings towards him.'

'She'll see his in those handsome eyes that she talks about, and then it will be all up with her. She's got such a soft heart, it will melt like butter in the sun if anyone looks sentimentally at her. She read the short reports he sent more than she did your letters, and pinched me when I spoke of it, and likes brown eyes, and doesn't think John an ugly name, and she'll go and fall in love, and there's an end of peace and fun, and cosy times together. I see it all! they'll go lovering around the house, and we shall have to dodge; Meg will be absorbed, and no good to me any more; Brooke will scratch up a fortune somehow, carry her off, and make a hole in the family; and I shall break my heart, and everything will be abominably uncomfortable. Oh, dear me! why weren't we all boys, then there wouldn't be any bother.'

Jo leaned her chin on her knees, in a disconsolate attitude, and shook her fist at the reprehensible John. Mrs March sighed, and Jo looked up with an air of relief.

'You don't like it, Mother? I'm glad of it. Let's send him about his business, and not tell Meg a word of it, but all be happy together as we always have been.'

'I did wrong to sigh, Jo. It is natural and right you should all go to homes of your own, in time; but I do want to keep my girls as long as I can; and I am sorry that this happened so soon, for Meg is only seventeen, and it will be some years before John can make a home for her. Your father and I have agreed that she shall not bind herself in any way, nor be married, before twenty. If she and John love one another, they can wait, and test the love by doing so. She is conscientious, and I have no fear of her treating him unkindly. My pretty, tender-hearted girl! I hope things will go happily with her.'

'Hadn't you rather have her marry a rich man?' asked Jo, as her mother's voice faltered a little over the last words.

'Money is a good and useful thing, Jo; and I hope my girls will never feel the need of it too bitterly, nor be tempted by too much. I should like to know that John was firmly established in some good business, which gave him an income large enough to keep free from debt and make Meg comfortable. I'm not ambitious for a splendid fortune, a fashionable position, or a great name for my girls. If rank and money come with love and virtue, also, I should accept them gratefully, and enjoy your good fortune; but I know, by experience, how much genuine happiness can be had in a plain little house, where the daily bread is earned, and some privations give sweetness to the few pleasures. I am content to see Meg begin humbly, for, if I am not mistaken, she will be rich in the possession of a good man's heart, and that is better than a fortune.'

'I understand, Mother, and quite agree; but I'm disappointed about Meg, for I'd planned to have her marry Teddy by and by, and sit in the lap of luxury all her days. Wouldn't it be nice?' asked Jo, looking up, with a brighter face.

'He is younger than she, you know,' began Mrs March; but Jo broke in: 'Only a little; he's old for his age, and tall; and can be quite grown-up in his manners if he likes. Then he's rich and generous and good, and loves us all; and *I* say it's a pity my plan is spoilt.'

'I'm afraid Laurie is hardly grown up enough to Meg, and altogether too much of a weathercock, just now, for anyone to depend on. Don't make plans, Jo; but let time and their own hearts mate your friends. We can't meddle safely in such matters, and had better not get "romantic rubbish", as you call it, into our heads, lest it spoil our friendship.'

'Well, I won't; but I hate to see things going all criss-cross and getting snarled up, when a pull here and a snip there would straighten it out. I wish wearing flat-irons on our heads would keep us from growing up. But buds will be roses, and kittens, cats – more's the pity!'

'What's that about flat-irons and cats?' asked Meg, as she crept into the room, with the finished letter in her hand.

'Only one of my stupid speeches. I'm going to bed; come, Peggy,' said Jo, unfolding herself, like an animated puzzle.

'Quite right, and beautifully written. Please add that I send my love to John,' said Mrs March, as she glanced over the letter, and gave it back.

'Do you call him "John"?' asked Meg, smiling, with her innocent eyes looking down into her mother's.

'Yes; he has been like a son to us, and we are very fond of him,' replied Mrs March, returning the look with a keen one.

'I'm glad of that, he is so lonely. Good night, Mother dear. It is so inexpressibly comfortable to have you here,' was Meg's quiet answer.

The kiss her mother gave her was a very tender one; and, as she went away, Mrs March said, with a mixture of satisfaction and regret, 'She does not love John yet, but will soon learn to.'

CHAPTER 21

Laurie Makes Mischief,
and Jo Makes Peace

Jo's face was a study next day, for the secret rather weighed upon her, and she found it hard not to look mysterious and important. Meg observed it, but did not trouble herself to make inquiries, for she had learned that the best way to manage Jo was by the law of contraries, so she felt sure of being told everything if she did not ask. She was rather surprised, therefore, when the silence remained unbroken, and Jo assumed a patronizing air, which decidedly aggravated Meg, who in her turn assumed an air of dignified reserve, and devoted herself to her mother. This left Jo to her own devices; for Mrs March had taken her place as nurse, and bade her rest, exercise, and amuse herself after her long confinement. Amy being gone, Laurie was her only refuge; and, much as she enjoyed his society, she rather dreaded him just then, for he was an incorrigible tease, and she feared he would coax her secret from her.

She was quite right; for the mischief-loving lad no sooner suspected a mystery than he set himself to find it out, and led Jo a trying life of it. He wheedled, bribed, ridiculed, threatened, and scolded; affected indifference, that he might surprise the truth from her; declared he knew, then that he didn't care; and, at last, by dint of perseverance, he satisfied himself that it concerned Meg and Mr Brooke. Feeling indignant that he was not taken into his tutor's confidence, he set his wits to work to devise some proper retaliation for the slight.

Meg meanwhile had apparently forgotten the matter, and was absorbed in preparations for her father's return; but all of a sudden a change seemed to come over her, and, for a day or two, she was quite unlike herself. She started when spoken to, blushed when looked at, was very quiet, and sat over her sewing, with a timid, troubled look on her face. To her mother's inquiries she answered that she was quite well, and Jo's she silenced by begging to be let alone.

'She feels it in the air – love, I mean – and she's going very fast. She's got most of the symptoms – is twittery and cross, doesn't eat, lies awake, and mopes in corners. I caught her singing that song he gave her, and once she said "John", as you do, and then turned as red as a poppy. Whatever shall we do?' said Jo, looking ready for any measures, however violent.

'Nothing but wait. Let her alone, be kind and patient, and Father's coming will settle everything,' replied her mother.

'Here's a note to you, Meg, all sealed up! How odd! Teddy never seals mine,' said Jo, next day, as she distributed the contents of the little post-office.

Mrs March and Jo were deep in their own affairs, when a sound from Meg made them look up to see her staring at her note with a frightened face.

'My child, what is it?' cried her mother, running to her, while Jo tried to take the paper which had done the mischief.

'It's all a mistake – he didn't send it. Oh, Jo, how could you do it?' and Meg hid her face in her hands, crying as if her heart was quite broken.

'Me! I've done nothing! What's she talking about?' cried Jo, bewildered.

Meg's mild eyes kindled with anger as she pulled a crumpled note from her pocket, and threw it at Jo, saying reproachfully: 'You wrote it, and that bad boy helped you. How could you be so rude, so mean, and cruel to us both?'

Jo hardly heard her, for she and her mother were reading the note, which was written in a peculiar hand.

> MY DEAREST MARGARET – I can no longer restrain my
> passion and must know my fate before I return. I dare
> not tell your parents yet, but I think they would
> consent if they knew that we adore one another. Mr
> Laurence will help me to some good place, and then,
> my sweet girl, you will make me happy. I implore you
> to say nothing to your family yet, but to send one
> word of hope through Laurie to Your devoted
> JOHN.

'Oh, the little villain! that's the way he meant to pay me for keeping my word to Mother. I'll give him a hearty scolding, and bring him over to beg pardon,' cried Jo, burning to execute immediate justice. But her mother held her back, saying, with a look she seldom wore: 'Stop, Jo, you must clear yourself first. You have played so many pranks, that I am afraid you have had a hand in this.'

'On my word, Mother, I haven't! I never saw that note before, and I don't know anything about it, as true as I live!' said Jo, so earnestly that they believed her. 'If I *had* taken a part in it I'd have done it better than this, and have written a sensible note. I should think you'd have known Mr Brooke wouldn't write such stuff as that,' she added, scornfully tossing down the paper.

'It's like his writing,' faltered Meg, comparing it with the note in her hand.

'Oh, Meg, you didn't answer it?' cried Mrs March, quickly.

'Yes, I did!' and Meg hid her face again, overcome with shame.

'Here's a scrape! *Do* let me bring that wicked boy over to explain, and be lectured. I can't rest till I get hold of him'; and Jo made for the door again.

'Hush! let me manage this, for it is worse than I thought. Margaret, tell me the whole story,' commanded Mrs March, sitting down by Meg, yet keeping hold of Jo, lest she should fly off.

'I received the first letter from Laurie, who didn't look as if he knew anything about it,' began Meg, without looking up. 'I was worried at first, and meant to tell you; then I remembered how you liked Mr Brooke, so I thought you wouldn't mind if I kept my little secret for a few days. I'm so silly that I liked to think no one knew; and, while I was deciding what to say I felt like the girls in books, who have such things to do. Forgive me, Mother, I'm paid for my silliness now; I never can look him in the face again.'

'What did you say to him?' asked Mrs March.

'I only said I was too young to do anything about it yet; that I didn't wish to have secrets from you, and he must speak to Father. I was very grateful for his kindness, and would be his friend, but nothing more, for a long while.'

Mrs March smiled, as if well pleased, and Jo clapped her hands, exclaiming, with a laugh:

'You are almost equal to Caroline Percy, who was a pattern of prudence! Tell on, Meg. What did he say to that?'

'He writes in a different way entirely, telling me that he never sent any love letter at all, and is very sorry that my roguish sister, Jo, should take such liberties with our names. It's very kind and respectful, but think how dreadful for me!'

Meg leaned against her mother, looking the image of despair, and Jo tramped about the room, calling Laurie names. All of a sudden, she stopped, caught up the two notes, and, after looking at them closely, said decidedly, 'I don't believe Brooke ever saw either of these letters. Teddy wrote both, and keeps yours to crow over me with, because I wouldn't tell him my secret.'

'Don't have any secrets, Jo; tell it to Mother, and keep out of trouble, as I should have done,' said Meg, warningly.

'Bless you, child! Mother told me.'

'That will do, Jo. I'll comfort Meg while you go and get Laurie. I shall sift the matter to the bottom, and put a stop to such pranks at once.'

Away ran Jo, and Mrs March gently told Meg Mr Brooke's real feelings. 'Now, dear, what are your own? Do you love him enough to wait till he can make a home for you, or will you keep yourself quite free for the present?'

'I've been so scared and worried, I don't want to have anything to do with lovers for a long while – perhaps never,' answered Meg, petulantly. 'If John *doesn't* know anything about this nonsense, don't tell him, and make Jo and Laurie hold their tongues. I won't be deceived and plagued and made a fool of – it's a shame!'

Seeing that Meg's usually gentle temper was roused, and her pride hurt by this mischievous joke, Mrs March soothed her by promises of entire silence, and great discretion for the future. The instant Laurie's step was heard in the hall, Meg fled into the study, and Mrs March received the culprit alone. Jo had not told him why he was wanted, fearing he wouldn't come; but he knew the minute he saw Mrs March's face, and stood twirling his hat, with a guilty air which convicted him at once. Jo was dismissed, but chose to march up and down the hall like a sentinel, having some fear that the prisoner might bolt. The sound of voices in the parlour rose and fell for half an hour; but what happened during that interview the girls never knew.

When they were called in, Laurie was standing by their mother, with such a penitent face that Jo forgave him on the spot, but did not think it wise to betray the fact. Meg received his humble apology, and was much comforted by the assurance that Brooke knew nothing of the joke.

'I'll never tell him to my dying day – wild horses shan't drag it out of me; so you'll forgive me, Meg, and I'll do anything to show how out-and-out sorry I am,' he added, looking very much ashamed of himself.

'I'll try; but it was a very ungentlemanly thing to do. I didn't think you could be so sly and malicious, Laurie,' replied Meg, trying to hide her maidenly confusion under a gravely reproachful air.

'It was altogether abominable, and I don't deserve to be spoken to for a month; but you will, though, won't you?' and Laurie folded his hands together with such an imploring gesture, as he spoke in his irresistibly persuasive tone, that it was impossible to frown upon him, in spite of his scandalous behaviour. Meg pardoned him, and Mrs March's grave face relaxed, in spite of her efforts to keep sober, when she heard him declare that he would atone for his sins by all sorts of penances and abase himself like a worm before the injured damsel.

Jo stood aloof, meanwhile, trying to harden her heart against him, and succeeding only in primming up her face into an expression of entire disapprobation. Laurie looked at her once or twice, but, as she showed no sign of relenting, he felt injured, and turned his back on her till the others were done with him, when he made her a low bow, and walked off without a word.

As soon as he had gone, she wished she had been more forgiving; and when Meg and her mother went upstairs she felt lonely and longed for Teddy. After resisting for some time, she yielded to the impulse and, armed with a book to return, went over to the big house.

'Is Mr Laurence in?' asked Jo, of a housemaid, who was coming downstairs.

'Yes, miss; but I don't believe he's seeable just yet.'

'Why not? is he ill?'

'La, no, miss, but he's had a scene with Mr Laurie, who is in one of his tantrums about something, which vexes the old gentleman, so I dursn't go nigh him.'

'Where is Laurie?'

'Shut up in his room, and he won't answer, though I've been a-tapping. I don't know what's to become of the dinner, for it's ready, and there's no one to eat it.'

'I'll go and see what the matter is. I'm not afraid of either of them.'

Up went Jo, and knocked smartly at the door of Laurie's little study.

'Stop that, or I'll open the door and make you!' called out the young gentleman, in a threatening tone.

Jo immediately knocked again; the door flew open, and in she bounced, before Laurie could recover from his surprise. Seeing that he really *was* out of temper, Jo, who knew how to manage him, assumed a contrite expression, and going artistically down upon her knees, said meekly, 'Please forgive me for being so cross. I came to make it up, and can't go away till I have.'

'It's all right. Get up, and don't be a goose, Jo,' was the cavalier reply to her petition.

'Thank you; I will. Could I ask what's the matter? You don't look exactly easy in your mind.'

'I've been shaken, and I won't bear it!' growled Laurie, indignantly.

'Who did it?' demanded Jo.

'Grandfather; if it had been anyone else I'd have –' And the injured youth finished his sentence by an energetic gesture of the right arm.

'That's nothing; I often shake you, and you don't mind,' said Jo, soothingly.

'Pooh! you're a girl, and it's fun; but I'll allow no man to shake *me*.'

'I don't think anyone would care to try it, if you looked as much like a thundercloud as you do now. Why were you treated so?'

'Just because I wouldn't say what your mother wanted me for. I'd promised not to tell, and of course I wasn't going to break my word.'

'Couldn't you satisfy your grandpa in any other way?'

'No; he *would* have the truth, the whole truth, and nothing but the truth. I'd have told my part of the scrape, if I could without bringing Meg in. As I couldn't, I held my tongue, and bore the scolding till the old gentleman collared me. Then I got angry, and bolted, for fear I should forget myself.'

'It wasn't nice, but he's sorry, I know; so go down and make up. I'll help you.'

'Hanged if I do! I'm not going to be lectured and pummelled by everyone, just for a bit of a frolic. I *was* sorry about Meg, and begged pardon like a man; but I won't do it again, when I wasn't in the wrong.'

'He didn't know that.'

'He ought to trust me, and not act as if I was a baby. It's no use, Jo; he's got to learn that I'm able to take care of myself, and don't need anyone's apron strings to hold on by.'

'What pepper-pots you are!' sighed Jo. 'How do you mean to settle this affair?'

'Well, he ought to beg pardon, and believe me when I say I can't tell him what the fuss is about.'

'Bless you! he won't do that.'

'I won't go down till he does.'

'Now, Teddy, be sensible; let it pass, and I'll explain what I can. You can't stay here, so what's the use of being melodramatic?'

'I don't intend to stay here long, anyway. I'll slip off and take a journey somewhere, and when grandpa misses me he'll come round fast enough.'

'I dare say; but you ought not to go and worry him.'

'Don't preach. I'll go to Washington and see Brooke; it's gay there, and I'll enjoy myself after the troubles.'

'What fun you'd have! I wish I could run off too,' said Jo, forgetting her part of Mentor in lively visions of martial life at the capital.

'Come on, then! Why not? You go and surprise your father, and I'll stir up old Brooke. It would be a glorious joke; let's do it, Jo. We'll leave a letter saying we are all right, and trot off at once. I've got money enough; it will do you good, and be no harm, as you go to your father.'

For a moment Jo looked as if she would agree; for, wild as the plan was, it just suited her. She was tired of care and confinement, longed for change, and thoughts of her father blended temptingly with the novel charms of camps and hospitals, liberty and fun. Her eyes kindled as they turned wistfully toward the window, but they fell on the old house opposite. And she shook her head with sorrowful decision.

'If I was a boy, we'd run away together, and have a capital time; but as I'm a miserable girl, I must be proper, and stop at home. Don't tempt me, Teddy, it's a crazy plan.'

'That's the fun of it,' began Laurie, who had got a wilful fit on him, and was possessed to break out of bounds in some way.

'Hold your tongue!' cried Jo, covering her ears. '"Prunes and prisms" are my doom, and I may as well make up my mind to it. I came here to moralize, not to hear about things that make me skip to think of.'

'I know Meg would wet-blanket such a proposal, but I thought you had more spirit,' began Laurie, insinuatingly.

'Bad boy, be quiet! Sit down and think of your own sins, don't go making me add to mine. If I get grandpa to apologize for the shaking, will you give up running away?' asked Jo, seriously.

'Yes, but you won't do it,' answered Laurie, who wished to 'make up', but felt that his outraged dignity must be appeased first.

'If I can manage the young one I can the old one,' muttered Jo, as she walked away, leaving Laurie bent over a railroad map, with his head propped up on both hands.

'Come in!' and Mr Laurence's gruff voice sounded gruffer than ever, as Jo tapped at his door.

'It's only me, sir, come to return a book,' she said, blandly, as she entered.

'Want any more?' asked the old gentleman, looking grim and vexed, but trying not to show it.

'Yes, please. I like old Sam so well, I think I'll try the second volume,' returned Jo, hoping to propitiate him by accepting a second dose of Boswell's *Johnson* as he had recommended that lively work.

The shaggy eyebrows unbent a little, as he rolled the steps towards the shelf where the Johnsonian literature was placed. Jo skipped up, and sitting on the top step, affected to be searching for her book, but was really wondering how best to introduce the dangerous object of her visit. Mr Laurence seemed to suspect that something was brewing in her mind; for, after taking several brisk turns about the room, he faced round on her, speaking so abruptly that *Rasselas* tumbled faced downward on the floor.

'What has that boy been about? Don't try to shield him. I know he has been in mischief by the way he acted when he came home. I can't get a word from him; and when I threatened to shake the truth out of him he bolted upstairs, and locked himself into his room.'

'He did do wrong, but we forgave him, and all promised not to say a word to anyone,' began Jo, reluctantly.

'That won't do; he shall not shelter himself behind a promise from you softhearted girls. If he's done anything amiss, he shall confess, beg pardon, and be punished. Out with it, Jo! I won't be kept in the dark.'

Mr Laurence looked so alarming, and spoke so sharply, that Jo would gladly have run away, if she could, but she was perched aloft on the steps, and he stood at the foot, a lion in the path, so she had to stay and brave it out.

'Indeed, sir, I cannot tell; Mother forbade it. Laurie has confessed, asked pardon, and been punished quite enough. We don't keep silence to shield him, but someone else, and it will make more trouble if you interfere. Please don't; it was partly my fault, but it's all right now; so let's forget it, and talk about the *Rambler*, or something pleasant.'

'Hang the *Rambler*! come down and give me your word that this harum-scarum boy of mine hasn't done anything ungrateful or impertinent. If he has, after all your kindness to him, I'll thrash him with my own hands.'

The threat sounded awful, but did not alarm Jo, for she knew the irascible old gentleman would never lift a finger against his grandson, whatever he might say to the contrary. She obediently descended, and made as light of the prank as she could without betraying Meg or forgetting the truth.

'Hum – ha – well, if the boy held his tongue because he promised, and not from obstinacy, I'll forgive him. He's a stubborn fellow, and hard to manage,' said Mr Laurence, rubbing up his hair till it looked as if he had been out in a gale, and smoothing the frown from his brow with an air of relief.

'So am I; but a kind word will govern me when all the king's horses and all the king's men couldn't,' said Jo, trying to say a kind word for her friend, who seemed to get out of one scrape only to fall into another.

'You think I'm not kind to him, hey?' was the sharp answer.

'Oh, dear, no, sir; you are rather too kind sometimes, and then just a trifle hasty when he tries your patience. Don't you think you are?'

Jo was determined to have it out now, and tried to look quite placid, though she quaked a little after her bold speech. To her great relief and surprise, the old gentleman only threw his spectacles on to the table, with a rattle, and exclaimed frankly: 'You're right, girl, I am! I love the boy, but he tries my patience past bearing, and I don't know how it will end, if we go on so.'

'I'll tell you, he'll run away.' Jo was sorry for that speech the minute it was made; she meant to warn him that Laurie would not bear much restraint, and hoped he would be more forbearing with the lad.

Mr Laurence's ruddy face changed suddenly, and he sat down, with a troubled glance at the picture of a handsome man, which hung over his table. It was Laurie's father, who *had* run away in his youth, and married against the imperious old man's will. Jo fancied he remembered and regretted the past, and she wished she had held her tongue.

'He won't do it unless he is very much worried, and only threatens it sometimes, when he gets tired of studying. I often think I should like to, especially since my hair was cut; so, if you ever miss us, you may advertise for two boys, and look among the ships bound for India.'

She laughed as she spoke, and Mr Laurence looked relieved, evidently taking the whole thing as a joke.

'You hussy, how dare you talk in that way? Where's your respect for me, and your proper bringing up? Bless the boys and girls! What torments they are; yet we can't do without them,' he said, pinching her cheeks good-humouredly. 'Go and bring that boy down to his dinner, tell him it's all right, and advise him not to put on tragedy airs with his grandfather. I won't bear it.'

'He won't come, sir; he feels badly because you didn't believe him when he said he couldn't tell. I think the shaking hurt his feelings very much.'

Jo tried to look pathetic, but must have failed, for Mr Laurence began to laugh, and she knew the day was won.

'I'm sorry for that, and ought to thank him for not shaking *me*, I suppose. What the dickens does the fellow expect?' and the old gentleman looked a trifle ashamed of his own testiness.

'If I were you, I'd write him an apology, sir. He says he won't come down till he has one, and talks about Washington, and goes on in an absurd way. A formal apology will make him see how foolish he is, and bring him down quite amiable. Try it; he likes fun, and this way is better than talking. I'll carry it up, and teach him his duty.'

Mr Laurence gave her a sharp look, and put on his spectacles, saying slowly, 'You're a sly puss, but I don't mind being managed by you and Beth. Here, give me a bit of paper, and let us have done with this nonsense.'

The note was written in the terms which one gentleman would use to another after offering some deep insult. Jo dropped a kiss on the top of Mr Laurence's bald head, and ran up to slip the apology under Laurie's door, advising him, through the keyhole, to be submissive, decorous, and a few other agreeable impossibilities. Finding the door locked again, she left the note to do its work, and was going quietly away, when the young gentleman slid down the bannisters, and waited for her at the bottom, saying, with his most virtuous expression of countenance, 'What a good fellow you are, Jo! Did you get blown up?' he added, laughing.

'No; he was pretty mild, on the whole.'

'Ah! I got it all round; even you cast me off over there, and I felt just ready to go to the deuce,' he began, apologetically.

'Don't talk in that way; turn over a new leaf and begin again, Teddy, my son.'

'I keep turning over new leaves, and spoiling them, as I used to spoil my copy-books; and I make so many beginnings there never will be an end,' he said, dolefully.

'Go and eat your dinner; you'll feel better after it. Men always croak when they are hungry,' and Jo whisked out at the front door after that.

'That's a "label" on my "sect",' answered Laurie, quoting Amy, as he went to partake of humble-pie dutifully with his grandfather, who was quite saintly in temper, and overwhelmingly respectful in manner, all the rest of the day.

Everyone thought the matter ended and the little cloud blown over; but the mischief was done, for, though others forgot it, Meg remembered. She never alluded to a certain person, but she thought of him a good deal, dreamed dreams more than ever; and once Jo, rummaging her sister's desk for stamps, found a bit of paper scribbled over with the words, 'Mrs John Brooke'; whereat she groaned tragically, and cast it into the fire, feeling that Laurie's prank had hastened the evil day for her.

CHAPTER 22

Pleasant Meadows

Like sunshine after storm were the peaceful weeks which followed. The invalids improved rapidly, and Mr March began to talk of returning early in the new year. Beth was soon able to lie on the study sofa all day, amusing herself with the well-beloved cats at first, and, in time, with dolls' sewing, which had fallen sadly behindhand. Her once active limbs were so stiff and feeble that Jo took her a daily airing about the house in her strong arms. Meg cheerfully blackened and burnt her white hands cooking delicate messes for the 'dear'; while Amy, a loyal slave of the ring, celebrated her return by giving away as many of her treasures as she could prevail on her sisters to accept.

As Christmas approached, the usual mysteries began to haunt the house, and Jo frequently convulsed the family by proposing utterly impossible or magnificently absurd ceremonies, in honour of this unusually merry Christmas. Laurie was equally impractical, and would have had bonfires, sky-rockets, and triumphal arches, if he had had his own way. After many skirmishes and snubbings, the ambitious pair were considered effectually quenched, and went about with forlorn faces, which were rather belied by explosions of laughter when the two got together.

Several days of unusually mild weather fitly ushered in a splendid Christmas Day. Hannah 'felt in her bones' that it was going to be an unusually fine day, and she proved herself a true prophetess, for everybody and everything seemed bound to produce a grand success. To begin with, Mr March wrote that he should soon be with them; then Beth felt uncommonly well that morning, and, being dressed in her mother's gift – a soft crimson merino wrapper – was borne in triumph to the window to behold the offering of Jo and Laurie. The Unquenchables had done their best to be worthy of the name, for, like elves, they had worked by night, and conjured up a comical surprise. Out in the garden stood a stately snow-maiden, crowned with holly, bearing a basket of fruit and flowers in one hand, a great roll of new music in the other, a perfect rainbow of an Afghan round her chilly shoulders, and a Christmas carol issuing from her lips, on a pink paper streamer:

THE JUNGFRAU TO BETH

God bless you, dear Queen Bess!
May nothing you dismay,
But health and peace and happiness
Be yours, this Christmas Day.

Here's fruit to feed our busy bee,
And flowers for her nose;
Here's music for her pianee,
An Afghan for her toes.

A portrait of Joanna, see,
By Raphael No. 2,
Who laboured with great industry
To make it fair and true.

Accept a ribbon red, I beg,
For Madam Purrer's tail;
And ice-cream made by lovely Peg –
A Mont Blanc in a pail.

Their dearest love, my makers laid
Within my breast of snow:
Accept it, and the Alpine maid,
From Laurie and from Jo.

How Beth laughed when she saw it, how Laurie ran up and down to bring in the gifts, and what ridiculous speeches Jo made as she presented them!

'I'm so full of happiness, that, if Father was only here, I couldn't hold one drop more,' said Beth, quite sighing with contentment, as Jo carried her off to the study to rest after the excitement and to refresh herself with some of the delicious grapes the 'Jungfrau' had sent her.

'So am I,' added Jo, slapping the pocket wherein reposed the long-desired *Undine and Sintram.*

'I'm sure I am,' echoed Amy, poring over the engraved copy of the Madonna and Child, which her mother had given her, in a pretty frame.

'Of course I am!' cried Meg, smoothing the silvery folds of her first silk dress; for Mr Laurence had insisted on giving it.

'How can *I* be otherwise?' said Mrs March, gratefully, as her eyes went from her husband's letter to Beth's smiling face, and her hand caressed the brooch made of grey and golden, chestnut and dark brown hair, which the girls had just fastened on her breast.

Now and then, in this workaday world, things do happen in the delightful story-book fashion, and what a comfort that is. Half an hour after everyone had said they were so happy they could only hold one drop more, the drop came. Laurie opened the parlour door, and popped his head in very quietly. He might just as well have turned a somersault and uttered an Indian war-whoop; for his face was so full of suppressed excitement and his voice so treacherously joyful, that everyone jumped up, though he only said, in a queer breathless voice, 'Here's another Christmas present for the March family.'

Before the words were well out of his mouth, he was whisked

away somehow, and in his place appeared a tall man, muffled up to the eyes, leaning on the arm of another tall man, who tried to say something and couldn't. Of course there was a general stampede; and for several minutes everybody seemed to lose their wits, for the strangest things were done, and no one said a word. Mrs March became invisible in the embrace of four pairs of loving arms; Jo disgraced herself by nearly fainting away, and had to be doctored by Laurie in the china-closet; Mr Brooke kissed Meg entirely by mistake, as he somewhat incoherently explained; and Amy, the dignified, tumbled over a stool, and, never stopping to get up, hugged and cried over her father's boots in the most touching manner. Mrs March was the first to recover herself, and held up her hand with a warning, 'Hush! remember Beth!'

But it was too late; the study door flew open, the little red wrapper appeared on the threshold – joy put strength into the feeble limbs – and Beth ran straight into her father's arms. Never mind what happened just after that; for the full hearts overflowed, washing away the bitterness of the past, and leaving only the sweetness of the present.

It was not at all romantic, but a hearty laugh set everybody straight again, for Hannah was discovered behind the door, sobbing over the fat turkey, which she had forgotten to put down when she rushed up from the kitchen. As the laugh subsided, Mrs March began to thank Mr Brooke for his faithful care of her husband, at which Mr Brooke suddenly remembered that Mr March needed rest, and, seizing Laurie, he precipitately retired. Then the two invalids were ordered to repose, which they did, by both sitting in one big arm-chair, and talking hard.

Mr March told how he had longed to surprise them, and how when the fine weather came, he had been allowed by his doctor to take advantage of it; how devoted Brooke had been, and how he was altogether a most estimable and upright young man. Why Mr March paused a minute just there, and, after a glance at Meg, who was violently poking the fire, looked at his wife with an inquiring lift of the eyebrows, I leave you to imagine; also why Mrs March gently nodded her head, and asked, rather abruptly, if he wouldn't have something to eat. Jo saw and understood the look; and she stalked grimly away to get beef-tea, muttering to herself, as she slammed the door, 'I hate estimable young men with brown eyes!'

There never *was* such a Christmas dinner as they had that day. The fat turkey was a sight to behold, when Hannah sent him up, stuffed, browned, and decorated; so was the plum-pudding, which quite melted in one's mouth; likewise the jellies, in which Amy revelled like a fly in a honey-pot. Everything turned out well; which was a mercy, Hannah said, 'For my mind was that flustered, mum, that it's a merrycle I didn't roast the pudding, and stuff the turkey with raisins, let alone bilin' of it in a cloth.'

Mr Laurence and his grandson dined with them, also Mr Brooke – at whom Jo glowered darkly, to Laurie's infinite amusement. Two easy-chairs stood side by side at the head of the table, in which sat Beth and her father, feasting modestly on chicken and a little fruit. They drank healths, told stories, sang songs, 'reminisced', as the old folk say, and had a thoroughly good time. A sleigh-ride had been planned, but the girls would not leave their father; so the guests departed early, and, as twilight gathered, the happy family sat together round the fire.

'Just a year ago we were groaning over the dismal Christmas we expected to have. Do you remember?' asked Jo, breaking a short pause which had followed a long conversation about many things.

'Rather a pleasant year on the whole!' said Meg, smiling at the fire, and congratulating herself on having treated Mr Brooke with dignity.

'I think it's been a pretty hard one,' observed Amy, watching the light shine on her ring, with thoughtful eyes.

'I'm glad it's over, because we've got you back,' whispered Beth, who sat on her father's knee.

'Rather a rough road for you to travel, my little pilgrims, especially the latter part of it. But you have got on bravely; and I think the burdens are in a fair way to tumble off very soon,' said Mr March, looking with fatherly satisfaction at the four young faces gathered round him.

'How do you know? Did Mother tell you?' asked Jo.

'Not much; straws show which way the wind blows, and I've made several discoveries today.'

'Oh, tell us what they are!' cried Meg, who sat beside him.

'Here is one!' and taking up the hand which lay on the arm of his chair, he pointed to the roughened forefinger, a burn on the back, and two or three little hard spots on the palm. 'I remember a time when this hand was white and smooth, and your first care was to keep it so. It was very pretty then, but to me it is much prettier now – for in these seeming blemishes I read a little history. A burnt-offering has been made of vanity; this hardened palm has earned something better than blisters; and I'm sure the sewing done by these pricked fingers will last a long time, so much goodwill went into the stitches. Meg, my dear, I value the womanly skill which keeps home happy more than white hands or fashionable accomplishments. I'm proud to shake this good, industrious little hand, and hope I shall not soon be asked to give it away.'

If Meg had wanted a reward for hours of patient labour, she received it in the hearty pressure of her father's hand, and the approving smile he gave her.

'What about Jo? Please say something nice; for she has tried so hard, and been so very, very good to me,' said Beth, in her father's ear.

He laughed, and looked across at the tall girl who sat opposite, with an unusually mild expression in her brown face.

'In spite of the curly crop, I don't see the "son Jo" whom I left a year ago,' said Mr March. 'I see a young lady who pins her collar straight, laces her boots neatly, and neither whistles, talks slang, nor lies on the rug as she used to do. Her face is rather thin and pale, just now, with watching and anxiety; but I like to look at it, for it has grown gentler, and her voice is lower; she doesn't bounce, but moves quietly, and takes care of a certain little person in a motherly way which delights me. I rather miss my wild girl;

but if I get a strong, helpful, tender-hearted woman in her place, I shall feel quite satisfied. I don't know whether the shearing sobered our black sheep, but I do know that in all Washington I couldn't find anything beautiful enough to be bought with the five-and-twenty dollars which my good girl sent me.'

Jo's keen eyes were rather dim for a minute, and her thin face grew rosy in the firelight, as she received her father's praise, feeling that she did deserve a portion of it.

'Now, Beth,' said Amy, longing for her turn, but ready to wait.

'There's so little of her, I'm afraid to say much, for fear she will slip away altogether, though she is not so shy as she used to be,' began their father cheerfully; but recollecting how nearly he *had* lost her, he held her close, saying tenderly, with her cheek against his own, 'I've got you safe, my Beth, and I'll keep you so, please God.'

After a minute's silence, he looked down at Amy, who sat on the cricket at his feet, and said, with a caress of the shining hair:

'I observed that Amy took drumsticks at dinner, ran errands for her mother all the afternoon, gave Meg her place tonight, and has waited on everyone with patience and good-humour. I also observe that she does not fret much nor look in the glass, and has not even mentioned a very pretty ring which she wears; so I conclude that she has learned to think of other people more and of herself less, and has decided to try and mould her character as carefully as she moulds her little clay figures. I am glad of this; for though I should be very proud of a graceful statue made by her, I shall be infinitely prouder of a lovable daughter, with a talent for making life beautiful to herself and others.'

'What are you thinking of, Beth?' asked Jo, when Amy had thanked her father and told about her ring.

'I read in *Pilgrim's Progress* today, how, after many troubles, Christian and Hopeful came to a pleasant green meadow, where lilies bloomed all the year round, and there they rested happily, as we do now, before they went on to their journey's end,' answered Beth; adding, as she slipped out of her father's arms, and went slowly to the instrument, 'It's singing time now, and I want to be in my old place. I'll try to sing the song of the shepherd-boy which the pilgrims heard. I made the music for Father, because he likes the verses.'

So, sitting at the dear little piano, Beth softly touched the keys, and, in the sweet voice they had never thought to hear again, sung to her own accompaniment the quaint hymn, which was a singularly fitting song for her:

'He that is down need fear no fall,
He that is low no pride;
He that is humble ever shall
Have God to be his guide.

'I am content with what I have,
Little be it or much;
And, Lord! contentment still I crave,
Because thou savest such.

'Fulness to them a burden is,
That go on pilgrimage;
Here little, and hereafter bliss,
Is best from age to age!'

CHAPTER 23

Aunt March Settles the Question

Like bees swarming after their queen, mother and daughters hovered about Mr March the next day, neglecting everything to look at, wait upon, and listen to the new invalid, who was in a fair way to be killed by kindness. As he sat propped up in a big chair by Beth's sofa, with the other three close by, and Hannah popping in her head now and then to 'peek at the dear man', nothing seemed needed to complete their happiness. But something was needed, and the elder ones felt it, though none confessed the fact. Mr and Mrs March looked at one another with an anxious expression, as their eyes followed Meg. Jo had sudden fits of sobriety, and was seen to shake her fist at Mr Brooke's umbrella, which had been left in the hall; Meg was absent-minded, shy, and silent, started when the bell rang, and coloured when John's name was mentioned; Amy said, 'Everyone seemed waiting for something, and couldn't settle down, which was queer, since Father was safe at home,' and Beth innocently wondered why their neighbours didn't run over as usual.

Laurie went by in the afternoon, and, seeing Meg at the window, seemed suddenly possessed with a melodramatic fit, for he fell down upon one knee in the snow, beat his breast, tore his hair, and clasped his hands imploringly, as if begging some boon; and when Meg told him to behave himself and go away, he wrung imaginary tears out of his handkerchief, and staggered round the corner as if in utter despair.

'What does the goose mean?' said Meg, laughing, and trying to look unconscious.

'He's showing you how your John will go on by and by. Touching, isn't it?' answered Jo, scornfully.

'Don't say *my John*, it isn't proper or true'; but Meg's voice lingered over the words as if they sounded pleasant to her. 'Please don't plague me, Jo; I've told you I don't care *much* about him, and there isn't to be anything said, but we are all to be friendly, and go on as before.'

'We can't, for something *has* been said, and Laurie's mischief has spoilt you for me. I see it, and so does Mother; you are not like your old self a bit, and seem ever so far away from me. I don't mean to plague you, and will bear it like a man, but I do wish it was all settled. I hate to wait; so if you mean ever to do it, make haste and have it over quickly,' said Jo, pettishly.

'*I* can't say or do anything till he speaks, and he won't, because Father said I was too young,' began Meg, bending over her work, with a queer little smile, which suggested that she did not quite agree with her father on that point.

'If he did speak, you wouldn't know what to say, but would cry or blush, or let him have his own way, instead of giving a good, decided No.'

'I'm not so silly and weak as you think. I know just what I should say, for I've planned it all, so I needn't be taken unawares; there's no knowing what may happen, and I wish to be prepared.'

Jo couldn't help smiling at the important air which Meg had unconsciously assumed, and which was as becoming as the pretty colour varying in her cheeks.

'Would you mind telling me what you'd say?' asked Jo, more respectfully.

'Not at all; you are sixteen now, quite old enough to be my confidante, and my experience will be useful to you by-and-by, perhaps, in your own affairs of this sort.'

'Don't mean to have any; it's fun to watch other people

philander, but I should feel like a fool doing it myself,' said Jo, looking alarmed at the thought.

'I think not, if you liked anyone very much, and he liked you.' Meg spoke as if to herself, and glanced out at the lane, where she had often seen lovers walking together in the summer twilight.

'I thought you were going to tell your speech to that man,' said Jo, rudely shortening her sister's little reverie.

'Oh, I should merely say, quite calmly and decidedly, "Thank you, Mr Brooke, you are very kind, but I agree with Father that I am too young to enter into any engagement at present; so please say no more, but let us be friends as we were."'

'Hum! that's stiff and cool enough. I don't believe you'll ever say it, and I know he won't be satisfied if you do. If he goes on like the rejected lovers in books, you'll give in, rather than hurt his feelings.'

'No, I won't. I shall tell him I've made up my mind, and shall walk out of the room with dignity.'

Meg rose as she spoke, and was just going to rehearse the dignified exit, when a step in the hall made her fly into her seat and begin to sew as if her life depended on finishing that particular seam in a given time. Jo smothered a laugh at the sudden change, and, when someone gave a modest tap, opened the door with a grim aspect, which was anything but hospitable.

'Good afternoon. I came to get my umbrella – that is, to see how your father finds himself today,' said Mr Brooke, getting a trifle confused as his eye went from one tell-tale face to the other.

'It's very well, he's in the rack, I'll get him, and tell it you are here,' and having jumbled her father and the umbrella well together in her reply, Jo slipped out of the room to give Meg a chance to make her speech and air her dignity. But the instant she vanished, Meg began to sidle towards the door, murmuring, 'Mother will like to see you. Pray sit down, I'll call her.'

'Don't go; are you afraid of me, Margaret?' and Mr Brooke looked so hurt that Meg thought she must have done something very rude. She blushed up to the little curls on her forehead, for he had never called her Margaret before, and she was surprised to find how natural and sweet it seemed to hear him say it. Anxious to appear friendly and at her ease, she put out her hand with a confiding gesture, and said gratefully: 'How can I be afraid when you have been so kind to Father? I only wish I could thank you for it.'

'Shall I tell you how?' asked Mr Brooke, holding the small hand fast in both his own, and looking down at Meg with so much love in the brown eyes, that her heart began to flutter, and she both longed to run away and to stop and listen.

'Oh no, please don't – I'd rather not,' she said, trying to withdraw her hand, and looking frightened in spite of her denial.

'I won't trouble you, I only want to know if you care for me a little, Meg. I love you so much, dear,' added Mr Brooke tenderly.

This was the moment for the calm, proper speech, but Meg didn't make it; she forgot every word of it, hung her head, and answered, 'I don't know,' so softly, that John had to stoop down to catch the foolish little reply.

He seemed to think it was worth the trouble, for he smiled to himself as if quite satisfied, pressed the plump hand gratefully, and said, in his most persuasive tone, 'Will you try and find out? I want to know *so* much; for I can't go to work with any heart until I learn whether I am to have my reward in the end or not.'

'I'm too young,' faltered Meg, wondering why she was so fluttered, yet rather enjoying it.

'I'll wait; and in the meantime, you could be learning to like me. Would it be a very hard lesson, dear?'

'Not if I chose to learn it, but –'

'Please choose to learn, Meg. I love to teach, and this is easier than German,' broke in John, getting possession of the other hand, so that she had no way of hiding her face, as he bent to look into it.

His tone was properly beseeching; but, stealing a shy look at him, Meg saw that his eyes were merry as well as tender, and that he wore the satisfied smile of one who had no doubt of his success. This nettled her; Annie Moffat's foolish lessons in coquetry came into her mind, and the love of power, which sleeps in the bosoms of the best of little women, woke up all of a sudden and took possession of her. She felt excited and strange, and, not knowing what to do, followed a capricious impulse, and, withdrawing her hands, said petulantly, 'I *don't* choose. Please go away and let me be!'

Poor Mr Brooke looked as if his lovely castle in the air was tumbling about his ears, for he had never seen Meg in such a mood before, and it rather bewildered him.

'Do you really mean that?' he asked, anxiously, following her as she walked away.

'Yes, I do; I don't want to be worried about such things. Father says I needn't; it's too soon and I'd rather not.'

'Mayn't I hope you'll change your mind by-and-by? I'll wait, and say nothing till you have had more time. Don't play with me, Meg. I didn't think that of you.'

'Don't think of me at all. I'd rather you wouldn't,' said Meg, taking a naughty satisfaction in trying her lover's patience and her own power.

He was grave and silent now, and looked decidedly more like the novel heroes whom she admired; but he neither slapped his forehead nor tramped about the room, as they did; he just stood looking at her so wistfully, so tenderly, that she found her heart relenting in spite of her. What would have happened next I cannot say, if Aunt March had not come hobbling in at this interesting minute.

The old lady couldn't resist her longing to see her nephew; for she had met Laurie as she took her airing, and, hearing of Mr March's arrival, drove straight out to see him. The family were all busy in the back part of the house, and she had made her way quietly in, hoping to surprise them. She did surprise two of them so much that Meg started as if she had seen a ghost, and Mr Brooke vanished into the study.

'Bless me, what's all this?' cried the old lady, with a rap of her cane, as she glanced from the pale young gentleman to the scarlet young lady.

'It's Father's friend. I'm *so* surprised to see you!' stammered Meg, feeling that she was in for a lecture now.

'That's evident,' returned Aunt March, sitting down. 'But what is Father's friend saying to make you look like a peony? There's mischief going on, and I insist upon knowing what it is,' with another rap.

'We were merely talking. Mr Brooke came for his umbrella,' began Meg, wishing that Mr Brooke and the umbrella were safely out of the house.

'Brooke? That boy's tutor? Ah! I understand now. I know all about it. Jo blundered into a wrong message in one of your father's letters, and I made her tell me. You haven't gone and accepted him, child?' cried Aunt March, looking scandalized.

'Hush! he'll hear. Shan't I call Mother?' said Meg, much troubled.

'Not yet. I've something to say to you, and I must free my mind at once. Tell me, do you mean to marry this Cook? If you do, not one penny of my money ever goes to you. Remember that, and be a sensible girl,' said the old lady, impressively.

Now Aunt March possessed in perfection the art of rousing the spirit of opposition in the gentlest people, and enjoyed doing it. The best of us have a spice of perversity in us, especially when we are young and in love. If Aunt March had begged Meg to accept John Brooke, she would probably have declared she couldn't think of it; but as she was peremptorily ordered *not* to like him, she immediately made up her mind that she would. Inclination as well as perversity made the decision easy, and, being already much excited, Meg opposed the old lady with unusual spirit.

'I shall marry whom I please, Aunt March, and you can leave your money to anyone you like,' she said, nodding her head with a resolute air.

'Highty tighty! Is that the way you take my advice, miss? You'll be sorry for it, by and by, when you've tried love in a cottage, and found it a failure.'

'It can't be a worse one than some people find in big houses,' retorted Meg.

Aunt March put on her glasses and took a look at the girl, for she did not know her in this new mood. Meg hardly knew herself, she felt so brave and independent – so glad to defend John, and assert her right to love him, if she liked. Aunt March saw that she had begun wrong, and, after a little pause, made a fresh start, saying, as mildly as she could, 'Now, Meg, my dear, be reasonable, and take my advice. I mean it kindly, and don't want you to spoil your whole life by making a mistake at the beginning. You ought to marry well, and help your family; it's your duty to make a rich match, and it ought to be impressed upon you.'

'Father and Mother don't think so; they like John, though he *is* poor.'

'Your parents, my dear, have no more worldly wisdom than two babies.'

'I'm glad of it,' cried Meg, stoutly.

Aunt March took no notice, but went on with her lecture, 'This Rook is poor, and hasn't got any rich relations, has he?'

'No, but he has many warm friends.'

'You can't live on friends; try it, and see how cool they'll grow. He hasn't any business, has he?'

'Not yet; Mr Laurence is going to help him.'

'That won't last long. James Laurence is a crotchety old fellow, and not to be depended upon. So you intend to marry a man without money, position, or business, and go on working harder than you do now, when you might be comfortable all your days by minding me and doing better? I thought you had more sense, Meg.'

'I couldn't do better if I waited half my life! John is good and wise; he's got heaps of talent; he's willing to work, and sure to get on, he's so energetic and brave. Everyone likes and respects him, and I'm proud to think he cares for me, though I'm so poor and young and silly,' said Meg, looking prettier than ever in her earnestness.

'He knows *you* have got rich relations, child; that's the secret of his liking, I suspect.'

'Aunt March, how dare you say such a thing? John is above such meanness, and I won't listen to you a minute if you talk so,' cried Meg, indignantly, forgetting everything but the injustice of the old lady's suspicions. 'My John wouldn't marry for money, any more than I would. We are willing to work, and we mean to wait. I'm not afraid of being poor, for I've been happy so far and I know I shall be with him, because he loves me, and I –'

Meg stopped there, remembering all of a sudden that she hadn't made up her mind; that she had told 'her John' to go away, and that he might be overhearing her inconsistent remarks.

Aunt March was very angry, for she had set her heart on having her pretty niece make a fine match, and something in the girl's happy young face made the lonely old woman feel both sad and sour.

'Well, I wash my hands of the whole affair. You are a wilful child, and you've lost more than you know by this piece of folly. No, I won't stop; I'm disappointed in you, and haven't spirits to see your father now. Don't expect anything from me when you are married; your Mr Book's friends must take care of you. I've done with you for ever.'

And, slamming the door in Meg's face, Aunt March drove off in high dudgeon. She seemed to take all the girl's courage with her; for, when left alone, Meg stood a moment, undecided whether to laugh or cry. Before she could make up her mind, she was taken possession of by Mr Brooke, who said, all in one breath, 'I couldn't help hearing, Meg. Thank you for defending me and Aunt March for proving that you *do* care for me a little bit.'

'I didn't know how much till she abused you,' began Meg.

'And I needn't go away, but may stay and be happy, may I, dear?'

Here was another fine chance to make the crushing speech and the stately exit, but Meg never thought of doing either, and disgraced herself for ever in Jo's eyes by meekly whispering, 'Yes, John,' and hiding her face on Mr Brooke's waistcoat.

Fifteen minutes after Aunt March's departure, Jo came softly downstairs, paused an instant at the parlour door, and, hearing no sound within, nodded and smiled, with a satisfied expression, saying to herself, 'She has sent him away as we planned, and that affair is settled. I'll go and hear the fun, and have a good laugh over it.'

But poor Jo never got her laugh, for she was transfixed upon the threshold by a spectacle which held her there, staring with her mouth nearly as wide open as her eyes. Going to exult over a fallen enemy, and to praise a strong-minded sister for the banishment of an objectionable lover, it certainly *was* a shock to behold the aforesaid enemy serenely sitting on the sofa, with the strong-minded sister enthroned upon his knee, and wearing an expression of the most abject submission. Jo gave a sort of gasp as if a cold shower-bath had suddenly fallen upon her – for such an unexpected turning of the tables actually took her breath away. At the odd sound the lovers turned and saw her. Meg jumped up, looking both proud and shy; but 'that man', as Jo called him, actually laughed, and said coolly, as he kissed the astonished newcomer, 'Sister Jo, congratulate us!'

That was adding insult to injury – it was altogether too much – and making some wild demonstration with her hands, Jo vanished without a word. Rushing upstairs, she startled the invalids by exclaiming tragically, as she burst into the room:

'Oh, *do* somebody go down quick; John Brooke is acting dreadfully, and Meg likes it!'

Mr and Mrs March left the room with speed; and, casting herself upon the bed, Jo cried and scolded tempestuously, as she told the awful news to Beth and Amy. The little girls, however, considered it a most agreeable and interesting event, and Jo got little comfort from them; so she went up to her refuge in the garret, and confided her troubles to the rats.

Nobody ever knew what went on in the parlour that afternoon, but a great deal of talking was done, and quiet Mr Brooke astonished his friends by the eloquence and spirit with which he pleaded his suit, told his plans, and persuaded them to arrange everything just as he wanted it.

The tea-bell rang before he had finished describing the paradise which he meant to earn for Meg, and he proudly took her in to supper, both looking so happy that Jo hadn't the heart to be jealous or dismal. Amy was very much impressed by John's devotion and

Meg's dignity, Beth beamed at them from a distance, while Mr and Mrs March surveyed the young couple with such tender satisfaction that it was perfectly evident Aunt March was right in calling them as 'unworldly as a pair of babies'. No one ate much, but everyone looked very happy, and the old room seemed to brighten up amazingly when the first romance of the family began there.

'You can't say nothing pleasant ever happens now, can you, Meg?' said Amy, trying to decide how she would group the lovers in the sketch she was planning to make.

'No, I'm sure I can't. How much has happened since I said that! It seems a year ago,' answered Meg, who was in a blissful dream, lifted far above such common things as bread and butter.

'The joys come close upon the sorrows this time, and I rather think the changes have begun,' said Mrs March. 'In most families there comes, now and then, a year full of events; this has been such a one, but it ends well after all.'

'Hope the next will end better,' muttered Jo, who found it very hard to see Meg absorbed in a stranger before her face; for Jo loved a few persons very dearly, and dreaded to have their affection lost or lessened in any way.

'I hope the third year from this *will* end better; I mean it shall, if I live to work out my plans,' said Mr Brooke, smiling at Meg, as if everything had become possible to him now.

'Doesn't it seem very long to wait?' asked Amy, who was in a hurry for the wedding.

'I've got so much to learn before I shall be ready, it seems a short time to me,' answered Meg, with a sweet gravity in her face, never seen there before.

'You have only to wait; *I* have to do the work,' said John, beginning his labours by picking up Meg's napkin, with an expression which caused Jo to shake her head, and then say to herself, with an air of relief, as the front door banged, 'Here comes Laurie. Now we shall have a little sensible conversation.'

But Jo was mistaken; for Laurie came prancing in, overflowing with spirits, bearing a great bridal-looking bouquet for 'Mrs John

Brooke', and evidently labouring under the delusion that the whole affair had been brought about by his excellent management.

'I knew Brooke would have it all his own way, he always does; for when he makes up his mind to accomplish anything, it's done, though the sky falls,' said Laurie, when he had presented his offering and his congratulations.

'Much obliged for that recommendation. I take it as a good omen for the future, and invite you to my wedding on the spot,' answered Mr Brooke, who felt at peace with all mankind, even his mischievous pupil.

'I'll come if I'm at the ends of the earth; for the sight of Jo's face alone on that occasion would be worth a long journey. You don't look festive, ma'am; what's the matter?' asked Laurie, following her into a corner of the parlour, whither all had adjourned to greet Mr Laurence.

'I don't approve of the match, but I've made up my mind to bear it, and shall not say a word against it,' said Jo, solemnly. 'You can't know how hard it is for me to give up Meg,' she continued, with a little quiver in her voice.

'You don't give her up. You only go halves,' said Laurie, consolingly.

'It never can be the same again. I've lost my dearest friend,' sighed Jo.

'You've got me, anyhow. I'm not good for much, I know; but I'll stand by you, Jo, all the days of my life; upon my word I will!' and Laurie meant what he said.

'I know you will, and I'm ever so much obliged; you are always a great comfort to me, Teddy', returned Jo, gratefully shaking hands.

'Well, now, don't be dismal, there's a good fellow. It's all right, you see. Meg is happy; Brooke will fly round and get settled immediately; grandpa will attend to him, and it will be very jolly to see Meg in her own little house. We'll have capital times after she is gone, for I shall be through college before long, and then we'll go abroad on some nice trip or other. Wouldn't that console you?'

'I rather think it would; but there's no knowing what may happen in three years,' said Jo, thoughtfully.

'That's true. Don't you wish you could take a look forward and see where we shall all be then? I do,' returned Laurie.

'I think not, for I might see something sad; and everyone looks so happy now, I don't believe they could be much improved'; and Jo's eyes went slowly round the room, brightening as they looked, for the prospect was a pleasant one.

Father and Mother sat together, quietly re-living the first chapter of the romance which for them began some twenty years ago. Amy was drawing the lovers, who sat apart in a beautiful world of their own, the light of which touched their faces with a grace the little artist could not copy. Beth lay on her sofa, talking cheerily with her old friend, who held her little hand as if he felt that it possessed the power to lead him along the peaceful way she walked. Jo lounged in her favourite low seat, with the grave, quiet look which best became her; and Laurie, leaning on the back of her chair, his chin on a level with her curly head, smiled with his friendliest aspect, and nodded at her in the long glass which reflected them both.

So grouped, the curtain falls upon Meg, Jo, Beth, and Amy. Whether it ever rises again, depends upon the reception given to the first act of the domestic drama called

LITTLE WOMEN.

Classic Literature: Words and Phrases

adapted from the Collins English Dictionary

Accoucheur NOUN a male midwife or doctor ❑ *I think my sister must have had some general idea that I was a young offender whom an Accoucheur Policemen had taken up (on my birthday) and delivered over to her* (*Great Expectations* by Charles Dickens)

addled ADJ confused and unable to think properly ❑ *But she counted and counted till she got that addled* (*The Adventures of Huckleberry Finn* by Mark Twain)

admiration NOUN amazement or wonder ❑ *lifting up his hands and eyes by way of admiration* (*Gulliver's Travels* by Jonathan Swift)

afeard ADJ afeard means afraid ❑ *shake it – and don't be afeard* (*The Adventures of Huckleberry Finn* by Mark Twain)

affected VERB affected means followed ❑ *Hadst thou affected sweet divinity* (*Doctor Faustus 5.2* by Christopher Marlowe)

aground ADV when a boat runs aground, it touches the ground in a shallow part of the water and gets stuck ❑ *what kep' you? – boat get aground?* (*The Adventures of Huckleberry Finn* by Mark Twain)

ague NOUN a fever in which the patient has alternate hot and cold shivering fits ❑ *his exposure to the wet and cold had brought on fever and ague* (*Oliver Twist* by Charles Dickens)

alchemy ADJ false or worthless ❑ *all wealth alchemy* (*The Sun Rising* by John Donne)

all alike phrase the same all the time ❑ *Love, all alike* (*The Sun Rising* by John Donne)

alow and aloft phrase alow means in the lower part or bottom, and aloft means on the top, so alow and aloft means on the top and in the bottom or throughout ❑ *Someone's turned the chest out alow and aloft* (*Treasure Island* by Robert Louis Stevenson)

ambuscade NOUN ambuscade is not a proper word. Tom means an ambush, which is when a group of people attack their enemies, after hiding and waiting for them ❑ *and so we would lie in ambuscade, as he called it* (*The Adventures of Huckleberry Finn* by Mark Twain)

amiable ADJ likeable or pleasant ❑ *Such amiable qualities must speak for themselves* (*Pride and Prejudice* by Jane Austen)

amulet NOUN an amulet is a charm thought to drive away evil spirits. ❑ *uttered phrases at once occult and familiar, like the amulet worn on the heart* (*Silas Marner* by George Eliot)

amusement NOUN here amusement means a strange and disturbing puzzle ❑ *this was an amusement the other way* (*Robinson Crusoe* by Daniel Defoe)

ancient NOUN an ancient was the flag displayed on a ship to show which country it belongs to. It is also called the ensign ❑ *her ancient and pendants out* (*Robinson Crusoe* by Daniel Defoe)

antic ADJ here antic means horrible or grotesque ❑ *armed and dressed after a very antic manner* (*Gulliver's Travels* by Jonathan Swift)

antics NOUN antics is an old word meaning clowns, or people who do silly things to make other people laugh ❑ *And point like antics at his triple crown* (*Doctor Faustus 3.2* by Christopher Marlowe)

appanage NOUN an appanage is a living allowance ❑ *As if loveliness were not the special prerogative of woman*

– *her legitimate appanage and heritage!* (*Jane Eyre* by Charlotte Brontë)

appended VERB appended means attached or added to ❏ *and these words appended* (*Treasure Island* by Robert Louis Stevenson)

approver NOUN an approver is someone who gives evidence against someone he used to work with ❏ *Mr. Noah Claypole: receiving a free pardon from the Crown in consequence of being admitted approver against Fagin* (*Oliver Twist* by Charles Dickens)

areas NOUN the areas is the space, below street level, in front of the basement of a house ❏ *The Dodger had a vicious propensity, too, of pulling the caps from the heads of small boys and tossing them down areas* (*Oliver Twist* by Charles Dickens)

argument NOUN theme or important idea or subject which runs through a piece of writing ❏ *Thrice needful to the argument which now* (*The Prelude* by William Wordsworth)

artificially ADJ artfully or cleverly ❏ *and he with a sharp flint sharpened very artificially* (*Gulliver's Travels* by Jonathan Swift)

artist NOUN here artist means a skilled workman ❏ *This man was a most ingenious artist* (*Gulliver's Travels* by Jonathan Swift)

assizes NOUN assizes were regular court sessions which a visiting judge was in charge of ❏ *you shall hang at the next assizes* (*Treasure Island* by Robert Louis Stevenson)

attraction NOUN gravitation, or Newton's theory of gravitation ❏ *he predicted the same fate to attraction* (*Gulliver's Travels* by Jonathan Swift)

aver VERB to aver is to claim something strongly ❏ *for Jem Rodney, the mole catcher, averred that one evening as he was returning homeward* (*Silas Marner* by George Eliot)

baby NOUN here baby means doll, which is a child's toy that looks like a small person ❏ *and skilful dressing her baby* (*Gulliver's Travels* by Jonathan Swift)

bagatelle NOUN bagatelle is a game rather like billiards and pool ❏ *Breakfast had been ordered at a pleasant little tavern, a mile or so away upon the rising ground beyond the green; and there was a bagatelle board in the room, in case we should desire to unbend our minds after the solemnity.* (*Great Expectations* by Charles Dickens)

bah exclam Bah is an exclamation of frustration or anger ❏ *"Bah," said Scrooge.* (*A Christmas Carol* by Charles Dickens)

bairn NOUN a northern word for child ❏ *Who has taught you those fine words, my bairn?* (*Wuthering Heights* by Emily Brontë)

bait VERB to bait means to stop on a journey to take refreshment ❏ *So, when they stopped to bait the horse, and ate and drank and enjoyed themselves, I could touch nothing that they touched, but kept my fast unbroken.* (*David Copperfield* by Charles Dickens)

balustrade NOUN a balustrade is a row of vertical columns that form railings ❏ *but I mean to say you might have got a hearse up that staircase, and taken it broadwise, with the splinter-bar towards the wall, and the door towards the balustrades: and done it easy* (*A Christmas Carol* by Charles Dickens)

bandbox NOUN a large lightweight box for carrying bonnets or hats ❏ *I am glad I bought my bonnet, if it is only for the fun of having another bandbox* (*Pride and Prejudice* by Jane Austen)

barren NOUN a barren here is a stretch or expanse of barren land ❏ *a line of upright stones, continued the length of the barren* (*Wuthering Heights* by Emily Brontë)

basin NOUN a basin was a cup without a handle ❏ *who is drinking his tea* out of a basin (*Wuthering Heights* by Emily Brontë)

battalia NOUN the order of battle ❑ *till I saw part of his army in battalia* (*Gulliver's Travels* by Jonathan Swift)

battery NOUN a Battery is a fort or a place where guns are positioned ❑ *You bring the lot to me, at that old Battery over yonder* (*Great Expectations* by Charles Dickens)

battledore and shuttlecock NOUN The game battledore and shuttlecock was an early version of the game now known as badminton. The aim of the early game was simply to keep the shuttlecock from hitting the ground. ❑ *Battledore and shuttlecock's a wery good game vhen you an't the shuttlecock and two lawyers the battledores, in which case it gets too excitin' to be pleasant* (*Pickwick Papers* by Charles Dickens)

beadle NOUN a beadle was a local official who had power over the poor ❑ *But these impertinences were speedily checked by the evidence of the surgeon, and the testimony of the beadle* (*Oliver Twist* by Charles Dickens)

bearings NOUN the bearings of a place are the measurements or directions that are used to find or locate it ❑ *the bearings of the island* (*Treasure Island* by Robert Louis Stevenson)

beaufet NOUN a beaufet was a sideboard ❑ *and sweet-cake from the beaufet* (*Emma* by Jane Austen)

beck NOUN a beck is a small stream ❑ *a beck which follows the bend of the glen* (*Wuthering Heights* by Emily Brontë)

bedight VERB decorated ❑ *and bedight with Christmas holly stuck into the top.* (*A Christmas Carol* by Charles Dickens)

Bedlam NOUN Bedlam was a lunatic asylum in London which had statues carved by Caius Gabriel Cibber at its entrance ❑ *Bedlam,*

and those carved maniacs at the gates (*The Prelude* by William Wordsworth)

beeves NOUN oxen or castrated bulls which are animals used for pulling vehicles or carrying things ❑ *to deliver in every morning six beeves* (*Gulliver's Travels* by Jonathan Swift)

begot VERB created or caused ❑ *Begot in thee* (*On His Mistress* by John Donne)

behoof NOUN behoof means benefit ❑ *"Yes, young man," said he, releasing the handle of the article in question, retiring a step or two from my table, and speaking for the behoof of the landlord and waiter at the door* (*Great Expectations* by Charles Dickens)

berth NOUN a berth is a bed on a boat ❑ *this is the berth for me* (*Treasure Island* by Robert Louis Stevenson)

bevers NOUN a bever is a snack, or small portion of food, eaten between main meals ❑ *that buys me thirty meals a day and ten bevers* (*Doctor Faustus 2.1* by Christopher Marlowe)

bilge water NOUN the bilge is the widest part of a ship's bottom, and the bilge water is the dirty water that collects there ❑ *no gush of bilge-water had turned it to fetid puddle* (*Jane Eyre* by Charlotte Brontë)

bills NOUN bills is an old term meaning prescription. A prescription is the piece of paper on which your doctor writes an order for medicine and which you give to a chemist to get the medicine ❑ *Are not thy bills hung up as monuments* (*Doctor Faustus 1.1* by Christopher Marlowe)

black cap NOUN a judge wore a black cap when he was about to sentence a prisoner to death ❑ *The judge assumed the black cap, and the prisoner still stood with the same air and gesture.* (*Oliver Twist* by Charles Dickens)

boot-jack NOUN a wooden device to help take boots off ❑ *The speaker appeared to throw a boot-jack, or some such article, at the person he addressed* (*Oliver Twist* by Charles Dickens)

booty NOUN booty means treasure or prizes ❑ *would be inclined to give up their booty in payment of the dead man's debts* (*Treasure Island* by Robert Louis Stevenson)

Bow Street runner phrase Bow Street runners were the first British police force, set up by the author Henry Fielding in the eighteenth century ❑ *as would have convinced a judge or a Bow Street runner* (*Treasure Island* by Robert Louis Stevenson)

brawn NOUN brawn is a dish of meat which is set in jelly ❑ *Heaped up upon the floor, to form a kind of throne, were turkeys, geese, game, poultry, brawn, great joints of meat, sucking-pigs* (*A Christmas Carol* by Charles Dickens)

bray VERB when a donkey brays, it makes a loud, harsh sound ❑ *and she doesn't bray like a jackass* (*The Adventures of Huckleberry Finn* by Mark Twain)

break VERB in order to train a horse you first have to break it ❑ *"If a high-mettled creature like this," said he, "can't be broken by fair means, she will never be good for anything"* (*Black Beauty* by Anna Sewell)

bullyragging VERB bullyragging is an old word which means bullying. To bullyrag someone is to threaten or force someone to do something they don't want to do ❑ *and a lot of loafers bullyragging him for sport* (*The Adventures of Huckleberry Finn* by Mark Twain)

but prep except for (this) ❑ *but this, all pleasures fancies be* (*The Good-Morrow* by John Donne)

by hand phrase by hand was a common expression of the time meaning that baby had been fed either using a spoon or a bottle rather than by breast-feeding ❑ *My sister, Mrs. Joe Gargery, was more than twenty years older than I, and had established a great reputation with herself . . . because she had bought me up 'by hand'* (*Great Expectations* by Charles Dickens)

bye-spots NOUN bye-spots are lonely places ❑ *and bye-spots of tales rich with indigenous produce* (*The Prelude* by William Wordsworth)

calico NOUN calico is plain white fabric made from cotton ❑ *There was two old dirty calico dresses* (*The Adventures of Huckleberry Finn* by Mark Twain)

camp-fever NOUN camp-fever was another word for the disease typhus ❑ *during a severe camp-fever* (*Emma* by Jane Austen)

cant NOUN cant is insincere or empty talk ❑ *"Man," said the Ghost, "if man you be in heart, not adamant, forbear that wicked cant until you have discovered What the surplus is, and Where it is."* (*A Christmas Carol* by Charles Dickens)

canty ADJ canty means lively, full of life ❑ *My mother lived til eighty, a canty dame to the last* (*Wuthering Heights* by Emily Brontë)

canvas VERB to canvas is to discuss ❑ *We think so very differently on this point Mr Knightley, that there can be no use in canvassing it* (*Emma* by Jane Austen)

capital ADJ capital means excellent or extremely good ❑ *for it's capital, so shady, light, and big* (*Little Women* by Louisa May Alcott)

capstan NOUN a capstan is a device used on a ship to lift sails and anchors ❑ *capstans going, ships going out to sea, and unintelligible sea creatures roaring curses over the bulwarks at respondent lightermen* (*Great Expectations* by Charles Dickens)

case-bottle NOUN a square bottle designed to fit with others into a case ❑ *The spirit being set before him in a huge case-bottle, which had originally come out of some* ship's locker (*The Old Curiosity Shop* by Charles Dickens)

casement NOUN casement is a word meaning window. The teacher in Nicholas Nickleby misspells window showing what a bad teacher he is ❑ *W-i-n, win, d-e-r, der, winder, a casement.'* (*Nicholas Nickleby* by Charles Dickens)

cataleptic ADJ a cataleptic fit is one in which the victim goes into a trancelike state and remains still for a long time ❑ *It was at this point in their history that Silas's cataleptic fit occurred during the prayer-meeting* (*Silas Marner* by George Eliot)

cauldron NOUN a cauldron is a large cooking pot made of metal ❑ *stirring a large cauldron which seemed to be full of soup* (*Alice's Adventures in Wonderland* by Lewis Carroll)

cephalic ADJ cephalic means to do with the head ❑ *with ink composed of a cephalic tincture* (*Gulliver's Travels* by Jonathan Swift)

chaise and four NOUN a closed four-wheel carriage pulled by four horses ❑ *he came down on Monday in a chaise and four to see the place* (*Pride and Prejudice* by Jane Austen)

chamberlain NOUN the main servant in a household ❑ *In those times a bed was always to be got there at any hour of the night, and the chamberlain, letting me in at his ready wicket, lighted the candle next in order on his shelf* (*Great Expectations* by Charles Dickens)

characters NOUN distinguishing marks ❑ *Impressed upon all forms the characters* (*The Prelude* by William Wordsworth)

chary ADJ cautious ❑ *I should have been chary of discussing my guardian too freely even with her* (*Great Expectations* by Charles Dickens)

cherishes VERB here cherishes means cheers or brightens ❑ *some*

philosophic song of Truth that cherishes our daily life (*The Prelude* by William Wordsworth)

chickens' meat phrase chickens' meat is an old term which means chickens' feed or food ❑ *I had shook a bag of chickens' meat out in that place* (*Robinson Crusoe* by Daniel Defoe)

chimeras NOUN a chimera is an unrealistic idea or a wish which is unlikely to be fulfilled ❑ *with many other wild impossible chimeras* (*Gulliver's Travels* by Jonathan Swift)

chines NOUN chine is a cut of meat that includes part or all of the backbone of the animal ❑ *and they found hams and chines uncut* (*Silas Marner* by George Eliot)

chits NOUN chits is a slang word which means girls ❑ *I hate affected, niminy-piminy chits!* (*Little Women* by Louisa May Alcott)

chopped VERB chopped means come suddenly or accidentally ❑ *if I had chopped upon them* (*Robinson Crusoe* by Daniel Defoe)

chute NOUN a narrow channel ❑ *One morning about day-break, I found a canoe and crossed over a chute to the main shore* (*The Adventures of Huckleberry Finn* by Mark Twain)

circumspection NOUN careful observation of events and circumstances; caution ❑ *I honour your circumspection* (*Pride and Prejudice* by Jane Austen)

clambered VERB clambered means to climb somewhere with difficulty, usually using your hands and your feet ❑ *he clambered up and down stairs* (*Treasure Island* by Robert Louis Stevenson)

clime NOUN climate ❑ *no season knows nor clime* (*The Sun Rising* by John Donne)

clinched VERB clenched ❑ *the tops whereof I could but just reach with my fist clinched* (*Gulliver's Travels* by Jonathan Swift)

close chair NOUN a close chair is a sedan chair, which is an covered chair which has room for one person. The sedan chair is carried on two poles by two men, one in front and one behind ❑ *persuaded even the Empress herself to let me hold her in her close chair* (*Gulliver's Travels* by Jonathan Swift)

clown NOUN clown here means peasant or person who lives off the land ❑ *In ancient days by emperor and clown* (*Ode on a Nightingale* by John Keats)

coalheaver NOUN a coalheaver loaded coal onto ships using a spade ❑ *Good, strong, wholesome medicine, as was given with great success to two Irish labourers and a coalheaver* (*Oliver Twist* by Charles Dickens)

coal-whippers NOUN men who worked at docks using machines to load coal onto ships ❑ *here, were colliers by the score and score, with the coal-whippers plunging off stages on deck* (*Great Expectations* by Charles Dickens)

cobweb NOUN a cobweb is the net which a spider makes for catching insects ❑ *the walls and ceilings were all hung round with cobwebs* (*Gulliver's Travels* by Jonathan Swift)

coddling VERB coddling means to treat someone too kindly or protect them too much ❑ *and I've been coddling the fellow as if I'd been his grandmother* (*Little Women* by Louisa May Alcott)

coil NOUN coil means noise or fuss or disturbance ❑ *What a coil is there?* (*Doctor Faustus 4.7* by Christopher Marlowe)

collared VERB to collar something is a slang term which means to capture. In this sentence, it means he stole it [the money] ❑ *he collared it* (*The Adventures of Huckleberry Finn* by Mark Twain)

colling VERB colling is an old word which means to embrace and kiss ❑ *and no clasping and colling at all*

(*Tess of the D'Urbervilles* by Thomas Hardy)

colloquies NOUN colloquy is a formal conversation or dialogue ❑ *Such colloquies have occupied many a pair of pale-faced weavers* (*Silas Marner* by George Eliot)

comfit NOUN sugar-covered pieces of fruit or nut eaten as sweets ❑ *and pulled out a box of comfits* (*Alice's Adventures in Wonderland* by Lewis Carroll)

coming out VERB when a girl came out in society it meant she was of marriageable age. In order to 'come out' girls were expecting to attend balls and other parties during a season ❑ *The younger girls formed hopes of coming out a year or two sooner than they might otherwise have done* (*Pride and Prejudice* by Jane Austen)

commit VERB commit means arrest or stop ❑ *Commit the rascals* (*Doctor Faustus 4.7* by Christopher Marlowe)

commodious ADJ commodious means convenient ❑ *the most commodious and effectual ways* (*Gulliver's Travels* by Jonathan Swift)

commons NOUN commons is an old term meaning food shared with others ❑ *his pauper assistants ranged themselves behind him; the gruel was served out; and a long grace was said over the short commons.* (*Oliver Twist* by Charles Dickens)

complacency NOUN here complacency means a desire to please others. Today complacency means feeling pleased with oneself without good reason. ❑ *Twas thy power that raised the first complacency in me* (*The Prelude* by William Wordsworth)

complaisance NOUN complaisance was eagerness to please ❑ *we cannot wonder at his complaisance* (*Pride and Prejudice* by Jane Austen)

complaisant ADJ complaisant means polite ❑ *extremely cheerful and* *complaisant to their guest* (*Gulliver's Travels* by Jonathan Swift)

conning VERB conning means learning by heart ❏ *Or conning more* (*The Prelude* by William Wordsworth)

consequent NOUN consequence ❏ *as avarice is the necessary consequent of old age* (*Gulliver's Travels* by Jonathan Swift)

consorts NOUN concerts ❏ *The King, who delighted in music, had frequent consorts at Court* (*Gulliver's Travels* by Jonathan Swift)

conversible ADJ conversible meant easy to talk to, companionable ❏ *He can be a conversible companion* (*Pride and Prejudice* by Jane Austen)

copper NOUN a copper is a large pot than can be heated directly over a fire ❏ *He gazed in stupefied astonishment on the small rebel for some seconds, and then clung for support to the copper* (*Oliver Twist* by Charles Dickens)

copper-stick NOUN a copper-stick is the long piece of wood used to stir washing in the copper (or boiler) which was usually the biggest cooking pot in the house ❏ *It was Christmas Eve, and I had to stir the pudding for next day, with a copper-stick, from seven to eight by the Dutch clock* (*Great Expectations* by Charles Dickens)

counting-house NOUN a counting house is a place where accountants work ❏ *Once upon a time – of all the good days in the year, on Christmas Eve – old Scrooge sat busy in his countinghouse* (*A Christmas Carol* by Charles Dickens)

courtier NOUN a courtier is someone who attends the king or queen – a member of the court ❏ *next the ten courtiers;* (*Alice's Adventures in Wonderland* by Lewis Carroll)

covies NOUN covies were flocks of partridges ❏ *and will save all of the*

best covies for you (*Pride and Prejudice* by Jane Austen)

cowed VERB cowed means frightened or intimidated ❏ *it cowed me more than the pain* (*Treasure Island* by Robert Louis Stevenson)

cozened VERB cozened means tricked or deceived ❏ *Do you remember, sir, how you cozened me* (*Doctor Faustus 4.7* by Christopher Marlowe)

cravats NOUN a cravat is a folded cloth that a man wears wrapped around his neck as a decorative item of clothing ❏ *we'd'a' slept in our cravats to-night* (*The Adventures of Huckleberry Finn* by Mark Twain)

crock and dirt phrase crock and dirt is an old expression meaning soot and dirt ❏ *and the mare catching cold at the door, and the boy grimed with crock and dirt* (*Great Expectations* by Charles Dickens)

crockery NOUN here crockery means pottery ❏ *By one of the parrots was a cat made of crockery* (*The Adventures of Huckleberry Finn* by Mark Twain)

crooked sixpence phrase it was considered unlucky to have a bent sixpence ❏ *You've got the beauty, you see, and I've got the luck, so you must keep me by you for your crooked sixpence* (*Silas Marner* by George Eliot)

croquet NOUN croquet is a traditional English summer game in which players try to hit wooden balls through hoops ❏ *and once she remembered trying to box her own ears for having cheated herself in a game of croquet* (*Alice's Adventures in Wonderland* by Lewis Carroll)

cross prep across ❏ *The two great streets, which run cross and divide it into four quarters* (*Gulliver's Travels* by Jonathan Swift)

culpable ADJ if you are culpable for something it means you are to blame ❏ *deep are the sorrows that spring from false ideas for which no man is culpable.* (*Silas Marner* by George Eliot)

cultured ADJ cultivated ❑ *Nor less when spring had warmed the cultured Vale* (*The Prelude* by William Wordsworth)

cupidity NOUN cupidity is greed ❑ *These people hated me with the hatred of cupidity and disappointment.* (*Great Expectations* by Charles Dickens)

curricle NOUN an open two-wheeled carriage with one seat for the driver and space for a single passenger ❑ *and they saw a lady and a gentleman in a curricle* (*Pride and Prejudice* by Jane Austen)

cynosure NOUN a cynosure is something that strongly attracts attention or admiration ❑ *Then I thought of Eliza and Georgiana; I beheld one the cynosure of a ballroom, the other the inmate of a convent cell* (*Jane Eyre* by Charlotte Brontë)

dalliance NOUN someone's dalliance with something is a brief involvement with it ❑ *nor sporting in the dalliance of love* (*Doctor Faustus Chorus* by Christopher Marlowe)

darkling ADV darkling is an archaic way of saying in the dark ❑ *Darkling I listen* (*Ode on a Nightingale* by John Keats)

delf-case NOUN a sideboard for holding dishes and crockery ❑ *at the pewter dishes and delf-case* (*Wuthering Heights* by Emily Brontë)

determined ◼ VERB here determined means ended ❑ *and be out of vogue when that was determined* (*Gulliver's Travels* by Jonathan Swift) ◾ VERB determined can mean to have been learned or found especially by investigation or experience ❑ *All the sensitive feelings it wounded so cruelly, all the shame and misery it kept alive within my breast, became more poignant as I thought of this; and I determined that the life was unendurable* (*David Copperfield* by Charles Dickens)

Deuce NOUN a slang term for the Devil ❑ *Ah, I dare say I did. Deuce take me, he added suddenly, I know I did. I find I am not quite unscrewed yet.* (*Great Expectations* by Charles Dickens)

diabolical ADJ diabolical means devilish or evil ❑ *and with a thousand diabolical expressions* (*Treasure Island* by Robert Louis Stevenson)

direction NOUN here direction means address ❑ *Elizabeth was not surprised at it, as Jane had written the direction remarkably ill* (*Pride and Prejudice* by Jane Austen)

discover VERB to make known or announce ❑ *the Emperor would discover the secret while I was out of his power* (*Gulliver's Travels* by Jonathan Swift)

dissemble VERB hide or conceal ❑ *Dissemble nothing* (*On His Mistress* by John Donne)

dissolve VERB dissolve here means to release from life, to die ❑ *Fade far away, dissolve, and quite forget* (*Ode on a Nightingale* by John Keats)

distrain VERB to distrain is to seize the property of someone who is in debt in compensation for the money owed ❑ *for he's threatening to distrain for it* (*Silas Marner* by George Eliot)

Divan NOUN a Divan was originally a Turkish council of state – the name was transferred to the couches they sat on and is used to mean this in English ❑ *Mr Brass applauded this picture very much, and the bed being soft and comfortable, Mr Quilp determined to use it, both as a sleeping place by night and as a kind of Divan by day.* (*The Old Curiosity Shop* by Charles Dickens)

divorcement NOUN separation ❑ *By all pains which want and divorcement hath* (*On His Mistress* by John Donne)

dog in the manger, a phrase this phrase describes someone who prevents you from enjoying something that they themselves have no need for ❑ *You are a dog in the manger, Cathy, and desire no one to be loved but yourself* (*Wuthering Heights* by Emily Brontë)

dolorifuge NOUN dolorifuge is a word which Thomas Hardy invented. It means pain-killer or comfort ❑ *as a species of dolorifuge* (*Tess of the D'Urbervilles* by Thomas Hardy)

dome NOUN building ❑ *that river and that mouldering dome* (*The Prelude* by William Wordsworth)

domestic phrase here domestic means a person's management of the house ❑ *to give some account of my domestic* (*Gulliver's Travels* by Jonathan Swift)

dunce NOUN a dunce is another word for idiot ❑ *Do you take me for a dunce? Go on?* (*Alice's Adventures in Wonderland* by Lewis Carroll)

Ecod exclam a slang exclamation meaning 'oh God!' ❑ *"Ecod," replied Wemmick, shaking his head, "that's not my trade."* (*Great Expectations* by Charles Dickens)

egg-hot NOUN an egg-hot (see also 'flip' and 'negus') was a hot drink made from beer and eggs, sweetened with nutmeg ❑ *She fainted when she saw me return, and made a little jug of egg-hot afterwards to console us while we talked it over.* (*David Copperfield* by Charles Dickens)

encores NOUN an encore is a short extra performance at the end of a longer one, which the entertainer gives because the audience has enthusiastically asked for it ❑ *we want a little something to answer encores with, anyway* (*The Adventures of Huckleberry Finn* by Mark Twain)

equipage NOUN an elegant and impressive carriage ❑ *and besides, the equipage did not answer to any of their neighbours* (*Pride and Prejudice* by Jane Austen)

exordium NOUN an exordium is the opening part of a speech ❑ *"Now, Handel," as if it were the grave* beginning of a portentous business exordium, he had suddenly given up that tone (*Great Expectations* by Charles Dickens)

expect VERB here expect means to wait for ❑ *to expect his farther commands* (*Gulliver's Travels* by Jonathan Swift)

familiars NOUN familiars means spirits or devils who come to someone when they are called ❑ *I'll turn all the lice about thee into familiars* (*Doctor Faustus* 1.4 by Christopher Marlowe)

fantods NOUN a fantod is a person who fidgets or can't stop moving nervously ❑ *It most give me the fantods* (*The Adventures of Huckleberry Finn* by Mark Twain)

farthing NOUN a farthing is an old unit of British currency which was worth a quarter of a penny ❑ *Not a farthing less. A great many back-payments are included in it, I assure you.* (*A Christmas Carol* by Charles Dickens)

farthingale NOUN a hoop worn under a skirt to extend it ❑ *A bell with an old voice – which I dare say in its time had often said to the house, Here is the green farthingale* (*Great Expectations* by Charles Dickens)

favours NOUN here favours is an old word which means ribbons ❑ *A group of humble mourners entered the gate: wearing white favours* (*Oliver Twist* by Charles Dickens)

feigned VERB pretend or pretending ❑ *not my feigned page* (*On His Mistress* by John Donne)

fence ■ NOUN a fence is someone who receives and sells stolen goods ❑ *What are you up to? Ill-treating the boys, you covetous, avaricious, in-sa-ti-a-ble old fence?* (*Oliver Twist* by Charles Dickens) ■ NOUN defence or protection ❑ *but honesty hath no fence against superior cunning* (*Gulliver's Travels* by Jonathan Swift)

fess ADJ fess is an old word which means pleased or proud ❑ *You'll be* *fess enough, my poppet* (*Tess of the D'Urbervilles* by Thomas Hardy)

fettered ADJ fettered means bound in chains or chained ❏ *"You are fettered," said Scrooge, trembling. "Tell me why?"* (*A Christmas Carol* by Charles Dickens)

fidges VERB fidges means fidgets, which is to keep moving your hands slightly because you are nervous or excited ❏ *Look, Jim, how my fingers fidges* (*Treasure Island* by Robert Louis Stevenson)

finger-post NOUN a finger-post is a sign-post showing the direction to different places ❏ *"The gallows," continued Fagin, "the gallows, my dear, is an ugly finger-post, which points out a very short and sharp turning that has stopped many a bold fellow's career on the broad highway."* (*Oliver Twist* by Charles Dickens)

fire-irons NOUN fire-irons are tools kept by the side of the fire to either cook with or look after the fire ❏ *the fire-irons came first* (*Alice's Adventures in Wonderland* by Lewis Carroll)

fire-plug NOUN a fire-plug is another word for a fire hydrant ❏ *The pony looked with great attention into a fire-plug, which was near him, and appeared to be quite absorbed in contemplating it* (*The Old Curiosity Shop* by Charles Dickens)

flank NOUN flank is the side of an animal ❏ *And all her silken flanks with garlands dressed* (*Ode on a Grecian Urn* by John Keats)

flip NOUN a flip is a drink made from warmed ale, sugar, spice and beaten egg ❏ *The events of the day, in combination with the twins, if not with the flip, had made Mrs. Micawber hysterical, and she shed tears as she replied* (*David Copperfield* by Charles Dickens)

flit VERB flit means to move quickly ❏ *and if he had meant to flit to Thrushcross Grange* (*Wuthering Heights* by Emily Brontë)

floorcloth NOUN a floorcloth was a hard-wearing piece of canvas used instead of carpet ❏ *This avenging phantom was ordered to be on duty at eight on Tuesday morning in the hall (it was two feet square, as charged for floorcloth)* (*Great Expectations* by Charles Dickens)

fly-driver NOUN a fly-driver is a carriage drawn by a single horse ❏ *The fly-drivers, among whom I inquired next, were equally jocose and equally disrespectful* (*David Copperfield* by Charles Dickens)

fob NOUN a small pocket in which a watch is kept ❏ *"Certain," replied the man, drawing a gold watch from his fob* (*Oliver Twist* by Charles Dickens)

folly NOUN folly means foolishness or stupidity ❏ *the folly of beginning a work* (*Robinson Crusoe* by Daniel Defoe)

fond ADJ fond means foolish ❏ *Fond worldling* (*Doctor Faustus* 5.2 by Christopher Marlowe)

fondness NOUN silly or foolish affection ❏ *They have no fondness for their colts or foals* (*Gulliver's Travels* by Jonathan Swift)

for his fancy phrase for his fancy means for his liking or as he wanted ❏ *and as I did not obey quick enough for his fancy* (*Treasure Island* by Robert Louis Stevenson)

forlorn ADJ lost or very upset ❏ *you are from that day forlorn* (*Gulliver's Travels* by Jonathan Swift)

foster-sister NOUN a foster-sister was someone brought up by the same nurse or in the same household ❏ *I had been his foster-sister* (*Wuthering Heights* by Emily Brontë)

fox-fire NOUN fox-fire is a weak glow that is given off by decaying, rotten wood ❏ *what we must have was a lot of them rotten chunks that's called fox-fire* (*The Adventures of Huckleberry Finn* by Mark Twain)

frozen sea phrase the Arctic Ocean ❏ *into the frozen sea* (*Gulliver's Travels* by Jonathan Swift)

gainsay VERB to gainsay something is to say it isn't true or to deny it ❑ *"So she had," cried Scrooge. "You're right. I'll not gainsay it, Spirit. God forbid!"* (*A Christmas Carol* by Charles Dickens)

gaiters NOUN gaiters were leggings made of a cloth or piece of leather which covered the leg from the knee to the ankle ❑ *Mr Knightley was hard at work upon the lower buttons of his thick leather gaiters* (*Emma* by Jane Austen)

galluses NOUN galluses is an old spelling of gallows, and here means suspenders. Suspenders are straps worn over someone's shoulders and fastened to their trousers to prevent the trousers falling down ❑ *and home-knit galluses* (*The Adventures of Huckleberry Finn* by Mark Twain)

galoot NOUN a sailor but also a clumsy person ❑ *and maybe a galoot on it chopping* (*The Adventures of Huckleberry Finn* by Mark Twain)

gayest ADJ gayest means the most lively and bright or merry ❑ *Beth played her gayest march* (*Little Women* by Louisa May Alcott)

gem NOUN here gem means jewellery ❑ *the mountain shook off turf and flower, had only heath for raiment and crag for gem* (*Jane Eyre* by Charlotte Brontë)

giddy ADJ giddy means dizzy ❑ *and I wish you wouldn't keep appearing and vanishing so suddenly; you make one quite giddy.* (*Alice's Adventures in Wonderland* by Lewis Carroll)

gig NOUN a light two-wheeled carriage ❑ *when a gig drove up to the garden gate: out of which there jumped a fat gentleman* (*Oliver Twist* by Charles Dickens)

gladsome ADJ gladsome is an old word meaning glad or happy ❑ *Nobody ever stopped him in the street to say, with gladsome looks* (*A Christmas Carol* by Charles Dickens)

glen NOUN a glen is a small valley; the word is used commonly in Scotland ❑ *a beck which follows the bend of the glen* (*Wuthering Heights* by Emily Brontë)

gravelled VERB gravelled is an old term which means to baffle or defeat someone ❑ *Gravelled the pastors of the German Church* (*Doctor Faustus 1.1* by Christopher Marlowe)

grinder NOUN a grinder was a private tutor ❑ *but that when he had had the happiness of marrying Mrs Pocket very early in his life, he had impaired his prospects and taken up the calling of a Grinder* (*Great Expectations* by Charles Dickens)

gruel NOUN gruel is a thin, watery cornmeal or oatmeal soup ❑ *and the little saucepan of gruel (Scrooge had a cold in his head) upon the hob.* (*A Christmas Carol* by Charles Dickens)

guinea, half a NOUN a half guinea was ten shillings and sixpence ❑ *but lay out half a guinea at Ford's* (*Emma* by Jane Austen)

gull VERB gull is an old term which means to fool or deceive someone ❑ *Hush, I'll gull him supernaturally* (*Doctor Faustus 3.4* by Christopher Marlowe)

gunnel NOUN the gunnel, or gunwhale, is the upper edge of a boat's side ❑ *But he put his foot on the gunnel and rocked her* (*The Adventures of Huckleberry Finn* by Mark Twain)

gunwale NOUN the side of a ship ❑ *He dipped his hand in the water over the boat's gunwale* (*Great Expectations* by Charles Dickens)

Gytrash NOUN a Gytrash is an omen of misfortune to the superstitious, usually taking the form of a hound ❑ *I remembered certain of Bessie's tales, wherein figured a North-of-England spirit, called a 'Gytrash'* (*Jane Eyre* by Charlotte Brontë)

hackney-cabriolet NOUN a two-wheeled carriage with four seats for hire and pulled by a horse ❑ *A hackney-cabriolet was in waiting; with the same vehemence which she had exhibited in addressing Oliver, the girl pulled him in with her, and drew the curtains close.* (Oliver Twist by Charles Dickens)

hackney-coach NOUN a four-wheeled horse-drawn vehicle for hire ❑ *The twilight was beginning to close in, when Mr. Brownlow alighted from a hackney-coach at his own door, and knocked softly.* (Oliver Twist by Charles Dickens)

haggler NOUN a haggler is someone who travels from place to place selling small goods and items ❑ *when I be plain Jack Durbeyfield, the haggler* (Tess of the D'Urbervilles by Thomas Hardy)

halter NOUN a halter is a rope or strap used to lead an animal or to tie it up ❑ *I had of course long been used to a halter and a headstall* (Black Beauty by Anna Sewell)

hamlet NOUN a hamlet is a small village or a group of houses in the countryside ❑ *down from the hamlet* (Treasure Island by Robert Louis Stevenson)

hand-barrow NOUN a hand-barrow is a device for carrying heavy objects. It is like a wheelbarrow except that it has handles, rather than wheels, for moving the barrow ❑ *his sea chest following behind him in a hand-barrow* (Treasure Island by Robert Louis Stevenson)

handspike NOUN a handspike was a stick which was used as a lever ❑ *a bit of stick like a handspike* (Treasure Island by Robert Louis Stevenson)

haply ADV haply means by chance or perhaps ❑ *And haply the Queen-Moon is on her throne* (Ode on a Nightingale by John Keats)

harem NOUN the harem was the part of the house where the women lived ❑ *mostly they hang round the harem* (The Adventures of Huckleberry Finn by Mark Twain)

hautboys NOUN hautboys are oboes ❑ *sausages and puddings resembling flutes and hautboys* (Gulliver's Travels by Jonathan Swift)

hawker NOUN a hawker is someone who sells goods to people as he travels rather than from a fixed place like a shop ❑ *to buy some stockings from a hawker* (Treasure Island by Robert Louis Stevenson)

hawser NOUN a hawser is a rope used to tie up or tow a ship or boat ❑ *Again among the tiers of shipping, in and out, avoiding rusty chain-cables, frayed hempen hawsers* (Great Expectations by Charles Dickens)

headstall NOUN the headstall is the part of the bridle or halter that goes around a horse's head ❑ *I had of course long been used to a halter and a headstall* (Black Beauty by Anna Sewell)

hearken VERB hearken means to listen ❑ *though we sometimes stopped to lay hold of each other and hearken* (Treasure Island by Robert Louis Stevenson)

heartless ADJ here heartless means without heart or dejected ❑ *I am not heartless* (The Prelude by William Wordsworth)

hebdomadal ADJ hebdomadal means weekly ❑ *It was the hebdomadal treat to which we all looked forward from Sabbath to Sabbath* (Jane Eyre by Charlotte Brontë)

highwaymen NOUN highwaymen were people who stopped travellers and robbed them ❑ *We are highwaymen* (The Adventures of Huckleberry Finn by Mark Twain)

hinds NOUN hinds means farm hands, or people who work on a farm ❑ *He called his hinds about him* (Gulliver's Travels by Jonathan Swift)

histrionic ADJ if you refer to someone's behaviour as histrionic, you are being critical of it because it is dramatic and exaggerated

❏ *But the histrionic muse is the darling* (*The Adventures of Huckleberry Finn* by Mark Twain)

hogs NOUN hogs is another word for pigs ❏ *Tom called the hogs 'ingots'* (*The Adventures of Huckleberry Finn* by Mark Twain)

horrors NOUN the horrors are a fit, called delirium tremens, which is caused by drinking too much alcohol ❏ *I'll have the horrors* (*Treasure Island* by Robert Louis Stevenson)

huffy ADJ huffy means to be obviously annoyed or offended about something ❏ *They will feel that more than angry speeches or huffy actions* (*Little Women* by Louisa May Alcott)

hulks NOUN hulks were prison-ships ❏ *The miserable companion of thieves and ruffians, the fallen outcast of low haunts, the associate of the scourings of the jails and hulks* (*Oliver Twist* by Charles Dickens)

humbug NOUN humbug means nonsense or rubbish ❏ *"Bah," said Scrooge. "Humbug!"* (*A Christmas Carol* by Charles Dickens)

humours NOUN it was believed that there were four fluids in the body called humours which decided the temperament of a person depending on how much of each fluid was present ❏ *other peccant humours* (*Gulliver's Travels* by Jonathan Swift)

husbandry NOUN husbandry is farming animals ❏ *bad husbandry were plentifully anointing their wheels* (*Silas Marner* by George Eliot)

huswife NOUN a huswife was a small sewing kit ❏ *but I had put my huswife on it* (*Emma* by Jane Austen)

ideal ADJ ideal in this context means imaginary ❏ *I discovered the yell was not ideal* (*Wuthering Heights* by Emily Brontë)

If our two phrase if both our ❏ *If our two loves be one* (*The Good-Morrow* by John Donne)

ignis-fatuus NOUN ignis-fatuus is the light given out by burning marsh gases, which lead careless travellers into danger ❏ *it is madness in all women to let a secret love kindle within them, which, if unreturned and unknown, must devour the life that feeds it; and, if discovered and responded to, must lead ignis-fatuus-like, into miry wilds whence there is no extrication.* (*Jane Eyre* by Charlotte Brontë)

imaginations NOUN here imaginations means schemes or plans ❏ *soon drove out those imaginations* (*Gulliver's Travels* by Jonathan Swift)

impressible ADJ impressible means open or impressionable ❏ *for Marner had one of those impressible, self-doubting natures* (*Silas Marner* by George Eliot)

in good intelligence phrase friendly with each other ❏ *that these two persons were in good intelligence with each other* (*Gulliver's Travels* by Jonathan Swift)

inanity NOUN inanity is sillyness or dull stupidity ❏ *Do we not wile away moments of inanity* (*Silas Marner* by George Eliot)

incivility NOUN incivility means rudeness or impoliteness ❏ *if it's only for a piece of incivility like to-night's* (*Treasure Island* by Robert Louis Stevenson)

indigenae NOUN indigenae means natives or people from that area ❏ *an exotic that the surly indigenae will not recognise for kin* (*Wuthering Heights* by Emily Brontë)

indocible ADJ unteachable ❏ *so they were the most restive and indocible* (*Gulliver's Travels* by Jonathan Swift)

ingenuity NOUN inventiveness ❏ *entreated me to give him something as an encouragement to ingenuity* (*Gulliver's Travels* by Jonathan Swift)

ingots NOUN an ingot is a lump of a valuable metal like gold, usually shaped like a brick ❏ *Tom called the hogs 'ingots'* (*The Adventures of Huckleberry Finn* by Mark Twain)

inkstand NOUN an inkstand is a pot which was put on a desk to contain either ink or pencils and pens ❏ *throwing an inkstand at the Lizard as she spoke* (*Alice's Adventures in Wonderland* by Lewis Carroll)

inordinate ADJ without order. Today inordinate means 'excessive'. ❏ *Though yet untutored and inordinate* (*The Prelude* by William Wordsworth)

intellectuals NOUN here intellectuals means the minds (of the workmen) ❏ *those instructions they give being too refined for the intellectuals of their workmen* (*Gulliver's Travels* by Jonathan Swift)

interview NOUN meeting ❏ *By our first strange and fatal interview* (*On His Mistress* by John Donne)

jacks NOUN jacks are rods for turning a spit over a fire ❏ *It was a small bit of pork suspended from the kettle hanger by a string passed through a large door key, in a way known to primitive housekeepers unpossessed of jacks* (*Silas Marner* by George Eliot)

jews-harp NOUN a jews-harp is a small, metal, musical instrument that is played by the mouth ❏ *A jews-harp's plenty good enough for a rat* (*The Adventures of Huckleberry Finn* by Mark Twain)

jorum NOUN a large bowl ❏ *while Miss Skiffins brewed such a jorum of tea, that the pig in the back premises became strongly excited* (*Great Expectations* by Charles Dickens)

jostled VERB jostled means bumped or pushed by someone or some people ❏ *being jostled himself into the kennel* (*Gulliver's Travels* by Jonathan Swift)

keepsake NOUN a keepsake is a gift which reminds someone of an event or of the person who gave it to them. ❏ *books and ornaments they had in their boudoirs at home: keepsakes that different relations had presented to them* (*Jane Eyre* by Charlotte Brontë)

kenned VERB kenned means knew ❏ *though little kenned the lamplighter that he had any company but Christmas!* (*A Christmas Carol* by Charles Dickens)

kennel NOUN kennel means gutter, which is the edge of a road next to the pavement, where rain water collects and flows away ❏ *being jostled himself into the kennel* (*Gulliver's Travels* by Jonathan Swift)

knock-knee ADJ knock-knee means slanted, at an angle. ❏ *LOT 1 was marked in whitewashed knock-knee letters on the brewhouse* (*Great Expectations* by Charles Dickens)

ladylike ADJ to be ladylike is to behave in a polite, dignified and graceful way ❏ *No, winking isn't ladylike* (*Little Women* by Louisa May Alcott)

lapse NOUN flow ❏ *Stealing with silent lapse to join the brook* (*The Prelude* by William Wordsworth)

larry NOUN larry is an old word which means commotion or noisy celebration ❏ *That was all a part of the larry!* (*Tess of the D'Urbervilles* by Thomas Hardy)

laths NOUN laths are strips of wood ❏ *The panels shrunk, the windows cracked; fragments of plaster fell out of the ceiling, and the naked laths were shown instead* (*A Christmas Carol* by Charles Dickens)

leer NOUN a leer is an unpleasant smile ❏ *with a kind of leer* (*Treasure Island* by Robert Louis Stevenson)

lenitives NOUN these are different kinds of drugs or medicines: lenitives and palliatives were pain relievers; aperitives were laxatives; abstersives caused vomiting; corrosives destroyed human tissue; restringents caused constipation; cephalalgics stopped headaches;

icterics were used as medicine for jaundice; apophlegmatics were cough medicine, and acoustics were cures for the loss of hearing ❑ *lenitives, aperitives, abstersives, corrosives, restringents, palliatives, laxatives, cephalalgics, icterics, apophlegmatics, acoustics* (*Gulliver's Travels* by Jonathan Swift)

lest CONJ in case. If you do something lest something (usually) unpleasant happens you do it to try to prevent it happening ❑ *She went in without knocking, and hurried upstairs, in great fear lest she should meet the real Mary Ann* (*Alice's Adventures in Wonderland* by Lewis Carroll)

levee NOUN a levee is an old term for a meeting held in the morning, shortly after the person holding the meeting has got out of bed ❑ *I used to attend the King's levee once or twice a week* (*Gulliver's Travels* by Jonathan Swift)

life-preserver NOUN a club which had lead inside it to make it heavier and therefore more dangerous ❑ *and with no more suspicious articles displayed to view than two or three heavy bludgeons which stood in a corner, and a 'life-preserver' that hung over the chimney-piece.* (*Oliver Twist* by Charles Dickens)

lighterman NOUN a lighterman is another word for sailor ❑ *in and out, hammers going in ship-builders' yards, saws going at timber, clashing engines going at things unknown, pumps going in leaky ships, capstans going, ships going out to sea, and unintelligible sea creatures roaring curses over the bulwarks at respondent lightermen* (*Great Expectations* by Charles Dickens)

livery NOUN servants often wore a uniform known as a livery ❑ *suddenly a footman in livery came running out of the wood* (*Alice's Adventures in Wonderland* by Lewis Carroll)

livid ADJ livid means pale or ash coloured. Livid also means very angry ❑ *a dirty, livid white*

(*Treasure Island* by Robert Louis Stevenson)

lottery-tickets NOUN a popular card game ❑ *and Mrs. Philips protested that they would have a nice comfortable noisy game of lottery tickets* (*Pride and Prejudice* by Jane Austen)

lower and upper world phrase the earth and the heavens are the lower and upper worlds ❑ *the changes in the lower and upper world* (*Gulliver's Travels* by Jonathan Swift)

lustres NOUN lustres are chandeliers. A chandelier is a large, decorative frame which holds light bulbs or candles and hangs from the ceiling ❑ *the lustres, lights, the carving and the guilding* (*The Prelude* by William Wordsworth)

lynched VERB killed without a criminal trial by a crowd of people ❑ *He'll never know how nigh he come to getting lynched* (*The Adventures of Huckleberry Finn* by Mark Twain)

malingering VERB if someone is malingering they are pretending to be ill to avoid working ❑ *And you stand there malingering* (*Treasure Island* by Robert Louis Stevenson)

managing phrase treating with consideration ❑ *to think the honour of my own kind not worth managing* (*Gulliver's Travels* by Jonathan Swift)

manhood phrase manhood means human nature ❑ *concerning the nature of manhood* (*Gulliver's Travels* by Jonathan Swift)

man-trap NOUN a man-trap is a set of steel jaws that snap shut when trodden on and trap a person's leg ❑ *"Don't go to him," I called out of the window, "he's an assassin! A man-trap!"* (*Oliver Twist* by Charles Dickens)

maps NOUN charts of the night sky ❑ *Let maps to others, worlds on worlds have shown* (*The Good-Morrow* by John Donne)

mark VERB look at or notice ❏ Mark but this flea, and mark in this (The Flea by John Donne)

maroons NOUN A maroon is someone who has been left in a place which it is difficult for them to escape from, like a small island ❏ if schooners, islands, and maroons (Treasure Island by Robert Louis Stevenson)

mast NOUN here mast means the fruit of forest trees ❏ a quantity of acorns, dates, chestnuts, and other mast (Gulliver's Travels by Jonathan Swift)

mate VERB defeat ❏ Where Mars did mate the warlike Carthigens (Doctor Faustus Chorus by Christopher Marlowe)

mealy ADJ Mealy when used to describe a face meant palid, pale or colourless ❏ I only know two sorts of boys. Mealy boys, and beef-faced boys (Oliver Twist by Charles Dickens)

middling ADJ fairly or moderately ❏ she worked me middling hard for about an hour (The Adventures of Huckleberry Finn by Mark Twain)

mill NOUN a mill, or treadmill, was a device for hard labour or punishment in prison ❏ Was you never on the mill? (Oliver Twist by Charles Dickens)

milliner's shop NOUN a milliner's sold fabrics, clothing, lace and accessories; as time went on they specialized more and more in hats ❏ to pay their duty to their aunt and to a milliner's shop just over the way (Pride and Prejudice by Jane Austen)

minching un' munching phrase how people in the north of England used to describe the way people from the south speak ❏ Minching un' munching! (Wuthering Heights by Emily Brontë)

mine NOUN gold ❏ Whether both th'Indias of spice and mine (The Sun Rising by John Donne)

mire NOUN mud ❏ 'Tis my fate to be always ground into the mire under the iron heel of oppression (The Adventures of Huckleberry Finn by Mark Twain)

miscellany NOUN a miscellany is a collection of many different kinds of things ❏ under that, the miscellany began (Treasure Island by Robert Louis Stevenson)

mistarshers NOUN mistarshers means moustache, which is the hair that grows on a man's upper lip ❏ when he put his hand up to his mistarshers (Tess of the D'Urbervilles by Thomas Hardy)

morrow NOUN here good-morrow means tomorrow and a new and better life ❏ And now good-morrow to our waking souls (The Good-Morrow by John Donne)

mortification NOUN mortification is an old word for gangrene which is when part of the body decays or 'dies' because of disease ❏ Yes, it was a mortification – that was it (The Adventures of Huckleberry Finn by Mark Twain)

mought PARTICIPLE mought is an old spelling of might ❏ what you mought call me? You mought call me captain (Treasure Island by Robert Louis Stevenson)

move VERB move me not means do not make me angry ❏ Move me not, Faustus (Doctor Faustus 2.1 by Christopher Marlowe)

muffin-cap NOUN a muffin cap is a flat cap made from wool ❏ the old one, remained stationary in the muffin-cap and leathers (Oliver Twist by Charles Dickens)

mulatter NOUN a mulatter was another word for mulatto, which is a person with parents who are from different races ❏ a mulatter, most as white as a white man (The Adventures of Huckleberry Finn by Mark Twain)

mummery NOUN mummery is an old word that meant meaningless (or pretentious) ceremony ❏ When they were all gone, and when Trabb and his men – but not his boy: I *looked for him – had crammed their mummery into bags, and were gone too, the house felt wholesomer.* (*Great Expectations* by Charles Dickens)

nap NOUN the nap is the woolly surface on a new item of clothing. Here the surface has been worn away so it looks bare ❑ *like an old hat with the nap rubbed off* (*The Adventures of Huckleberry Finn* by Mark Twain)

natural ◼ NOUN a natural is a person born with learning difficulties ❑ *though he had been left to his particular care by their deceased father, who thought him almost a natural.* (David Copperfield by Charles Dickens) ◼ ADJ natural meant illegitimate ❑ *Harriet Smith was the natural daughter of somebody* (*Emma* by Jane Austen)

navigator NOUN a navigator was originally someone employed to dig canals. It is the origin of the word 'navvy' meaning a labourer ❑ *She ascertained from me in a few words what it was all about, comforted Dora, and gradually convinced her that I was not a labourer – from my manner of stating the case I believe Dora concluded that I was a navigator, and went balancing myself up and down a plank all day with a wheelbarrow – and so brought us together in peace.* (*David Copperfield* by Charles Dickens)

necromancy NOUN necromancy means a kind of magic where the magician speaks to spirits or ghosts to find out what will happen in the future ❑ *He surfeits upon cursed necromancy* (*Doctor Faustus chorus* by Christopher Marlowe)

negus NOUN a negus is a hot drink made from sweetened wine and water ❑ *He sat placidly perusing the newspaper, with his little head on one side, and a glass of warm sherry negus at his elbow.* (*David Copperfield* by Charles Dickens)

nice ADJ discriminating. Able to make good judgements or choices ❑

consequently a claim to be nice (*Emma* by Jane Austen)

nigh ADV nigh means near ❑ *He'll never know how nigh he come to getting lynched* (*The Adventures of Huckleberry Finn* by Mark Twain)

nimbleness NOUN nimbleness means being able to move very quickly or skillfully ❑ *and with incredible accuracy and nimbleness* (*Treasure Island* by Robert Louis Stevenson)

noggin NOUN a noggin is a small mug or a wooden cup ❑ *you'll bring me one noggin of rum* (*Treasure Island* by Robert Louis Stevenson)

none ADJ neither ❑ *none can die* (*The Good-Morrow* by John Donne)

notices NOUN observations ❑ *Arch are his notices* (*The Prelude* by William Wordsworth)

occiput NOUN occiput means the back of the head ❑ *saw off the occiput of each couple* (*Gulliver's Travels* by Jonathan Swift)

officiously ADJ kindly ❑ *the governess who attended Glumdalclitch very officiously lifted me up* (*Gulliver's Travels* by Jonathan Swift)

old salt phrase old salt is a slang term for an experienced sailor ❑ *a 'true sea-dog', and a 'real old salt'* (*Treasure Island* by Robert Louis Stevenson)

or ere phrase before ❑ *or ere the Hall was built* (*The Prelude* by William Wordsworth)

ostler NOUN one who looks after horses at an inn ❑ *The bill paid, and the waiter remembered, and the ostler not forgotten, and the chambermaid taken into consideration* (*Great Expectations* by Charles Dickens)

ostry NOUN an ostry is an old word for a pub or hotel ❑ *lest I send you into the ostry with a vengeance* (*Doctor Faustus 2.2* by Christopher Marlowe)

outrunning the constable phrase outrunning the constable meant spending more than you earn ❑ *but I shall by this means be able to* check your bills and to pull you up if I find you outrunning the constable. (*Great Expectations* by Charles Dickens)

over ADJ across ❑ *It is in length six yards, and in the thickest part at least three yards over* (*Gulliver's Travels* by Jonathan Swift)

over the broomstick phrase this is a phrase meaning 'getting married without a formal ceremony' ❑ *They both led tramping lives, and this woman in Gerrard-street here, had been married very young, over the broomstick (as we say), to a tramping man, and was a perfect fury in point of jealousy.* (*Great Expectations* by Charles Dickens)

own VERB own means to admit or to acknowledge ❑ *It's my old girl that advises. She has the head. But I never own to it before her. Discipline must be maintained* (*Bleak House* by Charles Dickens)

page NOUN here page means a boy employed to run errands ❑ *not my feigned page* (*On His Mistress* by John Donne)

paid pretty dear phrase paid pretty dear means paid a high price or suffered quite a lot ❑ *I paid pretty dear for my monthly fourpenny piece* (*Treasure Island* by Robert Louis Stevenson)

pannikins NOUN pannikins were small tin cups ❑ *of lifting light glasses and cups to his lips, as if they were clumsy pannikins* (*Great Expectations* by Charles Dickens)

pards NOUN pards are leopards ❑ *Not charioted by Bacchus and his pards* (*Ode on a Nightingale* by John Keats)

parlour boarder NOUN a pupil who lived with the family ❑ *and somebody had lately raised her from the condition of scholar to parlour boarder* (*Emma* by Jane Austen)

particular, a London phrase London in Victorian times and up to the 1950s was famous for having very dense fog – which was a combination of real fog and the

smog of pollution from factories ❑ *This is a London particular . . . A fog, miss'* (*Bleak House* by Charles Dickens)

patten NOUN pattens were wooden soles which were fixed to shoes by straps to protect the shoes in wet weather ❑ *carrying a basket like the Great Seal of England in plaited straw, a pair of pattens, a spare shawl, and an umbrella, though it was a fine bright day* (*Great Expectations* by Charles Dickens)

paviour NOUN a paviour was a labourer who worked on the street pavement ❑ *the paviour his pickaxe* (*Oliver Twist* by Charles Dickens)

peccant ADJ peccant means unhealthy ❑ *other peccant humours* (*Gulliver's Travels* by Jonathan Swift)

penetralium NOUN penetralium is a word used to describe the inner rooms of the house ❑ *and I had no desire to aggravate his impatience previous to inspecting the penetralium* (*Wuthering Heights* by Emily Brontë)

pensive ADV pensive means deep in thought or thinking seriously about something ❑ *and she was leaning pensive on a tomb-stone on her right elbow* (*The Adventures of Huckleberry Finn* by Mark Twain)

penury NOUN penury is the state of being extremely poor ❑ *Distress, if not penury, loomed in the distance* (*Tess of the D'Urbervilles* by Thomas Hardy)

perspective NOUN telescope ❑ *a pocket perspective* (*Gulliver's Travels* by Jonathan Swift)

phaeton NOUN a phaeton was an open carriage for four people ❑ *often condescends to drive by my humble abode in her little phaeton and ponies* (*Pride and Prejudice* by Jane Austen)

phantasm NOUN a phantasm is an illusion, something that is not real. It is sometimes used to mean ghost ❑ *Experience had bred no fancies in* *him that could raise the phantasm of appetite* (Silas Marner by George Eliot)

physic NOUN here physic means medicine ❑ *there I studied physic two years and seven months* (Gulliver's Travels by Jonathan Swift)

pinioned VERB to pinion is to hold both arms so that a person cannot move them ❑ *But the relentless Ghost pinioned him in both his arms, and forced him to observe what happened next.* (A Christmas Carol by Charles Dickens)

piquet NOUN piquet was a popular card game in the C18th ❑ *Mr Hurst and Mr Bingley were at piquet* (Pride and Prejudice by Jane Austen)

plaister NOUN a plaister is a piece of cloth on which an apothecary (or pharmacist) would spread ointment. The cloth is then applied to wounds or bruises to treat them ❑ *Then, she gave the knife a final smart wipe on the edge of the plaister, and then sawed a very thick round off the loaf: which she finally, before separating from the loaf, hewed into two halves, of which Joe got one, and I the other.* (Great Expectations by Charles Dickens)

plantations NOUN here plantations means colonies, which are countries controlled by a more powerful country ❑ *besides our plantations in America* (Gulliver's Travels by Jonathan Swift)

plastic ADV here plastic is an old term meaning shaping or a power that was forming ❑ *A plastic power abode with me* (The Prelude by William Wordsworth)

players NOUN actors ❑ *of players which upon the world's stage be* (On His Mistress by John Donne)

plump ADV all at once, suddenly ❑ *But it took a bit of time to get it well round, the change come so uncommon plump, didn't it?* (Great Expectations by Charles Dickens)

plundered VERB to plunder is to rob or steal from ❑ *These crosses stand for the names of ships or towns that they sank or plundered* (Treasure Island by Robert Louis Stevenson)

pommel ◼ VERB to pommel someone is to hit them repeatedly with your fists ❑ *hug him round the neck, pommel his back, and kick his legs in irrepressible affection!* (A Christmas Carol by Charles Dickens) ◼ NOUN a pommel is the part of a saddle that rises up at the front ❑ *He had his gun across his pommel* (The Adventures of Huckleberry Finn by Mark Twain)

poor's rates NOUN poor's rates were property taxes which were used to support the poor ❑ *"Oh!" replied the undertaker; "why, you know, Mr. Bumble, I pay a good deal towards the poor's rates."* (Oliver Twist by Charles Dickens)

popular ADJ popular means ruled by the people, or Republican, rather than ruled by a monarch ❑ *With those of Greece compared and popular Rome* (The Prelude by William Wordsworth)

porringer NOUN a porringer is a small bowl ❑ *Of this festive composition each boy had one porringer, and no more* (Oliver Twist by Charles Dickens)

postboy NOUN a postboy was the driver of a horse-drawn carriage ❑ *He spoke to a postboy who was dozing under the gateway* (Oliver Twist by Charles Dickens)

post-chaise NOUN a fast carriage for two or four passengers ❑ *Looking round, he saw that it was a post-chaise, driven at great speed* (Oliver Twist by Charles Dickens)

postern NOUN a small gate usually at the back of a building ❑ *The little servant happening to be entering the fortress with two hot rolls, I passed through the postern and crossed the drawbridge, in her company* (Great Expectations by Charles Dickens)

pottle NOUN a pottle was a small basket ❑ *He had a paper-bag under each arm and a pottle of* strawberries in one hand . . . (*Great Expectations* by Charles Dickens)

pounce NOUN pounce is a fine powder used to prevent ink spreading on untreated paper ❏ *in that grim atmosphere of pounce and parchment, red-tape, dusty wafers, ink-jars, brief and draft paper, law reports, writs, declarations, and bills of costs* (*David Copperfield* by Charles Dickens)

pox NOUN pox means sexually transmitted diseases like syphilis ❏ *how the pox in all its consequences and denominations* (*Gulliver's Travels* by Jonathan Swift)

prelibation NOUN prelibation means a foretaste of or an example of something to come ❏ *A prelibation to the mower's scythe* (*The Prelude* by William Wordsworth)

prentice NOUN an apprentice ❏ *and Joe, sitting on an old gun, had told me that when I was 'prentice to him regularly bound, we would have such Larks there!* (*Great Expectations* by Charles Dickens)

presently ADV immediately ❏ *I presently knew what they meant* (*Gulliver's Travels* by Jonathan Swift)

pumpion NOUN pumpkin ❏ *for it was almost as large as a small pumpion* (*Gulliver's Travels* by Jonathan Swift)

punctual ADJ kept in one place ❏ *was not a punctual presence, but a spirit* (*The Prelude* by William Wordsworth)

quadrille ▮ NOUN a quadrille is a dance invented in France which is usually performed by four couples ❏ *However, Mr Swiveller had Miss Sophy's hand for the first quadrille (country-dances being low, were utterly proscribed)* (*The Old Curiosity Shop* by Charles Dickens) ▮ NOUN quadrille was a card game for four people ❏ *to make up her pool of quadrille in the evening* (*Pride and Prejudice* by Jane Austen)

quality NOUN gentry or upper-class people ❏ *if you are with the quality*

(*The Adventures of Huckleberry Finn* by Mark Twain)

quick parts phrase quick-witted ❏ *Mr Bennet was so odd a mixture of quick parts* (*Pride and Prejudice* by Jane Austen)

quid NOUN a quid is something chewed or kept in the mouth, like a piece of tobacco ❏ *rolling his quid* (*Treasure Island* by Robert Louis Stevenson)

quit VERB quit means to avenge or to make even ❏ *But Faustus's death shall quit my infamy* (*Doctor Faustus 4.3* by Christopher Marlowe)

rags NOUN divisions ❏ *Nor hours, days, months, which are the rags of time* (*The Sun Rising* by John Donne)

raiment NOUN raiment means clothing ❏ *the mountain shook off turf and flower, had only heath for raiment and crag for gem* (*Jane Eyre* by Charlotte Brontë)

rain cats and dogs phrase an expression meaning rain heavily. The origin of the expression is unclear ❏ *But it'll perhaps rain cats and dogs to-morrow* (*Silas Marner* by George Eliot)

raised Cain phrase raised Cain means caused a lot of trouble. Cain is a character in the Bible who killed his brother Abel ❏ *and every time he got drunk he raised Cain around town* (*The Adventures of Huckleberry Finn* by Mark Twain)

rambling ADJ rambling means confused and not very clear ❏ *my head began to be filled very early with rambling thoughts* (*Robinson Crusoe* by Daniel Defoe)

raree-show NOUN a raree-show is an old term for a peep-show or a fairground entertainment ❏ *A raree-show is here, with children gathered round* (*The Prelude* by William Wordsworth)

recusants NOUN people who resisted authority ❏ *hardy recusants* (*The Prelude* by William Wordsworth)

redounding VERB eddying. An eddy is a movement in water or air which goes round and round instead of flowing in one direction ❑ *mists and steam-like fogs redounding everywhere* (*The Prelude* by William Wordsworth)

redundant ADJ here redundant means overflowing but Wordsworth also uses it to mean excessively large or too big ❑ *A tempest, a redundant energy* (*The Prelude* by William Wordsworth)

reflex NOUN reflex is a shortened version of reflexion, which is an alternative spelling of reflection ❑ *To cut across the reflex of a star* (*The Prelude* by William Wordsworth)

Reformatory NOUN a prison for young offenders/criminals ❑ *Even when I was taken to have a new suit of clothes, the tailor had orders to make them like a kind of Reformatory, and on no account to let me have the free use of my limbs.* (*Great Expectations* by Charles Dickens)

remorse NOUN pity or compassion ❑ *by that remorse* (*On His Mistress* by John Donne)

render VERB in this context render means give. ❑ *and Sarah could render no reason that would be sanctioned by the feeling of the community.* (*Silas Marner* by George Eliot)

repeater NOUN a repeater was a watch that chimed the last hour when a button was pressed – as a result it was useful in the dark ❑ *And his watch is a gold repeater, and worth a hundred pound if it's worth a penny.* (*Great Expectations* by Charles Dickens)

repugnance NOUN repugnance means a strong dislike of something or someone ❑ *overcoming a strong repugnance* (*Treasure Island* by Robert Louis Stevenson)

reverence NOUN reverence means bow. When you bow to someone, you briefly bend your body towards

them as a formal way of showing them respect ❑ *made my reverence* (*Gulliver's Travels* by Jonathan Swift)

reverie NOUN a reverie is a day dream ❑ *I can guess the subject of your reverie* (*Pride and Prejudice* by Jane Austen)

revival NOUN a religious meeting held in public ❑ *well I'd ben a-running' a little temperance revival thar' bout a week* (*The Adventures of Huckleberry Finn* by Mark Twain)

revolt VERB revolt means turn back or stop your present course of action and go back to what you were doing before ❑ *Revolt, or I'll in piecemeal tear thy flesh* (*Doctor Faustus 5.1* by Christopher Marlowe)

rheumatics/rheumatism NOUN rheumatics [rheumatism] is an illness that makes your joints or muscles stiff and painful ❑ *a new cure for the rheumatics* (*Treasure Island* by Robert Louis Stevenson)

riddance NOUN riddance is usually used in the form good riddance which you say when you are pleased that something has gone or been left behind ❑ *I'd better go into the house, and die and be a riddance* (*David Copperfield* by Charles Dickens)

rimy ADJ rimy is an ADJECTIVE which means covered in ice and frost ❑ *It was a rimy morning, and very damp* (*Great Expectations* by Charles Dickens)

riper ADJ riper means more mature or older ❑ *At riper years to Wittenberg he went* (*Doctor Faustus chorus* by Christopher Marlowe)

rubber NOUN a set of games in whist or backgammon ❑ *her father was sure of his rubber* (*Emma* by Jane Austen)

ruffian NOUN a ruffian is a person who behaves violently ❑ *and when the ruffian had told him* (*Treasure Island* by Robert Louis Stevenson)

sadness NOUN sadness is an old term meaning seriousness ❑ *But I* *prithee tell me, in good sadness* (*Doctor Faustus 2.2* by Christopher Marlowe)

sailed before the mast phrase this phrase meant someone who did not look like a sailor ❑ *he had none of the appearance of a man that sailed before the mast* (*Treasure Island* by Robert Louis Stevenson)

scabbard NOUN a scabbard is the covering for a sword or dagger ❑ *Girded round its middle was an antique scabbard; but no sword was in it, and the ancient sheath was eaten up with rust* (*A Christmas Carol* by Charles Dickens)

schooners NOUN A schooner is a fast, medium-sized sailing ship ❑ *if schooners, islands, and maroons* (*Treasure Island* by Robert Louis Stevenson)

science NOUN learning or knowledge ❑ *Even Science, too, at hand* (*The Prelude* by William Wordsworth)

scrouge VERB to scrouge means to squeeze or to crowd ❑ *to scrouge in and get a sight* (*The Adventures of Huckleberry Finn* by Mark Twain)

scrutore NOUN a scrutore, or escritoire, was a writing table ❑ *set me gently on my feet upon the scrutore* (*Gulliver's Travels* by Jonathan Swift)

scutcheon/ escutcheon NOUN an escutcheon is a shield with a coat of arms, or the symbols of a family name, engraved on it ❑ *On the scutcheon we'll have a bend* (*The Adventures of Huckleberry Finn* by Mark Twain)

sea-dog phrase sea-dog is a slang term for an experienced sailor or pirate ❑ *a 'true sea-dog', and a 'real old salt,'* (*Treasure Island* by Robert Louis Stevenson)

see the lions phrase to see the lions was to go and see the sights of London. Originally the phrase referred to the menagerie in the Tower of London and later in Regent's Park ❑ *We will go and see the lions for an hour*

or two – it's something to have a fresh fellow like you to show them to, Copperfield (*David Copperfield* by Charles Dickens)

self-conceit NOUN self-conceit is an old term which means having too high an opinion of oneself, or deceiving yourself ❑ *Till swollen with cunning, of a self-conceit* (*Doctor Faustus chorus* by Christopher Marlowe)

seneschal NOUN a steward ❑ *where a grey-headed seneschal sings a funny chorus with a funnier body of vassals* (*Oliver Twist* by Charles Dickens)

sensible ADJ if you were sensible of something you are aware or conscious of something ❑ *If my children are silly I must hope to be always sensible of it* (*Pride and Prejudice* by Jane Austen)

sessions NOUN court cases were heard at specific times of the year called sessions ❑ *He lay in prison very ill, during the whole interval between his committal for trial, and the coming round of the Sessions.* (*Great Expectations* by Charles Dickens)

shabby ADJ shabby places look old and in bad condition ❑ *a little bit of a shabby village named Pikesville* (*The Adventures of Huckleberry Finn* by Mark Twain)

shay-cart NOUN a shay-cart was a small cart drawn by one horse ❑ "I were at the Bargemen t'other night, Pip;" whenever he subsided into affection, he called me Pip, and whenever he relapsed into politeness he called me Sir; "when there come up in his shay-cart Pumblechook." (Great Expectations by Charles Dickens)

shilling NOUN a shilling is an old unit of currency.There were twenty shillings in every British pound ❑ *"Ten shillings too much," said the gentleman in the white waistcoat.* (*Oliver Twist* by Charles Dickens)

shines NOUN tricks or games ❑ *well, it would make a cow laugh to see the* *shines that old idiot cut* (*The Adventures of Huckleberry Finn* by Mark Twain)

shirking VERB shirking means not doing what you are meant to be doing, or evading your duties ❏ *some of you shirking lubbers* (*Treasure Island* by Robert Louis Stevenson)

shiver my timbers phrase shiver my timbers is an expression which was used by sailors and pirates to express surprise ❏ *why, shiver my timbers, if I hadn't forgotten my score!* (*Treasure Island* by Robert Louis Stevenson)

shoe-roses NOUN shoe-roses were roses made from ribbons which were stuck on to shoes as decoration ❏ *the very shoe-roses for Netherfield were got by proxy* (*Pride and Prejudice* by Jane Austen)

singular ADJ singular means very great and remarkable or strange ❏ *"Singular dream," he says* (*The Adventures of Huckleberry Finn* by Mark Twain)

sire NOUN sire is an old word which means lord or master or elder ❏ *She also defied her sire* (*Little Women* by Louisa May Alcott)

sixpence NOUN a sixpence was half of a shilling ❏ *if she had only a shilling in the world, she would be very lilkely to give away sixpence of it* (*Emma* by Jane Austen)

slavey NOUN the word slavey was used when there was only one servant in a house or boarding-house – so she had to perform all the duties of a larger staff ❏ *Two distinct knocks, sir, will produce the slavey at any time* (*The Old Curiosity Shop* by Charles Dickens)

slender ADJ weak ❏ *In slender accents of sweet verse* (*The Prelude* by William Wordsworth)

slop-shops NOUN slop-shops were shops where cheap ready-made clothes were sold. They mainly sold clothes to sailors ❏ *Accordingly, I took the jacket off, that I might learn to do without it; and carrying it under my arm, began a tour of inspection of the various slop-shops.* (*David Copperfield* by Charles Dickens)

sluggard NOUN a lazy person ❏ *"Stand up and repeat 'Tis the voice of the sluggard,'" said the Gryphon.* (*Alice's Adventures in Wonderland* by Lewis Carroll)

smallpox NOUN smallpox is a serious infectious disease ❏ *by telling the men we had smallpox aboard* (*The Adventures of Huckleberry Finn* by Mark Twain)

smalls NOUN smalls are short trousers ❏ *It is difficult for a large-headed, small-eyed youth, of lumbering make and heavy countenance, to look dignified under any circumstances; but it is more especially so, when superadded to these personal attractions are a red nose and yellow smalls* (*Oliver Twist* by Charles Dickens)

sneeze-box NOUN a box for snuff was called a sneeze-box because sniffing snuff makes the user sneeze ❏ *To think of Jack Dawkins – lummy Jack – the Dodger – the Artful Dodger – going abroad for a common twopenny-halfpenny sneeze-box!* (*Oliver Twist* by Charles Dickens)

snorted VERB slept ❏ *Or snorted we in the Seven Sleepers' den?* (*The Good-Morrow* by John Donne)

snuff NOUN snuff is tobacco in powder form which is taken by sniffing ❏ *as he thrust his thumb and forefinger into the proffered snuff-box of the undertaker: which was an ingenious little model of a patent coffin.* (*Oliver Twist* by Charles Dickens)

soliloquized VERB to soliloquize is when an actor in a play speaks to himself or herself rather than to another actor ❏ *"A new servitude! There is something in that," I soliloquized (mentally, be it understood; I did not talk aloud)* (*Jane Eyre* by Charlotte Brontë)

sough NOUN a sough is a drain or a ditch ❑ *as you may have noticed the sough that runs from the marshes* (*Wuthering Heights* by Emily Brontë)

spirits NOUN a spirit is the nonphysical part of a person which is believed to remain alive after their death ❑ *that I might raise up spirits when I please* (*Doctor Faustus 1.5* by Christopher Marlowe)

spleen **1** NOUN here spleen means a type of sadness or depression which was thought to only affect the wealthy ❑ *yet here I could plainly discover the true seeds of spleen* (*Gulliver's Travels* by Jonathan Swift) **2** NOUN irritability and low spirits ❑ *Adieu to disappointment and spleen* (*Pride and Prejudice* by Jane Austen)

spondulicks NOUN spondulicks is a slang word which means money ❑ *not for all his spondulicks and as much more on top of it* (*The Adventures of Huckleberry Finn* by Mark Twain)

stalled of VERB to be stalled of something is to be bored with it ❑ *I'm stalled of doing naught* (*Wuthering Heights* by Emily Brontë)

stanchion NOUN a stanchion is a pole or bar that stands upright and is used as a buidling support ❑ *and slid down a stanchion* (*The Adventures of Huckleberry Finn* by Mark Twain)

stang NOUN stang is another word for pole which was an old measurement ❑ *These fields were intermingled with woods of half a stang* (*Gulliver's Travels* by Jonathan Swift)

starlings NOUN a starling is a wall built around the pillars that support a bridge to protect the pillars ❑ *There were states of the tide when, having been down the river, I could not get back through the eddy-chafed arches and starlings of old London Bridge* (*Great Expectations* by Charles Dickens)

startings NOUN twitching or night-time movements of the body ❑ *with midnight's startings* (*On His Mistress* by John Donne)

stomacher NOUN a panel at the front of a dress ❑ *but send her aunt the pattern of a stomacher* (*Emma* by Jane Austen)

stoop VERB swoop ❑ *Once a kite hovering over the garden made a swoop at me* (*Gulliver's Travels* by Jonathan Swift)

succedaneum NOUN a succedaneum is a substitute ❑ *But as a succedaneum* (*The Prelude* by William Wordsworth)

suet NOUN a hard animal fat used in cooking ❑ *and your jaws are too weak For anything tougher than suet* (*Alice's Adventures in Wonderland* by Lewis Carroll)

sultry ADJ sultry weather is hot and damp. Here sultry means unpleasant or risky ❑ *for it was getting pretty sultry for us* (*The Adventures of Huckleberry Finn* by Mark Twain)

summerset NOUN summerset is an old spelling of somersault. If someone does a somersault, they turn over completely in the air ❑ *I have seen him do the summerset* (*Gulliver's Travels* by Jonathan Swift)

supper NOUN supper was a light meal taken late in the evening. The main meal was dinner which was eaten at four or five in the afternoon ❑ *and the supper table was all set out* (*Emma* by Jane Austen)

surfeits VERB to surfeit in something is to have far too much of it, or to overindulge in it to an unhealthy degree ❑ *He surfeits upon cursed necromancy* (*Doctor Faustus chorus* by Christopher Marlowe)

surtout NOUN a surtout is a long close-fitting overcoat ❑ *He wore a long black surtout reaching nearly to his ankles* (*The Old Curiosity Shop* by Charles Dickens)

swath NOUN swath is the width of corn cut by a scythe ❑ *while thy* *hook Spares the next swath* (*Ode to Autumn* by John Keats)

sylvan ADJ sylvan means belonging to the woods ❑ *Sylvan historian* (*Ode on a Grecian Urn* by John Keats)

taction NOUN taction means touch. This means that the people had to be touched on the mouth or the ears to get their attention ❑ *without being roused by some external taction upon the organs of speech and hearing* (*Gulliver's Travels* by Jonathan Swift)

Tag and Rag and Bobtail phrase the riff-raff, or lower classes. Used in an insulting way ❑ *"No," said he; "not till it got about that there was no protection on the premises, and it come to be considered dangerous, with convicts and Tag and Rag and Bobtail going up and down."* (*Great Expectations* by Charles Dickens)

tallow NOUN tallow is hard animal fat that is used to make candles and soap ❑ *and a lot of tallow candles* (*The Adventures of Huckleberry Finn* by Mark Twain)

tan VERB to tan means to beat or whip ❑ *and if I catch you about that school I'll tan you good* (*The Adventures of Huckleberry Finn* by Mark Twain)

tanyard NOUN the tanyard is part of a tannery, which is a place where leather is made from animal skins ❑ *hid in the old tanyard* (*The Adventures of Huckleberry Finn* by Mark Twain)

tarry ADJ tarry means the colour of tar or black ❑ *his tarry pig-tail* (*Treasure Island* by Robert Louis Stevenson)

thereof phrase from there ❑ *By all desires which thereof did ensue* (*On His Mistress* by John Donne)

thick with, be phrase if you are 'thick with someone' you are very close, sharing secrets – it is often used to describe people who are planning something secret ❑ *Hasn't he been thick with Mr*

Heathcliff lately? (*Wuthering Heights* by Emily Brontë)

thimble NOUN a thimble is a small cover used to protect the finger while sewing ❑ *The paper had been sealed in several places by a thimble* (*Treasure Island* by Robert Louis Stevenson)

thirtover ADJ thirtover is an old word which means obstinate or that someone is very determined to do want they want and can not be persuaded to do something in another way ❑ *I have been living on in a thirtover, lackadaisical way* (*Tess of the D'Urbervilles* by Thomas Hardy)

timbrel NOUN timbrel is a tambourine ❑ *What pipes and timbrels?* (*Ode on a Grecian Urn* by John Keats)

tin NOUN tin is slang for money/cash ❑ *Then the plain question is, an't it a pity that this state of things should continue, and how much better would it be for the old gentleman to hand over a reasonable amount of tin, and make it all right and comfortable* (*The Old Curiosity Shop* by Charles Dickens)

tincture NOUN a tincture is a medicine made with alcohol and a small amount of a drug ❑ *with ink composed of a cephalic tincture* (*Gulliver's Travels* by Jonathan Swift)

tithe NOUN a tithe is a tax paid to the church ❑ *and held farms which, speaking from a spiritual point of view, paid highly-desirable tithes* (*Silas Marner* by George Eliot)

towardly ADJ a towardly child is dutiful or obedient ❑ *and a towardly child* (*Gulliver's Travels* by Jonathan Swift)

toys NOUN trifles are things which are considered to have little importance, value, or significance ❑ *purchase my life from them bysome bracelets, glass rings, and other toys* (*Gulliver's Travels* by Jonathan Swift)

tract NOUN a tract is a religious pamphlet or leaflet ❑ *and Joe*

Harper got a hymn-book and a tract (*The Adventures of Huckleberry Finn* by Mark Twain)

train-oil NOUN train-oil is oil from whale blubber ❑ *The train-oil and gunpowder were shoved out of sight in a minute* (*Wuthering Heights* by Emily Brontë)

tribulation NOUN tribulation means the suffering or difficulty you experience in a particular situation ❑ *Amy was learning this distinction through much tribulation* (*Little Women* by Louisa May Alcott)

trivet NOUN a trivet is a three-legged stand for resting a pot or kettle ❑ *a pocket-knife in his right; and a pewter pot on the trivet* (*Oliver Twist* by Charles Dickens)

trot line NOUN a trot line is a fishing line to which a row of smaller fishing lines are attached ❑ *when he got along I was hard at it taking up a trot line* (*The Adventures of Huckleberry Finn* by Mark Twain)

troth NOUN oath or pledge ❑ *I wonder, by my troth* (*The Good-Morrow* by John Donne)

truckle NOUN a truckle bedstead is a bed that is on wheels and can be slid under another bed to save space ❑ *It rose under my hand, and the door yielded. Looking in, I saw a lighted candle on a table, a bench, and a mattress on a truckle bedstead.* (*Great Expectations* by Charles Dickens)

trump NOUN a trump is a good, reliable person wo can be trusted ❑ *This lad Hawkins is a trump, I perceive* (Treasure Island by Robert Louis Stevenson)

tucker NOUN a tucker is a frilly lace collar which is worn around the neck ❑ *Whereat Scrooge's niece's sister the plump one with the lace tucker: not the one with the roses blushed.* (*A Christmas Carol* by Charles Dickens)

tureen NOUN a large bowl with a lid from which soup or vegetables are served ❑ *Waiting in a hot tureen!* (*Alice's Adventures in Wonderland* by Lewis Carroll)

turnkey NOUN a prison officer; jailer ❑ *As we came out of the prison through the lodge, I found that the great importance of my guardian was appreciated by the turnkeys, no less than by those whom they held in charge.* (*Great Expectations* by Charles Dickens)

turnpike NOUN the upkeep of many roads of the time was paid for by tolls (fees) collected at posts along the road. There was a gate to prevent people travelling further along the road until the toll had been paid. ❑ *Traddles, whom I have taken up by appointment at the turnpike, presents a dazzling combination of cream colour and light blue; and both he and Mr. Dick have a general effect about them of being all gloves.* (*David Copperfield* by Charles Dickens)

twas phrase it was ❑ *twas but a dream of thee* (*The Good-Morrow* by John Donne)

tyrannized VERB tyrannized means bullied or forced to do things against their will ❑ *for people would soon cease coming there to be tyrannized over and put down* (*Treasure Island* by Robert Louis Stevenson)

'un NOUN 'un is a slang term for one – usually used to refer to a person ❑ *She's been thinking the old 'un* (*David Copperfield* by Charles Dickens)

undistinguished ADJ undiscriminating or incapable of making a distinction between good and bad things ❑ *their undistinguished appetite to devour everything* (*Gulliver's Travels* by Jonathan Swift)

use NOUN habit ❑ *Though use make you apt to kill me* (*The Flea* by John Donne)

vacant ADJ vacant usually means empty, but here Wordsworth uses it to mean carefree ❑ *To vacant musing, unreproved neglect* (*The Prelude* by William Wordsworth)

valetudinarian NOUN one too concerned with his or her own health. ❑ *for having been a valetudinarian all his life* (*Emma* by Jane Austen)

vamp VERB vamp means to walk or tramp to somewhere ❑ *Well, vamp on to Marlott, will 'ee* (*Tess of the D'Urbervilles* by Thomas Hardy)

vapours NOUN the vapours is an old term which means unpleasant and strange thoughts, which make the person feel nervous and unhappy ❑ *and my head was full of vapours* (*Robinson Crusoe* by Daniel Defoe)

vegetables NOUN here vegetables means plants ❑ *the other vegetables are in the same proportion* (*Gulliver's Travels* by Jonathan Swift)

venturesome ADJ if you are venturesome you are willing to take risks ❑ *he must be either hopelessly stupid or a venturesome fool* (*Wuthering Heights* by Emily Brontë)

verily ADJ verily means really or truly ❑ *though I believe verily* (*Robinson Crusoe* by Daniel Defoe)

vicinage NOUN vicinage is an area or the residents of an area ❑ *and to his thought the whole vicinage was haunted by her.* (*Silas Marner* by George Eliot)

victuals NOUN victuals means food ❑ *grumble a little over the victuals* (*The Adventures of Huckleberry Finn* by Mark Twain)

vintage NOUN vintage in this context means wine ❑ *Oh, for a draught of vintage!* (*Ode on a Nightingale* by John Keats)

virtual ADJ here virtual means powerful or strong ❑ *had virtual faith* (*The Prelude* by William Wordsworth)

vittles NOUN vittles is a slang word which means food ❑ *There never was such a woman for givin' away vittles and drink* (*Little Women* by Louisa May Alcott)

voided straight phrase voided straight is an old expression which means emptied immediately ❑ *see the rooms be voided straight* (*Doctor Faustus 4.1* by Christopher Marlowe)

wainscot NOUN wainscot is wood panel lining in a room so wainscoted means a room lined with wooden panels ❑ *in the dark wainscoted parlor* (*Silas Marner* by George Eliot)

walking the plank phrase walking the plank was a punishment in which a prisoner would be made to walk along a plank on the side of the ship and fall into the sea, where they would be abandoned ❑ *about hanging, and walking the plank* (*Treasure Island* by Robert Louis Stevenson)

want VERB want means to be lacking or short of ❑ *The next thing wanted was to get the picture framed* (*Emma* by Jane Austen)

wanting ADJ wanting means lacking or missing ❑ *wanting two fingers of the left hand* (*Treasure Island* by Robert Louis Stevenson)

wanting, I was not phrase I was not wanting means I did not fail ❑ *I was not wanting to lay a foundation of religious knowledge in his mind* (*Robinson Crusoe* by Daniel Defoe)

ward NOUN a ward is, usually, a child who has been put under the protection of the court or a guardian for his or her protection ❑ *I call the Wards in Jarndyce. The are caged up with all the others.* (*Bleak House* by Charles Dickens)

waylay VERB to waylay someone is to lie in wait for them or to intercept them ❑ *I must go up the road and waylay him* (*The Adventures of Huckleberry Finn* by Mark Twain)

weazen NOUN weazen is a slang word for throat. It actually means shrivelled ❑ *You with an uncle too! Why, I knowed you at Gargery's when you was so small a wolf that I could have took your weazen betwixt this finger and thumb and chucked* *you away dead* (*Great Expectations* by Charles Dickens)

wery **1** ADV very ❑ *Be wery careful o' vidders all your life* (*Pickwick Papers* by Charles Dickens) **2** See wibrated

wherry NOUN wherry is a small swift rowing boat for one person ❑ *It was flood tide when Daniel Quilp sat himself down in the wherry to cross to the opposite shore.* (*The Old Curiosity Shop* by Charles Dickens)

whether prep whether means which of the two in this example ❑ *we came in full view of a great island or continent (for we knew not whether)* (*Gulliver's Travels* by Jonathan Swift)

whetstone NOUN a whetstone is a stone used to sharpen knives and other tools ❑ *I dropped pap's whetstone there too* (*The Adventures of Huckleberry Finn* by Mark Twain)

wibrated VERB in Dickens's use of the English language 'w' often replaces 'v' when he is reporting speech. So here 'wibrated' means 'vibrated'. In Pickwick Papers a judge asks Sam Weller (who constantly confuses the two letters) 'Do you spell is with a 'v' or a 'w'?' to which Weller replies 'That depends upon the taste and fancy of the speller, my Lord' ❑ *There are strings . . . in the human heart that had better not be wibrated* (*Barnaby Rudge* by Charles Dickens)

wicket NOUN a wicket is a little door in a larger entrance ❑ *Having rested here, for a minute or so, to collect a good burst of sobs and an imposing show of tears and terror, he knocked loudly at the wicket;* (*Oliver Twist* by Charles Dickens)

without CONJ without means unless ❑ *You don't know about me, without you have read a book by the name of The Adventures of Tom Sawyer* (*The Adventures of Huckleberry Finn* by Mark Twain)

wittles **1** NOUN vittles is a slang word which means food ❑ *I live on broken wittles – and I sleep on the coals* (*David Copperfield* by Charles Dickens) **2** See wibrated

woo VERB courts or forms a proper relationship with ❑ *before it woo* (*The Flea* by John Donne)

words, to have phrase if you have words with someone you have a disagreement or an argument ❑ *I do not want to have words with a young thing like you.* (*Black Beauty* by Emily Brontë)

workhouse NOUN workhouses were places where the homeless were given food and a place to live in return for doing very hard work ❑ *And the Union workhouses? demanded Scrooge. Are they still in operation?* (A Christmas Carol by Charles Dickens)

yawl NOUN a yawl is a small boat kept on a bigger boat for short trips. Yawl is also the name for a small fishing boat ❑ *She sent out her yawl, and we went aboard* (*The Adventures of Huckleberry Finn* by Mark Twain)

yeomanry NOUN the yeomanry was a collective term for the middle classes involved in agriculture ❑ *The yeomanry are precisely the order of people with whom I feel I can have nothing to do* (*Emma* by Jane Austen)

yonder ADV yonder means over there ❑ *all in the same second we seem to hear low voices in yonder!* (*The Adventures of Huckleberry Finn* by Mark Twain)